PROFIT WI

by the same author

SPYSHIP
EARTHRACE
THE FUSE
SKYSHROUD

PROFIT WITHOUT HONOUR

Tom Keene

COLLINS
8 Grafton Street, London W1
1986

William Collins Sons & Co Ltd.
London · Glasgow · Sydney · Auckland
Toronto · Johannesburg

ISBN 0 00 223035 6

First published in 1986

Made and printed in Great Britain by
Robert Hartnoll Ltd., Bodmin

For Annie.
Who shared Plumstead, Lima,
Dunkeswell and other adventures.
With much love.

My special thanks and admiration
to members of Search and Rescue Flight,
22 Squadron, RAF Chivenor,
who carried a passenger one busy August.

CHAPTER ONE

Three men in a boat. Four if you counted the corpse.

'A bit further,' Jackman ordered quietly from the stern, and the dark shadows that were Steevenson and Calvert hunched forward over their oars. There was no moon. Only the faint swirl of phosphorescence and the drip of liquid silver from the blade of an oar marked their passage as they slid silently out over the deep, gleaming waters of Loch Linnhe.

They had taken the rowing boat from the old wooden jetty beside the oil storage tanks near the laboratories of Highland Pharmaceuticals Limited where Professor Highcroft had died. The boat was sometimes used by members of the company's angling club. Now it carried a different burden as the shrouded body of the Professor lay wedged awkwardly across the thwarts, a dark mound sensed rather than seen as the men pulled on their oars to the accompaniment of just three sounds: the faint murmur of water beneath their painter, the dry squeal of the oars in their rowlocks, and the harsh, steady exhale of the men's breathing through the filters of their respirators.

The three men in the rowing boat had been joined by a fourth as they carried their burden down through the woods, stumbling and panting in the darkness, the body-bag jolting and banging against their thighs as they made their way to the jetty. But the boat had been too small to take them all, and they had left Parsons waiting nervously on the shore. Just as they had cast off, a faint breeze had sprung up and a soft, sibilant sigh had moaned eerily through the tops of the firs like some keening dirge to the departed.

Yet the evening had begun innocently enough . . .

The presentation ceremony at Highland Pharmaceuticals

was well into its stride as Bob Harris, the overweight Editor and chief reporter of the weekly *Gleninver Times*, helped himself to another free Scotch from the row of glasses on the table and slipped a creased notebook out of his pocket with a dexterity born of much practice in both these essential journalistic skills.

Harris was one of sixty visitors enjoying the company's hospitality in the staff canteen. Jostling at his shoulders, glasses raised, were a number of local councillors and their wives with perhaps twenty business colleagues from smaller concerns elsewhere in the valley. Among them all circulated HPL executives, each with a smile of welcome and a plastic identity tag on his lapel that proclaimed name, position and corporate allegiance.

The focus of all this hospitable attention stood beside the raised dais at the far end of the canteen, looking awkward and ill at ease. A loner by both instinct and calling, Sandy Tulloch was more at home running marathons than collecting pledges from his sponsors in best suit and tie. Flash guns popped in his face as he shook hands with a bewildering succession of HPL executives and hearty local dignitaries. He had come a very creditable sixty-third in the recent London Marathon – but he had first run the four hundred and eighty-five miles south from Gleninver to the capital. That, together with the fact that he was fifty-five years old, made him news. Hearing he was raising money for a clutch of local charities, Highland Pharmaceuticals had offered to sponsor him at two pounds a mile every step of the way. Which made them news too.

The motive for such open-handed generosity was both complex and covert.

Complex, because although HPL was held in high regard by the local community as both saviour and benefactor, no pharmaceutical company seriously engaged in the manufacture of more than four and a half million pills, tablets and preparations a year could afford to ignore the smallest opportunity to enhance its reputation with a notoriously fickle public.

Covert, because, in the sober, calculating opinion of a

small inner coterie of HPL directors, such *bonhomie* provided the best possible camouflage.

Beside Bob Harris stood Hamish Owen. Tall and thin and just twenty-one years old, Hamish Owen had been in the job as junior reporter for eleven weeks. Before that he had been at university. Now Harris dug him in the ribs and flicked his notebook under his nose. 'Get it out, laddie, get it out!' he hissed. 'You're not here because they've taken a liking to your face, for the love of Christ.'

Hamish fumbled for notebook and pencil as, around them, the chatter of voices and the clink of glasses fell away and a spare-framed man in his late fifties with swept-back grey hair strode briskly to the centre of the dais and stooped to the microphone.

'Ladies and gentlemen – good evening. I don't intend to hold up the celebrations for more than a moment, I assure you.' The accent was English, his words greeted by a ripple of well-disposed laughter. 'I just want to thank you all for coming here tonight to join us in paying tribute to a particularly gallant gentleman who's done so much over the last few weeks to raise money for local charities here in Gleninver. Sandy, as I'm sure all of you are aware by now . . . '

The relaxed voice ran on, and Hamish Owen's pencil kept pace over the pages of his notebook. He wrote in shorthand, a skill that endeared him still less to a chief reporter who disapproved of all trainee reporters in general, and smart-aleck twenty-one-year-old graduate shorthand-writers in particular. Now, as the man on the dais paused, Hamish glanced up. 'Who's the speaker?' he whispered.

Harris picked up another glass and shot Hamish a withering glance. 'Have you learned nothing in the weeks you've been here? The man's name, laddie, is Engel – Harold Engel,' Harris supplied, watching Engel over the rim of his glass. 'He's the Sassenach who dragged this town back from the mouth of the grave when you were still away learning to pick your nose, so just be good and sure you spell his name right.'

'What's his position?'

'Chairman, Chief Executive, Lord God Almighty,' Harris muttered succinctly. 'It's his company, laddie. You can take your pick.' Wrong, of course, but Harris wasn't to know that. Not then.

'Ah, Mr Harris – everything all right?' asked a sudden voice at their shoulder.

Harris swung round. 'Oh, aye, Mr Jackman. Everything's just dandy, thank you very much. We'll get this one on the front page for you, no worry.'

Jackman nodded. 'Excellent. What I believe you people call a good human interest story, is that not so?' A flicker of a smile touched Jackman's eyes. He was in his early forties with pale, straight hair receding from a high, domed forehead and wore light-reactive spectacles that added to an indefinable air of clinical, academic detachment. Now he removed those spectacles and began polishing them carefully with a spotless folded handkerchief.

'Right enough, Mr Jackman, right enough. Oh – by the way.' Harris waved his notebook towards Hamish Owen dismissively. 'This is the new junior I was telling you about. What Head Office calls a trainee.' Harris laid heavy, disparaging emphasis on the last two vowels. 'He started a few weeks back. Before that he was away at college studying journalism, so you'll ken he knows bugger all about the newspaper business.' He turned towards Hamish. 'Mr Jackman here is HPL's Project Development Manager.'

Jackman held out his hand. The young reporter took it eagerly. 'Hamish Owen, Mr Jackman. Pleased to meet you.'

Jackman gave a formal little nod. 'Welcome to Highland Pharmaceuticals, Mr Owen. I hope you'll visit us for a look round one of these days. We have a number of exciting new projects coming up soon that should provide good copy.'

One of those projects was housed on the second and third floors of the three-storey Research and Development block three-quarters of a mile from the canteen and administrative buildings where Jackman, Harris and Hamish Owen stood talking. The OMAHA project, however, would never be included in any reference to commercial activity; it would not appear in any shareholders' annual report, nor would its laboratories be part of any guided tour, although what was happening at that moment would undoubtedly have made extremely good copy. And very chilling, very frightening reading.

Douglas Parsons was Duty Shift Manager in an area known simply as RD7. He sat alone now in front of the monitors with the sheen of fear glistening on his forehead, his eyes moving with mounting alarm from left to right across the display in front of him as orange CONTAM panels flashed into life.

Parsons glanced up at the television monitor above his head. Whatever had gone wrong in Section Nine had done so with terrifying swiftness. And for one man at least, it was already too late.

Professor Malcolm Highcroft lay on his back in an aisle between two stools next to the laboratory workbench, his arms flung wide, his white coat torn askew as his body twitched spastically in a widening pool of yellow liquid on the tiled floor and the breath sawed noisily in his throat.

Parsons looked away hurriedly. Beyond the glass partition on the far side of the control console two floors below where the Professor lay dying, Steevenson and Calvert were already struggling into protective clothing, pulling on with practised haste the thick boots and rubber gloves, the hoods and full-face respirators that would give them individual protection inside the contaminated area. As Parsons watched, one eye on the clock as the seconds ticked away, both men screwed filter canisters on to the side of their respirators, swiftly checked the integrity of one another's protective clothing, and then exchanged thumbs-up signals with Parsons behind his glass screen. Then they moved with slow, deliberate care towards the isolation chamber and the lift beyond that would take them to the third floor and, after they had passed through two separate airlocks, into Section Nine itself.

At the console, Parsons breathed a sudden sigh of relief.

Two of the orange CONTAM panels had flickered and then turned green. Orange had told him Section Nine was contaminated and in airtight isolation from the rest of the third floor; green told him the air filtration plant was already extracting, scrubbing clean and recycling the contaminated air within.

Calvert and Steevenson stepped inside the lift and the steel doors closed soundlessly behind them. Parsons watched his bank of indicators as the lift lights winked up to the third floor, then reached for the telephone. 'Page Mr Jackman, please. Quick as you can.'

'Do all your products come in pill form, then?' asked Hamish Owen, the new reporter, notebook poised.

Jackman shook his head. 'Oh, no. I should estimate no more than sixty per cent leave our warehouse as tablets, Mr Owen. The rest go out as capsules, drops, sachets, skin preparations – in all we market seventy-nine different medical . . . '

'Aye, and you do a nice line in suppositories too, don't you, Mr Jackman?' Harris interrupted, his natural belligerence increasing in direct proportion to his blood alcohol level.

Jackman stifled a sudden flicker of annoyance. 'That is correct, yes.' He turned to Hamish. 'There are some drugs, Mr Owen, which, if taken orally, are broken down by stomach acid and digestive juices *before* they enter the blood stream. Enteral administration bypasses that danger—'

'He means, laddie, that they ram them up your arse,' elaborated Harris crudely.

There are some words that can cut across cocktail chatter like a hot knife. Harris had just used one of them, and people turned. So did Jackman.

'Look, Mr Harris. If you must—' He broke off then and glanced down as a pocket pager began to cheep from his breast pocket. He switched it off and glanced up at the two reporters. 'You'll have to excuse me.' He smiled briefly. 'Nice talking to you, Mr Owen. Don't forget now – come and see us soon.' He shook hands with Hamish, nodded briefly at Harris, and turned on his heel to move smoothly through the press of guests. He plucked a telephone off the wall, dialled the operator and waited, a hand pressed against his ear to block out the clamour of voices behind him.

'Switchboard.'

'This is Jackman. You paged me.'

'Oh, yes, Mr Jackman. Would you please call extension 645? Right away?'

Jackman replaced the receiver. 645. That placed the summons inside RD7. He thought for a moment, then, instead of dialling the extension from where he was, he moved quietly out of the canteen and down the corridor to a vacant office. He closed and locked the door behind him and sat down in front of a bare desk. His call was answered immediately.

'We've gone to Condition Orange on the third floor, Mr Jackman,' stated Parsons without preamble.

'You've *what*?' Jackman felt the hair begin to rise on the nape of his neck.

'Condition Orange, Mr Jackman. Sections Seven, Eight and Nine. There's at least one casualty.'

'Right, I'm on my way over,' snapped Jackman. 'Warn the gate to expect me. No one else is to enter or leave the compound until I arrive, is that clearly understood?'

'What about an ambulance, Mr Jackman? Shouldn't I—?'

'No! No ambulance! Wait until I get there!' Jackman slammed down the receiver and sat back, breathing deeply. Then he took off his spectacles and began polishing the lenses with quick, practised movements. Call an ambulance? With half the Council and all the local Press knocking back free drinks as it went screaming past the window with its siren going? Sweet Jesus.

Jackman replaced his spectacles, switched off the light and went out into the corridor. Engel ought to be told, warned at least. Except that Engel, Simmons and Bathgate were all in the canteen playing dutiful host. Better deal with it himself, do what had to be done and tell Engel about it afterwards. The first priority was secrecy. The second, to assess and contain the damage. He hurried outside, slipped behind the wheel of his company Rover and drove slowly out of the crowded car park. Only when he had turned on to the private perimeter road past the warehouse and the bulk chemical store did he turn his headlights to full beam and send the car surging forward.

Highland Pharmaceuticals leased a forty-seven-acre site that stretched north and south along the wooded eastern bank of Loch Linnhe. The Research and Development wing was more than three-quarters of a mile from the company's main administrative buildings. The whole area was restricted to those not working in one of seven different Research and Development categories and was screened from sight from both land and water by a thick plantation of fir, rowan and beech. The three-storey building where the accident had happened, standing out now like a lighthouse from the surrounding darkness with lights blazing from all three floors, was the heart of the company's endeavour, the key to its very existence here in western Scotland. Locked behind its own chain-link fence, access was by special pass through a gate guarded night and day by the company's own security specialists. In an industry where the theft of a single chemical formula could invalidate a decade of expensive research, such precautions against trespass, theft and the industrial curiosity of a rival company had long ceased to excite comment.

The guard had the gate open before Jackman's car had rolled to a halt. He swept past and brought the Rover to a smooth halt outside the illuminated building. Then he took a plastic card from his wallet and presented this face downwards across the scanner eye set into a metal plate beside the heavy, smoked-glass doors. The electronic eye passed his code sequence to the computer, which acknowledged Jackman's authority instantly. The doors opened. Ninety seconds later, the lift doors sighed back on the first floor. Parsons was standing there to meet him, looking pale and anxious in his white lab coat, a metal clipboard clutched tightly in both hands. His Adam's apple bobbed nervously.

'He's . . . he's dead, Mr Jackman.'

'Who's dead?' snapped Jackman.

'Professor Highcroft. Steevenson and Calvert injected atropine into his thigh as soon as they reached him, but he'd . . . he'd already gone. They're bringing him down now.'

Jackman nodded. Highcroft had been one of their senior microbiologists and, as such, would be hard to replace. He was also a married man with three children, although that piece of domestic information did not spring to the forefront of Jackman's clinical, professional mind.

'All right – what else?'

'It was horrible. I . . . I watched it here, on the monitor.' He pointed. 'All we could—'

'All right – forget about Highcroft. Just tell me: what else?'

Parsons stared at him for a moment, then pulled himself together with a conscious effort.

'All three sections – that's Seven, Eight and Nine on the third floor – have downgraded to Condition Green.'

'Good.'

Both men turned as the lift doors at the far end of the sterile area opened and Steevenson and Calvert emerged awkwardly, the stretcher with its grisly burden wedged vertically between them. They swung the stretcher down to the ground, snapped its wheels into place and began wheeling it towards the glass partition. Both men on the far side of the sterile area were in full protective clothing and respirators. Professor Highcroft's body was enclosed in a grey, heavy-duty, plastic body-bag strapped tightly on to the stretcher cradle.

Jackman moved swiftly to the control desk and pressed the microphone switch. 'Hold it there, I'll come to you.' One of the men raised a black-gloved hand in acknowledgement as Jackman opened a cupboard, took down two vacuum-sealed packets of protective clothing and began ripping them open. He started dressing rapidly in loose-fitting smock and over-trousers. As he bent to tie the last of the tapes, the phone began to ring on the control desk. Parsons, who was nearest, reached for the call.

'Research and Development.' He listened for a moment. 'Er . . . one moment, please.' He covered the mouthpiece and lowered the phone slowly. 'It's Mrs Highcroft,' he whispered, visibly shaken.

There was a moment of brief, frozen silence. Then Jackman stepped forward and took the receiver. 'Good evening, Mrs Highcroft,' he began easily. 'It's Maurice Jackman. What can I do for you?' With her husband lying trussed in a body-bag ten feet away.

'Oh. I . . . I was hoping to speak to Malcolm,' began a woman's voice brightly. There was only the briefest of pauses before Jackman spoke.

'Your husband?' he queried, with just the right amount of puzzled surprise in his voice. 'I was under the impression he left some hours ago. One moment and I'll check.' Jackman lowered the receiver slowly to his side, gazed at Parsons with blank, cold eyes for several seconds and then raised the receiver once more. 'No, I'm sorry, Mrs Highcroft. Your husband left here at the usual time.' Beyond the partition, Steevenson and Calvert exchanged inscrutable glances, their expressions lost behind their respirators.

'Oh, that's strange.' Mrs Highcroft gave an apologetic little laugh. 'He promised he'd be home at half past eight at the latest.' Jackman filed away the fact that she sounded puzzled. Puzzled but not worried. Not yet. 'Oh, well. Sorry I troubled you.'

'Not at all, Mrs Highcroft. Good-night.'

Jackman replaced the receiver slowly and looked up to see Parsons gazing at him with a mixture of disbelief and horror. 'Is there something you wish to say?' invited Jackman with silky menace.

Parsons swallowed. 'That . . . that was his wife,' he managed. Jackman nodded. 'You gave her the impression everything was all right. That her husband was still alive . . .'

'That was the intention.'

'But when she finds out that—'

'She won't find out. Not unless you tell her.' He turned to face the two men on the far side of the glass partition. 'Not unless any of you tell her.'

'But that's madness!' Parsons burst out. 'You can't seriously expect to keep his death a secret, for God's sake! There'll have to be an inquest! And when they discover . . .'

'There will only be a Fatal Accident Inquiry, Mr Parsons, if there is a body. And there will only be a body—' Jackman glanced slowly at the shrouded corpse lying trussed and silent on the stretcher – 'if Professor Highcroft is allowed to die.'

Three miles away in a neat, detached, modern house on the outskirts of the town, Helen Highcroft closed the oven door, wiped her hands on her apron and went through into the sitting-room where Sarah, Mark and Simon were sprawled in front of the sofa, watching television and drawing. 'Right, kids: who wants to eat?' she asked brightly, unease pushed to the back of her mind. He'd probably forgotten, that was all. In nineteen years' marriage she had become accustomed to the irregularities of her brilliant, absent-minded husband. If Sarah wanted charcoal for sketching, she always said she had only to ask Dad to watch the toast under the grill. It was a family joke, much worn with use and polished with the easy familiarity that goes with a happy household. Now Sarah twisted round, a pencil clenched between her teeth.

'Aren't we going to wait for Dad?'

Her mother shook her head. 'No, he'll be back later on. I've put his in the oven. Come on, it's on the table.' There was, as usual, no response. Helen marched in front of the television and switched it off. 'Come on.' She pointed, a General marshalling the troops. 'Eat!'

They went through to the kitchen, sat down at the table and ate. No one seemed to notice the empty place at the head of the table.

It was cold on the loch and Jackman hunched forward, rubbing his hands together as he looked round. The nearest lights were more than a mile away. Somewhere on the far shore a car horn sounded angrily. Then there was complete silence.

Jackman moved unsteadily down the length of the dinghy, crouched down beside the corpse, groped around the covered head and dragged down the zipper until the body-bag gaped open. He looked round over his shoulder towards Calvert and Steevenson, the gesture infinitely sinister as the reflected gleam of the water flashed against the opaque lenses of his respirator. 'Come on – what are you waiting for?' he hissed, the words muffled and distorted. They hesitated. Then Steevenson crouched down, picked up the first of the heavy stones they had loaded into the boat and passed it across to Jackman without a word. Jackman stuffed it inside the body-bag and gestured impatiently for another. Calvert paused a moment longer, then he too bent down for a stone. Jackman was scientist enough to know that the corpse would rise after three days as latent gases expanded inside the body, unless he added extra weight. Eight, ten, a dozen heavy stones were pressed down tight against the corpse. Finally, Jackman was satisfied. 'That'll do,' he said and, bending forward, began tugging the zipper closed. As he did so, the moon slid from behind a bank of cloud, and Jackman started violently as he found himself staring into eyes that bulged from their sockets as they stared unblinking up at the heavens for the last time. Then the moon slid from sight again, and Jackman jerked up the zipper savagely, as though thus he might shut out the memory of what he had seen. 'Help me,' he ordered roughly, dragging the body sideways towards the gunwale.

With Steevenson acting as counterweight, Jackman and Calvert hauled the weighted body towards the side, grunting with the effort. It was heavy and awkward, snagging against every obstruction as though fighting to delay the ignominy of such dismissal from the sight of men. Then, with a final heave, it slid over the side and disappeared down into the dark depths of the loch with a silent ripple and a trail of tiny silver bubbles.

CHAPTER TWO

Jenny Macrae came up the narrow, twisting lane above the town, swung her Citroën Dyane between the imposing granite gateposts and drove past deep thickets of rhododendron, the gravel crunching beneath her wheels, the twin pools of light thrown by her headlights lancing out into the darkness ahead.

The house came into view, and Jenny braked to a halt beside a new registration hatchback and switched off the engine. The beautifully kept gardens, the new car, the dark pile of the weathered granite mansion overlooking Loch Linnhe – all these things made Jenny suddenly conscious of the dent in the Dyane's wing and of what she chose to see as the shortcomings of her own appearance.

Or perhaps it was just that she was tired. She sat for a moment behind the wheel without moving, gathering strength from the stillness and silence after the telephones, the tensions, and the unceasing demands of another long day at the clinic. Then she sighed and glanced briefly at her own reflection in the driving mirror, frowning in accustomed irritation as she raked slim fingers through thick, unruly brown hair. Jenny was twenty-four, with a natural, glowing complexion that testified to a childhood spent sailing, climbing and walking this same rugged, gale-swept coastline. No one had ever told her she was beautiful, but the level, grey-green eyes that gazed back from the mirror held a directness that spoke of character and a stubborn determination. In view of her errand that was perhaps just as well.

Jenny scooped up her shoulder bag from the passenger seat, walked briskly across the gravel and up the porch steps to the front door. She rang the bell and waited, steeling herself for confrontation, vowing that this time she would . . . A light snapped on above her head, there was the click of a lock going back and the door opened.

'Oh. It's you.'

'Me again, I'm afraid, Mrs Ennis,' Jenny admitted cheerfully. 'I thought I'd better just give it one more try.' She smiled with more confidence than she felt, the Scottish lilt softening the edges of her voice. Yet even as she spoke, Jenny sensed she was wasting her time, saw it in the tight line of Mrs Ennis' mouth as she stood there, a hand across the door jamb.

Although there was less than a decade between them, the two women were a study in contrasts. Mrs Ennis, the company executive wife: suburban, maternal, and with not a lacquered hair out of place, impeccably dressed in a gown that could only have come from Edinburgh or Glasgow – and Jenny, the working girl: slim, mid-twenties, standing outside on the porch in skirt and sweater, thick brown hair ruffled into disarray by the wind as she waited for Mrs Ennis to close the door in her face.

Almost subconsciously, Mrs Ennis half turned and glanced up at the bedrooms on the first floor. 'He's asleep. I don't want to wake him.'

'It's you I want to see, Mrs Ennis, not Jamie.' Jenny paused. 'Is your husband in just now?'

The older woman shook her head. 'He's out on Council business, I'm afraid. Some civic presentation or other up at Highland Pharmaceuticals.'

Highland Pharmaceuticals: the biggest employer in Gleninver and the company whose sudden arrival in the valley four years previously had set the declining fishing town back on the long road from the brink of financial extinction. Now Jenny remembered that, apart from various business interests in the town, John Ennis was also a prominent local councillor.

'May I step inside just one moment?' Jenny asked quietly. 'I'll not keep you long.'

Mrs Ennis sighed and then relented. The door opened wider. 'Yes – yes, of course. Do come in.' She stood aside, and Jenny crossed the threshold. Mrs Ennis led her into a wide, carpeted hall where an ancient grandfather clock boomed solemnly from a corner. They went through to a spacious drawing-room with a high ceiling and tall french windows that, in daylight, overlooked a wide expanse of lawn and offered a glimpse of the loch in the distance.

Mrs Ennis gestured Jenny towards one of two armchairs on either side of the wide marble fireplace and sat down opposite. 'Before we go any further, Miss Macrae,' she began, twisting her fingers together nervously, 'I . . . I feel I owe you an apology.'

Jenny frowned. 'An apology? Whatever for?' As if she couldn't guess.

'For . . . ah . . . ending our conversation so abruptly on the telephone this morning. I do hope you'll forgive me. I'm not usually so rude to people who, after all, are only trying to help.'

Yes you are, thought Jenny. You're also patronizing and over-protective. You're half Jamie's problem. But she said none of these things. Instead, she smiled.

'There's no need to apologize, Mrs Ennis, really. All that's forgotten.' For the first time, Jenny noticed the framed photograph of Jamie on the occasional table at his mother's elbow. The boy was smiling directly into the camera, a shock of fair hair falling down across his forehead. He looked almost normal. It was only when you studied the eyes that you noticed the vacant look that told of some deep, inner isolation.

'Nevertheless, I was rude and I apologize,' persisted Mrs Ennis.

Jenny saw her opportunity. 'Does that mean—?'

Mrs Ennis shook her head before the request was even made, and they were back where they had started. 'The answer, I'm afraid, is still no. I can't let him go. I just can't.'

'Can't?' challenged Jenny.

Mrs Ennis shrugged. 'Won't, then, if you prefer it.'

Jenny leaned forward and tried to curb her growing exasperation. 'But why, for goodness' sake? It would only be for a few hours. I could pick him up mid-morning and . . . '

'Because I do not consider it necessary,' retorted Mrs Ennis primly. 'Jamie is not like other children, Miss Macrae. He needs special care, special attention. Left on his own . . . ' She shuddered as an over-active imagination took hold. 'Anything could happen.'

'But he won't *be* on his own, don't you see?' Jenny insisted with quiet intensity. 'He'll be with me. Away from all this.' She swept a hand around the immaculate drawing-room.

Mrs Ennis sat a little straighter in her chair. 'The "this" you refer to is Jamie's home, Miss Macrae. He is happy here. Secure. It's all he knows.'

'That's exactly my point, Mrs Ennis. It's *all* he knows.' Jenny took a deep breath. 'Just tell me: when was the last time Jamie went out to play with other children? When did you last take him to a . . . to a fairground? A circus? When did he last play football with children his own age who—'

'He's not ready yet,' Mrs Ennis interrupted, with a note of protective desperation creeping into her voice. 'Look, Miss Macrae. I know you mean well, but I really *must* be permitted to know what is best for my child. Perhaps if you had children of your own you would understand. If you knew how—'

'Your son is deaf, Mrs Ennis,' Jenny interrupted bluntly, deliberately. 'And because he is deaf he has no natural comprehension of speech, of words – *but that is all*. In every other respect, Jamie is perfectly normal.' She looked up. 'Visual stimulation is everything to your son. Every single thing he understands, everything he learns, arrives at his brain by the same route: through his eyes. Yes – he is making progress; yes – his vocabulary is growing all the time. But it is growing much, much too slowly. Jamie is eight years old, Mrs Ennis. He isn't a baby any more.'

'What are you trying to tell me?' demanded Mrs Ennis with haunted eyes.

'I am trying to tell you that we are running out of time. Jamie isn't my only concern. The department has forty, fifty other children with speech delay and communication difficulties between here and Fort William. Anywhere else in Britain you'd have an audiologist *and* a speech therapist. Here, I'm doing both jobs at the same time and, frankly, there isn't enough me to go round. There has to be a limit to the amount of time I can spend with any one child.'

'I'm not interested in other children,' said Mrs Ennis dully. 'All I care about is Jamie. I know that sounds cruel and selfish but—'

'I *have* to care about other children,' Jenny countered reasonably. 'That's part of my job. Another year, eighteen months at the outside, and Jamie will have to go away for special schooling – unless, between now and then, he shows signs of major improvement.' She paused, watching the words sink home like daggers. 'I'm sorry,' she added more quietly, 'but we both know that's the law. There will be nothing more that either I or the primary school will be able to do for him. And the nearest special school for someone with Jamie's disability . . . ' Jenny didn't bother to finish.

'Yes, I know,' said Mrs Ennis, her voice almost a whisper. 'It's in East Kilbride.' East Kilbride was eighty-five miles to the south-east. The far side of the moon. There was a silence that lasted several seconds, then – 'And you really believe this . . . this sort of outing you propose could stimulate a breakthrough?'

Jenny held up a hand. 'It would be a start, that's all. A step in the right direction.'

Mrs Ennis studied Jenny for a long moment. 'He thinks the world of you, you know,' she offered, inconsequently.

Jenny smiled. 'I think the world of him, too. That's why I want to help.'

There was another silence, then Mrs Ennis sighed. 'What do you want me to do?' she asked in a subdued voice.

Jenny felt no elation at her victory, only relief and sympathy for a mother anxious to protect a vulnerable child from the outside world for as long as possible. 'Let go a little, that's all,' she urged. 'Let him spread his wings a bit.'

Still Mrs Ennis hesitated, loath to commit herself now that the moment of decision had arrived. 'Tell me,' she stalled. 'What does Mrs Ross think of this idea of yours?' Pamela Ross was Jenny's nominal superior at the health clinic.

'I don't know,' Jenny replied simply. 'I haven't told her. Not in any detail, anyway.'

'Why not?' demanded Mrs Ennis sharply, all her old fears flooding back as she clutched blindly at some dangerous, imagined irregularity.

Jenny shrugged. She was quite used to making her own decisions without referral. 'I just hadn't got round to telling her, that's all.'

'But surely, Miss Macrae, if you intend to take my son—'

'I haven't told her yet because, officially, tomorrow was to have been my half day,' explained Jenny patiently.

Mrs Ennis looked embarrassed. 'You mean you're giving up your afternoon off? To take my son to the seaside?'

Now it was Jenny's turn to look uncomfortable. 'It's no trouble. I'd probably have gone to the beach anyway . . . ' She shrugged. 'Forget it. Now, I must be off.' She rose abruptly to her feet before Mrs Ennis had her canonized. 'I'll be round for Jamie at about eleven-fifteen, if that's all right. I've got one or two appointments first, but that should leave us plenty of time to catch the bus from the square at half past.'

'A *bus*?' Mrs Ennis echoed, faintly alarmed. 'Jamie's never been on a bus before. I'm not sure that—' Then she caught the look in Jenny's eye and laughed at last at the irrationality of her own fears as Jenny held up an admonishing finger, only half in jest.

'Outside stimulation, Mrs Ennis, remember? Outside stimulation.' She turned to the front door and then stopped as Mrs Ennis laid a hand on her arm.

'Oh, Miss Macrae—?'

'Yes?'

'Thank you. For taking so much trouble. With Jamie, I mean.' She smiled awkwardly. 'And with me. He's . . . he's all we have, you see,' she confided. 'We nearly lost him once, shortly after he was born. I suppose that's why I'm so

bottom of the picture in what he hoped was a generous, loving scrawl, he wrote: 'To my darling Malcolm – with all my love until we can be together. Your adoring Monica.'

He followed this with three large kisses and sat back slowly to inspect his handiwork. Yes, that caught the mood; that would do nicely. He slowly screwed the cap back on to his fountain pen, picked up the photograph by a corner and waved it gently backwards and forwards until the ink was dry. Then he slipped the photograph inside Professor Highcroft's diary and reached for the telephone. He would make two calls. One would be local. And one would be to London.

' . . . in Northern Ireland, western and central Scotland, the showers will die away overnight leaving tomorrow mainly dry with a fair amount of sunshine.' The television weatherman moved across to the side of the chart. 'Winds? Well, nothing much to worry about: south-westerly two to three, temperatures still up there in the early twenties – that's seventy-one, seventy-two degrees Fahrenheit . . . ' Jenny Macrae rosc from her bean-bag cushion in the lounge and switched off the television. As she went back into her tiny kitchen to finish cutting the sandwiches she and Jamie would take with them to Ardtornish the next afternoon, she was humming happily to herself. It looked as though it was going to be another beautiful day.

There was a sudden tapping on the ceiling, as though someone was hitting the floor above with a walking-stick or broom handle. Jenny banged down her kitchen knife and groaned. 'Bugger!' she muttered under her breath. 'All right, Mrs Proctor. All *right*. I'm coming!' she called, drying her hands on a tea towel.

Jenny rented a self-contained flat on the ground floor of what had once been a substantial detached family house on the eastern outskirts of the town. Granite, severe, four-square, with symmetrical Victorian bay windows on either side of the front door, the property had been divided into flats in the late sixties. The owner, Mrs Proctor, lived on the first floor. Widowed many years earlier, Mrs Proctor had a heart condition – she had told Jenny that much when Jenny had first called, flat-hunting. Hoping to secure the flat on the strength of her upright character and professional training, Jenny had let slip that she was a speech therapist. Mrs Proctor's eyes had lit up. That meant Jenny was some kind of nurse. She got the flat on the spot. And rather more besides.

Her landlady, she discovered belatedly, was a hypochondriac who saw herself as a bed-bound invalid hovering forever in Doctor Death's waiting-room. She remained indoors awaiting that final summons for weeks at a time, venturing outside only as far as the chemist or the doctor's surgery for a resupply of prescriptions and pills. She looked about ninety but was nearer seventy. And, thought Jenny bleakly as she went up the stairs, chances are she'll outlive us all. She knocked on the door. 'Hello? Mrs Proctor? It's Jenny – Jenny Macrae.' There was no reply. Jenny called again and tried the handle. The door was locked. Pushing back the letterbox, she reached inside for the key dangling on a length of ribbon. She let herself in and stepped cautiously into the hall.

Mrs Proctor believed in neither exercise nor fresh air. The windows had not been opened for years and the flat smelt of stale perfume, old pictures, and ancient clothes from a different age, of an old woman clinging obstinately to the memories of former years. The hall was in darkness. Jenny moved carefully towards the glow of light coming from the old woman's bedroom. 'Hello? Mrs Proctor . . . ?'

'Jen . . . ? Is that you, dearie?' wavered a thin, frail voice. Jenny hurried into the bedroom, a room cluttered with dark lumps of furniture too large for its reduced dimensions, the window hidden behind a fall of thick, heavy brocade. Mrs Proctor lay in her nightdress on her side between the bed and the hand basin, a walking-stick clenched in one thin, bony hand. Somehow in her falling she had managed to drag the lamp off the bedside table. The lamp had fallen to the floor scattering pills, bottles and tablets in all directions.

'Whatever happened?' Jenny demanded anxiously, dropping to one knee beside the old woman as an eyelid fluttered open and Mrs Proctor grimaced with pain as she hauled herself heavily on to one elbow. She looked pale and shaken, her face a lined ruin in the harsh, bright glare of the unshaded bedside light. Jenny pulled an eiderdown across the floor towards her, padded it into a pillow and wedged it tightly behind Mrs Proctor's back. The old woman gripped her wrist as she coughed a dry, tight little cough.

'I . . . I don't remember . . . '

'Can you move? D'you want me to call Dr Erskine?' Mrs Proctor shook her head and managed to pull herself a little straighter on to the eiderdown. Jenny settled her, felt her pulse, and then fetched a glass of water from the basin. Mrs Proctor nodded her thanks and sipped cautiously.

'I . . . I must have passed out,' she managed. 'I . . . I remember getting up to get a drink of water and . . . that's all.'

'Can you move your arms? Your legs?' There was a cautious moment of experimentation. 'Good . . . good. And the other one? That's grand. Now – are you sure you don't want me calling Dr Erskine?' Jenny pressed.

Mrs Proctor shook her head. 'If you could just help me back to my bed . . . '

They managed it between them, eventually, with Mrs Proctor leaning heavily on Jenny's shoulder. With the bed covers pulled up around the old woman's shoulders, Jenny replaced the lamp and began picking up the pills and tablets scattered on the carpet around Mrs Proctor's heavy wooden bedstead.

Some of the pills came in a little, green, tinfoil strip.

It was an hour later, and Helen Highcroft was on the telephone talking to the duty Sergeant at Gleninver police station. 'I see . . . Yes . . . Yes . . . Thank you very much. No, I've already tried Casualty. Yes, I will. If he doesn't turn up soon. Thank you.' She replaced the receiver and turned slowly. Sarah, their thirteen-year-old daughter, was watching her gravely from the sofa in slippers and dressing-gown, her hair held back by an elastic band and her feet curled up beneath her. She smiled a tense little smile at her mother and, in that moment, she was woman, not child, as she read the worry in her mother's eyes with an adult's awareness.

'Perhaps he's still at the office, Mum – you know, working late,' she offered.

Mrs Highcroft shook her head. 'It's after midnight, darling. Anyway, I tried there first. They said he left at half past five.'

Both women turned as there was a sudden scuff of feet on the stairs and nine-year-old Simon, tousle-haired and still half asleep, wandered into the sitting-room, his pyjamas halfway down his bottom. He rubbed his eyes and yawned sleepily. 'Where's Daddy, Mummy?'

His mother dragged a hand through her hair as Sarah gathered her youngest brother into her arms, rocked him gently from side to side, and then hugged him close as their mother shook her head, not trusting herself to speak as a feeling of cold dread, of sudden precognition, settled over her heart. 'I don't know, darling,' she managed finally, her voice a husky whisper. 'I just don't know. Nobody seems to know.'

'You can't be serious,' muttered Harold Engel, ashen with shock as he listened, appalled, to the latest of Jackman's remorseless disclosures. 'You mean to tell me the three of you dumped his body in the loch? Just weighed him down with stones and . . . and threw him over the side?'

Jackman sipped his Scotch and nodded, massively untroubled by the reaction of his nominal superior. 'There wasn't any choice.'

'Choice?' Engel whirled round angrily from the drinks' cabinet that took up one corner of his book-lined study, and set his glass down with a crack. 'Choice? Of course you had a *choice*! You could have moved him out of Section Nine at the same time as you called the ambulance! OMAHA would never have been compromised, and the Professor might still be alive!'

'It would not have made the slightest difference,' corrected Jackman quietly, his eyes on his drink as he swirled the Scotch carefully around the bottom of his glass. 'Professor Highcroft was a doomed man the moment he placed his hands inside the glove box and saw that the rubber seal had perished. Better than anyone else, he knew what that meant. He knew then that he had only a few minutes, at best.'

'What d'you mean, "he knew"?' Engel demanded harshly. 'How can you be so sure?'

'How can I be so sure?' echoed Jackman. 'Because he told me.' He fished in the pocket of his jacket and held out a small cassette tape. 'Or rather, he told us all. On the monitor tape fed through automatically to Master Control the moment RD7 went to Condition Orange.'

'He actually *told* you he was dying?'

'He monitored his own collapse, yes. It's all here – on tape.' He laid the cassette carefully on a side table and Harold Engel stared at it, mesmerized. 'Calling an ambulance would have ensured only one thing, Mr Engel: a public inquest. By the time Section Nine went to Condition Orange, Professor Highcroft was already in spasm; by the time Calvert and Steevenson reached him, he was dead. Faced with that fact . . . ' Jackman shrugged. 'I did what had to be done, that's all.'

'But to just throw his body in the loch like that . . . it's, well, it's . . . inhuman,' Engel protested, running his hands through his hair distractedly as he stalked the length of the carpet. He turned suddenly as a new thought struck him. 'And his wife, Helen? What will you tell her?'

'Yes. I have thought about that,' Jackman admitted quietly. Briefly he told Engel about the photograph he had taken from the personnel department and what he expected Engel to do in support of his actions. When he had finished, Engel just stared at him.

'You'd do that?' he whispered. 'You'd put the man's family through that sort of hell?'

Jackman shrugged. 'They will be shocked at first, naturally. But after that I believe they will adjust. Come to terms with the new reality.'

'*Come to terms with the new reality?*' echoed Harold Engel, aghast. 'This may come as a surprise to you, Mr Jackman, but the man you and your cronies *disposed* of so efficiently out there was a friend of mine. Someone I liked, trusted! And you . . . you have the nerve, the sheer cold-blooded effrontery to sit here, to drink my drink—' he plucked Jackman's glass from his fingers and set it down with a crack – 'and tell me his family must "come to terms with the new reality"? What sort of a man are you?' Shaking his head as though unable to believe the evidence of his own ears, Harold Engel turned away, crossed to his desk and picked up the phone. 'This madness has gone far enough.' He began tapping in a number with quick, angry movements.

Jackman rose from his chair, crossed to the phone and placed his forefinger gently across the arm of the receiver. As Engel swung round – 'Tell me something,' Jackman invited quietly, his eyes hard and cold as round black pebbles – 'before you appease that self-righteous conscience of yours by calling the police or whoever it is you think you ought to call.'

'What?' demanded Engel.

'You really believe in this company of yours, don't you?' Jackman waved a languid hand at the world outside. 'In the research and the laboratories? In your hand-picked bunch of scientists; in that pretty little helicopter of yours?' Engel piloted the company's Bell-Jet Ranger Executive four-seat helicopter. It was one of the few perks he permitted himself. Jackman, on the other hand, loathed flying.

'It's my life, you know that,' Engel replied shortly, suspicious where Jackman's logic was leading him.

'And this new drug of yours?' persisted Jackman. 'You believe in that too, don't you?'

'Cardocol? Of course!' snapped Harold Engel impatiently. 'Get to the point.'

Jackman's nod affected a certain weariness. 'Indeed,' he

said, gently mocking. 'You wear that belief like a badge on your sleeve. Or would a hair-shirt be more . . . appropriate?'

'What d'you mean?'

'Oh – come now, Mr Engel! It's your chance of vindication, isn't it? A second chance? An opportunity to wave two fingers at the world. To wipe the slate clean.'

'I . . . I don't . . . '

'I've read the Bookham file, Mr Engel, remember? All right – so, very properly, you alert the authorities to the fate of the unfortunate Professor. Excellent. Duty done, conscience appeased.' He paused. 'And so – what happens? I shall tell you exactly what happens. This dream of yours, this second chance – it's over. Finished. No Cardocol. No life-giving new heart drug for the needy thousands whose lives you are about to transform. And why?' asked Jackman softly, rhetorically. 'Because the company, HPL, will cease to exist.' He shrugged. 'Me? Oh, they'll probably put me in gaol for a few months until all the fuss has died down – but you? *You*? You'll be finished, along with that breakthrough drug of yours. Or do you seriously imagine you could build up again from scratch? For the *third* time? Forget it. Without government support, government backing, government *permission*?' Jackman sighed regretfully. 'And all those people, all those thousands of people you so desperately want to help will just have to go on suffering – all because you put the death of one man before them. One solitary, single man.' He turned and gestured at the telephone. 'However, if you want to make that call, please: go right ahead. You are at perfect liberty to do so.' Jackman waited a moment, savouring the silence, the victory. Then he took his glass over to Harold Engel's drinks' cabinet and poured himself another Scotch with slow, unhurried deliberation.

As a gesture of moral domination, its timing was perfect.

CHAPTER THREE

'Good, Angus! That was very good – now: we'll try again, OK? Right from the top of the page. Are you ready?' Angus Frazer looked up and nodded, little jaw clenched tight with determination. He was seven years old; a ginger-haired lad with a shock of freckles and a delayed speech impediment that brought him here to Jenny Macrae at Gleninver's wooden-walled, single-storey health clinic once a week. Jenny smiled encouragingly at Angus as they sat close together with the book open on the table between them, Angus's mother watching carefully from a chair by the door. After months of effort and repetitive tuition, the lad was at last making real progress. 'Set?' asked Jenny, leaning forward conspiratorially and forcing Angus to smile, to turn corrective learning into fun, into a game. He nodded, and Jenny took an elaborate deep breath. 'Go!'

'*Ch*air . . . *Ch*ain . . . *Ch*ocolate,' managed Angus, concentrating for all he was worth as he forced out his lips to shape each word, a finger tracing slowly along the brightly coloured page. Jenny nodded patiently as he cleared each new hurdle. '*Ch*ildren . . . *Ch*eese . . . *Ch*icken!' He sat back then, grinning triumphantly, and Jenny squeezed his arm.

'There, you see? You can do it! I knew you could!' She twisted round. 'What d'you think, Mrs Frazer?'

The boy's mother smiled. 'Aye, he's coming along now, Miss Macrae, there's no doubt about it. He's coming along just fine.'

Jenny ruffled the boy's hair. 'Well done, Angus. I think that's maybe worth a little reward, don't you?' Angus nodded, his eyes sliding away towards the top drawer of Jenny's desk. She watched him speculatively for a moment and then reached down, took out a bag of lollies and offered it towards him. After a moment's hesitation, Angus plumped for a green one and began tearing off the wrapper. He always seemed to win a lolly, somehow. Right at the end of each session.

Jenny rose to her feet, smoothed down her white coat and turned towards the boy's mother. 'That's fine, Mrs Frazer. If you'd like to bring Angus back at the same time next week, we'll have another go. And Angus—' She waited for the boy to join them by the door, the lolly bulging in one cheek, as she dropped a hand naturally to his shoulder. 'See if you can't bring me a few *W*s, all right?' He nodded readily. 'Right you are then – see you next week.' Mother and son nodded their thanks and set off down the corridor. The door closed quietly behind them.

Alone in her office, Jenny sighed and walked slowly back to her desk and sat down, her shoulders slumped beneath a weight of sadness Mrs Frazer and her son would never have imagined. But speech therapists have private lives too – and hopes that can be dashed, feelings that can be hurt. Jenny sat for a moment, staring vacantly at the far wall. Then she reached into her coat pocket, took out Danny's letter and unfolded it again slowly. It had arrived that same morning.

> . . . I've given it a great deal of thought, Jen, believe me, and I know in my heart it could never really have worked. Perhaps, if we'd met five years from now, things might have worked out differently, I don't know. The easy thing would be just to let things slide, to go on pretending everything was still the same and that one day you'll come down to work in Newcastle or I'll come back up to Gleninver, but that kind of compromise wouldn't be fair to either one of us. Besides, Gleninver hospital just doesn't offer the sort of long-term challenge I feel I need. I know that must sound terribly selfish, Jen, but it's the truth.
>
> We discussed it often enough, didn't we? I haven't met anyone else, Jen, and I'll never forget the last five months, not as long as I live, but I just don't see how

we can go on, not at this distance, seeing each other for perhaps one weekend in eight. I think we're both too sure of what we want to give up what we have for one another, without turning that sacrifice into bitterness and resentment. Although this letter may come as a shock to begin with, I'm sure that in a few weeks' time you will see it as the right, the only thing to do. I know it's trite and corny to say I hope we can remain friends, Jen, but I really do. You're a wonderful girl and, from the bottom of my heart, I wish you every happiness in the world.

With my love, always,
Danny.

Jenny folded away the letter slowly. Bastard, she thought dully. Oh, you bastard, Danny. But the words lacked feeling and conviction and Jenny sat back numbly, remembering the laughter and the meals together, the picnics and the long walks over the hills that had started earlier in the year, when Danny had begun his mandatory six months as junior houseman at County Royal Hospital, and September had seemed impossibly far away. They had met in the hospital car park, of all places, arguing over the last parking space and, in the weeks that had followed when they had become lovers, he had filled her life in a way she had never dreamed possible. Now, instead of the kindness, the warmth and easy laughter they had shared, she was alone. It was over, finished.

There was a soft tap on the door. Jenny thrust Danny's letter into her coat pocket, wiped swiftly at her eyes and pretended to be looking for something in the drawer of her desk as the door opened and Pam Ross bustled into the office. Short, grey-haired, married with three teenage children of her own, Pam was Jenny's superior at the clinic. But she was more than that, and in the three years since Jenny had qualified she had become both friend and confidante. 'Sorry to trouble you, love,' she said as she came in, 'but I wonder if you'd mind just keeping an eye open for . . . What's the matter?' Jenny had glanced round with a sudden, forced smile.

'Nothing – why?'

'You sure?' challenged Pam doubtfully.

'I'm fine, really.'

Pam studied her friend for a moment, then – 'You've heard from him, haven't you?' she decided with sudden intuition.

Jenny made to deny it, started to shake her head and then found herself nodding. She took Danny's letter from her pocket and held it up. 'He thinks it's best if we just . . . call it a day,' she whispered huskily, her eyes brimming with tears as she opened out the letter and let Pam read the final paragraph for herself.

Presently, Pam folded the letter slowly and handed it back. 'D'you want to go down there?' she asked. 'Take a few days off and sort things out?'

Jenny looked up. 'I can't just go running after him.'

'Why ever not?' challenged Pam. ''Course you can – if you feel enough for the man. Do you?'

Jenny sighed. 'God knows. I used to think I did. Now . . . ' She shook her head. 'No, I'm not going down there after him, Pam, there's no point. Besides, I'm supposed to be taking that Ennis kid off to the beach . . . '

'That's just an excuse,' Pam interrupted firmly. 'I can look after him, if that's all that's stopping you.'

'After the trouble I had persuading his mother to let him out of her sight in the first place? Not on your life!' retorted Jenny with a flash of her former self, as she glanced at her watch and then pushed to her feet. 'I'd . . . I'd better go, Pam. I promised I'd pick him up at eleven-fifteen and I've got to drop some stuff off at Dad's on the way through.' She made for the door and then paused as emotions shaped themselves into words. 'You're right,' she admitted finally. 'It is just an excuse. Danny doesn't want to put down roots in a picture-postcard little town like this, and I . . . I don't want to dig up roots for precisely the opposite reason. This is my home, Pam – I've known Gleninver all my life! I couldn't give it all up for somewhere like . . . Newcastle.' She made it sound like Grimsville-on-Sea.

'You wouldn't be giving it up for Newcastle or anywhere else,' corrected Pam, the traditional romantic from an earlier age. 'You'd be giving it up for him. Starting a new life together.'

'Roses round the door, you mean? Hubby off to work while the little woman waves a hanky from the doorstep and mewling infant burps over her shoulder?' Jenny pulled a face. 'Maybe one day, Pam, but not yet. I'm not ready for that.' She sighed. 'Men, Pam – bloody men: who needs them?'

Thirty minutes later, Jenny hauled on the handbrake of her Citroën, switched off the engine and lit a cigarette. She needed this moment of silence, of solitude, before walking round the corner to her father's bungalow. She gazed sightlessly out of the window and took a perverse, masochistic pleasure in defying the shrill medical logic of the anti-tobacco lobby as she drew the smoke deep down into her lungs. From where she had parked she could see most of the town stretched out in a wide, sweeping crescent below her. Hemmed in by gentle, fir-clad hills and by the long finger of Loch Linnhe to the west, the view from the bend in the road across the shelving terraces and sloping rooftops was as familiar as the feel of the latch-gate that led to her father's front door. Gleninver had once been a fish town, and the grey, four-square, granite buildings running back from the harbour and the quay attested to that early prosperity when the harbour had been choked with fishing boats and the air had been heavy with the smell of mackerel and herring, drying nets and Stockholm tar. Now Jenny finished her cigarette, picked up the basket of shopping from the passenger seat beside her, got out and walked round the corner and down the path towards her father's bungalow. She rattled the letterbox and opened the front door. 'Hello!' she called brightly. 'It's me! Dad?' There was no reply. Jenny walked slowly down the hall and into the back, where she placed her shopping basket with her father's groceries on the kitchen table. As she glanced round, she saw her father through the kitchen window. He was out in the garden, straightening up slowly from his vegetable patch, a hand pressed against the small of his back. Jenny made to call out and then hesitated, shocked by the pain she saw in the face he wore when he thought no one was looking, as he stood there gazing down at his cabbages, the breeze ruffling his sparse grey hair. You're getting old, thought Jenny with a sudden shiver of realization: you're getting old, and I am all the family you have left. Not for the first time she realized it was more than just memories that kept her here in Gleninver. Jenny went up to the window, tapped on the glass and waved cheerfully.

'And when did you last see your husband, Mrs Highcroft?' asked the young police Sergeant, pencil poised above the incident book as he leaned across the station counter in shirtsleeve order and blue serge trousers. There was no reply. 'Did you not hear my question, Mrs Highcroft?' he repeated patiently. 'When did you last see your husband?'

Helen Highcroft looked pale and dishevelled. She would not remember a yard of the drive to the police station nor, later, would she recall taking the children to neighbours and leaving them there with some mumbled, inarticulate explanation. She had spent half the night on the telephone and the rest of the time dozing fitfully in an armchair, starting awake every few minutes to stare at the clock. Half a dozen times she had gone to the front door and just stood on the step in the darkness, willing her husband's headlights to swing down the road towards her. She had telephoned the hospital three times, the police station twice. Now she was here to make the report official. She stirred. 'I'm sorry, Sergeant. What did you say?' He repeated the question a third time, and Helen sighed heavily. 'Breakfast. Breakfast-time yesterday.' It seemed much longer.

'That would be before he left for the office?' She nodded, and Sergeant McInnes made a careful note in his ledger. The door opened behind Mrs Highcroft and a young police cadet came in, balancing a cup of tea he had carried all the way down from the canteen. At a nod from his Sergeant, the cadet placed it carefully on the counter. Helen Highcroft looked round in surprise and gave a tired, wan smile. 'Thank you.' It was the first thing she had tasted since supper with the children the previous evening. The previous lifetime.

'You're most welcome, I'm sure. Tell me, Mrs Highcroft – your husband works as a scientist up at Highland Pharmaceuticals, is that not right?'

'That's right, yes.'

'What sort of work would that be, Mrs Highcroft?'

She looked blank. 'I've really no idea.' She caught his look, dragged a hand through her hair and sighed. 'I mean, I know he's engaged in pharmaceutical research, of course. I just don't happen to know what he's working on specifically.'

'You mean he hasn't told you?'

'I mean, Sergeant, that I wouldn't be any the wiser if he did. I'm not a scientist, you see. Never have been. Over the years I've just . . . stopped asking, I suppose.' Stated flatly like that, it sounded lame, implausible. As though she had ceased caring.

'Would you say your husband was under particular stress just now, Mrs Highcroft?'

'Stress?'

'Pressure, maybe. There's been a lot of talk in the town about this new wonder drug that's on its way. I'd have thought that if perhaps your husband—'

'No, not particularly. He's always busy, of course, but then that's only natural. They all are.'

Sergeant McInnes made another careful entry in the incident book and looked up. 'Tell me, Mrs Highcroft . . . ' He paused to clear his throat as he pondered the best way across the domestic minefield that stretched in front of him. 'Everything was quite all right when he left yesterday morning? Between the two of you, I mean?' Eighty-five per cent of domestic disputes result in husband and wife joining forces against the investigating police officer one of them has called in to arbitrate over their differences. Now Mrs Highcroft set down her teacup and frowned.

'Between the two of us? What do you mean . . . ?'

'I mean, you hadn't had a row with your husband? An argument, say, just before he left?'

She shook her head emphatically. 'No, definitely not. Nothing like that.'

'You're sure now?'

'Quite sure.'

'I'm sorry, Mrs Highcroft, but these are questions I have to ask. You understand?'

'I suppose so, yes.'

'Then can I ask you this, Mrs Highcroft. Would you say that the pair of you were happily married?'

Helen Highcroft found the spirit somewhere to bridle at that. 'Yes, if you must know, Sergeant. Yes, I would say we are very happily married, strange as that may seem,' she replied defensively, irritated that the questions of an objective, professional outsider should force her to scrutinize a relationship that had been the private, unchallenged touchstone of her happiness, of her life, for the last nineteen years. That, she was discovering, was the most unsettling thing of all . . .

'There now, Mrs Hamilton. If you'd just like to take this along to the chemist, I'm quite sure he'll be able to fix you up in no time at all.' In his cluttered, ancient little surgery tucked away behind Gleninver's Market Hall Square, Stanley Erskine pulled a pad of blank prescription forms towards him, unscrewed the cap of his fountain pen and filled in the form with a practised flourish. He blotted the prescription carefully and handed it across his roll-top desk with the same reassuring smile that had been comforting patients for years. Dr Erskine was a craggy, fifty-nine-year-old Scot with salt-and-pepper hair who had been born in the Highlands and trained in Edinburgh. Apart from five miserable months in the freezing mud of north-west Europe during the last year of the war, he had been in Gleninver ever since.

In the years since his arrival, two more GPs had moved into the town, younger men with a practice of their own in newer, grander premises. Yet Dr Erskine felt no urge to modernize, no desire to exchange the warm, panelled, wooden walls and frosted glass windows of the last century for wipe-clean Formica and greater efficiency. In his parochial view, pharmaceutical representatives and monthly medical journals, free hand-outs and the occasional buffet lunch given by one of the drug companies, kept him sufficiently up to date with medical developments and, although the names of some of the modern drugs might seem to change with bewildering, irritating frequency, it was his firm opinion that the patient who came into his consulting-room remained basically unchanged: a patient who, six times out of ten, needed not so much medical treatment as someone to talk to; a sympathetic ear. Like Mrs Hamilton, for example, sitting across the desk there with her handbag clutched firmly on her knees. With a husband continually out of work and three teenage sons at frequent odds with the law, she would regularly wait more than an hour for a five-minute chat about her husband, her rheumatism and her sleeplessness, and then go on her way perfectly content with one of his prescriptions for a few mild sleeping tablets. Prescriptions, Dr Erskine had long realized, were the key: if people didn't leave the surgery with a prescription they felt he hadn't bothered, that somehow they'd been short-changed. Now Mrs Hamilton took the proffered slip of paper, folded it carefully into her purse, closed her handbag with a loud snap and rose heavily to her feet.

'I'll be on my way then, Doctor. Thank you once again, I'm sure.'

Dr Erskine rose from behind his desk and shook her hand. 'Not at all, Mrs Hamilton, not at all – it's what I'm here for, after all.'

'Aye, that's as maybe. It's a great help, I do know, just having someone to talk to now and awhile. That Michael of mine . . . ' She shook her head and pursed her lips into a thin line of disapproval, the worst better left unsaid. 'See you again, Doctor.'

'Good day to you, Mrs Hamilton.' The door closed

behind her and the doctor sat back behind his desk with a sigh. He made a routine entry in Mrs Hamilton's case notes and pressed the buzzer on his desk. 'Send in the next patient, please.'

'That's the last just now, Doctor. Oh – and there's a Mr Ransome waiting outside to see you.' Roger Ransome, one of the clinical trials' team from Highland Pharmaceuticals. Dr Erskine brightened.

'Send him in, lassie – send him in.' Presently there was a brief knock on the door. 'Come along in,' Erskine called. The door, surprisingly, did not open. Instead, there came another brief tap. Frowning, Dr Erskine rose from behind his desk and opened the door himself.

Roger Ransome was standing outside smiling, both hands gripping the handles of a lightweight metal trolley tipped back towards him. On the trolley's platform rested a large, heavy parcel bound with string. Behind Ransome stood Dr Erskine's receptionist. She was smiling too, obviously privy to the surprise. The doctor looked from Ransome to the parcel on the trolley and back again.

'They've arrived?'

Ransome nodded. 'Came up from London this morning. Thought I'd better bring them over right away.'

Dr Erskine nodded. He was actually rubbing his hands together. 'Come along in, come along in. Here – can you manage?' Ransome edged awkwardly into the consulting-room, tipped the trolley upright and eased the heavy parcel on to Erskine's threadbare carpet. The doctor bent down, inspected the label and nodded his head in quiet satisfaction. 'I don't mind admitting I feel just like a child at Christmas-time, Mr Ransome.' He shook his head. 'Oh, but it's very generous, you know – very generous indeed. All I did—'

Ransome held up a hand good-naturedly. 'Now, don't start that again, Doctor, please.' He glanced round. 'D'you think you could find some scissors?' Erskine offered a pair towards the man from Highland Pharmaceuticals, but Ransome shook his head. 'Go on, Doctor – they're your books.'

Two minutes later the carpet was scattered with brown paper, string and corrugated cardboard. On his desk, stacked almost two feet high, stood all nine volumes of Albert Groesner's medical classic, *The Wisdom of Healing*. Individually, each leather-bound and lavishly illustrated volume retailed at £49.50. Dr Erskine picked up the top copy and let his fingers linger over the crisp, glossy pages, his face that of a man who has seen his dreams come true. 'I've been promising myself a set of Groesners for almost as long as I can remember,' he murmured.

Ransome smiled. 'We're delighted to have been able to help.'

That 'we' brought the doctor back to earth with a bump. He replaced the book on the pile with exaggerated care, opened one of the drawers and took out a pair of pale green cards.

'I almost forgot – here's a couple more Stage Threes for those analysts of yours. You can tell Mr Summers I'll be sending on the paperwork in a day or so.' Ransome glanced briefly at the medical data cards and then slipped them into a pocket as Dr Erskine turned back to his books, still stunned by the generosity of the gift. 'Please – you must let me make a . . . a contribution, at least.'

But the man from Highland Pharmaceuticals shook his head. 'Absolutely not. You've been very good to us over the last few months with this Cardocol business, Dr Erskine. It's just our way of showing our appreciation, that's all.'

The doctor made a small gesture of self-depreciation. 'One does what one can, you know. One does what one can.' It never occurred to him that he was being bought. Or bribed.

Jenny leaned back against the smooth, rounded stones of the breakwater and felt their warmth soak through her thin blouse. She closed her eyes, tilted her face towards the glare of the sun and welcomed the strength of its rays against her closed lids. She felt drained, worn-out by the emotional hammer-blow of Danny's letter as she tried unsuccessfully to push him to the back of her mind and listen instead to Jamie prattling away happily to himself nearby. The outing to Ardtornish was working, at least. She could sense it every time Jamie turned to point out something new in the little fishing village, his eyes sparkling with an animation she had never seen before, not once in the empty vastness of the mansion that was his home. Her hunch was paying off.

When Jenny had called at the house at eleven-fifteen, Jamie had been ready, waiting in the hall. His mother, however, had not finished packing what she considered to be the essentials for a day away from maternal care. The result suggested her son was off to some cold, inhospitable climate for at least a week, and Jenny had filleted his things with swift, ruthless fingers. By the time she had finished they were running late – and it was then that Mrs Ennis had announced she would accompany them as far as the bus stop. Through gritted teeth, Jenny had agreed: the bus stop but no further.

There, eight-year-old Jamie had waited quietly at Jenny's side, and only the thin, bony little fingers tightly clutching her hand had told of some inner animation, some excitement bubbling away beneath the surface as his mother smoothed a hand over his shock of fair hair and fussed with the nylon straps of the phonic ear he always wore strapped across his chest. Jenny found she had almost to prise their beach-bag away from Mrs Ennis' grasp as the bus came to a halt, yet the beach-bag was a vital part of her strategy for, apart from their sandwiches, it contained their sketchbooks, crayons and paintbrushes. Give Jamie a sheet of paper and a coloured crayon, Jenny had discovered, and you unlocked a small door to his silent world.

The bus doors had folded back and Jamie had scrambled on ahead without a backward glance, scampering up the twisting stairs to the top deck, sandalled feet reaching mightily for the high steps. They had sat at the front as the bus moved off, leaving Mrs Ennis waving unnoticed from the pavement. Freed from his mother's apron strings at last, Jamie had bounced up and down on the front seat, turned to Jenny and given her the biggest smile she had seen all week.

Now there came a sudden shout from below, and Jenny stirred from her comfortable position resting back against the warm stones of the breakwater and looked down, a raised hand shielding her eyes from the sun.

'How am I looking, then?' The question came in the form of a good-natured shout from an elderly, silver-haired fisherman in baggy grey sweater and old, paint-flecked trousers, tending his lobster pots in the stern of a twenty-five-foot fishing boat moored just inside Ardtornish harbour. Jenny grinned, pushed to her feet and crossed to Jamie's side. The boy was sitting with his back against a weathered, pitted bollard, his bare toes dangling over the edge of the breakwater, his drawing-book open on his knees and a bag of coloured crayons at his side. Jenny glanced down at the picture and then up at the old man working in the stern of his boat.

'A vast improvement, Robbie,' she called. 'A vast improvement on the original!' Robbie gave a wave of amused dismissal and bent back to his lobster pots, as Jenny crouched down beside Jamie, rested a hand on his shoulder and studied the picture in more detail. For a boy of eight, the drawing was remarkably adult. There was no mistaking which boat he was drawing, nor the figure standing in the stern, pipe clenched between his teeth: Jamie's pencil lines were firm and decisive, the sense of scale and distance, proportion and perspective, those you might expect from a child of eleven or twelve. With painting, sketching and coloured crayons, Jenny had built the first fragile bridge between their two worlds.

'Good, Jamie – very good,' she encouraged. Jamie looked up into her face and smiled, nodding vigorously. 'Can you tell me what it is?'

He couldn't say: 'It's a man in a fishing boat, stupid!' but he came close. Jenny pointed down at Robbie. 'Go on – show him what you've done. Show Robbie the picture.' For a moment the boy was overcome by suitable artistic shyness, then he suddenly reversed the drawing and held it up for the fisherman's inspection. Although he was still too far away, Robbie nodded approvingly.

'Aye, that's very good, laddie – very good indeed, although I didn't know I looked quite like that!' Jamie couldn't hear. He started forward and shook his head angrily, bending over the controls on his chest set and straining to break through, to understand. The old man saw him struggle and his face softened. He hauled on a line and deftly drew the stern in towards an iron ladder set into a channel running up the side of the breakwater, its lower rungs green and slippery with seaweed. When Jenny and Jamie had first arrived, the tip of the boat's mast had been below the top of the causeway. Now, as the pleasure craft, yachts, tenders and fishing boats that filled the cluttered anchorage rose inexorably on the tide, fisherman and artist had been drawn closer together so that, over the last half-hour, there had been several such one-sided exchanges between the boy sitting against the iron bollard and the man unravelling his lobster lines. It was exactly, precisely, the sort of encounter Jamie needed. Now the old fisherman hauled himself heavily up the rungs of the ladder, paused at the top to catch his breath, grinned at Jamie as he walked over and bent down to give both boy and picture the attention they deserved. He studied the sketch in silence for several seconds. Finally—

'Aye, you've got something there, laddie – no doubt about it.' Jamie looked up into the man's face and smiled happily. Then, as the fisherman straightened to his feet and ruffled Jamie's hair, the boy bent over his sketch with renewed energy. Close-up, he had seen that the old man's jaw was flecked with silver stubble; that too would have to appear on the picture. The fisherman watched for a moment, then turned towards Jenny, his boots clumping on the smooth granite of the breakwater. 'He's a good eye for a picture, that one.' He nodded, adding with a quizzical smile, 'Another of your stray lambs, Jen?' They'd known one another on and off for years. Some of Jenny's happiest memories had been built around this harbour, these boats, this old man who seemed as solid, as unchanging, as the weathered granite beneath his feet.

'He needed a change – outside stimulation. A chance to get out from under his mum's feet.' She glanced at Jamie, hunched industriously over his drawing. 'Out here, he's like a different child.'

'Aye, thanks to you.'

Jenny shrugged. 'Me – you – all of this. You always used to say the air was worth a pound a gulp.'

Robbie nodded absently and crouched down, something important weighing on his mind. 'So it is, Jen – so it is.' He paused. 'I was wondering, watching the lad just then . . . ' He paused again, puffing gently on that pipe of his. 'I'm away out to check the lobster pots in a wee while. Just out round the island there.' He pointed to a whaleback hump of land sticking out of the sparkling sea a mile or so offshore. 'I thought . . . if the lad there had a mind to come along, I could maybe show him a lobster or two – what d'you say?'

Jenny paused before replying, a natural professional reluctance to entrust her charge into the care of another vying with the knowledge that just such an experience – away from both mother *and* speech therapist – was exactly what the child needed to bolster his meagre store of self-confidence.

'We wouldn't be gone more than an hour . . .'

Still Jenny hesitated, irresolute. Then she shook her head. 'It's very kind of you, Robbie, but I really think I'd better say no. Thanks all the same.'

'Oh. Oh, well, just as you will. It was only a suggestion.' The hurt was plain to see in the old man's eyes as he turned and pointed out to sea. 'If it's the weather you're worried about, there's no need.' He began coughing then – a dry, rasping cough that went on for several seconds as he banged a large hand against his chest and shook his head. Finally it stopped and he gestured back to sea. 'It's as flat as a millpond, Jen. There's not been more than a breath of wind all morning. We could—'

'It isn't the weather, Robbie, it—'

'What stops you, then?'

'It's just that—'

'Has he caught a lobster before?'

Jenny shook her head. 'I don't think he's even *seen* a lobster before – not alive, anyway. Not unless it was in his mother's freezer . . . '

Robbie bent closer, sensing the battle might still go his way. 'Well then, don't you see? Now's his chance.' He paused as though reading her mind and added seriously: 'You can trust me, you know, Jen. I'm not about to go running off with the lad. You're welcome to come too, if you like.'

The suggestion that she *didn't* trust him, that after all the years of easy, casual friendship between them she might still harbour some private reservation, tipped the balance. Besides, hadn't she brought Jamie here for just such an experience, to soak up and enjoy whatever opportunity placed before him? She was getting as bad as his mother . . .

'All right,' Jenny agreed suddenly. 'Why not?' She nodded over towards the boy. 'You'd best go and ask him.'

The battered old face creased into a sudden smile. 'Aye. Grand. Right you are then.' He turned and hurried off along the breakwater. Jenny watched him bend down as he laid a hand on Jamie's shoulder and began to talk, pointing first at the boat, then out into the bay, and make a circular motion. It was as though someone had touched a switch. Jamie scrambled to his feet, sketchbook and crayons forgotten as he rushed up to Jenny, eyes on fire with excitement, head bobbing violently as he wrestled to control his excitement and marshal his scattered, kaleidoscopic vocabulary all at the same time. With a gigantic effort—

'Jen . . . pl-pl-please can I g-g-go? In the . . . in the boat?'

After that there was, of course, only one possible answer.

Ten minutes later, Jenny stood on the breakwater as the little fishing boat headed bravely out between the steep harbour walls, the deep vee of her bow-wave sending ripples chasing and slapping against the quay. Robbie turned and waved, one hand on the tiller as, in the bows, Jamie Ennis leaned forward into the breeze, Robbie's binoculars slung importantly around his neck.

The boat moved out into deep water.

Management meetings at Highland Pharmaceuticals Limited were invariably held in the boardroom on the top floor of the administrative centre. This morning, a dozen senior executives sat around the polished oval table in their shirtsleeves, their jackets discarded over the backs of their chairs. The windows faced due east and, although the fanlights had been opened, the room was very warm.

The double doors at the far end of the boardroom had been closed and hung with the 'Meeting in Progress' sign since shortly after ten o'clock, when Harold Engel had tersely called the meeting to order and taken his customary place at the head of the table without, noticed one or two of his colleagues, his customary exchange of morning pleasantries. Unaware of what had happened the previous night, they attributed their Chairman's ill-humour to pre-launch tension.

For months now, Highland Pharmaceuticals had been focusing its corporate attentions upon just one date – 28 September. That was the launch date for Cardocol, HPL's new heart drug. The twenty-eighth was now less than one week away. So if, at yet one more pre-launch marketing and promotions conference, Harold Engel showed signs of stress, then that, after all, was no more than his prerogative. As Chairman and Chief Executive, much of the final responsibility for the success or failure of a product and sales campaign aimed with mathematical precision at a tiny chink in the lucrative heart-drug market, rested upon his shoulders.

Noting Engel's tension but misreading its cause, Matthew Simmons smiled wryly to himself and jotted the brand name Theporal on his jotter. Theporal was an anti-cholineric prescribed for peptic ulcers and manufactured, under patent, by Highland Pharmaceuticals.

Sitting opposite, Jackman watched Simmons doodle

something on his jotter, cross it out and then turn towards David Eckett, the Marketing and Promotions Manager for the company's pharmaceutical division, and the in-house co-ordinator for the Cardocol launch campaign. Eckett rose to his feet, picked up a pointer and crossed to his display board once more. Slim, fair-haired, and in his mid-thirties, David Eckett owed fifty per cent of his success to suave, well-groomed good looks, and the other fifty per cent to a shrewd combination of organizational genius, carefully sheathed ambition and sheer drive. 'Gentlemen – to re-cap,' he went on, tapping his pointer gently against a chart projected on to a neatly captioned viewfoil. 'This week's BMJ will carry our five-page colour supplement for Cardocol, the copy for which you have already seen and which has been cleared by both pharmacological and legal departments. Tomorrow, every one of Britain's twenty thousand prescribing GPs and hospital doctors will receive one of these—' He held up a glossy coloured brochure. Printed across the top in neat, gold-embossed letters set against an emerald-green background, were the words: FROM HPL: CARDOCOL – A HEARTBEAT CLOSER. David Eckett turned slowly around the table, the brochure held up for display. Then he laid it carefully on the table and looked up.

'The day *after* tomorrow, two thousand four hundred selected hospital registrars, GPs and senior housemen will receive, through the post, addressed to them personally, a simple, returnable, pre-paid quiz requiring the answers to six straightforward questions about Cardocol's therapeutic trials and physiological effects. The answers, of course, can be found easily enough in the brochure they will have already received.' He paused for the pay-off. 'With a dozen prizes of a fortnight's all-expenses-paid holiday for two in the Caribbean island of their choice, I think we can look forward to a . . . healthy response.' There was a chuckle of agreement.

'Good. We come then, gentlemen, to launch minus 1: the reception for three hundred guests at the Grand Metropole, the Albany and the Great Northern hotels in and around Glasgow. Guests will be arriving between – yes, Peter?' A hand had been raised across the table.

'Three hundred?' frowned Peter Lawner. 'I thought the figure agreed was nearer one hundred and fifty?'

'One hundred and fifty GPs and hospital doctors, yes.' Eckett smiled. 'Plus, of course, their wives.'

'Ah, yes. Yes, of course. I'm sorry.'

'Before I touch upon the schedules for the visit here to Gleninver – the coach trip to the airport at Glasgow, the helicopter shuttle flights, the symposia and so on – let me just say a word or two about those hotel bedrooms, gentlemen.' He looked round the table, pausing until he had everyone's attention. 'Waiting for our guests in each room will be a chilled bottle of champagne, a bouquet of flowers, and a pure silk Italian headscarf bearing the company motif. That motif, gentlemen, will, at that stage, be the single solitary reminder that we are their hosts.' Heads nodded approvingly. The pharmaceutical industry had long tumbled to the fact that 'inducements' to the medical profession were digested rather more easily if the hand that held the sugar-coated spoon was kept at a discreet distance.

Not a single man seated around the boardroom table at Highland Pharmaceuticals considered it passing strange that they were about to spend fifteen per cent more promoting their new product than they had spent upon research into its risks and benefits.

'Here he comes . . . here he comes – ready, laddie?' warned Robbie Roberts, hauling in wet line as Jamie Ennis stood beside him, staring over the side of the boat into the clear, cold depths as the lobster pot came up, hand over hand. Robbie glanced at the boy out of the corner of his eye, then suddenly pushed the wet line towards him. 'Come on, Jamie – you bring this one in!' Jamie shied away in alarm. 'Go on – haul him in!'

'No. No, I—'

'Sure you can! Nothing to it – here.' He grasped Jamie's hand in his, placed the line between his fingers and began hauling in once more, his arms doing Jamie's work for him as the wet line snaked aboard and coiled between their feet. 'Good, good – keep it coming, Jamie boy,' Robbie encouraged him, leaning out over the gunwale and staring down into the water. 'Here he comes, laddie. Just a few more feet and he's yours!' The lobster pot broke surface, Robbie reached over the side and swept pot, line and startled lobster into the bottom of the boat in a cascade of seawater that had Jamie laughing delightedly as Robbie bent down to inspect their catch. Already there were two other lobsters in the plastic crate beneath the for'ard bench, their claws scratching at the walls of their prison as they blew out angry bubbles of saltwater. 'Now then, me beauty, let's have a look at you.' Reaching inside the trap to pin the lobster deftly behind the creases of its thick, encrusted carapace, he lifted it, snapping and flapping, into the sunlight, its antennae waving indignantly.

Robbie shook his head. It was too small, too young; it would have to go back. He held it towards Jamie. 'Here. D'you want to hold it, Jamie?' The boy shook his head and stepped back hurriedly, eyes fixed in fascination upon those long, wavering stalks and snapping claws. Robbie laughed. 'OK, then, Jamie – but this one's got to go back – understand what I'm saying?' He pointed at the sea. 'It's too small for the table. We'll come back for it next year maybe, eh?' He lowered the lobster gently over the side, and they both watched as it slid away into the depths and vanished from sight. Robbie straightened up.

'Right then, Cap'n – find us the next one,' he ordered, falling happily into the role of hired hand as Jamie twisted round, scrambled into the bows and began searching the sea for the next tell-tale orange marker-float. They were perhaps a mile and a half from the mainland just then, working their way slowly round the western side of the island so that the harbour was hidden behind a shoulder of land.

'There!' Jamie pointed excitedly. Robbie nodded as he began to cough once more.

'Aye, Jamie lad – that's the one.' Robbie moved slowly

back to the stern and pressed the starter button. The petrol engine coughed into life, Robbie swung the tiller, and they began curving away over the sunlit, rolling sea towards the next lobster pot. Jamie picked up the boathook and pointed it at their target as they swung in as Robbie had taught him. Then he turned and grinned suddenly at the old fisherman, his teeth very white in the sunlight. He'd never had so much fun, never in all his life. Pipe clenched contentedly between his teeth, Robbie nodded and shouted words of encouragement, his voice lost against the buzz of the engine.

And then, quite suddenly, the engine spluttered and died.

They ran on for a few more yards before the rudder went slack and they fell away off course, to wallow silently on the easy swell between the waves. Standing poised like Captain Ahab in the bows, Jamie turned to see Robbie stabbing impatiently at the starter button with his thumb. Nothing happened. Crouching down, Robbie unfastened the casing hatches at his feet, lifted back the engine cover and looked inside. Nothing was obviously wrong. He unscrewed the fuel tap and peered inside the tank. Plenty of juice, too. He looked up, sensing the boy might be worrying. 'Nothing to fret about, Jamie,' he shouted down the length of the boat. 'Robbie'll have this sorted through in a jiffy!'

It wasn't a fuel shortage, certainly – even if it was, there was still that spare can lashed under the seat beside the spare oars. Then Robbie remembered the engine had spluttered for a second before it died . . . perhaps it was the fuel after all; a blocked fuel line, maybe. He dropped to all fours with a grunt of effort, took a torch from his toolbox and played its beam carefully along the fuel feed to the carburettor. Ah! The thing was dry – blocked! Muttering beneath his breath at the unaccustomed, ungainly exertion, Robbie rummaged about for spanner and screwdriver and began uncoupling the jubilee clip. That came away easily enough and he tugged the plastic tubing free, got his mouth around the end, grimaced at the bitter taste of petrol and began sucking vigorously. There was a moment's resistance and then the stoppage freed itself and petrol gushed down the starved fuel line. Robbie jammed his thumb over the end, scrambled to his feet, spat hard over the side and raised a hand to Jamie in the bows. 'It's all right now, laddie, I've—' He got no further. Dark clouds of pain and dizziness seemed to press down suddenly upon the centre of his skull as his vision blurred and the world was reduced to a narrow band of agony.

Robbie opened his mouth to cry out, but no sounds came as he sagged weakly against the tiller, the fuel pipe dropping unheeded from his fingers. Petrol pumped out across the engine-space floorboards. Robbie clawed at the side of the boat and then slumped sideways, cracking his head as he fell against a varnished thwart and crumpled into a heap in the stern of the boat. His pipe fell from his mouth, and a plug of smouldering tobacco rolled across the floorboards towards that widening pool of petrol. Then the boat rolled to a gentle wave and petrol washed quietly across the decking.

With a sudden *whoomph!* of flame, Robbie's boat began to burn.

In the bows, Jamie cried out in fear as that first blast of fire blew gouts of blazing fuel half the length of the boat. He looked around wildly for help, but there was no boat in sight and the nearest land was two hundred metres away, its inhospitable, uninhabited shores rising in slabs of vertical cliff as the shags and guillemots rose in their wheeling clouds to caw at one another in alarm. Robbie lay where he had fallen, motionless on his side amid the silent, leaping flames.

Jamie scrambled aft, coughing in the smoke. He grabbed one of Robbie's feet and began pulling, shouting, begging him in his strange, private language to get up, to put out the fire, to make the flames, the smoke and the fear go away. Then the wind shifted suddenly, fanning the flames towards him, beating him back towards the bows. He backed away. His heel caught in the lobster crate and Jamie fell back against a thwart, the lobsters spilling out across the deck to slither and cackle towards him as the boat swayed and wallowed in the water. Jamie started to cry. He picked up the empty plastic crate and tried leaning over the side to scoop water on to the flames, but the crate was too heavy. The weight of the water knocked it from his fingers and it drifted away out of reach.

Alone on a sea of roaring flames, Jamie was very, very frightened. And only eight years old.

CHAPTER FOUR

'Hey, Steve – what's that smoke, then?'

'Smoke? Where?'

'You blind or something? There, ya daft sod. Out by the island.'

'Oh. Oh, yeah . . . '

The words drifted into Jenny's consciousness and wedged there as she lay back against the warm stones of the breakwater, her eyes closed. For long moments they seemed to hang dismembered before her eyes, sounds wholly without significance, disjointed. Then they clicked together with sudden, terrible clarity and Jenny was scrambling to her feet, heart pounding against her ribs.

Smoke. As in fire.

There were two teenagers in jeans and sleeveless T-shirts standing together by one of those slot-machine telescopes anchored to the breakwater. One of the boys was bending down and peering out to sea through the eyepiece. The other glanced at Jenny speculatively as she hurried up.

'Hello, darlin' – what's the rush, then? Want to—'

'Please – can I have a look? It's very urgent,' asked Jenny, suddenly aware of curious glances. She could see the smoke herself now with the naked eye as it rose in a thin, oily cloud towards the rim of the island.

The boy grinned. ''Ere – Steve – this could be your lucky day, mate. Bird here wants to get her hands on your telescope.'

'Dear God,' Jenny groaned. 'Look, please, I—'

The boy called Steve straightened up with a grin. Jenny brushed him impatiently aside and grin turned to frown.

'All right, all right – take it easy,' complained the boy, turning to his mate. 'What's up with her?' But Jenny wasn't listening. The smoke filled the telescope: a ragged banner of black against the blue of sea and sky that vanished behind a low hillock of island, hiding its cause from the mainland. Had to be a boat, thought Jenny with sick certainty: had to be. She panned the telescope quickly across the empty bay and prayed: please, God, let them be somewhere else – please. But the sea remained empty. When she picked up the smoke again it had drifted slightly, and her knuckles turned white against the knurled ring of the telescope as she saw something drifting low in the water at the base of the smoke column. Something that might once, at a pinch, have been a twenty-five-foot fishing boat . . .

'God, no!' This time the prayer was muttered aloud, and the two boys exchanged glances, realizing simultaneously that she was serious, that out there amid the smoke and the sea some larger catastrophe was about to unfold. Jenny swung towards the people on the breakwater: a cluster of small boys in swimming trunks with fishing rods and shrimp nets, families on holiday, couples strolling arm-in-arm looking at the boats, while out there . . . 'FIRE!' She pointed dramatically. 'There's a boat on fire!' They stared at her stupidly. 'She's on *fire*, don't you understand?' Jenny shouted.

People glanced at one another uneasily as though she was some kind of local lunatic let out for the day. The seconds ticked away. The bay was clear, anyway. There wasn't a boat in sight. Jenny turned suddenly to an urgent tap on the shoulder.

'You're *sure*?' It was Steve, the teenager. 'You're not pissin' about?'

Jenny shook her head vehemently. 'No. No, I'm not. There's . . . ' She swallowed. 'There's an old man and . . . and a boy. Only he's deaf and he can't—'

Steve pointed behind her. 'I'll call the Coastguard, right?' He broke into a run, and Jenny set off after him towards the phone-box, her sandals slapping urgently against the smooth cobbles as they weaved through the gaping, rooted onlookers.

'Hurry!' she panted. 'Hurry!'

They ran along the quay, dodged across the road and pulled up panting outside the call-box. There was a man inside already, making a call, a neat pile of ten-pence pieces on the shelf beside him. Steve didn't even hesitate. He glanced at Jenny, pulled open the door, grabbed the phone from the man's hand and jerked him out of the booth.

'Look – do you—' began the man indignantly. Then he saw the earring, the spiked haircut and the thick, bare shoulder muscles and thought better of it.

'Sorry, mate – emergency. Matter of life and death – know what I mean?' The man backed away uncertainly as Steve squeezed into the phone-box, banged the receiver rest up and down and then dialled three nines. Jenny watched from the door in an agony of impatience.

'Emergency. Which service do you require?'

'Coastguard, love. And get your skates on, all right? We've got a boat on fire.'

Even as Jenny listened, the emergency operator was connecting the call to the Marine Rescue Sub-Centre at Oban, thirty miles down the coast. The MRSC controls the use and deployment of the four RNLI lifeboats stationed at Islay, Oban, Mallaig and Barra. They also have direct radio access to the RAF helicopter rescue flights at RAF Leuchars, RAF Lossiemouth and RAF Glenhaddon. Now, as the call was patched through to the main desk Controller in Oban's Boswell Street, and Steve began blurting out details of the emergency, the Controller spun round in his chair and ran his eyes down the availability board to his left. In other circumstances he would get on the telephone to the local secretary of the RNLI and request a lifeboat launch. But it would still be fifty minutes, perhaps even longer, before the nearest volunteer-manned RNLI lifeboat could hope to launch and reach Ardtornish. But they didn't have an hour. What they did have, however, was a Royal Air Force Search and Rescue Wessex helicopter at fifteen minutes' readiness on the ground at RAF Glenhaddon. And Glenhaddon was eighteen minutes' flying time from Ardtornish.

The MRSC Controller at Oban had not been selected because he was slow-witted or indecisive. Even as he ordered the caller to hold, he was reaching forward to the radio and flipping a switch . . .

'Glenhaddon Rescue, this is Oban. Immediate.'

The crew of RESCUE 44 – pilot, navigator/winch operator and winchman – were lounging in the crewroom in dark green, one-piece flying overalls drinking coffee, their feet propped on the scarred and battered table between them. They were coming towards the end of their third consecutive twenty-four-hour duty shift and, apart from a false alarm to a missing climber who wasn't, and a short bumble up the coast to blow a drifting airbed and its oblivious owner back to shore and out of danger, it had been quiet. But now, before the Corporal writing up the log in Operations at the end of the corridor had even acknowledged Oban's opening preamble, the crew were on their feet, coffee forgotten. Phones could be ringing, the television could be on, and the crewroom swamped with visitors and raucous laughter – but the moment that 'Immediate' came over the air, the moment they detected that special, unmistakable edge of tension in the Controller's voice, they were moving, motivated by some sixth sense, some professional instinct culled from the years of training and endless waiting that told them this one was special. This one was a job.

They burst through into Operations with the pilot, Flight Lieutenant Dave Bourne, in the lead. Hard on his heels came navigator Pete Sleaman and Flight Sergeant Tony Lockhart, their winchman. Crossing straight to an open locker, Bourne shrugged into his Mae West lifevest. The Corporal acknowledged Oban MRSC on the radio, leant across the control desk and smashed the heel of his hand against the Scramble alarm. The bells rang out immediately all over Search and Rescue Flight, bringing blue-overalled ground-crew mechanics sprinting from the hangar across the concrete towards the bright yellow Wessex helicopter that stood in the exact centre of the landing circle, its rotor-blades dropping tiredly towards the ground. As the mechanics began dragging off the orange air intake covers, wheeling up the fire cart and switching external power through to the aircraft for start-up, Dave Bourne glanced up at the control desk. 'What have we got?' he demanded, fingers fastening the buttons of his Mae West as he slipped into the shoulder straps of his dinghy seat pack and snapped the locks home. There was a squawk-box on the desk that relayed his question directly to the Oban Controller.

'Glenhaddon, this is Oban. Fishing boat on fire approximately two nautical miles west of Ardtornish. Two on board. One's a child.'

Bourne nodded, swept up helmet and gloves and made for the door. His priority was to get out to the aircraft and start pre-takeoff checks. The door banged shut behind him and he broke into a run. SAR crewmen have a habit of running. Especially for children.

Inside Operations, navigator/winch operator Pete Sleaman grabbed helmet and gloves, glanced at the windspeed indicator and paused at the door to study the 1:50,000 scale map of the Western Highlands that dominated the far wall, as he computed in his head their rough heading to Ardtornish. Then he picked up his navbag containing charts, maps and aerial photographs of every town and hospital approach, together with pylons, powerlines and overhead obstructions in a two-hundred-mile radius, and turned to see how Tony was doing. 'Come on, Winchie – pull your finger out.' He grinned.

Tony looked round and cursed. As the winchman, Tony Lockhart was the one member of the crew required to leave the aircraft, to go down on the wire into the sea if necessary to rescue survivors. Because of this ever-present possibility, he was struggling into a one-piece total immersion suit of bright orange with integral boots and rubber seals at wrists and neck with a single diagonal zip that slashed from right shoulder to left buttock. It was this heavy-duty zip Tony struggled with now, jerking it savagely down across his body as the precious seconds ticked away. Then he too grabbed yellow helmet and dirty, chamois-leather gloves and followed Pete out towards the aircraft, his boots thumping heavily on the concrete.

Dave Bourne was already halfway through cockpit checks by now, and the two men paused at the pilot's two o'clock position outside the helicopter's rotor-disc, thumbs raised above their heads towards their pilot. There was an answering thumbs-up from Bourne, and they ran forward, both ducking low out of habit – Pete to climb nimbly into the left-hand seat beside the pilot, Tony to scramble into the open cabin, its sliding door dogged back. Throat-mike fastened in place, helmet on and pulled tight, Tony reached for the jack-plug behind his helmet and plugged himself into the aircraft's internal communications system on a trailing lead.

Instantly, Tony's ears filled with the sudden hiss of static overlaid with the murmur of the pilot's patter as he ran rapidly down his list of mandatory cockpit checks: start starboard engine, start port engine, auto-stabilizer, rotor start, anti-icing hydraulics . . . On a Scramble start there were permissible corners that could be cut, seconds that could be shaved off a checklist to save a life. Even so, the checklist took precious seconds as Dave Bourne raced to get them into the air, his litany interrupted every few moments by Pete Sleaman sitting on his left, smoothly checking, confirming, verifying. As he did so, Tony double-buckled a monkey-harness around his waist, sat down on the cabin dinghy pack and waited. Suddenly his head snapped up. Dave was calling up Air Traffic Control, warning them he was about to lift off and swing left across the airfield at two hundred feet before turning on to heading. Air Traffic confirmed they were clear and that the circuit was empty of other aircraft. The brakes came off, the collective lever at Dave's left hand was raised to increase the thrust of the main rotor, and Tony leaned out of the door and looked round.

'Clear right and behind.'

'Roger.' Tony scrambled across to the port bubble and repeated the check, not just glancing out of the window but *looking*, searching for danger. A whirling beret sucked into the rotor at the critical moment of takeoff was as good as a five-pound bird strike any day of the week.

'Clear left and behind.'

'Roger.' The ground dropped away suddenly and they were airborne, gaining little height as they skidded away across the airfield, the ground flashing past dizzily. An airwoman on a pushbike stopped and waved as they roared overhead, and Tony leant back against the sudden tilt of the cabin floor.

'Come left on two four zero degrees, Boss.' That was Pete, the navigator.

'Left on two four zero degrees,' acknowledged Dave Bourne as the aircraft banked sharply on to heading.

'Oban Coastguard, Oban Coastguard, this is RESCUE 44 airborne this time with three souls on board. ETA Ardtornish harbour eighteen repeat one eighter minutes. Listening out two five two eighter, over.'

'RESCUE 44, this is Oban Coastguard. All copied. Listening out.'

In the Wessex cabin, Tony hauled the door closed against the blasting wind and moved to the rear of the aircraft. A canvas bench seat ran down the starboard side of the aircraft and on this was stacked the winchman's emergency medical equipment. Tony pulled the first canvas valise towards him, tore back the Velcro fastening and lifted out the heavy oxygen cylinder and face mask. Cracking open the demand valve, he listened for a moment to the hiss of escaping gas, twisted the valve shut, laid the bottle on the bench beside him and reached for the next medical satchel. Flight Sergeant Tony Lockhart was 'thinking evil', preparing for the worst. Time and again, reality had justified such prudent, pessimistic planning.

The flames were closer now. Jamie's eyebrows were singed and the heat beat fiercely against his face as he scrambled up on to the scrap of decking in the very bows of the fishing boat, barking his shins on the hard planking in his haste, but he was too frightened to notice. Robbie had gone, lost somewhere behind a wall of flame and shimmering heat as the flames ate their way forward. Already the boat was awash, submerged up to mid-section as she sank slowly beneath him.

The wind gusted suddenly, and Jamie threw up a hand with a cry of pain as he tried to ward off the flames that licked greedily towards him. A few more seconds, a few more minutes, and he would be forced into the sea, for there was nowhere else left to go.

And swimming was something else his mother had omitted to teach him.

'Come on . . . come on,' muttered the middle-aged sailor, a faintly ridiculous figure in smart blue skipper's cap and expensive Breton sweater as he stood over his outboard motor, jerking impotently on the pull-start handle as the engine coughed, spluttered and refused to start. 'Can't understand it,' he panted, wiping a plump hand over his sweating brow. 'It worked perfectly less than an hour ago. All I—'

'Don't stop, don't stop – please. Keep trying!' Jenny pleaded from the stone steps of the jetty, adding in a whispered prayer under her breath: 'Please, please God, make it work. Please.' The harbour was full of boats, crammed with vessels of every size and description. But not all had owners on board, or engines, or engines that weren't in pieces, or fuel in their tanks. It had taken Jenny, Steve and his mate three minutes of frenzied yelling and running along the top of the breakwater before they had settled on the yacht tender *Saucy Knights* as the unlikely heroine of the hour. Only now the engine wouldn't start.

''Ere, guv – let's have a go,' decided Steve impatiently, jumping lightly down into the tender. The owner thought about objecting and then stood back as Steve brushed him aside, grasped the handle and pulled in one smooth, fluid movement. The engine burst instantly into life, over-revved for a moment, and then settled down to a sweet, even howl. Thank God. Jenny leapt into the boat, fended them away from the steps with a foot and crouched down in the bows as they swung towards the harbour entrance. The breakwater was crowded with sightseers now, for the burning boat had drifted obligingly into sight on the tide and the small boy clinging to the bows was just visible through a pair of binoculars. Jenny, Steve and the tender-owner passed through the harbour mouth and swung towards the distant pall of smoke. On the breakwater, someone started clapping.

'RESCUE 44, this is Oban Coastguard. Advise ETA Ardtornish harbour, over.'

Pete Sleaman, navigating from the left-hand seat of the Wessex, lifted his head from his maps, studied the twisting valley floor eight hundred feet below, checked bridge, power-lines and farm buildings to port against the map overprint on his lap and made a rapid calculation.

'Six minutes, Boss.'

Dave Bourne nodded and reached unerringly above and behind his helmet for the radio switch.

'Oban Coastguard, Oban Coastguard – this is RESCUE 44. ETA six minutes. Any up-date, over?'

There was a brief pause with just the rush and hiss of static, then: 'RESCUE 44, this is Oban Coastguard. Be advised one of the casualties is deaf, repeat deaf, over.'

'Jesus!' Pete and Dave exchanged glances. 'D'you hear that, Tony? One of 'em's deaf.'

Behind and below in the cabin, Tony nodded. 'Not blind too, is he, Boss? Terrific. That's all we need: rescue by braille. Get Oban to find out which one, will you?' A deaf survivor wouldn't hear them coming, wouldn't hear shouted instructions that might be vital. In a moment, back came the reply, adding refinement to a task already hazardous: the boy.

'Oban Coastguard, Oban Coastguard, this is RESCUE 44. All noted. ETA now five minutes, over.'

Tony stood up, unbuckled the wide canvas belt from around his waist and pushed it back towards the rear of the aircraft. Then he took a webbing harness and bo's'un's chair from a canvas bag behind him, stepped into the loops, hauled the webbing seat up around his waist and adjusted the shoulder straps, deliberately tightening the left side more than the right to counteract the torque of his body spinning on the winch cable. Jerking the straps tight, Tony checked the quick-release box, replaced the monkey-harness, moved to the edge of the door and tore it back. Light flooded into the cabin. They were now at six hundred feet and the valley floor was flattening out beneath them, the cars looking like matchbox toys on the winding ribbon of road far below. Leaning out of the door, the wind tearing at his immersion suit, Tony could see the flat gleam of the sea stretching ahead and the outskirts of a small town coming up directly on track: Ardtornish. The aircraft banked steeply and began to lose height.

Reaching up to the top left-hand corner of the door, Tony pressed the winch switch and the hook directly above the door began to unwind towards him with a low whine.

They carried three hundred feet of cable on the winch and another one hundred and twenty feet of tape. Tony drew the cable into the cabin, stopped the winch and snapped the hook through the eye of the strop attached to the bo's'un's harness and pushed home the pin.

'OK, Boss – I'm off downstairs.' That was Pete, about to change from redundant navigator to winch operator with Tony's life at the tip of his finger. He achieved this transformation by folding back his seat and wriggling backwards and down through a space little bigger than the door of a washing machine. He did it, moreover, without touching any interesting-looking knobs, buttons and levers. Pilots tended to be quite fussy about that, and Pete Sleaman made it look easy. He slithered down beside Tony, plugged himself into the intercom, strapped himself deftly into a monkey-harness and crouched down beside the door. 'All set?'

Tony gave him a thumbs-up, unbuckled his safety belt and wriggled forward until he was sitting on the edge of the door, boots dangling into space. 'All set downstairs, Boss.'

'Roger, Pete.'

'RESCUE 44, this is Coastguard Mobile at Ardtornish harbour, over.' New voice, new call-sign.

'Coastguard Mobile, this is RESCUE 44. Go ahead, over.'

'RESCUE 44, I have you visual south and west of the breakwater. Do you see casualty, over?'

'Anyone?' Dave demanded tersely, as three pairs of eyes quartered the sea. From six hundred feet there was a lot of it to search.

'Too much glare,' offered Pete presently.

Dave agreed. 'Coastguard Mobile, this is RESCUE 44. Negative, over.'

'Understood, RESCUE 44. Casualty positioned two nautical miles due west this location and drifting north. Watch for my orange smoke. Repeat: watch for my orange smoke, over.'

'Wilco, out.'

They banked sharply over the sea and turned back along a north-westerly bearing. Almost immediately—

'Orange smoke, Boss. Your two o'clock,' reported Tony, wasting not a word as he called out the heading. Pete had left the door and gone to the port bubble to search the sea to the west. Almost at the same moment he spotted a thin column of black smoke rising from the sea, hidden before against the dark bulk of the island. Now Dave saw it too and spun the helicopter towards the burning fishing boat, the Coastguard's orange smoke marker discarded. He put the burning hulk slightly ahead and to his right and the helicopter swooped down.

'Look!' yelled Steve, pointing from the stern of the tender *Saucy Knights*. 'There's a chopper! A bleeding great yellow chopper!'

They were still a mile from the smoke and making agonizingly slow progress against wind and tide. Jenny twisted round and watched as the Wessex rolled and turned in the sky, the clatter of its rotors the sweetest sound she had ever heard as RESCUE 44 roared overhead. She swallowed, a lump in her throat that might have been relief, or hope, or tears, or a combination of all three.

'Get them!' she whispered savagely. 'Go on – get them!'

The boat was empty. It wallowed in the swell almost awash, the flames confined now to a flickering glow at the bows where the seawater had yet to quench the fire.

RESCUE 44 came to the hover sixty feet overhead, the down-draught of its rotors ruffling the surface of the sea and whipping up tendrils of spray as three pairs of eyes hunted for survivors. Nothing. No one clinging to the wreckage, no one floundering in the water nearby. One circuit, another, and then Dave began crabbing the aircraft gently sideways, following tidal drift. Perhaps thirty seconds passed in complete silence as they moved slowly out across open water, then—

'Something in the sea, Dave. One hundred metres at four o'clock.'

'Roger.' RESCUE 44 swung round. 'Got him.' Arms spread out in a position of crucifixion, a bubble of air trapped under his shirt high above his shoulders, Jamie Ennis floated face down in the gentle swell.

'Preparing to winch out,' warned Pete over the intercom, as Tony clipped an orange lifting strop on to his harness, took off his helmet and signalled that he was ready. 'Winching out.' There was a sharp tug as Pete flicked up the switch and Tony was pulled off the sill and swung out of the door into space.

'Tony is clear of the door. Winching out . . . Ten feet of cable out . . . twenty . . . thirty . . . Holding it there.' Tony hung suspended below the aircraft, head buffeted by the down-draught as he swung in his harness, kicking his legs violently to swing himself round so that he faced the casualty. There was a jerk as the cable stopped. Tony waved one hand sharply downwards and the cable unwound as Pete leant out of the door, one eye on the position of the casualty, the other on Tony swinging thirty feet below him. 'Forward thirty.' Obediently, tail down and nose slightly up, the helicopter moved forward as Tony began walking his legs through the air to keep directional stability. He was six feet above the sea and thirty yards from the body floating face down in the water. High above, pilot and winch operator concentrated intently: Pete upon distance, direction and Tony's precise hand signals; Dave upon height, speed and his operator's patter, hands and feet feather-light upon controls and pedals.

'Height is good. Forward ten . . . Winching out—' Another hand signal from Tony, and Pete lowered him slowly until little feathers of spray told him Tony's boots were just breaking through the crests of the swell and he had begun trawling towards the casualty. 'Forward twenty . . . forward fifteen . . . ten . . . height is good . . . eight . . . six . . . five . . . four . . . three . . . two . . . one . . . and steady. Steady.' Pete flicked out another three feet of cable and Tony sank down into the sea. 'Tony is in the water. He is moving to the casualty. He is beside the casualty . . . now.'

Tony grasped the boy by the shoulder and hauled him over on to his back. His eyes were closed and a mop of fair hair fell forward across the pale, waxy forehead above lips that were already tinged with blue. Lifting Jamie's chin clear of the sea with the cup of his hand, Tony forced the boy's jaws apart, pushed a gloved finger inside his mouth and swept it round to clear away any debris. Then, still treading water and with the boy clutched to his chest, Tony bent forward and blew several quick, short breaths into his lungs. There was no response. Nothing. The chest expanded, deflated – but did not rise. Tony tried again, the taste of salt strong in his mouth as he tried to force his own exhaled oxygen into Jamie's lungs, oblivious to the roar of the helicopter overhead and the sting and slash of salt spray whipping into his face, oblivious to everything except the boy's reaction. And still the chest wouldn't rise. Right. Enough. Stop pissing about.

Tony looped the orange strop over Jamie's lolling head and arms, pushed the strop toggle closed against the boy's chest and waved urgently upwards. Instantly the cable started to winch in and they were hauled clear of the water, the strop catching beneath Jamie's shoulder blades, Tony's legs wrapped tightly around the boy's slim body as he hugged him close. And still, even as they swung upwards, Tony was bending forward, forcing air into those congested lungs, looking for signs of a pulse. Of life.

'Winching in . . . Twenty feet of cable to come . . . Ten feet of cable to come . . . They're by the sill.' Fending them off with both feet planted against the edge of the door, Tony cradled Jamie's lolling head against his chest, drew his feet suddenly together and swung them both neatly inside the cabin. Pete moved back from the door.

'They're inside. Inside and off the cable.'

Dave acknowledged as Pete helped Tony drag off the strop and haul Jamie to the rear of the cabin. Now Tony's foresight paid off. Within seconds, Pete had the sucker out of its plastic case and forced between Jamie's lips, running it quickly backwards and forwards as it cleared away the last of the detritus.

Unclipped from the winch cable, water streaming off his immersion suit, panting harshly from exertion, Tony pulled on his helmet, jammed his intercom lead into the jack-plug, tore off his sodden gloves and pressed flat fingers against the boy's jugular. Pete glanced up, oxygen bottle ready to slide into place. 'Pulse?'

Tony shook his head briefly. 'Can't find the bastard.'

At that moment, Jamie Ennis was clinically dead.

In the dinghy half a mile away, Jenny turned to the others with tears coursing down her cheeks, her eyes shining with excitement and relief. 'Did you see?' she pointed, not caring if they saw her tears, her hair torn back from her face by the wind. 'They've got him! Thank God . . . he's going to be all right!'

Inside the cabin of RESCUE 44, Tony and Pete were bending over Jamie's still body, trying desperately to revive him. Pete was at the head giving mouth-to-mouth resuscitation. Tony was working on the chest giving cardiac compression: five compressions of the chest – one inflation; five – and then one; five – and then one. Check for breathing: no breathing. Check for pulse. Pete looked up and Tony shook his head briefly. Tony leant forward and pressed two stiffened fingers down hard against the centre of the boy's rib-cage. Jamie quivered and lay still. Tony pressed again, harder this time but with great care. Still nothing.

'He isn't—' began Pete. And then stopped. For then, quite suddenly, he had seen the chest rise of its own accord. There it was again.

Pete grinned and thumped Tony on the shoulder. Beneath the visor of his helmet, Tony's face creased into a sudden smile. The thousand dollar moment. They were bringing him back.

With winchman and navigator both busy in the cabin, it was up to pilot Dave Bourne to quarter the sea ahead as they crabbed slowly north-west across the sky, searching for the second casualty. They had drifted perhaps five hundred metres when Dave spotted what in kinder times he might have taken for the back of a basking seal, as a ripple of tiny waves broke over something in the water. But it wasn't a seal. It was a grey sweater. And it belonged to the body of a man floating just below the surface, twisted over on to his left side as though resting back comfortably against the endless cushion of the sea.

'There's the other one,' reported Dave tersely over the intercom. 'Fifty metres at three o'clock.' That placed him opposite the door.

Bending over the unconscious boy, Pete and Tony exchanged a look that spoke volumes. Rescue work is full of stark, uncompromising choices, the stakes invariably high with lost lives the penalty for a wrong decision or momentary error of judgement. For Tony to go into the sea a second time, both winchman and winch operator would have to leave the boy unattended, for there was no way Tony could work the winch himself, no way Pete could attend to the casualty with Tony on the end of the wire. Experience told them it would take between three and five minutes to winch Tony down into the sea, pick up the second casualty and get back aboard. And in that time . . . a mental shrug: the child would have to take his chances, that was all. They had wrapped him in a blanket, inserted a plastic airway into his mouth and settled the oxygen mask over mouth and nose. As long as he remained unconscious, the airway would prevent him suffocating; as long as his heart kept beating, oxygen should keep him breathing and his condition stable. That, at least, was the theory. But for five minutes, perhaps longer? If they were lucky.

'Let's not hang about on this one, OK, Boss?' suggested Tony laconically, snapping himself on to the winch cable, pulling on wet gloves and sitting forward into the door as Pete began directing Dave on to the body in the water, and the casualty slid from the pilot's sight beneath the nose of the aircraft.

'Preparing to winch out . . . '

'Roger.'

'Winching out . . . Tony is clear of the door . . . Ten feet of cable out . . . Twenty feet of cable out. Height is good . . . '

Forty-five seconds later, Tony was splashing down into the water and grasping for the shoulder of the second casualty. He hauled him over on to his back and saw with a sudden slide of revulsion that most of the right side of the face, head and neck had been eaten away by fire. The man's false teeth had become dislodged and filled the slack, gaping mouth like a bad fit. The eyes were already glazed and cold. Almost certain that he was wasting his time, Tony made one or two quick checks of the kind that do not come out of the regulation first-aid handbook: but there was no deep reflex to the eyeball, no elasticity left in the heavy body as he struggled to force the awkward, lolling arms through the strop.

Tony jammed the toggle tight across the chest and turned the body in the water. Officially, of course, neither he nor anyone else aboard RESCUE 44 was qualified to pronounce death, although the harsh school of practical experience had taught them many times over to recognize the absence of life. It was absent here, now, beyond the point of recovery. That, in many ways, made things easier.

Tony twisted round to look up at Pete leaning out of the cabin door forty feet above his head. He gave the signal to hoist. A moment's pause and the living and the dead were rising together out of the sea, streaming water, locked together in a tight embrace on the end of the cable. Twenty . . . Ten . . . Up to the door and in, with Pete reading all he needed to know in the way Tony swung his burden forward on to the cabin floor. It had ceased to be a person and had become instead a cargo, an envelope of empty, discarded flesh awaiting delivery and clinical disposal.

Tony plugged in at the jack-point, pushed up his visor and turned a thumb briefly downwards over the old man who gazed sightlessly up at the roof, the water streaming from his limp hair. 'Wasting our time on this one, Pete,' he said, leaning forward. 'How's the boy?' They crouched their way aft as Dave banked RESCUE 44 steeply to starboard and sent them racing nose-down towards the shore at less than one hundred feet, the water flashing past below the open door.

They'd got away with it. The boy was still alive, still taking oxygen on demand – a pale, vulnerable shape lost in a swathe of thick white blanket, clinging to life on the floor of the noisy, vibrating helicopter. Pete watched Tony monitor the boy's condition for a moment. Then they both came forward and harnessed the corpse into the Neil Robertson stretcher they carried hooked up on to the aircraft's roof.

'One bagged and ready to go, Dave,' reported Tony with the affected cynicism they adopted to shield one another from involvement, from caring. 'But the kid's still hanging on by his fingernails.'

'Roger. Pete – you'd better get up here and start looking in that bag of yours. I'm gonna need Approach and Overhead Obstruction Clearances from here all the way to County Royal.'

'On my way, Boss.' County Royal was the nearest general hospital with a casualty department. Pete tapped Tony on the shoulder, unbuckled his monkey-harness, came off the intercom and wormed his way back up to the navigator's seat beside the pilot.

'Tony – better get on the blower to Coastguard Mobile. Get them to warn Casualty at County Royal.'

'Roger.' Tony could take over radio communications from a duplicated set of controls mounted on a panel to the left of the door. Switching to the Coastguard frequency – 'Coastguard Mobile, Coastguard Mobile, this is RESCUE 44. Do you read, over?'

'RESCUE 44, this is Coastguard Mobile. Send, over.'

'Coastguard Mobile, this is RESCUE 44. Mission completed with five passengers on board. One male adult, Code Purple. One male child, unconscious, hypothermic. Condition critical. Will fly direct County Royal. Alert Casualty. Our ETA that location . . . zero niner minutes, over.'

'RESCUE 44, this is Coastguard Mobile. All copied. Wilco. Listening out.'

RESCUE 44 raced towards the harbour wall, twisted away to starboard and began to climb as Pete took them on a course over the town and south towards Gleninver.

CHAPTER FIVE

Fifteen minutes later, the yacht tender *Saucy Knights* nosed back into Ardtornish harbour with Jenny Macrae crouched in the bows ready to leap ashore the second they reached the steps. Twenty feet to go and Jenny turned suddenly, her debts remembered. 'Thank you – both of you. For helping.'

'You gonna be OK?' demanded Steve doubtfully.

Jenny nodded. 'Me? 'Course I am. Only I must . . . must find out what's happened. To Jamie, I mean.'

The wealthy weekend sailor in the skipper's cap nodded. 'Of course. Off you go, then – hope everything's all right.'

'So do I.' Jenny jumped for the steps and climbed them two at a time as the tender swung away to her mooring. Jenny reached the top of the breakwater and glanced round. With the fire quenched, the boat sunk, the helicopter gone and the excitement over, the crowds had dispersed too. Even the ambulance and the Coastguard Land Rover had melted back into the brickwork, the only sign of officialdom an elderly traffic warden strolling along beside the parked cars on the quay, his hat tilted back. Jenny hurried up to his side. 'Excuse me,' she began.

The traffic warden turned. 'Aye?' Cautiously, as though she might be the recipient of one of his tickets.

'Where would they have taken them?' she panted. 'The . . . the helicopter, I mean?'

He peered at her thoughtfully in the bright sunlight. 'The helicopter?'

Jenny swung round and pointed impatiently out to sea. 'The yellow helicopter. The one that was here just a few minutes ago. Where would they take the people they'd rescued, d'you know?' She'd expected to see them set down on the breakwater.

'Well now . . . ' A pencil scratched thoughtfully at a closely cropped skull. 'I dare say you could try the County Royal – only that's away down in Gleninver.' The traffic warden shook his head doubtfully, folded his arms and settled down to give the matter serious thought. 'There's the Masonic here in Ardtornish, of course, but that hasn't got a casualty department. Mind you, if they'd—'

'County Royal, of course. Thank you. Thank you very much,' interrupted Jenny hastily. She turned away and then stopped: she'd left the car at home, hadn't she? They'd come by bus. Then Jenny saw a rank of taxis waiting over by the bus station, hurried across the road and leant down by the driver's window. 'County Royal Hospital in Gleninver, please. It's very urgent.'

Mrs Ennis was picking flowers in the garden at the side of the house when she heard the snick of the garden gate and looked up. A police officer was standing with one hand on the gate catch, his cap tucked formally under his arm. 'Mrs Ennis . . . ?' They'd identified Jamie after RESCUE 44 had sent them the serial number of the phonic ear still strapped to his chest.

'Yes, I'm Mrs Ennis.' She frowned, puzzled. And then rose slowly to her feet, a hand to her throat as she knew with instinctive, sickening, maternal certainty that something terrible had happened to her son. 'It's . . . it's Jamie, isn't it? Something's happened to Jamie, I just know it,' she whispered. The policeman began walking slowly down the garden path.

'I'm afraid so, yes, Mrs Ennis. There's . . . there's been a wee bit of an accident . . . '

In the shabby first-floor offices of the *Gleninver Times*, Hamish Owen pushed away the wedding report he had been typing up and craned his head out of the window as the yellow helicopter flashed overhead. That had never happened before. Hamish thought for a moment, flicked open a newly thumbed contact book and dialled Coastguard headquarters at Oban with a sudden stirring of excitement. He introduced himself and asked his questions. A minute later he was slamming down the phone, pulling his jacket off the back of his chair and scrabbling around for notebook and pencil.

The Editor's door was closed. When Hamish entered he was confronted by Bob Harris poring over a page layout in his shirtsleeves, beer gut bulging forward over his desk, hairy arms hidden in a welter of copy. It was not an edifying sight. There were dark stains at both armpits and his cluttered, airless office was thick with the smell of newsprint and tobacco. Harris frowned as he glanced up at the interruption. '*Now* what is it, laddie?'

'The helicopter that—'

'What helicopter?'

'The one that just flew overhead.'

'You finished that wedding I gave you?'

Hamish shook his head. 'Almost. I—'

Harris stabbed a thick finger towards his junior. 'Aye, I thought not. Get it finished, laddie – get it finished before you come blathering to me about any helicopter. You're holding up an early page.' He sighed. 'I don't suppose you have the slightest idea what—'

'I called the Coastguard. There's been a fire at sea off Ardtornish. They're taking two casualties to County Royal. One of them's Code Purple, he said.'

That stopped Harris, brought him up short. 'Purple, did you say?'

'That's what the Controller told me, yes.'

'You're sure, now?'

'Positive. I got him to repeat it.'

Harris nodded and then waved him away. He might have been waving off flies. 'Well, what are you waiting for, laddie – a starter's gun up your backside? Get on up there, get on up there.' But already Harris was talking to himself. Hamish was gone, racing down the back stairs to his Morris Minor.

Jenny's taxi swung round the last bend and entered the grounds of County Royal Hospital. It was set in a gentle fold of hills behind Gleninver town, its wards and administrative buildings scattered among a dozen acres of coniferous woodland and rhododendrons, interconnected by a smooth tarmac walkway lined with wooden benches where one or two elderly patients in dressing-gowns sat out in the late morning sunshine, tartan rugs drawn prudently over their knees.

They followed the white and red arrows towards the casualty department and then came suddenly upon a wide expanse of open grass. There, standing in its centre, stood the yellow rescue helicopter, its door dogged open, its rotors still and silent. A pair of hospital porters in grey coats with fire extinguishers at their feet were talking to a fair-haired young man in flying suit and dark-green lifevest who was sitting on one of the large rubber wheels with a mug in one hand and a yellow helmet dangling from its chin-strap in the other. A fire engine was parked on the far side of the grass, its crew lounging in the sun by the open doors. Now, as her taxi took her closer to this alien world of hospital and rescue services that had swept up her charge with such brisk efficiency, Jenny felt suddenly afraid. Apprehensive for Jamie, desperately worried about his safety, certainly – but scared, too, for herself. For what these people might think about her. She was responsible, in part. She was to blame for putting these people at risk, to so much trouble. Or so she told herself. She tapped the driver on the shoulder. 'Anywhere here's fine. How much do I owe you?'

He glanced down at the milometer. 'Four pounds fifty should about cover it.' Jenny nodded and snapped open her purse. If he'd said twenty-five pounds it would hardly have registered. 'D'you want me to wait?' he asked. Jenny shook her head, got out, pressed a fiver into the driver's outstretched hand and hurried towards Casualty without waiting for change. As she did so, a young nurse in blue-and-white uniform hurried out towards the helicopter, folding up a white blanket. Jenny began to frame a question, but the nurse was past and the moment had gone before she had decided what she was going to say. Jenny took a deep breath and pushed through the rubber-skirted double doors, passing from sunlight into that other world where the smell of floor polish, surgical dressings and centrally heated, antiseptic sterility is the hallmark of every British hospital from Penzance to Aberdeen.

There was a middle-aged receptionist sitting behind a glass partition that kept her in germ-free isolation from the contagious public. A row of canvas-backed metal chairs lined one wall a little further down the corridor leading to Intensive Care and the casualty wards. Beyond the receptionist, peering at her now over the top of flesh-coloured spectacles, Jenny saw two other crewmen from the rescue helicopter, both sitting hunched forward nursing paper cups of coffee, their yellow helmets on the empty chairs beside them. One wore an orange rubber suit, his dark hair pushed up into rough spikes by the sweat and exertion of the rescue. The other was of slight build and wore the same dark-green flying suit as the man waiting outside by the helicopter. Both men looked drawn, their faces lined by strain now that they were resting. Jenny began walking hesitantly towards them, planning what she would say, her shoes squeaking on the highly polished linoleum.

'Yes? Can I help you?' It was the receptionist behind her glass partition, her spectacles now hanging down on to her chest on a length of gold chain. She was really saying: no one gets past me without permission.

Jenny walked up to the desk: 'Oh, yes – good morning. I . . . er . . . I understand a young boy was brought in here just now by those . . . those gentlemen.' She gestured briefly down the corridor and the men glanced up, her words carrying clearly in a place of silence and sudden, distant echoes. 'I was wondering . . . Could you tell me how he is, please? His name is Jamie. Jamie Ennis. He's eight years old.'

A capable finger ran down an entry sheet in the ledger and stopped beside a time and a name. Then the receptionist looked up, her finger still marking the place. 'You're the boy's mother, I presume?'

Jenny shook her head. 'No. No, I'm not. I'm . . . I'm his teacher. His speech therapist. I was looking after him when . . . when the accident happened.'

'I see.' The first faint hint of disapproval as the ledger closed with a soft thud. 'I'm sorry, but we are not permitted to release information of that nature to anyone other than next of kin. However, if you—'

'But he is here, in this hospital?'

'He has been admitted, yes,' the woman conceded.

'Then surely I can—'

'He's in Intensive Care.'

Jenny absorbed this in shocked silence. 'Intensive Care? But I . . . I saw him lifted out of the water. He . . . '

'I'm sorry, that's all I can tell you. If you'd care to wait over there.' She pointed a pencil elegantly down the corridor at the line of chairs. 'I will tell the Casualty Officer that you're here. Perhaps, under the circumstances, if he has time . . . ' She left the sentence hanging dismembered in the air.

Jenny nodded and walked slowly down the polished corridor, dazed. Intensive Care. That meant it was serious. That Jamie could die. And she, Jenny Macrae – she was to blame. The two crewmen looked up as she came towards them. 'How is he?' she asked quietly. 'The boy, I mean. The boy you picked out of the water.'

Tony Lockhart shrugged. 'He'd been in the water a while when we got to him,' he said quietly. 'He was unconscious.'

'But he's alive?' pressed Jenny. 'He is going to be all right. Isn't he?' There was a fractional pause.

'When we brought him into Casualty? Yes, he was still alive.'

'And Robbie?'

'I'm sorry?'

'Robbie Roberts. The old man with him in the boat.' Pray God, let him be all right too. Please.

Tony paused, then – 'I'm sorry. He didn't make it.'

'He . . . '

'He'd drowned before we could reach him,' explained Tony quietly, sparing her the finer details.

'Oh. I . . . I see.' Jenny sat down slowly as that soaked in, thinking of that craggy, earnest face as he asked if he could take Jamie with him out to the lobster pots: 'You can trust me, you know, Jen. I'm not about to go running off with the lad.' All that warmth and kindness down through the years, just suddenly . . . gone. 'I . . . I watched you. From the dinghy,' Jenny said quietly, looking up. 'You . . . you were marvellous. You all were,' she said simply, too numbed for subtlety. Tony nursed his coffee and stared into the bottom of the paper carton. Marvellous? 'Course they were. Regular Action Men, the lot of them. Especially when someone got away, slipped through their hands. Like now. Like this man Roberts. Tony looked up suddenly as a door banged shut at the far end of the corridor.

'It . . . it was his idea,' Jenny explained suddenly, the words tumbling out almost against her will. 'He . . . he was going fishing, you see. Going to collect up his lobster pots just out in the bay. It looked so . . . so safe. There wasn't a breath of wind. When Robbie asked if he could take Jamie with him, I . . . ' She shrugged helplessly. 'I said yes. I never thought for one moment that—' They all turned suddenly as the double doors at the end of the corridor were pushed open and a policeman led the way into Casualty followed by a man and woman. It was Mr and Mrs Ennis.

Jenny rose slowly to her feet as the policeman spoke briefly to the receptionist and then ushered Jamie's parents politely ahead of him down the corridor towards the row of metal chairs. When Mrs Ennis saw Jenny her steps faltered, her face a mixture of battling emotions as Jenny hurried forward. 'Mrs Ennis, I'm terribly, terribly sorry . . . ' she began inadequately.

'Who're you?' demanded John Ennis sharply, a heavy-faced, straight-spoken businessman in three-piece suit.

'I'm Jenny Macrae,' Jenny explained, holding out a hand. 'Jamie's speech therapist.'

'Just tell me how he is,' began Mrs Ennis, her voice pitched low, her emotions under tight control. 'I'm not angry, I just want to know how he is.' She got no further as her husband stepped forward, brushing aside both his wife's question and Jenny's outstretched hand.

'I'll deal with this now, love, if you don't mind,' he interrupted sternly. 'Now then, Miss . . . Miss whatever your name is. Let's get one or two things straight from the start. As I understand it, you were supposed to be looking after my son, correct?'

Jenny swallowed. 'That is correct, yes, Mr Ennis.'

'Right. Now then: what the hell's going on?'

Jenny took a deep breath, aware that everyone was looking at her, everybody listening.

'Jamie went out in a fishing boat to pick up some lobsters. For some reason the boat caught fire. I . . . I don't know why. Jamie was picked up from the sea by that yellow helicopter you saw outside, by these men here.' She gestured at Tony and Pete. 'They brought him here.'

'Jamie – my son? In a fishing boat? Look, lassie – if you're having me on, let me assure you—'

'I'm not having you on, Mr Ennis,' Jenny replied wearily. 'I wish to God I was. A fisherman offered to take Jamie with him when he went to look at his lobster pots.'

'And you let him go?' demanded Mrs Ennis, aghast, as if Jenny had let a mentally subnormal child play alone with a loaded pistol.

Jenny nodded slowly. 'I . . . I thought it would be good experience for him,' she admitted quietly.

'Good experience for him?' echoed John Ennis incredulously, as though he could not believe his ears. 'The boy's stone deaf – you do know that, I suppose?'

'Yes, I am aware of that, Mr Ennis,' Jenny countered steadily, holding her ground. 'Your wife and I agreed outside stimulation would be a good thing.'

'Outside stimulation?' Ennis exploded. 'And who the hell—'

'I should never have agreed to it,' interrupted his wife dully. 'If I'd only—'

'And just where the hell were you all this time?' stormed the boy's father. 'You don't look like you've done much swimming in the sea!'

'I . . . I was on the breakwater. We'd been sketching and—'

'Mr and Mrs Ennis?' asked a quiet voice behind them. They all turned. 'Might I have a word, please? In private.' With John Ennis storming on at Jenny, no one had noticed the doctor walk quietly down the corridor towards them from Casualty, both hands jammed into the pockets of his white coat. Sandy-haired, with pale-blue eyes behind metal-framed spectacles, he looked too young to be a doctor. Jamie's parents exchanged glances.

'Yes. Yes, of course . . . '

'I'm Dr Dorman. Would you both like to come this way, please?' He turned and led them politely towards the glass doors leading to his department. Jenny, the policeman and the two helicopter crewmen watched the figures recede in silence. Then Pete pushed to his feet.

'Come on, Winchie,' he said quietly. ''Nother day, 'nother dollar.'

Tony crushed his coffee carton in his fist and tossed it wearily into the wastebasket. 'Oh, God,' he groaned, 'I thought we'd got him.' He stood up slowly, and Jenny looked from one crewman to another, puzzled. Like the police, Pete and Tony were well versed in the formalities of bereavement. They knew what lay behind that casual, oh-so-casual invitation to accompany the doctor to the far end of the corridor. Only Jenny was left in brief, merciful ignorance as the men moved away.

Jenny watched the young doctor pause out of earshot on the far side of the glass screen, turn to Jamie's parents and begin to talk. Gradually, very gradually, a terrible suspicion took root in her mind, blossoming into certainty like some malignant cancer of despair that was confirmed in the sudden slump of Mrs Ennis' shoulders, in the impotent crash of her husband's open palm against the glass screen, in the sad, final shake of the doctor's head as he turned and walked away, leaving them to come to terms with a grief so sudden, so huge that they could not recognize it.

'No . . . ' whispered Jenny. 'Oh, please . . . no.'

Long seconds of frozen time inched by as Jenny stood in

the empty corridor, her eyes locked on the two figures on the far side of the glass doors, her world reduced to a numb, dull ache of pain and despair. The doors opened at last and Jamie's parents came slowly down the corridor towards her, one of John Ennis' arms about his wife's shoulders as she stumbled beneath a weight of grief too heavy to support unaided. Mrs Ennis stopped in front of the woman who had persuaded her to part with her only son, and looked into Jenny's face with eyes that were blank, dazed, disbelieving. 'He's . . . he's dead,' she whispered in the stillness, the words too new for meaning. 'Jamie's . . . dead.'

CHAPTER SIX

Jackman pushed quietly through the double glass doors into the main concourse at Glasgow Airport, his arrival passing unnoticed amid the bustle of the busy terminal as the doors swung shut behind him and the small executive jet that had flown him in from Gleninver was lost from view. He melted into the crowd and moved towards the north-western corner of the building where, as he had been told, he found a cluster of newsmen grouped around the familiar, portly figure of the Right Honourable James Belcher MP, Secretary of State for Industry. Belcher was standing in front of a display of heavy plant and machinery, the cameras flashing busily as the reporters' pencils raced over their notebooks. Jackman edged closer until he too could hear what the Minister from London was saying.

' . . . the closure of Lairds Shipyard and the loss of three thousand jobs is, of course, a matter of the utmost concern to this government,' Belcher explained gravely, with that look of palpable sincerity that is the true hallmark of the career politician. 'That is why I have come here today. It is my hope that, in close consultation with both management and union officials, we will be able to hammer out a plan of campaign that will go some way towards alleviating the hardship and suffering such a closure brings in its wake. You may rest assured I will do everything in my power . . . ' Belcher talked on, the empty, well-used words bouncing off the wall of solid, disenchanted Scots faces like paper darts off the side of a tank, his flanks protected by a uniformed police Inspector and a small party of officials from Whitehall and the Scottish Office.

Jackman moved unobtrusively around the outer ring of

reporters, his eyes not upon the Minister but upon one of the men who had come up with him on the Shuttle from London.

Ewan Baxter was in his early fifties with short, iron-grey hair brushed hard and flat across a wide forehead above pale, piercing, blue eyes. A former regular officer in the Royal Engineers, Baxter had been moved discreetly sideways into the shadows of SIS five years earlier for what was still euphemistically referred to as 'additional duties'. Now, as Jackman watched and waited, Baxter glanced up, saw Jackman standing at the back of the group and glanced away without a flicker of recognition. Jackman turned and walked casually towards a kiosk where he bought a newspaper. He was standing there reading when Baxter stepped quietly to his side a few minutes later.

'How's Engel taking it?' he asked without preamble, not offering to shake hands. Jackman folded his newspaper carefully, dropped it into a litter bin and looked up.

'Predictably, I'm afraid. Wanted to wash his hands of the whole business to begin with. Even threatened to call the police until I reminded him of certain . . . papers; certain commitments. Professor Highcroft was a personal friend of the family. That hardly helped.'

'Oh dear, I see. And now?'

'Now?' Jackman smiled briefly. 'Now I suppose you could say he's going through an equally predictable period of self-loathing.' Baxter made to speak but Jackman held up a hand. 'Don't worry, he'll get over it. I've seen his type before. He's too far in for second thoughts at this stage.'

Baxter nodded. 'Right, let's get on then, shall we? Porton want all the sordid details, I'm afraid. They're hopping mad.' Porton Down, the government chemical and biological research establishment on the edge of Salisbury Plain.

'I'm not surprised,' agreed Jackman candidly. He glanced round. 'You've time for a coffee, I take it? We can talk over there.' He gestured towards the cafeteria as Baxter shot back a cuff and glanced at the face of a watch turned to the inside of his wrist.

'Belcher's just launched into that "you have my solemn word" routine of his. On past showing, I can give you exactly twenty minutes.' He smiled briefly.

Ten of those minutes had gone before Ewan Baxter had the salient events of the previous night fixed firmly in his neat, military mind. Jackman had told him about the reception for Sandy Tulloch, about the sudden emergency summons to RD7, the disposal of Professor Highcroft's body, and the steps he had taken to hide the fact of his death from the Professor's wife and family. Now, as they sat together over their coffee in a quiet corner of the cafeteria with the nearest occupied table safely out of earshot – 'Those three men you mentioned,' Baxter mused idly, glancing at the names he had written on a small, leather-framed memo pad – 'Parsons, Calvert and Steevenson. You're sure they're the only ones who actually *saw* what happened to Highcroft? The only witnesses?'

Jackman nodded. 'Quite sure. No one else entered the compound until 07.00 this morning. I checked the log myself.'

'And they can be trusted, these men?'

'I assume so, otherwise they'd never have been cleared by your people to work on OMAHA. Steevenson has been with us a long time. He was PV'd long before he came up from Porton. The same goes for Calvert, by and large.'

'I wouldn't put too much store by that if I were you,' advised Baxter dryly, the Prime business at GCHQ still fresh in his mind.

Jackman shrugged. 'Anyway, they both know the score. Besides, by now both men will be aware that they're in line for an additional incentive to erase the matter completely from their minds.'

'Incentive?' Baxter asked sharply. 'What sort of incentive?'

'Two thousand. Each. In cash. To . . . bind them to the cause, as it were.'

Baxter nodded slowly. 'All right. That seems fair enough. What about Parsons, the third man? What about him?'

Jackman hesitated. 'He . . . hasn't been with us as long,' he replied at last, carefully.

'You sound unsure.' An observation, not criticism.

'A question mark, that's all,' admitted Jackman, remembering Parsons' face as he had stepped out of the lift on to the first floor of HPL's Research and Development block.

Baxter hunched forward. 'London don't want question marks,' he said quietly. 'They want this Highcroft business locked up. Tight.'

Jackman stirred his coffee slowly. 'What was I supposed to do – heave him over the side as well?'

Baxter sat back in his chair, pencil tapping slowly against the three names on the pad in front of him. Then he looked up and regarded Jackman in speculative silence for several moments.

'All right,' he said finally. 'Point taken. My report will show that there was nothing more you could reasonably have done given the time and facilities at your disposal. However—' he made a little note on his pad and looked up – 'there are still too many mouths.' He laid heavy emphasis on the last word. 'I think we should put someone in on the ground, don't you? Just for a few days. Just in case you need someone close at hand to keep an eye on things. It'll probably blow itself out soon enough. But if it doesn't . . . well, he'd be there, wouldn't he? Just in case.'

'Anyone particular in mind?' Jackman asked.

Baxter sighed as though the whole awkward business was deeply regrettable. 'There's a chap I sometimes use,' he replied.

They were back on the ground at RAF Glenhaddon, rotors windmilling to a stop. Blessed silence.

Dave Bourne, the pilot of RESCUE 44, let his hands fall away from the controls and sat back with a groan. He twisted the quick-release box in his lap, banged a heavy hand against its centre and let the shoulder straps reel back into the bulkhead behind him. Sliding back the door to his right, Dave unplugged his helmet and climbed slowly down to the ground, suddenly conscious of the dull ache across his shoulders as he followed his winchman and navigator across the concrete landing pad towards the crewroom. No one spoke. They walked away from the aircraft without a backward glance as though it had failed them, each man alone with his thoughts. There was little satisfaction in rescue work just then and no glamour, no glamour at all. Just the sour taste of failure and the nagging suspicion that they ought, somehow, to have done more . . .

Standing at the control desk with its battery of telephones and its uninterrupted views west, north and south across the airfield, Warrant Officer 'Timber' Woods watched the crew of RESCUE 44 approach with experienced eyes. Forty-two years old and with a chest of ribbons attesting to almost twenty-five years unbroken service, Warrant Officer Woods was the human bolt that held Rescue Flight together and provided the vital administrative link between aircrew and ground personnel. Crowded here into the control room with the second Wessex wheeled out on to its landing circle and the standby crew called to Readiness to cover 44's absence, they had all heard the details of the mission's failure in the terse R/T transmissions between MRSC in Oban and RESCUE 44. Years of experience at just such a desk had taught Woods to read the mood of a returning crew with considerable sensitivity. The fact that there were two more deaths to write up on the tally board at the end of the corridor was bad enough; that one of them was a child made it infinitely worse. Dave Bourne and Pete Sleaman were both unmarried and had no children, but Tony Lockhart had a son of his own and he, Woods realized, would take it hardest of all.

Now, as the men from RESCUE 44 moved from First Crew to Second Standby and handed over to the three men lounging in the crewroom with *their* boots on the same scuffed coffee table, Warrant Officer Woods knew it would be a time of forced jokes, short tempers and private introspection until the next job, the next successful rescue. 'Better get the tea on, son,' he suggested quietly to one of the Corporals.

'Already on its way,' replied the Corporal without

turning round. He too had learnt to read the signs.

The outside door banged open suddenly and Tony, Pete and Dave pushed into Operations. Tony was still wearing the one-piece orange immersion suit and held the sodden bo's'un's harness in one gloved hand. He crossed to the open wooden locker where he kept his flying gear, unclipped his throat mike and eased off his helmet with a groan of relief, his ears still ringing from the flight. As he turned he saw Woods watching him from amid the cluster of silent people around the control desk. In theory, Woods was the senior NCO although, on Rescue Flight, such distinctions were meaningless.

'Sounded like a right bastard from here,' offered Woods sympathetically, tapping the radio.

'Bad enough,' Tony agreed curtly, pushing his helmet violently towards the back of his locker as though he never wanted to see it again. 'We were too late, that's all,' he told the listening room, his voice pitched low with frustrated anger. 'Just too sodding late.' He turned and went through the swing door, the thick rustle of his rubber immersion suit filling the narrow corridor as he almost collided with an airman coming towards him carrying a tray of steaming mugs. Tony took one without a word and strode on towards the washroom. The airman turned indignantly and was about to object until, just in time, he caught Woods' warning shake of the head.

The washroom had drying pipes set at head height across one end. At the other, there was a large, square, tiled bath filled with fresh water. Tony threw bo's'un's harness and leather gloves into the water and sat down on the edge of the bath, both hands cupped around his mug of hot sweet tea, his eyes and thoughts in some far-off place only he could see. Presently he pushed himself to his feet, clambered out of the orange immersion suit and dumped this too into the bath to rinse off the salt. There was a sudden burst of laughter from the crewroom and Tony looked up, prodding the sluggish, bloated immersion suit moodily with a broom handle as he finished his tea. Then he padded barefoot in his underwear through to the shower-room across the corridor.

Tony pulled open his locker, reached automatically for towel and washing things and then paused, hand outstretched, suddenly shocked by his own reflection in the steel mirror on the inside of the door. He looked old and lined, brown eyes sunk back into their sockets, cheeks and forehead furrowed below a sweat-streaked mat of black hair. He slammed the metal door shut with a crash. Sod it. So what? So bloody what? He felt old, just now. They'd done a long shift.

He stripped off and stood for long minutes under the powerful shower, turning his face up into the lancing needles of hot water as though soap and washing alone might somehow purge the memory of that small, frail body lolling face downwards to the gentle motion of the waves, as he trawled towards it on the end of the wire. Death was something he could never get used to, not deep down beneath the rough jokes and macabre stories that sustained them all at the necessary level of professional detachment. Cliff fallers and cliff jumpers, drowned swimmers and lost climbers, heart-attack victims and careless adventurers who thought it could never happen to them – on balmy, treacherous summer afternoons, and in the midst of howling winter blizzards, he had clasped them all briefly in his arms, steadied them in the stretcher as they swung up into the helicopter, so that over the years death had become an old, familiar adversary cloaked in a dozen different disguises. Yet it still retained its ability to shock, to soil and degrade.

Tony stepped out of the shower and began dressing. Although he was coming off duty with the other two members of the crew after a total of twenty-five hours on call, including the Gleninver over-run, he would still be officially on Second Standby until dusk. Because of such insensitive rostering he was required to travel home in uniform. Adjusting his tie in the mirror, Tony slipped into the tunic blouse with the small golden eagle above the Sergeant's chevrons that was the jealously guarded symbol of operational aircrew status, and crammed his dirty clothes into a holdall, anxious now to be gone from such overly familiar surroundings. Hefting the bag, he went out across the tarmac and slid behind the wheel of his Ford Escort parked on the other side of the hangar. He had just begun to swing the car towards the perimeter road when the crewroom door opened and Pete Sleaman came sprinting across the grass towards him. He was still wearing flying gear. Tony stopped the car and wound down the window. 'Don't tell me,' he groaned. 'Four Three's unserviceable and we've just been slated for another twenty-four.'

Pete bent down to the car window, a hand resting on the Escort's warm roof. 'They'd have a bloody riot if they tried that . . . ' He paused. 'Dave and I reckon we'll sink a few down at the Dolphin a bit later on. Why don't you come along too?' After four days as First Crew and four evenings tethered to the station on the end of a telephone as Second Standby, tonight would be their first opportunity for serious drinking for almost a week. As bachelors living in the officers' mess with an historic reputation to uphold and minimal domestic overheads to worry about, both men intended to make the most of it. But Tony shook his head.

'No thanks, Pete. Not tonight.'

'Why not? Do you the power of good, mate. You can't just sit around on your own forever. Tell you what – there's this bird with the most—'

'Yeah, I know. Thanks, Pete.'

'See you there?'

'Definitely maybe, OK?' Tony smiled, reached down for the ignition and then paused. 'Know who I feel sorry for?'

'Who?'

'That girl. The bird with the brown hair waiting at the hospital.'

'The one getting all that stick from the kid's old man? Stupid cow – it was her bloody fault, wasn't it? He'd still be alive if she hadn't let him out of her sight.'

'Did you see her face?' asked Tony thoughtfully. 'The look in her eyes when she realized the doc was telling them their son had snuffed it?'

'What about it?'

'She doesn't have to wait until she dies to know what hell's like,' he said sombrely, easing off the handbrake. 'She's there already.'

Jenny pushed the front door closed behind her and walked slowly down the narrow hall of her flat towards the living-room, her mind a numb blur of grief and bitter self-recrimination. She had no recollection of talking to the police, of answering their questions and making a statement before leaving the hospital, no memory of walking out of Casualty past the flat, hostile glare of the receptionist and down the long, steep hill to the town; no awareness of pain in her shoulder as the rope handles of the beach-bags sawed cruelly through the thin cotton of her blouse. Just numbness. Trance-like, Jenny moved now through to the living-room where she dropped uncaring on to the sofa and sat staring at the bookcase for long minutes, her bags strewn forgotten in the shadows at her feet, unaware that although it was mid-afternoon the curtains were still drawn from the previous evening.

In the shock and pain of her guilt, Jenny had fastened upon one scene from the nightmare drama of events that had unfolded around her at Gleninver that hot summer's afternoon: the old man, Robbie Roberts, the man she'd known since childhood, crouching down with a hand on Jamie's shoulder as he studied the boy's drawing. And the look on Jamie's face as he'd turned round.

Now, into that sea of private agony there floated two other cameos: Mrs Ennis, Jamie's mother, coming slowly down the hospital corridor towards her with her husband's arm about her shoulders – and one of the men from the helicopter, the one with the black hair and wearing that orange suit, crumpling his coffee carton slowly in his fist and saying: 'I thought we'd got him.'

All those people, all that grief. And she was responsible.

Ten minutes went by, perhaps longer. Jenny neither knew nor cared. At length she stirred, rose to her feet and pulled back the curtains. Daylight flooded into her sitting-room. As she turned back into the silent room she saw the contents of both beach-bags spilled across the floor. Jenny went down on hands and knees to pick up the pathetic debris of their trip to the seaside, each item now charged with a terrible poignancy: Jamie's blue sweater and bag of crayons; a plastic box of left-over cheese sandwiches they had decided to save until the afternoon; a packet of seashells bought at a stall near the breakwater. And, at the bottom of the pile, Jamie's sketchbook. Jenny turned it over in her hands and then opened it slowly to the last picture, at the sketch of Robbie working over his nets in the sunlit harbour. She stared at that picture, unmoving for several seconds. Then something seemed to tear loose deep inside her and she groaned aloud, sinking back on her haunches to weep anguished, silent tears, her face screwed into a mask of pain. She was sitting there still with the tears coursing down her cheeks when the doorbell rang.

She thought she had imagined it at first. There was a pause and then there it was again, more insistent this time. Jenny stirred, got to her feet and looked round, crossing to the mirror and looking with dismay at her red-rimmed eyes and tear-blotched cheeks. The bell rang again and Jenny went slowly down the corridor. She stopped by the door. 'Who is it?' she called dully.

'Miss Macrae?' A man's voice. Nervous, unsure.

'Yes? What do you want?'

'It's . . . er . . . it's Hamish Owen, Miss Macrae. May I speak to you a moment, please?'

Jenny paused before replying, loath to keep shouting through the closed door with Mrs Proctor no doubt listening to every word from the floor above, loath to let whoever it was see her in such a state and wanting, above all else, to be left alone. She could have ignored the bell completely, but she never imagined for one moment that the caller had something to do with Jamie's death. She sighed, slipped up the catch and pulled the door open.

A tall young man was standing outside, a notebook held in one hand. Even then it didn't click. 'Yes?' she repeated steadily, seeing the sudden flicker of embarrassment in his face as he registered she had been weeping. 'What do you want?'

The young reporter swallowed. 'Hamish Owen, Miss Macrae. *Gleninver Times.*' Jenny felt a sudden sickening lurch in the pit of her stomach. 'I wonder if I might just—'

Jenny shook her head. 'I'm not . . . I don't want to talk to the Press. You'll have to excuse me.' She began to close the door.

'Please, Miss Macrae – it won't take a moment,' Hamish Owen pleaded hastily, as he suddenly saw himself facing Harris' wrath as he returned to the office empty-handed to tell him he had failed in this, his most important journalistic assignment to date. 'If you could just confirm a few details, that's all. The police did give me your address . . . ' Not strictly true, for he had lifted it out of the incident book when the desk Sergeant's back had been turned, but it did give his questions a certain superficial legitimacy.

Jenny wavered, a hand on the doorknob. 'Well, I . . . '

'Please, Miss Macrae – just two minutes. Just to set the record straight,' he pleaded. Jenny sighed. And gave in.

'All right, then – but only two minutes. I suppose you'd . . . you'd better come in.' If she had been able to see the newspaper headlines the next morning, however, she would never have opened the door.

Flight Sergeant Tony Lockhart turned his Ford Escort into the mouth of Bruneval Close and drove down between the rows of identical semi-detached houses towards his own married quarter at the bottom of the cul-de-sac. The road was busy with children, and Tony slowed to a crawl as he found himself scanning faces, looking for one small face in particular. Even now, after all these weeks. Recognizing the car, several small boys raced after the driver, for Tony was something of a local hero, the man who spent much of his time in the big yellow helicopter rescuing people and doing exciting stuff like that . . .

The kids knew all about rescue helicopters in Bruneval Close. Some weeks earlier, before Maureen had left him, the headmaster of the local primary school had asked

Tony's Flight Commander to put on a bit of a demonstration, hammer home the need for safety at the seaside before the summer holidays got into their stride. At the appointed hour, RESCUE 44 had swooped in across the playing fields with Tony dangling on the end of the cable, a smoke canister strapped to each boot. Seventy-five under elevens had gone delirious with excitement, hopping from one foot to the other as the yellow Wessex banked over the classrooms and trails of orange smoke drifted across the playing fields. As a direct result of that display, and the free flights that were the highlight of a memorable afternoon, at least half the road's population of small boys now wanted to be helicopter winchmen more than anything else in the world, and Paul, Tony's eight-year-old son, had found himself swept to a pinnacle of envy and popularity among his school-mates. It was a popularity that had been short-lived, Tony remembered bitterly: less than a week later Paul had gone, plucked away to some school in the south by his mother.

Tony drove up on to the concrete hard-standing in front of the garage. Hauling a bag of groceries off the passenger seat and pushing the door closed with his hip, he let himself in at the side door.

The silence of the place still hit him, every time he came through the door.

Dumping his groceries on the cluttered kitchen worktop, Tony immediately turned on the radio, needing the companionship of music, of voices, to fill the empty house. Ordinary, less stressed marriages might be torn apart by infidelity, by boredom, even, but Maureen Lockhart's 'other woman' had been a Royal Air Force Wessex Search and Rescue helicopter, fuelled by fear and weighed down by a payload of her own personal inadequacies. Other winchmen, with wives who were perhaps less sensitive, were able to come home after the stress and occasional horror of rescue work and unwind slowly, to talk or not talk as they chose. But not Tony. Maureen had to *know*: to hear every single detail. And it was that knowledge, coupled to her own imagination and Tony's professional dedication, that had torn their marriage apart. Events had reached their climax in early July: a student had been trapped on a narrow ledge of rock halfway up a sheer five-hundred-foot cliff. Not too difficult at first, they'd thought: almost routine – until the girl had lost her nerve, ignored their shouted advice and tried to climb away from danger. They had watched, helpless, as she slipped and fell to her death. Tony's helicopter had been forced in under the cliffs with the tip of its rotor just inches away from the rock-face, as Tony sank down on the wire to release the body. Before that it must have been the heart attack on the oil tanker – and before that, engine trouble on that private gin-palace of a yacht full of seasick businessmen out for a jolly with not a life-jacket or a spanner between them. Attempted rescues, some successful, some not. Stock in trade for a professional SAR winchman, but not to his wife. To Maureen, the procession of incidents had seemed endless. Just danger after danger, risk without end. With Tony always, always, putting his work, the job, before his family. Before her.

Towards the end she had even shunned the other aircrew wives, turning her back on their kindness, their collective support and outward cheerfulness, refusing to believe they could understand and share her fears yet still smile, still come to terms with the pride and the risk inherent in their husbands' chosen profession. She had come to dread the coming of the holiday season, the busy time; come to resent the arrival of the 'Birmingham Navy', the boat-mad, land-locked holiday-makers; begrudge them their happiness, their fortnight's carefree optimism. For one day, she knew, one of them would rob her of her husband. Not next week, or next month, or even next year, perhaps – but one day there would be the knock on the door. And she would be left alone.

Finally, after another terrible, bitter row, she had decided she could take no more of it. Tony had stormed out of the house back to work, slamming the door behind him. When he returned at the end of the shift she was gone, back to her parents in the south. Taking Paul with her.

Now Tony looked slowly around the domestic shambles of his kitchen, at the stack of dirty dishes piled in the sink and the mountain of creased clothes waiting for him on the ironing board, and then groaned aloud as his eyes settled on a child's drawing of a bright-yellow helicopter Sellotaped to the side of the fridge. A thick brown line connected a gangling, stick-like figure to the door of the helicopter. A big arrow pointed to the figure, and scrawled beside it was the one word, DADDY, followed by a long row of crosses. Tony turned away abruptly and began unpacking his groceries.

It was only later when he went through into the hall that he noticed the brown envelope lying on the doormat. From RAF Glenhaddon's Housing Officer, it advised him crisply and impersonally that married quarters were allocated on a 'need' basis to married members of HM Forces stationed at RAF Glenhaddon and, regretfully, not to separated aircrew Flight Sergeants living alone. Under the circumstances they would be grateful if Flight Sergeant Lockhart A.J. could make alternative arrangements and vacate the quarter by 12.00 hours, 12 October.

It was two hours later, and in his stale, airless little office on the first floor of the *Gleninver Times*, Editor Bob Harris was subbing Hamish Owen's story about the fire at sea and the deaths of Jamie Ennis and Robbie Roberts. Tragedy at sea always made good copy, but this one was magic. It had everything, even pictures, for the drama had been captured by any number of holiday-makers armed with their ubiquitous telephoto lenses: a child who was dead, deaf, *and* the son of a prominent local councillor; an heroic helicopter winchman; they even had a scapegoat, someone to blame for the tragedy – this speech therapist woman, Jennifer Macrae. He had been going to lead on the deckchair 'scandal' he had exhumed with some difficulty from the Council minutes, but now, with less than two hours to go before he put the paper to bed, he had re-jigged most of the front page. Reaching forward, he pulled out a sliding tray recessed into the top of his desk and consulted a long list of telephone numbers. A thick finger stopped at the number of the *Daily Mirror* in Manchester, and Harris began dialling: linage was one of the Editor's perks on the *Gleninver Times*. As Harris waited for his call to be answered, he ran an eye over the new front-page layout. The sea story, with its dramatic central picture, would run across six columns.

It quite swamped the other human interest story tucked away in a single column and headlined simply: HUSBAND MISSING.

CHAPTER SEVEN

'This is Radio Firth. The time is just coming up to fourteen minutes after four, and that was Neil Diamond with a track from his *Diamonds* album called "Mr Bojangles", one of my all-time personal favourites. And, talking of jangles, this is Mike Mitchell ready to take the next call on Mike's Open Line. Hello, who's that?' There was no reply. 'Hello?'

'Hello. My . . . my name is Helen. Helen Highcroft,' began a tired, hesitant voice.

'Yes, Helen, my darling – what can I do for you?' Tuned to ceaseless pop and holiday requests, DJ Mike Mitchell didn't realize at first that this one was different, older, troubled . . .

'I'm not . . . not sure. I've . . . I've never even thought of calling a radio station before. I . . . '

'Well, now – that leaves a lot of interesting options open, doesn't it, Helen? Where are you calling from, sweetheart?'

'From . . . from Gleninver. I'm in a call-box.'

'From a call-box in Gleninver. I see. Fine. You having a good holiday, Helen?'

'I . . . no. I . . . we live here. You see—'

'Do you? Well, some people have all the luck – smashing part of the world down there. Well now, Helen, what can I do for you?'

'I'm trying to find my . . . my husband,' explained Helen Highcroft in a tight, controlled voice. In the studio on the outskirts of Glasgow, the DJ glanced up with a frown at his producer, listening through headphones on the other side of the sound-proof screen.

'Trying to find your husband?' rattled on the DJ, thinking ahead to possible trouble for the station; legal action. 'Lot of people I know are trying to lose theirs,

Helen!' He laughed easily. 'Tell you what. If you—'

'Please, Mr Mitchell. This isn't a . . . a joke. I'm not some . . . some teenager whose holiday romance has blown up in her face. My husband has just . . . vanished. Disappeared. I thought perhaps if he was listening to your programme somewhere . . . if I told you a little bit about him, gave a description, then perhaps one of your listeners might—'

'What about the police, love? We're not really able to—'

'I've already been to the police. They told me it was a civil matter, nothing to do with them. I've tried all our friends, all our relatives. I . . . I was driving around just now with the radio on and I just thought . . . please, I'm desperate. I don't know what else to try,' she begged, her voice beginning to break up. At the radio station, people had stopped work and were staring up at the speakers on the walls. In strictly commercial terms, of course, it was riveting stuff. In the studio, the DJ glanced up at his producer, who nodded and gave a cautious thumbs-up.

'OK, Helen, why not? Helping people solve their problems is what it's all about, right? So let's give it a whirl – and all you Radio Firth listeners out there, why don't you stop what you're doing for a minute or two and just listen, OK? Helen – the floor's yours, as we say.'

'Thank you.' They all heard her give a long, shuddering sigh, as though struggling to keep emotion under tight control. 'My . . . my husband's name is Malcolm – Malcolm Highcroft. We've . . . we've been together almost twenty years. He's . . . forty-nine years old, about five feet ten inches tall, with brown hair although there's not . . . not a lot of that left.' She tried a nervous little laugh that didn't quite come off. 'We . . . we all had breakfast together at the usual time yesterday morning and then . . .'

Douglas Parsons, the man responsible for isolating Section Nine when the third floor of RD7 had gone to Condition Orange, was off duty and at home in the garden, mending the lawnmower in his shirtsleeves. His wife was weeding a flowerbed nearby, and Laura, his thirteen-year-old daughter, was lying on an airbed in a bikini, sunbathing, a small transistor radio on a towel beside her. It was tuned to Radio Firth. Now, as she heard the name of the company, she propped herself up on one elbow. 'Dad?' She frowned. 'Did you hear that? It's someone from the company.'

Her father nodded impatiently, sucking on a knuckle. At the first mention of the woman's name he had started violently, the spanner had slipped and he had skinned his hand on the bolt he was trying to loosen. 'Yes, yes – of course I heard. You have that thing on so loud—'

'Sssh!' ordered his wife, sitting back on her little green gardening mat, a trowel held in a gloved hand. 'Let's hear what she's saying, Doug.'

'— If you're listening somewhere, darling, if we've upset you in some way . . . I don't know what you're thinking about but, please, come back to us soon. Sarah, Mark and Simon love you very much, my darling, and I . . . I do too.'

Douglas Parsons crossed over to the radio and turned it off violently. 'That's quite enough of that, thank you very much! It's not enough that I have to work there morning, noon and bloody night, I get it in my own back garden as well!'

His wife twisted round. 'Doug? What's the matter?'

'Nothing! Nothing's the matter!' he snapped. 'Nothing at all.' He turned, dropped his spanner into the toolbox with an angry crash and strode quickly towards the house. Wife and daughter exchanged glances.

'Now what did I do?' demanded Laura, with all the weary resignation of her age. Mrs Parsons thrust her trowel into the well-groomed soil, rose to her feet and set off across the lawn after her husband.

'Nothing, darling,' she threw back over her shoulder. 'Nothing at all. I expect Daddy's just tired, that's all.'

'He's always tired,' moaned Laura, rolling back on to her stomach.

Mrs Parsons found her husband holding his hand under the cold tap in the kitchen, a tin of plasters on the drainer beside him. She closed the door softly behind her. 'Doug?

What's got into you? There was no need to pitch into Laura like that. All she—'

'Yes, I know. I'm sorry.'

'It's not me you should be apologizing to, it's Laura. What is it? What's the matter? It's not like you . . . '

'Nothing. I told you.'

'Ever since you got in you've been . . . oh, I don't know: het up about something or other. Now that thing on the radio . . . ' She reached forward suddenly. 'Here, let me do that.' She took the plaster from his hand and stripped it deftly over the raw knuckle. 'There. How's that?'

Her husband flexed his hand experimentally. 'Fine.'

'Do you know him? This Professor . . . whatshisname?'

'Highcroft?' Douglas Parsons nodded slowly, gazing out of the kitchen window at their well-kept flowerbeds as he dried his hands. 'Yes. Yes, I do, as a matter of fact. He was a keen gardener too.' He turned quickly away from the window. 'I've got to go out,' he announced suddenly, rolling down his sleeves. 'Won't be long.'

'What? But we've . . . we've got the Simpsons coming round! You said you'd help put up the barbecue—'

'I've just remembered something I've got to do back at the labs. Won't take a moment.'

His wife gave him a strange look. 'Are you *sure* there's nothing the matter, darling? Nothing you want to tell me?'

He shook his head. 'Nothing. Really.' He smiled a brief, automatic smile and reached for his jacket.

A minute later he slipped into the garden shed, moved over to the workbench and looked cautiously out of the window and down the length of the garden. Laura was still sunbathing. His wife had returned to her weeding. Parsons unlocked his tool cupboard, lifted down several heavy jamjars full of nuts, nails and screws and reached to the very back of the shelf. He took down an old Oxo tin and placed it carefully on his workbench as though it contained something rather dangerous, his breathing unusually loud in the warm garden shed. Another quick glance out of the window at wife and daughter, then he prised off the lid of the Oxo tin. A thick brown envelope lay in the bottom. He slid the contents out on to the palm of his hand and glanced round guiltily. Two thousand pounds. Enough for a new car or a holiday abroad for the whole family. Enough for a new lawnmower; enough for a dozen new lawnmowers . . .

Seeing the money piled on his hand like that crystallized all the worry and uncertainty that had been gnawing away at him ever since he had come home from work. Blood money, that's what it is, he told himself sternly: nothing more, nothing less. A bribe for keeping quiet, for saying nothing, so that Helen Highcroft went on believing her husband was still alive somewhere, that he had just run off and left them. Parsons thrust the money angrily into his coat pocket. Well, he'd had enough. He would go and see Jackman and return the money. Now.

The anguish with which Helen Highcroft had talked her way on to the radio had spurred Douglas Parsons into action. It acted upon Joyce Engel, wife of Highland Pharmaceuticals' founder and Managing Director, in much the same way. She had been in the kitchen arranging flowers with the radio on for company. A slim, vivacious woman in her late forties, she had sat down slowly at the pine table, the cut flowers lying forgotten in a widening pool of water as Helen Highcroft described the last time she had seen her husband and begged haltingly for the slightest scrap of information from anyone, anyone at all out there in that silent sea of listeners. When she had finished, Joyce was almost in tears, for Helen had been here, in this very kitchen just three hours earlier, twisting her fingers together nervously as she struggled to retain her composure.

Presently Joyce turned off the radio and crossed to the telephone on the dresser. The number she dialled was a private line through to her husband's desk on the first floor of the administrative building at Highland Pharmaceuticals. There was no reply. Joyce broke the connection, dialled the external switchboard number and waited.

She had missed her husband by less than two minutes. Until then he had been sitting at his desk surrounded by reports, files, expenditure estimates and promotional schedules. All of them needed if not his signature then at least his urgent consideration – yet he had been unable to concentrate, his mind dwelling instead upon the nightmarish events of the previous night, upon Professor Highcroft's death and all that had ensued.

Harold Engel groaned, sat back in his chair, linked his hands behind his head and gazed across the office at a picture on the far wall. The black-and-white photograph in its silver frame showed a younger Harold Engel shaking hands with the then Secretary of State for Health at the topping-out ceremony at Engel Laboratories in Bookham, Surrey. The photograph had been taken during the boom years of the early sixties, when Engel was just beginning to carve a reputation for himself as an independent pharmaceutical manufacturer by under-cutting the over-priced branded products of the big drug companies with his own generic, non-branded substitutes. For almost two years it had worked – and then one morning, one bright and sunny morning, he remembered bitterly, his secretary had brought him a letter marked private and confidential from something calling itself the Defence Procurement Secretariat. That had been the first step down the slippery path of professional compromise that, month by month, had robbed him of his integrity and made him what he was today: a rich, outwardly successful entrepreneur trapped in a secret, gilded cage . . .

Engel pushed suddenly to his feet, crossed to the hat stand, slipped into a white coat and clapped one of the ludicrous, mandatory white nylon hats on his head. He then left the office and went down the back stairs to the ground floor, to stand where he always stood when he needed to get away from the telephone and think: watching the production line.

If RD7 was the penalty for co-operation with the Defence Procurement Secretariat, then the smoothly efficient production line, running from right to left in front of him now, was undoubtedly one of the prizes. Gleaming, silent, totally efficient, it occupied almost two hundred and fifty feet, the line itself punctuated every few paces by a woman worker in white coat and hairnet monitoring the production run at one of fourteen different quality-control way stations. These were strategically placed between the bulk chemical store, where the individual chemicals were stacked in metal drums, and the finished goods compound on Engel's left.

Engel came down the last few steps on to the production level and walked slowly back along the length of the line. Several of the women glanced up and smiled a greeting as he walked by, for he was a popular employer. Engel reached on to the conveyor, let his fingers trickle through the production run, examined one of the tinfoil packets at random and walked on with the calm, confident smile of senior management masking thoughts that had nothing whatever to do with Cardocol's trouble-free production run. He glanced up at the digital display suspended above the centre of the run and saw that Cardocol had been on stream non-stop now for almost seven hours. In that time, thousands of white, oval tablets had vibrated their way down these shining steel ramps past final quality control, to be fed in tinfoil blister strips fourteen at a time into bright, emerald-green cartons that were labelled and then passed forward to the finished goods compound ready for shipment.

Engel pictured all the plant and machinery dispersed in clinical, ordered sterility around him – the hoppers and blenders, the dryers, granulators and compressing machines, the laboratories and coating plant – glanced up at the cartons stacked almost to the ceiling in Finished Goods and felt that old familiar stirring of excitement. He was responsible for all this. A few more days and thousands of *his* pills would be dispersed in warehouses across the length and breadth of Britain, poised to meet the demand created by HPL's skilful promotion and marketing campaign and by a series of carefully orchestrated leaks to a number of influential medical journals – leaks that hinted at the arrival of a genuinely new miracle drug. For with Cardocol, Harold Engel fervently believed, HPL's team of scientists, research chemists and pharmacologists had broken through one of the last great pharmacological barriers. More than just another new heart drug with a catchy name, another 'me-tooer', Cardocol was a heart drug with a stable therapeutic index that dilated the arterioles, increased the flow of blood to the heart, and decreased peripheral resistance. It would be the first adrenergic neurone-blocker on the market whose medical data sheet would *not* carry black-edged warnings about the risk of an adverse effect among the elderly known as postural hypotension, of a severe and sudden fall in blood pressure upon standing.

A packet of fourteen Cardocol tablets would cost the National Health Service £6.85 and would last just two weeks. With a British over-sixties population of almost seventeen million, forty-two per cent of whom, it was estimated, had some form of high blood pressure, Cardocol was about to make HPL a very great deal of money. And with that money, Engel knew, would come prestige and a new-found, hard-won status in the eyes of his rivals. With that money too would come a greater degree of autonomy, a chance to dictate terms from a position of strength before agreeing to any further 'co-operation' with people like the Defence Procurement Secretariat. People like Jackman.

Harold Engel turned and pushed through the high, heavy rubber doors leading to Dispatch, Delivery and, beyond that, the other love of his life, the company helicopter. He had learned to fly years ago when he was a junior management trainee, working for one of the large London pharmaceutical companies and commuting daily from his parents' home near the airfield at Biggin Hill in Kent. The flying bug had bitten deep during National Service and had stayed with him into civilian life. Now he flew whenever he felt able to justify it – which was never as often as he wished. He walked across the concrete towards the landing circle and felt that customary lift to his spirits as the helicopter came into view. Powered by a single jet turbine, the three-bladed, five-seat Aerospatiale Squirrel 350 had a range of just over 400 miles and a top speed of 150 m.p.h. The aircraft had come to synthesize for him all that was clean and good and wholesome about his business venture here in Gleninver. In direct contrast to the pervading demands of Jackman and the Defence Procurement Secretariat, the silver-and-white machine bearing the proud emerald initials of the company – his company – had come to represent, over the last few escalating months, more than just rapid transport from company headquarters to Glasgow or Edinburgh, Belfast or Newcastle: it had come to symbolize freedom – freedom from interference, from Whitehall, from Jackman. Harold Engel walked slowly round the aircraft and let his eyes linger on its slender, aerodynamic lines, the pleasing harmony of Perspex and metal. He moved to the pilot's door, saw the headset lying there, waiting for him on the seat, and glanced instinctively at his watch. A minute from now, two at the most and he could be—

'Mr Engel?'

He turned suddenly, wrenched back to reality. 'Yes, Martin?' Martin Lear, one of his managers, was hurrying towards him across the concrete.

'Call for you, Mr Engel. External. It's your wife.'

'Ask her to give me another couple of minutes, will you? I'll take it upstairs in my office.' Martin Lear raised a hand in acknowledgement and disappeared back inside.

When she rang back, he was waiting for her call.

'Sorry to disturb you, darling,' she began. 'I know how busy you must be, but I don't suppose you had the radio on just now, did you?'

Her husband glanced at the papers strewn across his desk and sighed. 'No, Joyce – I did *not* have the radio on just now. What did I miss?'

'Helen. Helen Highcroft,' Joyce replied simply. 'She was on the radio. Asking if anyone had seen Malcolm. Poor woman was almost in tears.'

Harold Engel sat forward abruptly. 'She was *what*?'

'I said she was on the radio. Some pop phone-in programme or other. Just called in out of the blue and asked for help.' Engel digested this in silence. And

Jackman thought it would all just blow over, did he . . . ?

'Hello? Harold? Are you still there?'

'Yes, of course I'm still here,' he replied testily. 'I was just thinking, that's all.'

'There's no news, I suppose?'

'News?'

'About Malcolm! He's one of your employees, remember? I've had Helen in with me this morning. Poor thing was beside herself.'

'I'm perfectly aware he's one of my employees, Joyce,' countered Harold Engel. 'What are you implying?'

'I'm not "*implying*" anything. Only that I think you have . . . responsibilities, that's all.'

'Responsibilities? Joyce – I have more than three thousand employees working here. If I made myself personally responsible every time one of the staff had a row with his wife, I—'

'That's just the point: they didn't have a row. That's what makes the thing so . . . so cruel! He's just disappeared. Surely you—'

Harold dragged a hand over his hair. 'Look, Joyce. I . . . I really can't talk now – someone's just come in.' He glanced up, and the empty office gave the lie to his words. 'I'll . . . I'll get back to you later.'

'Then will you at least promise me you'll—?' But she was talking to herself. Joyce Engel replaced the receiver slowly and frowned. She frowned not at the sudden termination of their conversation – that had been fairly typical in recent weeks as the pre-launch pressure had mounted – but at the sudden realization that there had been an edginess, an unfathomed tension between them ever since Malcolm Highcroft had disappeared.

In his office, Harold Engel sat looking at the telephone for long, thoughtful moments, conscious that when he went home it would not be so easy to distance himself from his wife's questions. Then, on sudden impulse, he reached out and stabbed at the intercom. 'Is Mr Jackman back yet?'

'I think so, yes, Mr Engel.'

'Ask him to step into my office one moment, will you?'

Two minutes later there was a tap on the door and Jackman entered. He did so without waiting for Engel's permission, and came in with that brief smile of urbane self-assurance that never ceased to remind Engel of his own impotence. 'Well?' he snapped, the humiliation of the previous evening still fresh in his mind. Jackman wouldn't know about the radio programme yet and that slight advantage gave Engel confidence.

Jackman looked puzzled. 'I'm sorry?'

'You saw your Mr Baxter at the airport, I assume?'

'Yes, I did.'

'And? You said you'd report back.'

'We agreed upon certain . . . precautions.'

'But you're not prepared to tell me what those precautions are, is that it?'

Jackman shrugged. 'There is no need. We feel it best if you are kept at a distance. Uninvolved.'

'What I don't know—'

'—You can't disclose. Precisely.'

'You told me last night, Mr Jackman,' Engel said slowly, 'that all this Highcroft business would just "blow over" – you remember?' Jackman nodded warily. 'Would it interest you to know that the widow of the man you . . . you disposed of so efficiently has been on the radio, asking total strangers to keep an eye open for her husband?' He paused to let that sink in. 'I hardly think London would call that "blowing over", do you?'

The story of the fire at sea and the two tragic deaths off the small Scottish fishing village of Ardtornish made the five o'clock news on national radio. Jenny Macrae was mentioned by name.

The telephone rang in her flat less than six minutes later. Jenny reached for the call automatically, for the telephone had yet to become an instrument of spite and vituperation.

'Yes?' Her voice sounded flat, dull, lacklustre.

'Miss Jennifer Macrae?'

'Speaking.'

'Bill Townson, Miss Macrae: *Daily Mirror* in Glasgow. We're running a story about the fire, the death of the boy and the old man, in tomorrow's editions. We've a quote here from a Mr John Ennis, the boy's father. I'd like to read it to you, OK?'

'I—'

'He says – and I quote: "Miss Macrae's behaviour was grossly irresponsible. I hold her directly to blame for the death of my son." ' There was a shocked silence. 'Hello? Are you there, Miss Macrae?'

'I'm . . . I'm still here,' Jenny answered in a small voice, her knuckles white around the phone as she sank down slowly on to the sofa, her eyes closed.

'Would you care to comment, Miss Macrae?'

'I . . . no. There's . . . there's nothing I can say.'

'Well – d'you agree with him?' pressed the reporter from Glasgow. 'D'you think he might have a point?'

'I . . . I suppose so,' she whispered huskily.

'I'm sorry? It's a bad line.'

'I said: Yes – yes, I suppose so.'

'As I understand it, the boy was deaf. He was also unable to swim. Is that true, Miss Macrae?'

'He couldn't swim, no. I mean, yes, that's right. He couldn't swim. He'd never—'

'You knew that?'

'Yes.'

'And did you ask this . . . this Mr Roberts if his boat carried any life-jackets?'

Jenny closed her eyes and swallowed. 'I can't . . . I don't think I did, no. You see when he—'

'Why not?' Silence. 'Why not?'

'I . . . I don't know.'

'I'm sorry?'

'I said: I don't know.'

'You don't know?' pressed the reporter, safe in Glasgow. 'But the boy was in your care! Surely, Miss Macrae, as a qualified—'

'I don't know, all right?' she flared suddenly. 'I don't bloody well know!' Jenny slammed down the receiver with a sob and fell sideways across the sofa, burying her head in the cushions.

The phone rang again less than a minute later. This time it was the Press Association. Jenny banged down the phone and hurried towards her bedroom to get away, to hide. 'Leave me alone!' she sobbed, hands pressed over her ears. 'Please! Just . . . leave me alone!'

'Jen? Jen? Are you in there?' The muffled voice came from outside the front door and was followed by quick, insistent tapping. 'It's me – Pam! Jen – answer me. Are you all right?'

Pam. Pam Ross. Jenny hurried down the corridor, fumbled the catch off the lock and tugged the door open.

'Hello, love,' Pam said simply. 'I heard on the radio and came straight over. I thought you might be able to use a friend.' No questions; no blame or accusation. Just support and friendship when she needed it most. Jenny nodded and held the door wide, too choked up to speak.

'Douglas Parsons is waiting outside to see you, Mr Jackman.' Jackman was sitting at his desk in the administration building, penning his name to a clutch of letters and internal memos. Now, as his secretary mentioned Parsons' name, Jackman paused fractionally.

'Show him in, please, Frances.' He sat back in his chair and swung round to face the door, a smile of welcome already in place. Parsons entered. He appeared awkward, ill at ease. Jackman beckoned him forward. 'Douglas. Come along in. Sit you down,' he invited, pointing at an easy chair beside his desk. But Parsons shook his head.

'No. I won't, thank you. This shouldn't take a moment,' he announced abruptly, glancing over his shoulder as Jackman's secretary closed the door softly behind her.

'Just as you wish,' nodded Jackman easily, sitting slowly back in his chair as the warning bells began to tremble at the back of his mind. He took off his spectacles and began polishing the lenses with slow, circular movements. 'So – what can I do for you?'

For answer, Parsons took the money out of the inside

pockets of his jacket and laid it hurriedly on Jackman's desk as though it was contaminated. 'You can take this back for a start,' he said.

Jackman sat forward. 'Oh? And why is that?'

'Isn't it obvious?'

'If it was, I wouldn't have asked. Tell me.'

Parsons shrugged uncomfortably. 'Because it's a buy-off, isn't it?'

'A buy-off?'

'All right, then – a bribe.'

'Nonsense!' snorted Jackman, relieved now that he believed he had identified the depth of Parsons' problem: the man needed someone to tell him it was all right, to soothe his suburban, middle-class conscience before he could spend the money. 'It's nothing of the sort! Your duties last night involved you in a certain . . . unpleasantness. You came under sudden and considerable pressure and performed very creditably. Look upon it as an efficiency bonus if you like, that's all.'

'My duties?' challenged Parsons bitterly. 'Is that what they were? Carrying him down to the loch and—'

'Keep your voice down! If you—'

'And Mrs Highcroft? Did she "perform" well, too? How much does she get?'

Jackman frowned. 'I'm afraid I don't follow.'

Parsons stepped closer. 'Man, she was on the radio – just this afternoon!'

'Ah, yes: the radio. I had heard about that.'

'She was pleading with her husband, begging him to come home! She thinks he's just . . . buggered off, left them in the lurch! I didn't feel any too proud of myself, I can tell you, listening to that and knowing all the time that . . . that . . . ' The words trailed away as he stepped up to Jackman's desk, face tight and determined. 'Look, Mr Jackman. Before we went home, before we agreed to accept your . . . efficiency bonus, as you call it, you promised she would be *told*. Today. We'd never have gone along with your crackpot scheme if we'd known you were going to keep her deliberately in the dark like this.' Parsons paused. 'We're just ordinary people, Mr Jackman, not secret agents, government . . . zombies.'

'You are also, indirectly, a government employee, Mr Parsons,' reminded Jackman quietly. 'And, as such, you are bound by the Official Secrets Act. It was made perfectly clear before you accepted this posting that—'

'Official Secrets Act?' exploded Parsons. 'What the hell has that got to do with Helen Highcroft? I know the woman – and her family! She's going quietly out of her mind with worry – surely you can see that? Or are you so cold-blooded that the question of "security" blots out everything else?'

'In this case, yes, I'm rather afraid that it does,' Jackman admitted calmly, quietly evaluating the man opposite by a set of new and sinister values. He had been wrong, guilty of a serious error of judgement: Parsons *was* a threat. 'Tell me. What about Calvert and Steevenson – have you been in touch with them? Do they share your views?'

Parsons shrugged. 'I've no idea. I'm just speaking for myself, that's all.'

'And your wife? Does she share this . . . ' Jackman gestured at the pile of money on his desk. 'This crisis of conscience?'

'Of course not! She doesn't even know the money exists,' Parsons replied contemptuously.

Jackman nodded, thankful for small mercies. 'So what do you expect me to do – apart, that is, from resuscitate the dead?'

Parsons leant forward and tapped a hand angrily against the pile of money. 'You can keep that, for a start. *And* you can give me your word that Mrs Highcroft will be told. Put out of her misery.' He shook his head. 'Oh, I don't mean told about her husband's work on OMAHA, told about the details of the accident. I just mean told that he's dead, that's all. That he won't be coming home.'

Jackman nodded. As though it all sounded very reasonable. 'I see. As simple as that. And when she asks about his body for burial, for an inquest? What do you suggest I tell her then?'

'That's your lookout, Mr Jackman – not mine. You're an

inventive man – you can think of something, I'm sure. All I know is that I am not prepared to be party to this sort of . . . of deception. Not indefinitely.'

'You make that sound dangerously like an ultimatum, Mr Parsons,' observed Jackman idly, in an attempt to gauge the strength of the threat Parsons represented.

'You can take it any way you like,' Parsons retorted recklessly. He stepped back. 'Well, I've said what I came here to say, got it off my chest, so to speak. Thank you for seeing me, Mr Jackman.' He turned towards the door, it closed beind him, and Jackman was alone.

He sat looking at that closed door for several moments, a finger tapping slowly on the desk in front of him. Then he locked Parsons' money in his own briefcase and lifted the telephone. He asked for an outside line and dialled an unlisted London number from memory. His call was answered almost immediately.

'Baxter.'

'This is Jackman.' He paused, swivelled round slowly in his chair and stared bleakly out towards the still waters of the loch that glittered flat and smooth in the late summer sunshine. 'We have a problem.'

CHAPTER EIGHT

'Then we . . . we saw the smoke. Through one of those beach telescope things,' Jenny remembered in a low voice, gazing sightlessly into her cup of tea as she relived once more that awful moment of realization on the quayside. 'We . . . we called the Coastguard and they sent a helicopter, but it was too late. When it arrived, Jamie was already . . . already dead.' Eyes swimming with tears, Jenny looked up at Pam, sitting listening silently in an armchair across the sitting-room. 'If only I'd gone with him, Pam!' she cried suddenly. 'I could at least—' The telephone rang and Jenny started violently. She made a hesitant move towards the receiver, but Pam waved her back to her seat on the sofa.

'I'll get it.' She lifted the receiver. 'Hello?' She listened for a moment. 'No. No, you can't,' she said firmly. 'No, I'm sorry, but that would be quite impossible. Yes – and the same to you, I'm sure. Goodbye.' She replaced the handset and brushed her fingers together daintily as though she was brushing off crumbs. 'There you are, you see, my dear – nothing to it.' She smiled a brisk smile that didn't fool Jenny for a moment.

'Who was it?' she asked dully. 'Another reporter?'

Pam gave an offhand shrug. 'I hardly think so. Even Fleet Street's not that rude.'

'Oh. Oh, I see.' Jenny went suddenly cold inside. 'My first obscene phone call, is that it? I suppose I should feel honoured,' she tried lightly. 'Fame at last.'

Pam pursed her lips. 'There'll be one or two more like that, I shouldn't wonder . . . '

'Thanks. Thanks a lot.'

'I'm just trying to prepare you, that's all. You know what it's like once the newspapers get hold of a name and address.' She paused, and then added with a little smile: 'You've left it a bit late to go ex-directory, I'd have thought.' She leant forward then, suddenly serious. 'Suppose . . . suppose, just for the sake of argument, Jamie *had* come back. Would you have told his parents? About the trip?'

'Of course I would have done – yes.'

'And you wouldn't have felt guilty?'

Jenny frowned. 'What about?'

'About letting Jamie go off in the boat? Without you beside him to hold his hand.'

There was silence for long moments while Jenny examined that question with scrupulous honesty. Then she looked up. 'No. I don't believe I would have felt guilty.'

A gleam appeared in Pam's eye. 'Why not?' probed counsel for the defence.

Jenny shrugged. 'Because . . . I don't know . . . because it was an adventure – something Jamie had set out to accomplish on his own without that mother of his hanging on to his shirt-tails.'

Pam nodded triumphantly. 'Exactly! Precisely – something he had done *on his own*! That was the whole point about letting him go out with that friend of yours, wasn't it? Well, wasn't it?'

'I'm not sure,' Jenny stalled uncertainly, distrusting any suggestion that might lighten her load of guilt, offer escape from blame.

'You almost went with them, didn't you? On the boat?' pressed Pam. Jenny nodded dumbly. 'But you didn't because you wanted that boy to be able to think: me! I did that – all on my own!'

'That's . . . that's right,' Jenny whispered, the tears once again very near the surface. 'That's *exactly* what I thought! How did you—?'

'How did I know? Because I've read Jamie's case notes too, remember?' Pam rose from her chair, crossed the room and crouched down beside Jenny to take both her hands in hers. 'If it makes you feel any better, I'd have done exactly the same thing, all right?' she said softly. 'I'd have let him go. Alone – with Robbie.'

Jenny looked up slowly. 'You're just saying that,' she whispered, not daring to believe that a friend, any friend, would reach down that far to help her.

Pam shook her head. 'I'm not, I promise you, Jenny. That's exactly what I would have done. Now then—' She stood up and went back to her seat, suddenly all brisk efficiency. 'The boat: it just burst into flames, isn't that what you said?'

'That's right, yes.'

'Why?'

Jenny looked blank. 'I've no idea,' she sighed. 'It doesn't matter, don't you see? It won't change—'

'Of course it matters,' corrected Pam stoutly. 'It matters very much! Fishing boats don't just burst into flames without a reason. Wouldn't you like to know *why* that boat caught fire?'

Jenny shrugged. 'Well, yes. But I don't see who—?'

'What about these helicopter people? That man who rescued the bodies from the sea – he was by the boat when it was on fire, wasn't he?'

'Yes, but I can't just—'

'—Phone up and ask? Why not?' She lifted the telephone off the table, carried it over to the sofa and plonked it down beside Jenny. 'What have you got to lose?'

Afterwards, Jenny would remember that moment as the crossroads, the turning-point when, thanks to Pam, she began to fight back. To start asking questions.

It was early evening and, in his low-roofed bungalow, Jenny's father sat in front of the television, the baked beans on toast forgotten on the tray in front of him as he stared mesmerized at the television screen. The reporter was now talking about some Minister's visit to the shipyards, but Len Macrae didn't hear a word. He saw instead the picture of his daughter that had been flashed on to the screen just a few moments before, linked to some story or other about a disaster at sea. It had been a good report, lashed together with speed by a news crew who knew their business:

amateur cine film and voice-over, vox pops with witnesses on the breakwater and with MRSC in Oban. They'd even had an interview with the pilot of the rescue helicopter. But Len Macrae had only been listening with half an ear as he waited for his favourite soap opera to start. Even when they'd mentioned Ardtornish he had paid only scant attention – until, suddenly, there had been that picture of his daughter coming up the breakwater steps; his Jen, plastered all over the screen with that voice saying something about her being responsible. His daughter.

Feet fumbling around for his carpet slippers, Len Macrae laid the unfinished supper tray aside, pulled himself slowly to his feet and looked round the cheaply furnished lounge for his jacket. As he turned to the door, there was a sudden impatient rattling of his letterbox at the end of the hall. 'Len – Len – are you in there?' He turned in annoyance as, without waiting to be invited inside, neighbour and fellow pensioner Brough Williams hurried down the hall towards him. 'Did you see her?' he demanded excitedly, a bony finger pointing at the screen. 'Did you see the girl there? It was your Jen, I know it was! They had her name and everything!'

Len Macrae nodded and reached for the flat cap on the hall table. 'Aye, Brough – I saw her. So why don't you stop blathering about like a silly bugger and drive me round there in that car of yours you're always polishing? She'll be needing company, I'm thinking, now that feller of hers has gone back south.'

Ten minutes later, Pam broke off in mid-sentence and glanced towards Jenny enquiringly as the doorbell rang again. 'Want me to see who it is?' she offered. 'If it's another of those *bloody* men from the newspapers . . . '

Still numb with shock, Jenny couldn't even raise a smile at Pam's unaccustomed venom. They seemed to have been sitting together for hours, drinking endless cups of tea and running over the tragedy again and again. Jenny shook her head, set down her mug and stood up.

'I'll get it. I can't hide from the world for ever.' She went down the corridor, let up the catch and pulled the door open, bracing herself for rudeness, intrusion, confrontation. Her father stood waiting outside, hands thrust deep into his pockets. 'Had the telly on,' he began awkwardly, unable to meet Jenny's eyes. 'Thought it best if I came right round.' He jerked a thumb over his shoulder. 'Brough brought me.'

'I . . . I was going to call, Dad. Just as soon as—'

'Aye, I know.' He wiped his feet unnecessarily on the doormat and looked up. 'D'you plan to keep me standing here in the hall all day or can I come in?'

Jenny forced a smile. 'Yes. Yes, of course, Dad. Sorry.' She closed the door behind him and led the way down the hall.

Pam rose from her chair and held out a hand. 'Hello, Mr Macrae.'

'You remember Pam, Dad? She works with me at the clinic.'

Her father nodded. 'Aye, of course.'

They made stilted conversation for a while and then there was an awkward silence. Sensing that she was now the intruder, that this had become a time for father and daughter, Pam glanced at her watch.

'Well, it's time I was getting along.' Gathering up her bag, she nodded goodbye and made for the door. 'I'll be at home if you need me, all right?' She turned in the hall to pat Jenny's hand reassuringly. 'I know it doesn't seem possible, Jen, not right now, but all this will pass, really,' she promised. 'And just remember – you're not alone.' Pam kissed Jenny impulsively on the cheek, and Jenny closed the door behind her. Then she walked slowly back into the living-room, trying to prepare what she would say to her father. She found him standing with his back towards her, paying close attention to the brown curtains in the bay window.

'Thought you said you were going to change these for the blue ones?' he remarked without turning round. Inwardly, Jenny groaned. Her father hadn't been in the flat for months. Although she saw him often, it was invariably at his bungalow where they talked about the price of the week's shopping, about the way the town had changed since the days when Jenny's mother had been alive, and about what had been on television the night before. But never about the things that mattered, not with any ease. Nor would they now about the accident or Jamie Ennis' death.

'I know. I haven't got round to it, that's all,' Jenny replied in a low voice. And still he wouldn't turn.

'You don't want to leave it too long, you know. I remember—'

'Dad—'

'I remember the time your mother and me decided to—'

'Dad! Look at me, will you – please!' He turned, at last. 'I don't want to hear about the price of curtains just now, all right? All right?' He nodded slowly, the lined, weathered face at a loss to cope with what had happened to his daughter.

'Aye, I know,' he sighed. 'It were all over the news. They had your picture and everything.'

Jenny nodded. 'The phone's hardly stopped ringing.'

'Brough saw it too. He was round like a flash.'

'He would be,' Jenny agreed bitterly.

Her father nodded. 'Aye. Nosy bugger.' He paused, and then went on as though unable to contain himself any longer. 'Is it true? About the boy – that you just let him go off on his own? Brough said they—'

'He wasn't on his own, Dad,' replied Jenny steadily. 'He was with Robbie.'

'But you didn't go with him! Why not, for God's sake? The boy was only seven years old! Didn't you realize the risk you were taking?'

'Eight. He was eight, not seven,' Jenny corrected dully, feeling herself start to choke up again. Even her own father wasn't prepared to listen, to understand. He had already decided she had been wrong, foolish, misguided. She could see it in his eyes. 'I . . . I really thought it was for the best, Dad. He—'

'For the best?' echoed her father, the bite to his words

denying her the comfort and support she so desperately needed. 'How in God's name could you do such a thing, woman!' he exploded. 'The man on the telly was saying—' He broke off then suddenly as the phone began to ring beside him.

'Could you answer that, please?'

'Me? But—'

'Please.'

He moved reluctantly to the phone. 'Hello?' He listened for a moment. 'Oh. It's you.' He covered the receiver. 'It's that doctor feller of yours.'

'Danny?' Her father nodded, and Jenny came out of her chair with a rush.

'Danny?'

'I . . . I was just watching the news,' he began, the shock still fresh in his mind. 'Jen – what happened? That . . . that was you they were talking about, wasn't it?'

She closed her eyes and gripped the phone a little tighter. 'Yes. That was me.'

'God – what a stupid thing to say. What I mean is—'

'I know what you mean. It's all right. You don't have to say anything.'

But he did. 'If there's anything I can do. You know . . . if you need someone to . . . '

'It's all right. Really.' She paused. 'And I . . . I got your letter. It arrived this morning.'

'Oh. Oh, I see. That was really why I was calling, Jen. That and the . . . the accident. That was really good timing, wasn't it?' he said bitterly. 'The letter, I mean.'

'It could have been better,' Jenny replied, with a lightness she did not feel.

'Would you like me to come up for a few days? So we could talk things over?' Jenny closed her eyes for a moment, wishing with all her heart that she could undo the events of the last twenty-four hours. 'Jen? You still there?'

'Yes. I'm just thinking, that's all.'

'Would you like me to come up?'

Yes, if he hadn't posted that letter. No, because he had.

'No, really.'

'You sure?' Was there just a hint of relief in his voice, a sense of duty done?

'There's no point, Danny.'

'Do you want to tell me about what happened? Talk it through over the phone?'

Jenny glanced round, conscious of her father listening to every word. 'I'll . . . drop you a line about it, OK? In a day or so.'

'You're *sure* there's nothing I can do?'

'Quite sure,' she managed huskily, her eyes brimming with tears. There was a wretched, dragging silence as Danny racked his brain for some way to bring things to a painless end. He didn't find it. You never can.

'Be . . . be in touch, OK? I . . . goodbye, Jenny.'

'See you,' she whispered. 'Take care.' She lowered the receiver slowly. And felt as if her heart would break.

CHAPTER NINE

In the spare bedroom at the top of the landing of his narrow, semi-detached, terraced house in Merton Avenue behind London's Chiswick High Road, Dennis Ridley sat alone and in complete silence at a wide worktable illuminated by a single pool of hard white light. A spare, fit-looking man in his late thirties, with short brown hair, Ridley sat hunched forward, peering intently through a pedestal-mounted magnifying glass at a white lead model of a soldier. The soldier lay face-up in a little padded vice of his own design. Now Dennis Ridley dipped the tip of his very thinnest sable paintbrush into a tin of silver enamel, wiped it almost dry against the lip of the tin and, bending forward, began painting the white piping that denoted infantry on to the soldier's dark-grey shoulder straps.

The model was less than three inches high, and the detail of the piping all but invisible to the naked eye, yet to Dennis Ridley it was a matter of great importance that every detail on every one of his miniature army of lead soldiers should be as accurate as meticulous care and painstaking research could make it. To the untutored eye, the model was just another German soldier in coal-scuttle helmet and Wehrmacht grey from the Second World War, but Dennis Ridley knew rather differently. Cast to perfection at a cost of eighteen pounds each, every one was historically accurate down to the position of the last button. Ridley was now putting the finishing touches to an Obergefreiter of 2. Kompanie, I Bataillon, Panzer Grenadier Regt. 394 of von Schweppenburg's XL Panzer Corps – an Obergefreiter whose jackboots were not just painted black, but coated with a thin layer of dust; whose helmet strap was not merely painted brown but finished at the buckle in gun-metal black. When the model was completed, the soldier, with his

9 mm. Schmeisser sub-machine-gun and Stielhandgranate 24-stick grenade, would take his place with the others of his ten-man section in the diorama that took up three-quarters of the rear of the bedroom, and which depicted a section of weary German riflemen resting in late August 1942 amid the shattered ruins of a Russian postal clerk's vegetable garden near Mozdok in the Caucasian foothills between the Caspian and Black Seas.

There. The piping was finished – done. Dennis Ridley sat back slowly and studied his handiwork critically from several angles, with eyes that seemed curiously cold, distant, passive . . .

A timid knock on the door. Ridley didn't hear it at first, so absorbed was he in his hobby, in his obsessive interest in the battles and dusty campaigns of recent history. The knock came again, a little louder this time, and Ridley frowned at the intrusion. His wife knew he insisted on absolute silence and stillness when he was working . . .

'Come,' he ordered. The door opened cautiously. Several months ago, his wife had hurried in without knocking. The resulting anger, she still remembered with a shudder, had been . . . quite terrifying. 'What is it?' he asked, without turning round or looking up. His wife hovered hesitantly in the doorway, a thin shape limned against the gloom of the landing.

'It's that man again, Dennis . . . '

'What man?'

'You know – the funny one. The one who was here last winter.' Funny as in mysterious, sinister. Ridley sat back, dipped his brush carefully into a little jar of spirit, waved it thoughtfully to and fro and smiled a little smile. So – he had come back.

'Where is he now?' he asked, drying his brush slowly on a clean rag.

'Downstairs. In the hall. I thought, seeing as how you're working . . . ' The sentence trailed off into nothing.

'Did he say what he wants?'

His wife pushed a wisp of hair behind her ear. 'It's not me he's come to see, is it?'

Ridley put down his paintbrush, turned round slowly and examined his wife with those same flat, distant eyes. Ten years ago she might have been quite attractive, almost vivacious . . .

'No. No, I don't suppose it is,' he said cruelly.

She said nothing. Just stood there, waiting for the next instruction. The next insult.

'Well?'

She stirred. 'Would you like me to—?'

'Show him up? Yes, why don't you?' suggested Ridley quietly. His wife turned, and he listened to the creak of the treads as she went back downstairs. Faintly, through the open door, Ridley heard the low murmur of voices and then the soft, measured tread of approaching footsteps. One pair only this time, coming carefully up the stairs towards him in the darkness. Ridley made no move to get up, to turn on more light. Instead, he affected to work on, bending forward over his desk so that the visitor would come upon him from behind. He peered through the magnifying glass and waited as the steps came to a halt behind him and there was another soft tap on the door.

'Mr Ridley? Might I come in?' Ewan Baxter waited politely in the doorway as Ridley pushed the magnifying glass away with slow, careful deliberation and turned towards him.

'Ah, Mr Baxter – I thought it must be about time for another one of your little visits,' Ridley opened conversationally. 'Please – take a chair.'

Baxter stepped into the bedroom, gathered his raincoat around him, and sat down warily as though it was Ridley's chair and not its owner that he could never wholly trust. He noticed the German soldier lying in the vice on the table.

'Still at it, I see . . . '

Ridley nodded and moved the soldier pointedly out of reach. 'That's right.' He smiled thinly. 'Keeps me out of trouble.' The soldier and his model-making were private, personal. They had nothing to do with business. And this, he sensed, was business. Quite definitely.

Baxter smiled. 'I've . . . er . . . brought you a little

present.' He took an oblong box out of his pocket and laid it gently on the worktable. It was wrapped carefully in brown paper and tied with string. Ridley lifted the box experimentally. It was quite heavy. He looked up.

'With strings attached, I see,' he said dryly.

Baxter smiled. 'No strings, I assure you. Please – open it.' He sat back and watched as Ridley took up a razor-sharp modelling knife and stroked its blade gently over the string. The knots parted, he unwrapped the paper and lifted up the lid. Below was a thick layer of tissue paper. He removed that too and sat back with a sudden sigh.

'You like it?' asked Baxter, watching his face carefully.

Ridley nodded. 'Magnificent. Where did you find it?' he breathed. It was very quiet at the back of the house and their voices now were no more than murmurs. Baxter held up a finger. Light glittered briefly on a gold signet ring.

'Ah! That would be telling! Shall we just say that it proved rather . . . elusive?' Inside the box, lying on its side in its original wrapping, lay another lead model. This one was not of a soldier but of a German army vehicle, a VW Kübelwagen with every spring, panel and bolt reproduced in the most faithful detail. Ridley lifted the model out of the box as though it was part of the Turin Shroud.

'I didn't think there were more than half a dozen left in Europe,' he murmured, turning the box over carefully and pointing at a yellowed label gummed to its base. 'There – you see? 1952. One of the originals.' He replaced the model carefully and looked up. 'I assume this is just the beckoner?'

'I'm sorry?'

'That there is something you would like done? Outside the . . . usual channels?'

Baxter inclined his head fractionally. 'Perhaps. If you were interested.'

'Where?'

Ewan Baxter shrugged almost apologetically. 'UK this time, I'm afraid. Scotland. Little hole-in-the-wall sort of place called Gleninver. Ever been there?'

Ridley thought for a moment, then shook his head. 'Gleninver? Never even heard of it.'

Baxter nodded slowly. 'Good. Excellent. Then we can start with a clear pool, can't we?'

Ridley looked momentarily puzzled as the allusion to fishing escaped him. He was a hunter, not a fisherman.

John Ennis stood alone in the centre of Jamie's bedroom.

It was a large, spacious room full of warmth and colour, with bright, cheerful wallpaper and cluttered with the sort of expensive toys and electronic aids and gadgets only the well-to-do can afford to lavish upon their children. Mrs Ennis was already in bed, heavily sedated. Now, before she awoke in the morning, her husband had gone into Jamie's bedroom to remove some of the more sensitive reminders of the child they had lost. It was a devastating experience. Wherever he turned, wherever he looked, there was some reminder of the past, of happy days wrenched from his grasp, of toys with private names and piercing, personal associations. The outside world might know John Ennis as a bluff, hard-headed businessman, as a brisk, efficient councillor with a strong, forthright personality whose views and opinions had a habit of prevailing across the Council chamber, but here, inside Jamie's bedroom, all that might never have existed. Here, with his son, he had been Captain Magic.

He moved quietly to the door, his arms full of toys, and with the tears no one would ever see running down his cheeks. He closed the bedroom door softly behind him. Out of habit.

Through the numbness of bereavement one name, one person, stood out head and shoulders above the rest: that speech therapist woman, Jennifer Macrae. The woman who had waited until he was safely out of the way at the HPL reception the previous evening before sneaking into his home behind his back to persuade his wife to let her take their son to the seaside as part of some trendy new experiment in audial awareness, or whatever it was called. And who had never brought him home again. Well, Jamie might have gone, but that was not the end of it. No, sir. He owed Jamie more than that. Owed it to him to make sure that she could never, ever wreck a young life again. He had friends, didn't he? Contacts at County Hall? Influence? 'You haven't heard the last of me, Miss Macrae,' he promised aloud, as he went slowly down the stairs. 'Not by a long chalk, you haven't.'

Jenny swung her Citroën off the lane, drove across the crowded car park and pulled quietly to a halt with her bumper almost touching a low stone wall. She turned off the ignition, and the sound of voices, of music and laughter, drifted towards her from the pub's open windows. The laughter sounded alien, unreal, a sound from some other world to which she had long been excluded. Jenny got out and locked the car door. Then she caught herself hesitating, suddenly scared to find again that same look of hostility and contempt she had encountered in the faces of strangers as she left the hospital where Jamie had died. She took a deep breath and walked firmly across the gravelled forecourt towards the pub.

The Dolphin was busy, crowded with red-faced holidaymakers and sun burned girls in skimpy halter-tops knocking back summer pints and Babycham. It was a comfortable, low-beamed freehouse, wedged between a fold of hills and a twisting lane that ran down to the sea. It did excellent bar snacks at reasonable prices and was less than three miles from RAF Glenhaddon. For that reason alone, the Dolphin was a popular watering-hole for off-duty aircrew from Rescue Flight. Jenny edged her way towards the bar . . .

Dave, Pete and Tony were sitting together over their pints at a low, copper-covered table in the corner. Pete and Dave had been drinking steadily together since early evening. Tony had joined them half an hour ago with some offhand remark about changing his mind. In truth, the silence of his empty married quarter had driven him from his own living-room. Now Dave drained his glass, set it down with a smack and exhaled gustily. 'Not a bad drop of wallop, that. Right then – same again, lads?' He gestured at their glasses, and was just about to push to his feet when one of the regulars eased his way through the noisy press of holiday-makers clustered around the Space Invaders machine, leant between Tony and Dave's shoulders, lowered a tray carefully into their midst and began solemnly distributing brimming pint glasses among the three members of RESCUE 44.

'There you go, boys – and good luck to you.'

Dave twisted round. 'George? You feeling all right? Won the pools or something?'

The old man clapped a calloused hand on the pilot's shoulder.

'You did all right,' he offered, with the slow deliberation of a drinker already well on his way. 'No worry, boys. It wasn't your fault, out there in the bay. Not at all. You did what you could, eh?' He leant closer, and a gust of beery breath fanned across Tony's face as he added conspiratorially. 'I seen you, man. On the telly. It was that lassie's fault – *she's* the one to blame, if you ask me.' He lifted his glass and drank deeply. 'Good health to you . . . '

It was not unusual for Glenhaddon aircrew to be brought drinks by the Dolphin's regulars. They had come to regard Rescue Flight with a certain proprietary pride and, when the job had gone well, the crews accepted the drinks with a clear conscience. Now, however, they felt as though they were taking money under false pretences, and there was a moment's uncomfortable hesitation before they reached for the brimming glasses.

'That's very good of you, George,' replied Dave after the pause, speaking for them all. 'Keep the lead in your sporran, eh? Cheers.' George gave a sudden cackle of laughter. It was a very long time indeed since the wife had found any lead under *his* sporran . . .

The barman edged towards Jenny at last. 'Yes, love – what can I do you for?' No recognition. Thank God.

'Oh. A . . . an orange juice, please.' As the barman bent to the row of bottles under the counter: 'I'm looking for Flight Sergeant Tony Lockhart,' she said loudly, forced to almost shout above the noise around her. 'I was told I might find him here.'

The barman clipped the cap off the orange juice and poured deftly.

'Ice?'

'No. No thank you.'

'Forty-five pence.' He looked up. 'One of the Glenhaddon lot, is he?'

Jenny nodded. 'That's right, yes. From RAF Glenhaddon. The crewroom said he might be here.'

The barman shrugged and gestured with his chin towards the far window. 'There's three of 'em over there, love. Just past Space Invaders.'

'Thanks.' Jenny left her money on the counter, picked up her glass and moved slowly across the crowded bar.

She recognized them straight away. Despite the fact that they were in a mixture of civilian clothes, despite the non-regulation length of their hair, all three men seated around that corner table were obviously comfortable in one another's company to a pitch seldom found among men who do not rely upon one another for their very lives. Sensing this oneness, Jenny paused at the periphery of the group until one of the men glanced up and saw her standing there, watching them uncertainly. He grinned, not recognizing her, for he had been outside on the grass beside the helicopter when they put down at the hospital.

'Hello, darling. Looking for somewhere to sit?' asked Dave, always on the lookout for fresh talent.

Jenny gave a quick shake of the head. 'No. No, thank you. I was looking for Flight Sergeant Lockhart.'

Dave gestured across the table as Tony swung round. 'There he is – the man himself.'

Jenny glanced to her right. His hair had been washed and combed so that it lay flat instead of sticking up in dark sweaty spikes, and he wore a jacket and open-necked shirt instead of that orange rubber suit, yet she recognized him instantly, every image pin-sharp from that nightmare moment of realization in the hospital corridor.

'Hello. I'm . . . I'm sorry to trouble you when you're

off-duty. We . . . we met briefly this afternoon . . . '

Tony nodded. 'I remember,' he said quietly. 'At the hospital, wasn't it?'

Jenny swallowed. 'That's right, yes.' She held out her hand formally and Tony shook it. 'I'm Jenny – Jenny Macrae.' Her fingers felt small, frail and very cold engulfed in his own. Tony made to get up.

'Tony. Tony Lockhart.' He gestured briefly around the table. 'Pete Sleaman – Dave Bourne. Please – take a seat.' Again, that nervous shake of the head as Pete and Dave nodded hello.

'No, really. I . . . I can't stay long. I just wanted to thank you – all of you. For what you did. What you – tried to do.' She took a sudden nervous sip of her orange juice.

'I'm sorry we couldn't have done more,' replied Tony, the flat, banal words of sympathy hiding the true depths of his feelings. It was an awkward, stilted exchange, with noisy drinkers jostling and pressing about them on every side, as Pete and Dave found a sudden interest in the beer mats on the table in front of them. They didn't like meeting participants after a rescue had failed, none of them did. It could never change the result. It succeeded only in turning safe statistics into flesh and blood. It made them partisan, involved.

'I would also like to . . . to apologize,' Jenny offered quietly, determined to see it through. 'For putting you all to so much trouble. At so much risk.'

Tony shrugged. 'No bother. It's what we're here for.'

'I suppose . . . I suppose you think it was all my fault, do you?' Jenny asked bitterly, the words out before she could recall them. 'I wouldn't blame you if you did. Everyone else seems to.'

'We're not in the business of allocating blame, Miss Macrae. We—' He broke off suddenly and twisted round as a hand landed heavily on his shoulder.

'That's her, isn't it?' demanded George incredulously, indignantly, leaning forward and peering up at Jenny as though she was Quasimodo down from the belfry. 'It's that bloody woman, cool as you please!' Jenny felt the colour drain from her cheeks as people stopped talking and began to turn towards her. 'It's her! The woman on the telly!' insisted George, his voice ringing out loudly across the crowded bar.

'Now, George – take it easy,' placated Tony. 'There's no need to—'

'Me? An' . . . and what about that poor wee lad drowned out there in the bay, eh? An' . . . an' here she is now, bold as brass, without so much—'

'I . . . I shouldn't have come,' Jenny managed in a broken voice, as she began to back away. 'Thank you . . . thank you for . . . ' She turned and pushed blindly through the crowd of listening, watching people, her face averted. She reached the door, pushed outside and broke into a run, her bag swinging wildly from her shoulder as she hurried across the car park. Behind her, Tony pushed abruptly to his feet.

'You pissed, bloody idiot, George,' he muttered, making for the door. There had surely been enough pain, enough suffering for one day . . .

Tony hurried outside and looked around for signs of the girl. Nothing. Not a thing. Just the gleam of parked cars beneath ornate coach lanterns, and the crunch of feet on gravel over to his left. Then an engine coughed into life over by the far wall, and a little Citroën reversed jerkily out of the car park. Tony raised a hand and then let it fall to his side as the car disappeared down the lane and the sound of its engine dwindled away into the night.

Helen Highcroft drove slowly forward into the garage, turned off the engine and doused the lights. She sat staring blankly ahead into the darkness, her hands like leaden weights upon the wheel. It had been a fruitless, wasted day with nothing achieved, nothing accomplished. Despite the radio interview and the hours spent sitting at home waiting for the telephone to ring with news of her husband – nothing. Malcolm had just vanished.

Finally she had been unable to stand the waiting any longer and had taken to driving aimlessly about town, scanning the faces of holiday-makers. Of strangers. Now she turned off the garage light, hauled down the up-and-over door, and began to walk back towards the house with slow, heavy steps. She had just begun to reach inside her handbag for the front-door keys, when the phone began to ring in the hall. Fumbling in her haste, she threw open the door and rushed to the phone, the corridor still in darkness as she swept up the receiver. 'Yes?' she panted breathlessly. 'Yes? Malcolm?'

'Mrs Highcroft?' Her shoulders slumped dejectedly. It was a man's voice, but it wasn't her husband's.

'Yes?'

'I . . . I heard you on the radio this afternoon. Asking about your husband.'

'Have you seen him?' she demanded instantly. 'Please – do you know where he is?'

There was a pause. 'He won't be coming home, Mrs Highcroft.'

She frowned. 'What did you say?'

'I was there, Mrs Highcroft. I saw it happen.'

'Saw what happen? Look, who is this—?'

'Your husband is dead, Mrs Highcroft.' There was a click, followed by the dialling tone, as the caller replaced the receiver.

CHAPTER TEN

In the Middle Ages they pilloried wrongdoers in the stocks and pelted them with rotten fruit and vegetables. Five hundred years later the technique is slightly more sophisticated though no less painful: they print your photograph on the front page of the tabloid dailies and strike at you with barbed headlines.

Jenny found that out the hard way when she went to the corner shop for some eggs shortly after 8.30 the following morning: no cheery greeting, no exchange of pleasantries about the weather from the woman behind the counter; just an embarrassed little mumble, a nod and a quick scurry into the private rooms at the back, leaving her alone in the shop. As she picked up her box of eggs, Jenny saw the newspaper lying there in ambush, waiting for her on the counter. DEAF BOY DIES IN RECKLESS GAMBLE screamed the headline, with below, in smaller print, BOAT TRIP ENDS IN TRAGEDY. There was a photograph of Jamie with, beside it, a smaller one of her. Jenny pushed the paper away and hurried outside.

A reporter and a photographer were waiting outside the clinic in Margaret Street, but she evaded them easily enough by driving round to the back and parking there. Through the swing doors and along the corridor past more embarrassed, turned-away faces, as people she had known for years evaded her eyes in this first moment of mutual recognition since the accident. Jenny paused at Pam's door, but her office was empty. She walked down the corridor.

'Jenny?' She turned. It was Mrs Metcalf, the clinic's receptionist. Friendly, capable, middle-aged, Margaret was a staunch ally . . . only now she too seemed to find it difficult to meet Jenny's eyes.

'Hello, Margaret.'

'Good morning,' the woman replied, seeking refuge behind a thin shield of unnecessary formality. 'Mrs . . . er . . . Bolton, your eleven o'clock appointment, with her daughter Heather?'

'What about her?' asked Jenny, knowing what was coming.

'She telephoned five minutes ago. She won't be coming. Not today.'

'Oh. Oh, I see. Oh well, not to worry.' A forced, bright smile. 'Did she make another appointment?'

Margaret looked embarrassed. 'I offered her several alternatives but they were all . . . unsuitable.' There was a small silence between them as they faced one another, then Mrs Metcalf added, as gently as she could: 'Mrs Shaw and Mrs Wallis called too . . . '

'They won't be coming either?'

Mrs Metcalf nodded, shamefaced, as though somehow it was all her fault. 'No. No, they won't.' She reached out impulsively and touched Jenny's arm. 'I . . . I heard it on the news last night, Jenny. I . . . I'm terribly sorry – we all are. If there's anything I can do . . . '

'Thanks. Thanks very much,' Jenny said quietly. At least Margaret had the courage to talk about what had happened, to bring it out into the open. 'What about the Foxton boy, my ten o'clock? I suppose his mother's cancelled too, has she?' Rude, unreasonable, uncouth and completely dominated by their bullying mechanic of a father, the Foxtons were not high on Jenny's list of favourite families. Now, surprisingly, Margaret shook her head.

'No, no – he's here. Actually arrived on time for once. He's outside your office. Mum's with him, too.'

Jenny felt her spirits rise. Not everyone, it seemed, was quite so ready to damn her without a hearing.

'Wonders will never cease. I'd have thought they'd have been at the front of the queue with the rotten apples.'

Margaret shrugged. 'Well, they're here. See for yourself.'

Jenny turned to go down the corridor, and then remembered something. 'Oh – any word from Corbett? I don't imagine he'll let much grass grow under his feet with something like this.' Corbett was the District Administrator for the Social Services department. A dry little man with no sense of humour or feel for the human frailties of those he administered, Corbett was someone both Pam and Jenny tried to keep at arm's length.

'There's a note on your desk. He's coming over later this morning.'

Jenny groaned. That was all she needed.

'Any message?'

'You're to start writing up your report.'

Jenny nodded. Her report; of course. Pure Corbett.

'How did he sound?'

Margaret pulled a face. 'Harassed. As though half County Hall was breathing down his neck.' She was right. On the first working morning since the death of his son, Councillor John Ennis had not been idle.

Jenny went down the corridor and found Ronald Foxton and his mother sitting reproachfully outside her office. 'Morning,' she smiled pleasantly, determined to return their unexpected faith with a little kindness and tolerance of her own. 'Sorry to keep you waiting.'

'Been here since ten. On the dot,' said Mrs Foxton righteously, arms folded. Jenny glanced at her watch. It was four minutes past.

'Well, as I said, Mrs Foxton, I'm sorry. Something came up. Now—' She smiled briskly. 'How're you today, Ronnie? All set?' The boy looked up with sullen disinterest, and Jenny stifled a sigh of exasperation. Oh well, at least the Family Grimm had turned up. That was something, she supposed. 'Good – let's go in, shall we?' She unlocked the door and led the way inside.

A quarter of an hour later, the laborious, uphill business of teaching Ronnie to pronounce his S's was interrupted as angry voices moved swiftly down the corridor. The door of Jenny's office was suddenly flung open and a man stood in the doorway in grimy mechanic's overalls, a morning paper held like a baton in a greasy hand. 'Come on, you,' he ordered, pointing the paper first at his wife, then at his son. 'Out!'

Mrs Foxton looked suitably startled. 'Harry? I—'

'Out, I said! Come on, move!' he ordered, stepping further into the room. Behind his shoulder, Jenny saw Margaret making ineffectual attempts to intervene.

'Mr Foxton, if you don't mind, I—' began Jenny. He whirled on her.

'You shut your mouth!' he ordered, unfurling the paper and smashing an open hand across the front-page headline. 'I'm not having my kid taught by the likes of you.' He turned back to his family. 'Didn't you hear what I said?' he snarled, cuffing his son around the ears and grabbing his wife roughly by the arm. 'Out!' As they gathered up their things and hurried through the door ahead of him – 'Bloody child murderer!' he said. The door slammed behind him.

Ridley parked in a side road and darted through the traffic across Chiswick's Southfield Road and into the post office on the opposite corner. They always used post offices for he had long insisted that nothing ever be delivered to his home. Post offices were easy, safe, anonymous. He eased past the postcard carousels and the cluttered little cardboard-backed displays of pencils and rubbers, bent down at the grille and smiled at the old lady sitting on a high padded stool surrounded by her ledgers of stamps and postal orders. 'Good morning. You have a parcel for me, I believe – poste restante. The name is Spackman.' Private joke. Hauptmann Spackman had commanded I Bataillon, Panzer Grenadier Regt. 394 at Mozdok in August 1942.

The old lady thought for a moment, got down awkwardly from her stool and vanished into the rear recesses of her shop. When she returned she was holding a brown package scored through with thick blue pencil. 'Here you are, Mr Spackman. It arrived only this morning.'

Ridley thanked her, took possession of the parcel and returned to his car. Making sure he was not being watched, Ridley took out a penknife and slit open the parcel. The two packets of ten-pound notes went into an inner pocket without a second glance. Ridley studied the air ticket briefly, looked at the map Baxter had thoughtfully included for the reconnaissance and placed it inside an attaché case on the empty seat beside him. Then he sat back, opened a brown envelope and tipped a single black-and-white photograph into the palm of his hand. He glanced inside the envelope but there was nothing else. No note, no letter – nothing. He was not in the least surprised.

Ridley studied the photograph for several seconds and then glanced at the back where a name had been written lightly in pencil: Douglas Parsons.

It was mid-morning as the swing doors of the health clinic banged shut and Jenny hurried down the steps to her car. Bag slung over her shoulder, a bundle of newspapers jammed under one arm, she unlocked the car, tossed papers and bag angrily on to the passenger seat and slid behind the wheel. She sat there for a moment, staring defiantly over the steering-wheel at the place where she had worked, seeing once again Corbett's anxious, bureaucratic little face and the tight, pursed line of his mouth as he read her report. Jenny banged her hand angrily against the steering-wheel, reached down and started the engine. She was just about to reverse out of the car park when Pam came hurrying down the steps towards her. Jenny hauled on the handbrake as Pam bent down to the window. 'I just heard,' she said. 'Jen – what can I say? I'm sorry: if there's anything I can do to—'

'Suspended!' said Jenny bitterly. 'The little shit had made up his mind before he even came through the door!'

'It's only temporary, you know that. A formality, Jen. Surely you expected—'

'I expected him to at least read Jamie's case notes before deciding I was guilty!'

'Suspended doesn't mean guilty, Jen. *Or* innocent. It means exactly what it says: suspended. In limbo. With nothing decided one way or the other.'

Jenny shook her head impatiently. 'You know what he said – Corbett? He said "a gesture" was needed. The department needed to be seen to be reacting to public concern. What do they think I am? Some sort of . . . of child molester who couldn't *wait* for the first opportunity to . . . to . . . '

'He does have a point, you know. About a gesture, I mean.'

Jenny looked up, tight-lipped. 'Oh, great – now you're on his side too, are you? That's all I need—'

'That's unfair, Jenny, and you know it.'

'Just look at these, will you?' Jenny gestured at the newspapers strewn on the seat beside her where half a dozen front-page paragraphs had been ringed in red. 'Corbett marked all those – see what I mean? Not one of them refers to Jamie, or to me, or to his parents – they all refer to Corbett. To the department. It makes you sick.'

'All right – what would you have done in his place?'

Jenny shrugged. 'About me, you mean? Christ, I don't know . . . '

'At least look on the bright side: at least you're still on full pay. It could be a lot worse.'

Jenny turned away impatiently and stared out of the window. 'And that's supposed to make everything all right, is that it?'

'What I mean is—'

Jenny swung round. 'This is my home, Pam! I've lived here all my life! Yet already it's as though I'm a . . . a non-person. People pretend not to see me, they cross the street when they see me coming, they look away, they won't talk to me—'

'I'm still talking to you.'

There was a flicker of a smile. 'You know what I mean.'

Pam nodded. ''Course I do. But it'll blow over, given time. These things always do.'

'With John Ennis on the Council, and Corbett twittering away and disowning me every time the phone rings from County Hall? You really think so?'

Pam shrugged. 'All right, then: go away. Just until the dust settles.'

'*Run* away, you mean, don't you? With my tail between my legs.' Jenny banged a hand gently, deliberately against the steering-wheel. 'Look: I feel sorry, OK? About what happened. Terribly, terribly sorry. But I don't feel *guilty*, not any more. I know I did yesterday – I didn't have room for anything else. But today . . . ?' She shrugged helplessly. 'I don't know – I must have used up all those guilt feelings or something, can you understand that?'

Pam nodded. 'Yes, I can understand that. It sounds to me as if you're beginning to come to terms with what happened; with yourself.' She paused. 'So – what are you going to do – now, I mean?'

Jenny reached down for the handbrake. 'Me? Haven't a clue.'

'Well, don't forget. If you want to talk or just have a good cry on someone's shoulder, give me a call, all right? Better still, just pop round. Jim's always asking after you.' Jim was her husband.

Jenny nodded, slipped the car into reverse and backed slowly out of the car park. She'd lied to Pam. Not over anything important, but she had lied nonetheless and had done so quite deliberately, although she didn't really understand why, for she knew exactly what she was going to do next. She was going to talk to Amy Roberts, Robbie Roberts' widow. Her name and address appeared in most of the papers the punctilious Mr Corbett had brought with him from Glasgow.

In the first-floor executive offices of Highland Pharmaceuticals, Marketing and Promotions Manager David Eckett was drawing to the close of yet another pre-launch presentation. It was neither the first nor the last that Managing Director Harold Engel would be obliged to attend, yet this one was particularly crucial for it dealt specifically with the company's distributive arrangements over the entire British Isles. It would be no use generating a sudden and explosive demand for their new drug only to find they were unable to meet the demand.

Eckett folded back the last of the transparent overlays and turned to face his Chairman, as Engel sat back and steepled his fingers beneath his chin. 'And what *that* means, Mr Chairman, is that the moment those primary distribution targets are met, these secondary arterial distribution centres will be linked by computer to our own bonded warehouses in Glasgow, Carlisle, Birmingham, Horsham and Bristol—' a hand moved fluently over the map, pausing at each name as it was spoken – 'which means that no dispensing chemist or hospital pharmacist will be less than *one working day* from whatever additional supplies he may require – or, of course, from any of our other products.' He stepped back. 'Taking even the most conservative demand assumptions as our base line—' He broke off then as a telephone sounded discreetly on his desk. 'Excuse me.' He lifted the receiver, listened for a moment, and then held the receiver towards Harold Engel. 'For you, sir.'

Engel rose and took the call. 'Harold Engel.'

'This is reception, sir.' The voice sounded cool, poised, guarded. 'I have Mrs Helen Highcroft in reception, Mr Engel. She has asked to speak to you. Under the circumstances I thought perhaps . . . '

Harold Engel was doing some rapid thinking of his own. 'Yes. Yes, of course. I'll be down in just a minute. Oh – and . . . er . . . make her comfortable, will you?'

'Yes, Mr Engel, of course.'

He put the phone down slowly and turned to face a cluster of waiting, attentive faces. What touched their Chairman affected them also – or so they thought.

'You'll have to continue without me for a minute or so, I'm afraid, David,' he said, forcing a smile. 'But on what I've heard so far – excellent; really excellent. Please: continue. Gentlemen—' Engel nodded to them all, walked to the door and stepped out into the corridor. With the door closed safely behind him and the corridor empty, Engel wiped a shaking hand over his forehead and tried to force himself to think positively, clearly. He couldn't go down and see her himself, that was out of the question – yet she was waiting for him. Think! This was Jackman's doing, Jackman's . . . mess: let him clear it up. He hurried down the corridor and into Jackman's office. The secretary looked up. 'Would you please tell Mr Jackman I have to see him immediately?'

'I'm afraid there's someone—'

'Just do it!' Engel snapped. The girl was not paid to argue the toss with the Managing Director. She swallowed, lifted the phone and did as she was told. A moment later Engel stood aside as Jackman's visitor slipped into the corridor, then strode into Jackman's office. The moment the door had closed behind him and they were alone: 'She's here,' he said tersely. 'Now. Downstairs in reception.'

Jackman sat back in his chair, took off his spectacles and began polishing them carefully. 'By "she", I take it you mean Mrs Highcroft?'

Engel swallowed and nodded. 'She's downstairs. Waiting for me.'

'So?' enquired Jackman mildly. 'All you have to do—'

'I can't.' He swallowed nervously. 'I . . . I won't . . . If you want to pull the wool over that woman's eyes, you'll have to do it without my help.'

There was silence. Jackman replaced his spectacles carefully and glanced up. 'All right,' he announced evenly. 'I'll go and see her. Go back to your office and stay there. I'll let you know when she's gone.'

With the taste of self-loathing like a copper penny at the back of his mouth, Engel went.

Jackman went quietly down the back stairs and along the lower corridor that led towards both the reception area and the empty office he had selected the night Professor Highcroft had died in RD7. The entire executive wing had been designed to match the company's expansion programme for the mid-1980s and, as a consequence, most of the offices were still under-utilized. Jackman paused outside the door and glanced up and down the corridor. It was deserted and he let himself in with a master key. Papers strewn across the desk, family photograph, appointment diary where he had left it – nothing had been changed, nothing moved. Jackman took a ready-printed name-tag from inside his wallet, opened the door and slipped this carefully behind the empty metal grille on the outside of the door. He glanced back inside and, on impulse, crossed to the windows and drew the curtains. Then he slipped up the catch, closed the door softly behind him and continued along the corridor towards the reception hall.

Helen Highcroft was sitting alone on one of the comfortable fawn sofas set just inside the main doors beside a pleasing array of ferns and summer heather. She had her face averted as he approached.

'Mrs Highcroft?'

'Yes?' She twisted round anxiously. She had changed and washed her hair but she looked tense, drawn and exhausted, with deep, plum-coloured shadows under her eyes.

'Maurice Jackman, Mrs Highcroft,' he introduced himself, sitting down beside her. 'Mr Engel asked me to see if there was anything I could do.'

'Have you . . . have you heard anything? From my husband?'

Jackman shook his head sadly. 'I'm afraid not, Mrs Highcroft – not a thing. We've made our own enquiries, naturally, but . . . nothing. It may well be that—'

'I . . . I had a telephone call. Last night,' Helen Highcroft admitted quietly.

Jackman leant forward. 'I'm sorry?'

'When I got home. I'd . . . I'd been driving around most of the evening – you know, just looking. When I got home the phone was ringing. The caller wouldn't say who he was, just . . . that Malcolm was . . . was dead. That he wouldn't be coming home,' she recounted, dark eyes staring into the past, white fingers gripping the top of her handbag. 'I'd been on the radio, you see, earlier in the afternoon. Asking anyone to contact me if they'd seen him.'

'And this . . . this caller told you he was *dead*?' Parsons, thought Jackman darkly. Douglas Parsons – got to be.

She nodded. 'That's right, yes. He said he was with my husband when he . . . when he was killed.'

'Good God!' said Jackman, genuinely shocked. 'How . . . what a monstrous thing to say! Did you . . . I mean, did you know who the man was, recognize his voice?' He watched Helen Highcroft shake her head and breathed a sigh of relief.

'Not that I am aware of, no.'

'I'm afraid people like that are everywhere nowadays, Mrs Highcroft. When you appeal for help like that, for every hundred people who listen sympathetically—'

'He . . . he didn't sound like a crank, Mr Jackman; someone with a . . . a twisted sense of humour. He sounded . . . oh, I don't know, just . . . genuine. As though he really *had* seen Malcolm die.' Anguished, she turned towards Jackman. 'But if he saw my husband die, why wouldn't he give me his name, tell me what happened?'

'I . . . what can I say, Mrs Highcroft? I really have no idea. Did you report this to the police?'

'No. No, I didn't.' She shrugged apologetically. 'I thought I'd better sleep on it first. Then, this morning . . . well, it seemed so . . . so incredible, so intangible. I thought I'd do better coming here instead.'

'I'm glad you did, although I'm not sure how we—'

'I . . . I was wondering if you would mind showing me Malcolm's office, let me look at his diaries, things like that? There might be something there . . . some clue . . . ' Jackman managed to look a little doubtful, and Helen Highcroft reached out and touched his arm. 'I know it isn't company policy to let families into the working area, Mr Jackman, but perhaps, under the circumstances . . . '

Jackman patted her arm kindly and rose to his feet. 'Of course. One moment, Mrs Highcroft, and I'll see what can be arranged.' Jackman might be ruthless, amoral and glacial with his own personal relationships, but he was also a superb chess player who had planned and plotted Mrs Highcroft's various moves and counter-moves with almost mathematical precision. He crossed over to a wall phone some distance out of earshot, dialled his own extension number and had a wholly one-sided conversation with himself. Then he replaced the receiver and walked back towards Helen Highcroft, who watched him anxiously. He smiled reassuringly. 'If you'd like to come with me, Mrs Highcroft, I think we can rely upon everyone looking the other way just for a few minutes.'

'Thank you. Thank you very much.'

Jackman led her down the corridor and stopped outside the office he had left so few minutes before. He paused just long enough to ensure she saw her husband's name on the door, turned the handle and pushed inside. 'Here you are.' He switched on the light, ushered her in ahead of him, crossed to the windows and drew back the curtains. He turned to watch Helen Highcroft gaze slowly around the office. 'Is . . . is anything the matter?' he asked, watching her look round with a small, puzzled frown.

'It's . . . it's not quite how I imagined it, that's all . . . '

'Oh? In what way?' asked Jackman casually, watching her closely behind veiled eyes. What in God's name had he missed? What had he overlooked?

'I don't know.' She shrugged tiredly. 'It's just . . . smaller, I suppose. More untidy.'

Jackman relaxed, reached across the desk for the framed family photograph and proffered it towards the dead man's widow. 'Well, I think you'll agree – this *is* where your husband worked,' he said gently.

'Yes. Yes, of course.' She smiled a strained smile as she studied their three children.

Jackman watched her a moment longer, then pushed Professor Highcroft's engagement diary casually across the desk towards her and bent down to begin opening the drawers of the desk. Helen Highcroft picked up her husband's diary and began leafing through the pages as Jackman watched her carefully out of the corner of his eye. Any moment now . . .

Helen Highcroft gave a sudden little strangled cry, and Jackman looked up. 'What is it?' he demanded sharply. Right on cue.

She just stood there, frozen with shock as the diary slipped from her fingers and fell to the floor with a thud. 'It's . . . it's this!' she whispered, holding out a photograph.

It was a black-and-white picture of an attractive young girl in her mid-twenties with the wind blowing her hair away from her face. Jackman didn't really have to ask about the inscription across the bottom of the photograph, for he had chosen the words himself with some care less than forty-eight hours earlier. He decided to go through the motions anyway . . .

'What does it say?'

'It says . . . it says,' she tried, in a small, choked voice, "To my darling Malcolm. With all my love until we can be together. Your adoring Monica."

Seaview Road turned out to be a narrow ribbon of terraced, white-washed fishermen's cottages clinging to the hills overlooking Ardtornish harbour. It took Jenny half an hour to drive back along the coast from Gleninver, and another ten before she had parked and climbed up the steep, cobbled lane to Mrs Roberts' home. Jenny rang the bell, stepped back, and turned to gaze out across the sunlit bay sparkling below in the late morning sunshine. Seagulls wheeled and screamed on the summer thermals, yet it was a scene that to Jenny was both treacherous and deceptive: there could never again be anything wholly innocent or harmless in a setting that had taken so much with such ease . . .

The door opened behind her, and Jenny swung round to find an elderly woman with untidy grey hair, wearing a shapeless mauve cardigan, watching her silently from the front step. Jenny hesitated, for the woman's dishevelled appearance was at odds with the polished brass door knocker and the neat, narrow hallway glimpsed beyond her shoulder. 'Mrs Roberts?' Jenny had not been to Robbie's house before, never pictured him with a wife, a family, people who cared about him. The realization that she had never bothered to look behind their easy, harbourside familiarity made her feel uneasy, that she had somehow betrayed the dead man's friendship.

The woman shook her head. 'She's away indoors just now. I'm the neighbour, Mrs Leity. You'd be calling after Robbie, I've no doubt?'

'That's right, yes.'

Mrs Leity nodded glumly. 'Aye. I thought as much. You were with the boy.'

'Is she in? Could I speak to Mrs Roberts, please?'

'You'd best step inside.' The door closed firmly behind her, and Jenny followed Mrs Leity down the quiet hall and into the sitting-room.

Amy Roberts was sitting in an armchair beside the unlit fire. A frail, bird-like woman in her seventies, whose white hair was scraped back from her forehead in a severe bun, she turned slowly at the sound of voices and looked up enquiringly with eyes that were red from weeping. Jenny stepped forward hesitantly.

'Mrs Roberts? I . . . I'm sorry to trouble you just now. I was with your husband on the breakwater yesterday afternoon just before the . . . accident. My name's Jenny . . . Jenny Macrae.'

Mrs Roberts nodded slowly. 'The wee boy,' she said quietly, so quietly that Jenny had to lean forward to catch what she was saying. 'The one who was deaf. He was in your care, wasn't he?' Jenny nodded silently. 'I . . . I thought so,' murmured the old woman. 'It's him I keep thinking of in my mind, you see, sitting here. Him with all of his life stretching out in front of him . . . ' Her voice trailed away, and Jenny followed her gaze to a photograph of Robbie in a cardboard frame on top of an old upright piano in the corner. 'We . . . we never managed any children of our own, you see, Miss Macrae,' Amy Roberts confided. 'But Robbie . . . oh, he loved them. Always . . . always being friendly, you see, like that. Taking them out for little trips and such. Just . . . being friendly.' She turned away so Jenny wouldn't see her tears.

'I know,' Jenny said softly, near to tears herself. 'I went out with him myself.'

Mrs Leity cleared her throat. 'I'll . . . I'll be next door if you need me,' she offered. Amy Roberts nodded without turning round, twisting a scrap of handkerchief between thin fingers. There was a fragile silence as the door closed, leaving Jenny and Mrs Roberts alone together. Jenny sat down slowly and leaned forward.

'Please, Mrs Roberts – no one's blaming Robbie for what happened.'

Mrs Roberts turned and smiled a sad, slow smile. 'No,

lass – they're blaming you, aren't they?'

Jenny nodded. 'The newspapers are, yes.'

'And are they right? To blame you for what happened?'

Jenny spread her hands in a gesture of helplessness. 'Jamie was my responsibility, certainly, but it's . . . it's not as simple as that. At least, it isn't to me. There was a special reason why I let him go off without me.' She told Mrs Roberts then about Jamie, and about his overly protective mother, and about her conversation with Robbie down on the breakwater, then – 'Can you tell me anything about Robbie's boat, Mrs Roberts? Anything that might explain why it suddenly caught fire like that?'

Mrs Roberts thought for a moment and then shook her head. 'I can't think of anything, no . . . '

'What about the . . . engine? Had he had it a long time?'

Again the old lady shook her head. 'I'm not very sure. I think so, yes. I do know that he looked after it himself . . . '

'And there'd been nothing wrong with it? Not recently?'

'No, no. I'm quite sure there wasn't. Robbie kept everything in very good order. He was always taking it to pieces, cleaning it and such. Then he'd come away home and try and wash his hands in that sink of mine, just as I was making his tea. My, the words we'd have about that . . . ' Her gaze shifted to his photograph on the piano and her eyes glistened suddenly. 'We were married fifty-seven years, Miss Macrae,' she whispered softly, fingers picking aimlessly at the worn nap on the arm of her chair. 'I'd known him, I'd . . . I'd loved that man ever since I was a fair-haired wee slip of a thing at chapel that first Sunday we met.' She sighed and turned towards her visitor. 'I'm sorry, dearie, what was it you asked me?'

'You were telling me about that boat of his. About the engine.'

'The boat? Oh, aye, so I was. It must have taken up most of his time after he retired – that and the lobsters and such, when the weather was kind and the wind didn't start him up coughing. Too much of his time, maybe.'

'Too much? Why do you say that?'

Mrs Roberts shrugged. 'Och – just that the doctor told

him to take it easy. Not to go overdoing things the first few weeks.'

Jenny leaned a little closer. 'First few weeks? After what?'

'After going to the doctor.'

'You mean Robbie had been ill?'

'Ill? Robbie? Och, no – he never had a day's illness in his life. Just a wee bit of blood pressure, that's all Dr Erskine said.'

'Dr Erskine? In Gleninver?'

Amy Roberts nodded. 'Aye, that's the man. D'you know him?'

'He attended my mother when I was born. He delivered me.'

Amy Roberts smiled. 'Did he now? How very interesting. Aye, he's a grand man. A grand man.'

'What did he do? About Robbie, I mean?'

'Och, the usual: gave him some pills and told him to take it easy, and said he'd soon be as right as rain. Robbie took that to mean spend all the time he could down there in the harbour, tinkering about with that boat of his.' She sighed and looked up, as though closing the door on more painful, private memories. 'Now then – you haven't come all this way to listen to an old woman blathering away, have you now? You'll join me in a cup of tea, Miss Macrae?'

'Thank you, I'd like that. I'd like that very much,' Jenny replied warmly. 'Here, let me help you.' Mrs Roberts pulled herself upright, and they went through together into the small kitchen at the back of the cottage where Mrs Roberts boiled a kettle and guided Jenny towards the cups and saucers.

It was only when Jenny was looking round for the sugar that she saw the bottle of cough-mixture and the packet of pills standing together on the kitchen table. The pills came in an emerald-green packet. Jenny turned the packet over slowly in her hands, trying to remember where she had seen them before. Mrs Roberts glanced over her shoulder.

'Aye, they're the ones,' she said. 'Made all the difference to Robbie, they did.'

CHAPTER ELEVEN

Jenny drove back through the outskirts of Gleninver, parked her Citroën outside the flat, turned off the ignition and sat back to stare vacantly over the dashboard towards the town. Her thoughts were miles away. She felt depressed, lonely. Even if the accident had been Robbie's fault, even if some mechanical failure or some oversight on his part *had* caused the fire, it didn't change a thing. Jamie had still been in her care – and some time soon she would have to go up the hill and return Jamie's possessions to his parents, meet Mr and Mrs Ennis face to face. She wasn't looking forward to that.

Jenny crossed the pavement, opened the outer door, and was just about to put the key in the door of her own flat when she heard movement upstairs. Looking up from the hallway she saw that Mrs Proctor's door was ajar. Frowning, Jenny went slowly up the stairs, a hand on the banister rail. 'Hello?' she called. 'Hello? Who's that?' There was no reply. Then the door at the top of the stairs opened and Jenny sighed with relief. 'Mrs Elliott – you gave me quite a shock. Today's not Tuesday.' Mrs Elliott came in once a week to tidy up and collect Mrs Proctor's laundry. A dour, dumpy package of a woman, she studied Jenny sternly from the top of the stairs.

'They've taken her, haven't they?'

'Who? Mrs Proctor?'

'Aye. And who else would you imagine?'

'Who's taken her?'

'It's a fortunate thing I came by to drop off the laundry, that's all I can say. There she was, just lying beside the bed. Gave me a proper fright, I can tell you. Thought at first, well . . . you know . . . '

'Who's taken her?' Jenny repeated impatiently.

'The ambulance people, of course. Not twenty minutes ago. I'm telling you, Miss Macrae, if I hadn't—' They both turned to a sudden tap on the glass door panelling downstairs.

'Good afternoon,' called a well-dressed man in his late thirties, in a dark business suit that spoke of one of the professions. Doctor or architect, perhaps. Or a lawyer.

'Can I help you?' called Jenny from the landing, as Mrs Elliott craned curiously over the banister rail. The man stepped into the hall and wiped his feet carefully. He was carrying a black briefcase.

'Where might I find Miss Jennifer Macrae?'

'You're speaking to her.'

'Oh.' He waited until Jenny had come down the stairs and then held out his hand. 'My name is Smithson, Miss Macrae. From the Sheriff-clerk's office. I'm the Fiscal.' The Procurator-fiscal, that peculiarly Scottish appointment that exists in the legal middle-ground between public prosecutor and clerk to the magistrates. 'I wonder if I could have a few words?' He glanced briefly up at Mrs Elliott, watching them with interest from the landing. 'In private?'

'Yes. Yes, of course.' Jenny opened the front door of her flat and ushered Smithson in ahead of her as she brushed Mrs Proctor temporarily from her mind. 'Down the hallway to your right,' she instructed, and they went through into the sitting-room where Jenny offered him a chair. 'Would you like some tea, Mr Smithson? Or coffee perhaps? I thought—'

'No. No, thank you, Miss Macrae,' he said, the civil servant strictly there on business, the black briefcase balanced precisely across his knees.

'Oh. Oh, fine. Just as you will. How can I help you?' Jenny asked, sitting down opposite.

'Well,' Smithson began carefully. 'As you may already be aware, whenever there is an . . . an incident, such as there was yesterday afternoon, it is my job to collect what we call "precognitions", that is, eye-witness accounts of what took place; to bring all relevant facts out into the open.'

'I'd have thought they were publicized enough. The accident was all over the television. And the newspapers.'

'Indeed. So it was. However, it is my task to try and formalize those statements, so to speak; to enter them upon the public record. It will then be up to the Sheriff to decide whether or not the public interest would be best served by the institution of criminal proceedings against any particular party.'

Jenny felt herself go suddenly cold. 'Against me. That's what you really mean, isn't it?' she challenged quietly.

The Fiscal shrugged. 'That is a possibility that cannot be excluded, no, Miss Macrae.'

Helen Highcroft drove away from her meeting at HPL in a daze, the photograph she and Jackman had discovered in Malcolm's diary on the front seat beside her. The children had spent the night with friends. Now she was going to collect them.

The front door was wrenched open almost as soon as she reached out to press the buzzer. It was opened by Sarah. Mark and Simon pressed tightly against her shoulders as all three Highcroft children waited for news of their father. 'Have they heard from Daddy?' Sarah asked immediately. 'What did they say?'

'No,' managed Helen. 'No, they haven't. There's still no news, I'm afraid.' She closed the door behind her and turned to watch three faces crumple dejectedly.

'But where *is* he?' Mark demanded plaintively. 'When's Daddy coming home?' Helen could only shrug. Then she looked up to see her friend and neighbour Elizabeth Chalice coming slowly down the hall towards her. 'Have they been good?' she asked over the children's heads.

Elizabeth nodded. 'Good as gold,' she said, seeing what it cost her friend to maintain that outward air of composure in the presence of her three children – then four, then five, then six as her own rushed in to add to the mêlée in the hallway. She clapped her hands together sharply. 'Right – out. Into the garden – now! Vamoose!' she ordered, turning shoulders and propelling children gently on their way. When the last of them was out of earshot: 'Nothing?' Elizabeth demanded quietly. 'Not a *word*?'

The mask cracked. Helen's shoulders slumped as she fumbled with the clasp of her handbag. Elizabeth guided her into the lounge and shut the door behind them. Then she led her to the sofa and sat her down, as Helen took out the photograph of the girl and held it out without a word, her head averted as though she could no longer bear to look at it. Elizabeth took the picture slowly and read the inscription.

'Oh, no,' she breathed. 'Oh, Helen . . . '

'It was in his diary. Malcolm had left it in his diary.'

'Do you know who she is?'

Helen shook her head. 'I've . . . no, I've never seen her before.'

'You're sure?' pressed Elizabeth gently.

Helen nodded rapidly. 'Quite sure, yes. I'd . . . I'd remember. She's . . . very pretty.'

'What about the name – Monica? Did you . . . what I mean is . . . did you suspect that perhaps Malcolm might be . . . you know . . . ?'

Helen looked up, the tears streaking the mascara into black tramlines down her cheeks. 'Be having an affair? No . . . no, never.' She banged a fist impotently against her thigh, and the words that came now seemed to be torn from deep within her. 'I thought we were so . . . so *happy*,' she groaned. 'He never said anything that made me think there . . . there was somebody else. Not for one moment.' She shook her head tiredly. 'After last night I just . . . I just don't know what to think any more . . . '

'Last night? What happened last night?'

Helen sighed. 'Oh, somebody phoned. Just as I got home, to say that . . . that Malcolm was dead. That they had been there when he died. Just some . . . some crank, I suppose.' She looked up, dazed by grief, by shock. 'How can people be so . . . so cruel, Lizzie?'

Elizabeth gestured at the photograph. 'Perhaps it's just . . . you know . . . an old flame. From before you met. You know what men are: sometimes they . . . ' But the lame words trailed away into silence as she looked at the photograph. The picture was new, they could both see that, tell it from the girl's hairstyle, from her clothes.

The sudden ringing of the telephone rescued Elizabeth Chalice from a lengthening silence. She crossed the room and picked up the receiver. 'Yes?'

'Mrs Chalice? Sorry to trouble you – it's Maurice Jackman here at Highland Pharmaceuticals. Mrs Highcroft left your number. I wonder – might I have a word if she's still with you?'

'Yes, of course. One moment.' She lowered the receiver and turned to Helen. 'It's for you: Maurice Jackman – HPL.'

Helen rushed from her seat and reached for the phone. 'Yes? Have you heard anything?'

'I'm afraid it's looking pretty definite, Mrs Highcroft. The police have just called. They've found your husband's car.'

'They have? Where?'

'Here in Gleninver, Mrs Highcroft. In the station forecourt, actually. Looks as though it has been there quite some time.'

'Oh. I see. Thank you,' she said dully, automatically, lowering the phone slowly. 'How . . . how could he?' she whispered, gazing unseeing across the room. 'How could he?' There was silence for a moment as she turned slowly towards her friend. 'They . . . they think they've found Malcolm's car down at the station. He . . . he must have caught a train.' She paused and looked down uncertainly at her hands. When she looked up again her eyes were swimming with tears. 'What am I going to tell them, Lizzie?' she faltered. 'What am I going to tell the children?'

On the main concourse of Glasgow's Hamilton Street station, the terminal for all trains to the west of Scotland, the fair-haired young student darted through the crowds and hurried along the line of phone booths searching for an empty call-box. There was one! Lugging his holdall at his side, he moved forward to take the phone when a tall man in his mid-thirties stepped into his path. 'That one's taken,' he announced shortly. The boy, a cheery, innocent youth, twisted past his outstretched hand.

'Too late, mate,' he threw back over his shoulder with a cheerful grin. 'I saw it first. Sorry – got a train to catch.' He dropped his bag at his feet, reached in his pocket for his change and lifted the receiver. A lean hand fastened suddenly on his elbow from behind and began to squeeze with great strength and exact, medical precision. The boy swung round in alarm and let out a cry of agony as the receiver dropped back on to the cradle from nerveless fingers.

'I don't care if you're catching the plague,' said the man quietly, conversationally. 'You can't have heard me, sonny. This one's taken.' He released the boy's elbow and the student rubbed away at the pain.

'All right, all right – why didn't you say so?' he grumbled, picking up his holdall and turning away into the crowd, his phone call forgotten. He glanced back only once, and then almost fearfully. There had been a look in the man's eyes, a bleak, feral hardness, that he had never seen before. Which was hardly surprising, for Ridley came from a very different background indeed.

The telephone rang presently and Ridley snapped up the receiver, the student brushed ruthlessly from his mind. 'Yes?'

'It's all right,' said Jackman. 'We can talk now.'

'You took your time, didn't you?'

'There were complications. It's not always easy to get away.'

'Right – let's have it. London say you've got a problem.'

'Nothing you can't take care of, I'm assured. You got the photograph all right, I take it?'

'Yes.'

'Good. When do you arrive in Oban?'

Ridley glanced at his watch. 'Four o'clock.'

'Ideal.' He paused. 'The job needs doing *soon*, d'you see?'

'How soon?'

'Would tonight be convenient?' Jackman asked mildly. They might have been talking about fitting double-glazing.

The Procurator-fiscal slipped Jenny's four-page handwritten statement into a clear plastic folder and placed it carefully inside his briefcase. 'Right then, Miss Macrae – that all seems straightforward enough.' He rose to leave. 'Thank you for answering my questions so . . . candidly. You're . . . ah . . . not planning to go away anywhere in the next few days, I take it?'

'Don't leave town, is that it?' challenged Jenny with a slight smile. She was rewarded by a faint flush of colour to Smithson's smooth cheeks.

'Not at all, Miss Macrae – not at all. I'd just like to know where I can reach you if I have any further questions, that's all.'

Jenny shook her head. 'No, I'm not planning on going anywhere.'

'Good. Fine. Excellent. Then I'll bid you good-day.'

Jenny got up too. 'Do you have any idea when you will decide? Whether or not there are to be criminal proceedings against . . . anyone?'

Smithson gave a non-committal shrug. He had been in the legal profession far too long to allow himself to be pinned down on something as sensitive as that.

'I'm sorry, Miss Macrae, that would be quite impossible to say. After the Fatal Accident Inquiry, anyway.' They walked down the hall together, shook hands, and Jenny watched as Smithson crossed the road and disappeared briskly from sight.

She turned back indoors and glanced up at the landing. Mrs Proctor's door was shut and there was now no sign of Mrs Elliott. On sudden impulse, Jenny went upstairs, fished the key out of the letterbox on its length of ribbon and let herself quietly into Mrs Proctor's flat. Halfway through the interview she had suddenly remembered where she had seen Robbie's pills before . . .

The bed had been made with clean sheets, and Mrs Elliott had given the room her usual perfunctory tidy. It seemed strange, silent, and almost menacing without Mrs Proctor propped up there on her pillows with her walking-stick beside her, ready to bang on the floor when she wanted her pillows turned or a fresh glass of water.

Jenny crossed to the bay window, pulled back the heavy brocade curtains, and light flooded into the cluttered bedroom, rare as sunshine in a pharaoh's tomb. She turned from the window, went over to Mrs Proctor's bedside table and looked down at the old lady's private pharmacy of pills, tablets and potions. The pills she was looking for were beside a bottle of cough-mixture. Jenny looked up suddenly as a movement caught her eye, and she saw her own reflection in the dressing-table mirror.

That pulled her up short. What on earth did she think she was doing, going through Mrs Proctor's possessions like some common burglar? She had no right to be up here without permission. She reached over to replace the pills and then hesitated, reluctant to turn her back on the only clue she had. A clue. Was that what it was?

Jenny sat down on the edge of the bed and tried to marshal all those vague, half-formed thoughts that were milling around inside her head: Mrs Proctor collapsed beside her bed with an emerald-green packet of Cardocol pills on the floor beside her; Robbie Roberts' boat catching fire for no obvious reason – and those same pills lying there on his kitchen table, waiting for the man who would never return. Coincidence? Of course it was. You're clutching at straws, Jenny told herself sternly. You haven't the courage to accept the blame for Jamie's death and so you're busy looking for a scapegoat; for something – anything – that will shift the blame. Even a packet of pills.

Jenny told herself all these things and yet . . . and yet . . . She got up, picked up one or two bottles of tablets from the bedside table and looked at the chemist's label gummed to the front. That shouldn't be too difficult, anyway: all the medicines had been supplied by Archie Hooper, the chemist opposite the post office . . .

Gleninver's only chemist was busy, with a little queue of

sufferers waiting patiently beside the counter as Archie Hooper dispensed their prescriptions from behind a high Formica screen at one end of the counter. Holiday-makers who'd been taken short, old women with varicose veins, harassed young mothers with runny-nosed children tugging at their skirts, an old man bent with rheumatism coughing intermittently into a grubby, crumpled handkerchief – the sick, the lame and the halt, all waiting in the queue as Jenny joined them, grateful for the fact that, immersed in their own suffering, no one spared her a second glance. The queue dwindled away gradually until at last the shop was empty except for an overweight schoolgirl sorting through the slimming aids.

'Can I help you?' asked the freckle-faced young assistant in her white coat as Jenny stepped up to the counter.

'Can I speak to Mr Hooper, please? It's . . . it's a private matter.' The girl disappeared behind the screen, and Jenny heard the low murmur of voices. Then there was the sound of water running into a basin, a tap was turned off, and a tall, bearded men in his mid-forties came round the screen drying his hands. It was a small town and Jenny knew him by sight.

'It's Jenny Macrae, isn't it?' he asked pleasantly. Not quite everyone, it appeared, believed everything they read in the newspapers.

'That's right, yes.'

'Thought so. What can I do for you? Brigit said it was personal.'

In answer, Jenny took out the emerald-green packet of Cardocol pills and laid it on the counter. 'D'you think you could tell me what these are for?' she asked. 'I'm sorry to sound so mysterious, but I've a particular reason for asking.'

Archie Hooper picked up the packet of Cardocol pills and turned it over briefly in his hands. Then he looked up and frowned. 'No, I can't.' He sounded surprised. 'Not offhand. Not without checking. They look like some sort of anti-hypertensive. Why?'

'You mean you don't prescribe them?'

He shook his head. 'Doctors do the prescribing, Miss Macrae. I'm just the lowly alchemist who tries to turn a doctor's random medical scribbles into pills and powders.'

'But if a doctor prescribes this Cardocol . . . ' She pointed at the packet. 'You mean to say you don't stock it?'

The chemist shook his head. 'Can't say I do, no.'

'Oh,' Jenny said, nonplussed. 'I assumed you did. You *are* the only chemist in Gleninver, aren't you?'

'Unless you know something I don't – yes. Have been for years.'

'Then I don't understand it. This . . . this person I know gets all her pills and things from here. Regularly.'

'Well, she didn't get these, I can promise you. Officially, I've never even seen them before.'

'But if she . . . wait a minute. What d'you mean, "officially"?'

The chemist shrugged and glanced down again at the packet. 'Cardocol. They're the new heart drug HPL's been burning the midnight oil about these last few months. I'm almost sure they're not yet listed. Hang on a second.' He went back behind the screen, returned with the current issue of MIMS and began leafing through the pages. He ran a finger rapidly down the long columns of anti-hypertensives, shook his head, flicked to the index and drew a blank. Then he turned to the British National Formulary and presently closed that book too with a snap. 'Nothing. Cardocol's not listed.'

'You're sure?'

'Positive.'

'Could my friend have bought them in some other chemist's? Is that possible?'

An emphatic shake of the head. 'No, it's not. As I said, we all carry the same drugs, order from the same stock lists.'

'Well then, could she . . . I don't know . . . could she have bought them over the counter somewhere else?'

Archie Hooper shook his head. 'Out of the question. These capsules each contain active ingredients of the most sophisticated kind.' He tapped the side of the packet. 'This isn't just aspirin in here, Miss Macrae – it's a powerful drug.' He paused. 'Perhaps you'd better tell me who's taking them, eh?'

'I'd . . . er . . . I'd rather not, if you don't mind,' Jenny replied stubbornly without really knowing why, knowing only that she needed time to think, to work out what it all meant. 'Not just now, anyway. Thanks for your help.' And with that she picked up Mrs Proctor's pills and turned for the door, her mind whirling.

Helen Highcroft was taking her children home from Mrs Chalice's where they had spent the previous night. They were clustered in the back behind her asking the same incessant, never-ending questions. Where was Daddy? When was he coming home? For the two younger ones at least, she had run out of answers a long time ago.

A little earlier she had taken a taxi alone to the police station where she had signed for her husband's car keys. Then she had gone to the railway station to find their Volvo neatly parked at the end of the station forecourt. She had approached the car almost with caution, as though there might even now be some note or letter propped against the dashboard to tell her where she had failed as a wife and companion. Instead there was nothing, and she had slipped behind the wheel to weep long and bitter tears, for that, in a way, had wounded deepest of all.

Now Helen was about to drive past their local garage on the way home. She glanced down automatically at the fuel gauge and saw that the needle was hovering around empty. She drew the heavy car over to the crown of the road, waited for a break in the traffic and then turned in across the forecourt with the children's bickering arguments a suitable counterpoint to her own bleak preoccupation. She waited until the garage-hand had filled the tank and then went over to the office to sign for their petrol on the monthly account. As she did so, a blue-overalled mechanic hurried from the workshops and raised a hand in cheery greeting.

'Afternoon, Mrs Highcroft – almost given you up. If you've the key handy I'll drive it round myself.'

She looked up, puzzled. 'I'm sorry?'

'The keys, Mrs Highcroft: the keys to the Volvo. I'll drive it round myself. To the service bay. Save you the trouble.'

She shook her head stupidly. Was she going mad? Was this what a broken marriage did to a woman who had once been perfectly sane?

'I'm sorry, Billy – I haven't the faintest idea what you're talking about.'

'The service, Mrs Highcroft,' explained Billy patiently. 'The twenty thousand service.' He came forward confidently, wiping his hands on the sleeves of his overalls, took a clipboard down from a hook behind the counter and ran a dirty thumbnail down the list of vehicle registration numbers. 'There you are. XOD 62X.' He twisted round and glanced up at the clock. 'Mind you, you've clipped it pretty fine. Any later and I couldn't promise we'd have the job finished today.'

'But I didn't book the car in for a service.'

Head bent over the clipboard, Billy grinned. 'Didn't he tell you? Och, he's always doing that.'

'Didn't who tell me?'

'Your husband – the Professor. Came in yesterday on his way in to work.' Helen gripped him suddenly by the arm, and he looked up, startled. 'All I—'

'No – please. Just . . . say that again, would you? When did he book the car in?'

'Yesterday.'

'You're *sure*?'

The mechanic nodded. 'Aye, I'm sure, right enough. I wrote it down myself. Here—' He swivelled the grubby works' diary towards her and an oil-stained finger marked the place. 'There, you see? I wrote that with him watching me, standing where you're standing now.' For the first time he noticed the pale face, the eyes etched by worry and fatigue. 'Is there anything wrong, Mrs Highcroft?'

Why would Malcolm bother to book the Volvo in for a service the following day if he knew he was going to abandon the car at the station less than twelve hours later? *Why*?

'Mrs Highcroft . . . ?'

She didn't even hear him.

Again Tony Lockhart told himself he was being a bloody idiot; that he was too old for this sort of thing; that he was going to elaborate lengths just to make a fool of himself. She'd probably slam the door in his face anyway. Which was probably no more than he deserved, he thought wryly, overtaking a caravan labouring up the hill on the approach to Gleninver town centre. Not only was he squandering an afternoon off when he should be looking round for somewhere else to live after that 12 October deadline from the Housing Officer at RAF Glenhaddon, but he was also about to break one of the cardinal rules of the professional rescue worker: the one that said, Never Get Involved.

To begin with he had been quite crafty. He had told himself it was all in the line of duty and that he simply wanted to tidy up loose-ends in the wake of George's drunken outburst in the Dolphin the previous evening; that his visit was just good public relations – until he caught himself choosing shirt and trousers with special care and splashing on the old aftershave. Then he swore at himself in the bathroom mirror. He was thirty-seven years old, for Chrissakes, not some aircraftsman kid out to get his rocks off at the station Friday night disco. Hadn't he learnt his lesson with Maureen? He had studied his face in the bathroom mirror then and thought bleak, bitter thoughts as he contemplated the alternatives: stay in and watch the telly; get quietly drunk with his own company and a six-pack or two of lager; another solitary, lonely afternoon and evening on his own, or, worse still, in the company of well-meaning friends in the service, couples who'd invite him along because they felt sorry for him and then wonder what the hell to talk about when someone mentioned kids or marriage or houses. And with the bachelors? He might be on safer, less sensitive ground there, but he was a good ten years older than most of them. They didn't want him cluttering up the action and staring morosely into his beer while they chatted up anything in a skirt . . . Even as Tony wavered in front of the mirror, he had remembered suddenly how she had looked, the way she had picked her way through a crowd of strangers just to thank them for trying. It must have taken courage, that. Some guts. That had decided him. He'd give it a try. And if she slammed the door in his face and didn't want to know, then so be it. He could always go house-hunting. And come home with a few cans of beer and sit down in front of the telly. Tony slowed down, changed gear and indicated he was turning right.

The truth was rather more complex than that, although Tony, of course, was the last to see it. In Jenny's loneliness, in her isolation, he had found a mirror-image of his own.

Jenny took her mug of coffee through from the kitchen at the back of her flat, sat down on the sofa and leaned forward towards the table where Mrs Proctor's Cardocol pills stood propped against an empty vase. With nothing else to do, no appointments to keep, she had taken the phone off the hook and sat back to try and piece together the fragments of fact and assorted, half-formed theory that skated elusively around her mind. Part of her knew she was just clutching at straws, casting around for some distraction, some crutch to help her through these first terrible days of adjustment and self-recrimination. And yet . . . and yet . . . there was something there, she was sure of it: something that might, just possibly, link Jamie's death to the pills she had found on Robbie Roberts' kitchen table – and to Mrs Proctor's collapse upstairs. Those pills somehow were the key. Pills that had been manufactured by Highland Pharmaceuticals Limited, but which had yet to be released to the local chemist, and which had yet to appear in any of the current pharmaceutical reference books.

The doorbell rang.

Jenny got up and went cautiously down the hall. 'Who is it?' she called warily. Because if just one more bloody newspaper reporter tried to . . .

'Miss Macrae?' A man's voice, vaguely familiar.

'Who wants her?'

'It's Flight Sergeant Tony Lockhart, Miss Macrae. From RAF Glenhaddon. We met last night.'

The winchman. The man who had tried to save Jamie, done his best to put her at ease before all those hostile faces started staring in the pub. She took the chain off the door, slipped up the catch and stood back.

'Sorry. I don't usually shout at people through the door like that. It's just that I've been a bit . . . you know . . . pestered.' She forced a wry smile. 'The . . . er . . . Gentlemen of the Press, I believe they're called.'

Tony nodded his sympathy and held up a copy of a morning paper.

'They got the address right, at least.' He let the paper fall to his side. 'I . . . ah . . . I was just passing, so I thought I'd call by and apologize. For what happened in the pub, I mean. You don't want to pay any attention to old George back there. Nobody else does. Especially when he's had a skinful.'

'That's very kind of you, Flight Sergeant, but there's no need for you to go out of your way on my account. I'm sorry I made such a fool of myself, running off like that,' Jenny said stiffly. 'Thank you for calling.' She began to close the door.

'Whoa – wait a minute, will you? Don't be in such a hurry. What's the matter?'

'Nothing. It's just that I don't need your pity, OK? I made a mistake, the boy died, and I'm going to pay for it, all right? The Fiscal came round this afternoon and took a statement.'

'Jesus! What's . . . ? Look, I didn't come here to offer pity, OK? I . . . I just thought you got a raw deal, that's all. If you want me to bugger off – fine. I'm on my way. Sorry I troubled you.' Tony turned angrily on his heel and set off down the path towards the gate. You see? he said to himself savagely. You see? To hell with her.

Jenny watched his retreating back, then – 'Flight Sergeant.' No response. She tried again, a little louder. 'Flight Sergeant.' He stopped. And turned.

'Yeah?'

'I'm . . . I'm sorry. I didn't mean to bite your head off.'

'That's OK,' he said gruffly. 'Happens all the time.' There was a pause.

'Look – I . . . Would you like to come in? I've just made some coffee. Peace offering?'

Tony hesitated, then – 'Fresh or instant?'

'Instant.'

He cracked out a smile. 'You're on.' Tony came back up the garden path. 'Oh – and the name's Tony, all right?'

She nodded. 'Jenny.' Another smile. 'I expect the papers got that right, too.'

Ridley pulled in to the side of the road and turned off the engine. It never took him very long to settle into a new area, pick up his bearings. Like much else that cloaked his clandestine, murderous calling, he had got it down to a fine art: half an hour to sort out a hire car, half an hour to book himself into some small, anonymous motel, hotel or country pub, half an hour spent poring over a map of the target area absorbing the topography, and he was ready.

He had just driven slowly past Douglas Parsons' neat, prosperous home, and had braked the car to a gentle halt at the end of the slip road. One quick glance as he drove past confirmed what the estate agents' map had told him: there was no garage adjacent to the property itself. A garden shed there had been, with a lawnmower resting on blocks outside, but no garage. That, he suspected, would be found behind the row of identical semi-detached properties in a special service area screened from the houses behind a high hedge. Convenient, that.

Ridley started the engine, eased into gear and followed the slip road round to the service area. It was as he had imagined: twelve identical, neatly numbered steel-doored garages. The area appeared to be deserted. Ridley parked and got out. One of the garages was empty, its door pushed up. At the back of the garage, among the rags and the old oilcans, Ridley saw there was a narrow door leading through to a paved walkway. On impulse, he walked through the garage and stepped out on to the path, on the far side of which ran a high wooden fence with wicket gates leading to the rear gardens of the properties he had just driven past. All very symmetrical, all very planned and suburban. Which made his task that much easier.

Two minutes more and he was driving away as anonymously as he had arrived, his reconnaissance completed.

All that remained now was the final phase of the operation: the execution.

CHAPTER TWELVE

Jenny glanced up at the clock on the mantelpiece and saw with a start of surprise that almost fifty minutes had slipped by since Tony Lockhart had accepted her invitation to come inside for coffee. Tony was sitting opposite, both hands cupped around his mug as he described how he had tried to revive Jamie in the strop as they were winched up into the helicopter. He told the story with quiet, understated authority, his words carrying the chill edge of conviction as the images of horror came flooding back. Jenny closed her eyes for a moment, seeing it all so vividly – and when she looked up she saw that Tony too had that same faraway look in his eyes. 'I'm sorry,' she apologized quietly. 'I shouldn't have asked you to relive it. I just . . . needed to know. When we saw you swoop down like that, we felt so *sure* he . . . ' She shrugged and let the words trail away, for they would bring nothing back. 'Do you mind talking about it? Now that it's all over, I mean?'

The question took Tony by surprise. With Maureen, his wife? Yes, he had minded intensely – it had been a major source of friction between them. But here, now, talking to this woman—

'No, I don't mind,' he admitted, surprised to discover it was true. 'Not if you find it helps.'

'I suppose you just get used to it?' Jenny said, without thinking.

Tony looked up and shook his head slowly. 'Used to it? Can't say I do, no. Some of the others may say they do, but not me.'

'That was a stupid thing to say. I'm sorry.' There was a brief silence. 'Why do you do it? Search and rescue work, I mean?'

'Because I love it. Because it's my life,' Tony admitted

simply. 'Show me any other sort of work with half the same job satisfaction and I'll jack this lot in tomorrow.' There was another silence, more comfortable this time.

'Yesterday: when you went out to Robbie's boat . . . '

'Robbie?'

'The old man, Robbie Roberts. Did you see anything that might have caused the fire?'

Tony shrugged. 'Could have been anything. The boat was almost awash when we got there.'

'And Robbie? You said at the hospital that he'd died before you got to him?'

Tony nodded. 'That's right, yes.'

'What happened to him?'

Tony looked at her doubtfully. 'You sure you want to know?'

'What d'you mean?'

'Well, he wasn't a very pretty sight. He'd been badly burned. Face and neck, mostly.'

'Around the *face*? But how—?'

'It looked as though he'd fallen into the flames.'

Jenny shuddered. 'But how would anyone do that – fall into the flames?'

'God knows. Perhaps the boat rolled and he slipped.'

Jenny shook her head. 'Robbie had been working with that boat of his for years. Besides, there wasn't any swell. It was a flat calm. Just . . . just a minute!' She hunched forward excitedly. 'The burns would have to come *before* he drowned, yes? Otherwise the water would have quenched the flames.' Tony nodded. 'And for Robbie to be badly burned,' continued Jenny slowly, feeling her way carefully up the ladder of logic, 'he'd . . . he'd have to be lying there, wouldn't he? In the bottom of the boat.'

'I suppose so, yes.'

'Could he . . . What I mean is: if for some reason he had been unconscious *first*, and had *then* fallen into the flames – that would account for those burns, wouldn't it?'

Tony thought for a moment, remembering that weathered, once-handsome face eaten away by fire as he grasped Robbie's shoulder and hauled him towards him.

'Yes,' he said quietly. 'Yes, that would have done it, all right.'

Jenny reached across for the packet of Cardocol pills and held it out. 'Ever seen these before?' she asked.

Twenty minutes later, Jenny was on her way to see Mrs Proctor in hospital. And by then it seemed perfectly natural that Tony should go with her.

The nurse paused outside the closed door of one of the smaller rooms off Charlotte ward, and turned to them both. 'She's in here,' she said quietly. 'But she's still very weak, so please keep your visit as brief as possible. And preferably, if only one of you . . . '

Tony nodded. 'It's OK. I'll wait here.'

'Fine.' The nurse nodded and moved off down the corridor, her shoes squeaking on the polished lino. Jenny glanced at Tony, eased open the door and slipped inside.

Mrs Proctor was lying back against her pillows, eyes closed, mouth slightly open. A tube ran from her forearm to a machine beside her bed. She looked shrunken and frail, vulnerable amid the starched sheets and impersonal medical sterility. Jenny bent forward.

'Mrs Proctor – can you hear me? It's Jenny – Jenny Macrae.' An eyelid fluttered open, and Mrs Proctor gazed up at the ceiling with that faraway look of the heavily sedated. She twisted her head on the crisp white pillow and saw Jenny standing beside her. A ghost of a smile touched those dry white lips, and a hand moved slowly across the sheets towards her. Jenny pressed it tightly and lifted the flowers she had brought with her so Mrs Proctor could see them without further effort. 'I've brought you these.' There was a tiny nod and flicker of the eyelids, but that was all. Jenny moved the chair from the side of the ward and sat down beside her. 'How're you feeling?' she tried, looking down at the pale, wasted face. A tongue moved slowly over dry lips.

'T . . . tired,' the old woman whispered.

Jenny nodded. 'You're going to be all right, understand? You're in good hands – the very best. I've just spoken to the nurse.' She paused, and then squeezed the old lady's hand once more. 'You had another one of your falls, didn't you?'

'Did . . . did I?'

'Mrs Elliott found you. Lying on the floor next to your bed. It's a good job she came round with the laundry, otherwise you might have stayed there all week.' Jenny smiled and patted the hand reassuringly. 'Anyway, all that's over now. You'll soon be as right as rain.' Mrs Proctor closed her eyes for a moment and Jenny thought she had drifted back to sleep, but presently they opened again. 'Do you remember what happened?' she pressed. 'Do you remember getting out of bed?' A tired, slow shake of the head. Jenny took out Mrs Proctor's Cardocol pills and held them up in front of the old woman. 'Did you take one of these this morning?'

'After . . . breakfast.'

'Where did you get them, Mrs Proctor? Who gave them to you?'

The eyelids fluttered, closed, and then opened again with great effort. 'Doctor . . . gave them to me,' she whispered. Jenny shook her head impatiently. Old people were always blurring the distinction between doctors and chemists, yet the distinction was crucial: doctors didn't give drugs, they gave prescriptions.

'No, no, Mrs Proctor – which *chemist*? Can you remember?'

'Doctor . . . Doctor Erskine,' she insisted weakly.

Jenny and Tony drove directly from the hospital to Dr Erskine's surgery in Market Hall Square, only to discover it had closed until the following morning. It was after six in the evening by then, the heat had gone from the day, and the lanes and roads were busy with the last of the season's holiday-makers returning weary and sunburned to their hotels and guest houses as Jenny hauled on the handbrake outside her flat and groaned aloud: 'That traffic gets worse every year. Roll on winter when we get the place back to ourselves.'

'Amen to that,' Tony agreed. 'Winter's our quiet time,

too.' He twisted towards her. 'What are you going to do now?'

Jenny had been thinking about that on the drive home, remembering with a sudden flutter of nerves that she had still to return Jamie's things to his parents.

'Now? I suppose I'd better go and see Mr and Mrs Ennis. There's . . . one or two things I have to return.' She gazed out of the window and added softly: 'I don't imagine they'll exactly welcome me with open arms.'

'Want me to come with you as moral support?'

The question took Jenny by surprise. She shook her head. 'No, thanks.'

'Fine,' replied Tony lightly, turning back and reaching for the door catch as they got out together. With Jenny bending to lock the door: 'Listen – Jenny. Don't take this the wrong way, all right?' She looked up over the roof of the car. 'I'm going into town for a while, then I'll be having a meal in that French place down by the quay—'

'*Chez Simone*?'

'That's the place. If after you've seen the kid's parents . . .I don't know . . . you fancy some company . . . ' He shrugged. 'Well, all I'm saying is I'll be there after eight-thirty, OK . . . ?'

Ten minutes later, Tony's invitation had been pushed to the back of Jenny's mind as she drove slowly down the drive towards the Ennis home with her dread of the encounter a physical pain in the pit of her stomach. She walked across the gravel and rang the doorbell. She waited. An age seemed to pass before the door opened to reveal Jamie's father standing in the doorway. Jenny swallowed. 'Mr Ennis, I—'

'What the hell d'you want?'

She held out the bag of toys and artwork, sweaters and personal possessions. 'I've . . . I've brought Jamie's things back.'

John Ennis made no move to take them, and Jenny had to stand there as his eyes blazed into her.

'John? Who is it?' A thin, wavering voice from inside. John Ennis pushed the door half closed so his wife would not see Jenny standing outside.

'Nothing, love,' he called over his shoulder. 'It's all right.' He stepped out on to the porch, pulled the door almost shut and tore the bag from her fingers. 'Haven't you done enough damage? Get away from here, d'you hear?'

'Please, Mr Ennis: all I can do is say—'

'Don't you "please Mr Ennis" me! I'll . . . I'll tell you what you *can* do, Missy, you can bugger off, all right? Just leave us alone! You've robbed us of the only thing we really cared about, understand? That . . . that social experiment of yours cost us our son!' he blurted, almost in tears.

'It wasn't a social experiment, Mr Ennis. I was trying to—'

'—And I'll let you into another little secret.' He wagged a finger under her nose. 'I've contacts, friends in high places – you understand what I'm saying? By the time I've finished with you, you won't be able to get work washing dishes, never mind looking after children!'

'You can save some of your anger, Mr Ennis,' Jenny replied evenly, determined to stand her ground. 'I've already been suspended, if that makes you feel any better.'

John Ennis thought for a moment and then nodded curtly. 'It's a start, Miss Macrae, I'll say that. It's a start.'

'Good-night, darlings. And try not to worry.' Helen Highcroft stood at the door of Mark and Simon's bedroom and looked back at their two dark shapes huddled beneath the covers, her hand on the light switch.

'Good-night,' answered Mark, a small, drowsy voice from the corner. A pause, then – 'Mummy?'

'Now what is it?'

'He will *be* coming home, won't he?'

'I . . . I expect so, darling. We'll just have to wait and see, won't we?' she tried, with as much lightness as she could muster. 'Now then – off to sleep, the pair of you.'

She pulled the door almost closed, went a few paces down the corridor and glanced in at Sarah working, head bowed, over her desk. Then Helen crossed the landing and went into the master bedroom, closed the door softly behind her and sat down on the edge of their double bed. She stared at her reflection in the wardrobe mirror, suddenly hating the age-lines and the wisps of grey hair that she was sure had not been there the year before. She was getting older, that was the trouble; she had sacrificed the best years of her life to raise a family and make a home, only to find . . . Helen gave a long, shuddering sigh and looked round at their bedroom, at the framed family photographs and the unfinished books on their matching bedside tables, their places kept with the bookmarks the children had made for them both last Christmas. Cherished possessions suddenly called into question; made empty, meaningless.

Helen got up, opened her husband's wardrobe, fingered the cloth of one of his jackets and cried aloud with the pain of her loss as the nightmare of these last two days closed in around her. Was it possible, was it really possible to share so much, such intimacy and laughter over so many years, and then suddenly just walk away from it all without a word or a backward glance? Had she really been that bad a wife? A lover and companion?

Presently Helen washed her face at the basin, tidied her hair and went downstairs. She had made supper for the children earlier and, although she didn't feel like eating herself, she decided she had better make the effort.

She was whisking eggs for an omelette when the phone rang. Starting violently, she wiped her hands on a tea towel, hurried into the hall and swept up the receiver. 'Yes? Hello?' Then her shoulders drooped and she sank back against the wall. 'Oh, hello, Frank. Yes . . . yes, I did. No . . . nothing. They found the Volvo this morning. Yes . . . that's right. Parked at the station.' She paused. 'It looks as though he may have gone off with . . . someone else. With a younger woman.' The voice broke off then, and she had to stop as the business of putting infidelity and betrayal into words opened fresh wounds. The conversation went on for another minute or two, and then Helen replaced the receiver. When she turned round she saw Sarah watching her gravely from halfway up the stairs.

'That . . . that was your Uncle Frank,' she explained. 'He's . . . he's coming over for a couple of days. Then the three of you can go down to Durham, stay with John and Angie. Would you like that?'

'How long for?' Sarah asked suspiciously.

'Oh, just a few days. Just till things get back to normal.'

'It's not true, is it? What you said to Uncle Frank. About Daddy and that other woman?'

'You . . . you weren't supposed to be listening,' her mother said lamely. It was all she could think of.

'I'm not a baby any more, Mummy – I'm thirteen years old! Rachel Harding's parents broke up. They got divorced last year, just before the holidays. Are you and Daddy getting divorced?' She made it sound like a desirable social option.

'It's . . . it's not as simple as that, Sarah. If—'

'But if Daddy's gone off with someone else, that means he doesn't love us any more, doesn't it?'

'Of course Daddy still loves you, darling! You mustn't say that. It's just that . . . well . . . when someone—'

'When what?'

'Well, when two people who have—'

'It means he doesn't love you, doesn't it? It must do! Otherwise he wouldn't have left, would he?'

'I . . . we'll talk about it in the morning.'

'I want to talk about it now!'

'In the morning, I said! Now, go on: upstairs.'

Sarah went slowly, resentfully, up the stairs, and Helen watched her go, bitterly conscious of the inadequacy of her answers, yet knowing she didn't have the strength to talk it through without breaking down. Not now, not yet. She went back into the kitchen, took one look at the half-beaten eggs and decided she couldn't face them. Closing her mind to the waste, she tipped the whole sticky yellow mess down the sink and went through into the sitting-room where she poured herself a stiff drink and sat down heavily in an armchair, her daughter's words ringing in her ears.

A little later she discovered her glass was empty. She helped herself to another. Then Helen took down the pile of photograph albums from the shelf over by the window, returned to her chair and began leafing through the thick pages. As though by flicking through the testimony of past happiness she might find some clue to what had gone wrong with the present.

Holidays and family groups in the garden, visits from uncles and aunts, nativity plays and seaside outings, blown-out cheeks frozen over guttering candles recorded for posterity as the photographs changed from black and white to colour, and Malcolm's hairline steadily receded.

Her glass was empty again. Helen balanced the album on the arm of the chair and rose to replenish her glass. As she sat down again, she knocked the album on to the floor, spilling loose across the carpet a cluster of pictures tucked in at the back, waiting to be mounted. Helen picked them up and began glancing idly through the pile, the drink blunting the edge of pain and turning memory into a maudlin exercise in self-pity.

The photographs had all been taken quite recently: there was Mark at Cubs' camp, and Sarah proudly holding up the drama cup she had won at the end of spring term – and a Polaroid of Malcolm at the Christmas office party, sitting at his desk surrounded by a cluster of colleagues all wearing paper hats and half-intoxicated smiles. Helen gazed sightlessly at the Polaroid as she felt all the tiredness and unhappiness well up inside her. One minute everything was fine and there didn't appear to be a cloud on the horizon. The next, it was as if – she sat up suddenly, picked up the Polaroid again and bent forward. The window: the window in Malcolm's office. It had a blind, not curtains.

A blind, not curtains.

Helen laid the photograph slowly aside. Malcolm hadn't changed offices in the past year, she was sure. Besides, she recognized the picture frame on his desk. Yet the office Jackman had taken her to earlier that morning had curtains, not blinds, she was certain. He'd drawn them as they went in. Hadn't he?

Helen leaned back in the armchair and closed her eyes, conscious of a sudden inner stillness that seemed to cut away some of the fog of confusion and despair that had swirled about her for so long. Then she remembered Billy, the mechanic at the garage, insisting Malcolm had booked the car in for a service less than twelve hours before he disappeared – and suddenly she wasn't sure of anything any more. Nothing beyond a tiny, gnawing suspicion.

'Come on, little chap – let's have a look at you,' Jackman coaxed, reaching down a rubber-gloved hand to pick up one of two pure-white house mice from the bottom of the stainless-steel cage. He held the squirming animal up towards the light and inspected it critically. Pink nose and white whiskers wrinkling inquisitively, eyes sparkling sharp as pins beneath the strong overhead light, the little animal was the picture of vitality and good health.

Jackman reached for one of the microphones suspended on adjustable stalks from the laboratory ceiling, bent it towards him, turned the mouse over on to its back and rubbed the pale, hairy little stomach thoughtfully. Then he placed the mouse on the scales and leaned forward. 'Weight: 27.5 grammes,' he announced, for the benefit of the machine that had recorded Professor Highcroft's death-throes so faithfully. 'Length—' he lifted the mouse off the scales and stretched it along the graduated metal strip set into the top of the laboratory workbench – 'ninety-seven millimetres. Length of tail: ninety-two millimetres. Gender: male.'

Now Jackman moved across to a set of electronic monitors and spent five minutes taping tiny electrode conduits to the animal's head, chest and stomach. The mouse hardly seemed to mind at all. Jackman than lowered the animal carefully to the bottom of another experimental chamber, turned back to the workbench and spent the next fifteen minutes carefully calibrating each machine to establish a reliable template of the mouse's heart and respiratory patterns. Only when he was quite satisfied did he slide home the lid of the chamber and seal it down tight, with slow, deliberate turns of the butterfly keys. Then he turned towards Douglas Parsons on the far side of the screen.

Parsons was standing beside the console on the third floor of RD7, watching Jackman closely through the glass screen. No mention of their earlier encounter had been made when Parsons had come on duty – Jackman had acknowledged his presence with a curt nod, and that had been all. Still, Parsons would be relieved when the new man arrived. There was something about Jackman that made him uneasy . . .

'Please confirm the experimental unit is now sealed and switched through to IC.' Internal circuit: its own internal air supply.

Parsons scanned his bank of indicators and bent to his microphone. 'That is confirmed,' he acknowledged formally. 'Airtight integrity established at 96 p.s.i. All lights show Condition Green.'

'Thank you. Just to be on the safe side, would you isolate Section Nine from the remainder of the third floor? No point in taking unnecessary risks.'

Parsons raised a hand. After Professor Highcroft's accident, no one needed reminding. Parsons pressed the keys and ran his eyes along the bank of dials as the coloured panels glowed all the right colours. 'Section Nine is now isolated,' he confirmed.

Jackman moved slowly over to the workbench, snapped back the clips on a heavy, lead-lined casket and removed a shining metal cylinder with exaggerated caution. The cylinder was ten inches long and five in circumference. The top tapered slightly and terminated in a universal screw fitting. Jackman now located this against a matching socket on the side of the experimental unit and screwed the cylinder slowly clockwise until it would go no further. He stepped back to the microphone. 'Ready.'

Unconcerned, the mouse snuffled about in a corner.

A final check from Parsons: 'Condition still Green. Green across the board.'

'Releasing . . . now.' Jackman twisted the canister firmly clockwise, and then crouched down beside the chamber to see what happened, a stopwatch in his hand.

For several seconds nothing happened at all, and the

monitors on the bench beside him showed no appreciable change. Then the gas began to take effect.

The mouse became suddenly uncoordinated. It wandered around in a little circle, fell down, got up, banged against the side of the chamber and vomited violently before collapsing sideways. There was a sudden thick, yellow, nasal discharge and the body began to quiver and shake. Breathing became laboured, pulse became weak, and there was a sudden smear across the glass wall of the chamber as the little animal lost muscular control of bowel and bladder. Jackman glanced at his stopwatch and nodded with satisfaction.

Muscular contraction in both animals and humans is caused by a chemical called acetylcholine. On its own, this chemical would send all the muscles of the body into continuous contraction, but the amount of acetylcholine is kept in balance by another chemical called cholinesterase. The gas Jackman had introduced into the experimental chamber had inhibited the action of that second chemical and made the body, in effect, poison itself by sending the muscular system into continuous and terminal contraction. Now Jackman glanced first at the monitors and then at his stopwatch as the mouse twitched once more and lay still. Jackman made a careful note on his clipboard and straightened up. Death had occurred after seventeen seconds' exposure to the chemical nerve agent Tabun GA.

Seventeen seconds, they had established, was about average.

On the second floor of the Seaview Motel on the hilly outskirts of Gleninver, Ridley finished his solitary meal, wiped his mouth and fingers carefully on the paper napkin provided and laid his cluttered tray on the floor of the corridor outside his room. Back inside, he locked the door behind him and looked at his watch. Parsons would be coming off duty soon. It was time to get ready.

Ridley undressed, bathed and shaved with great care, changed into fresh clothes and then sat for long minutes in front of the mirror, brushing his short hair with slow, hard strokes of the hairbrush as he thought about what he would shortly do, his eyes bleak and cold and distant in the reflection. At last he rose, lifted his suitcase from beneath the bed, unlocked it, took out a plastic bag and reached inside. Slowly, one by one, he placed the items he would need in a neat, straight line on the candlewick bedspread. Innocuous, harmless in themselves, they were nevertheless, collectively, the tools of the trade.

Douglas Parsons pushed through the double glass doors and stepped gratefully into the fresh air. He stretched, and craned his neck far back to gaze up at the clear, bright stars. Breathing in the cool night air, he relished the scent of pines and the faint tang of the sea, each smell clear and separate after the scrubbed, starved sterility of RD7. It always took him a few minutes to rejoin the human race after leaving the laboratory. He had long made it his practice to walk around the grounds in the darkness, away from the glow of lights from the building, and try to brush all thoughts of work from his mind before starting the drive home. It was a policy actively encouraged and recognized by them all: thinking about work and death all day and all night, you could go gently but definitely round the bend. He had seen it happen at Porton with that chap Anderson, who suddenly took it into his head to take a stroll down the centre of the A303 . . . But tonight something was nagging at his sense of well-being and, as he unlocked the car door, Parsons recalled his ultimatum to Jackman earlier that morning. He sighed and slid behind the wheel. Well, he had done all he could; he had done what he set out to do, and now he felt better for it. Parsons started the car and drove home in a better frame of mind. He was looking forward pleasantly to bed, to sleep.

It was a clear, dry night and there was little traffic on the winding road back into Gleninver. Shortly after eleven-twenty, Parsons drove quietly past the house and turned into the service road, bringing the car to a halt outside his garage. As usual, the area was deserted. He got out, sent the garage door rolling up and back, and then drove forward, his headlights turning the empty garage interior into a bright white box. He stopped the car, hauled on the handbrake, switched off the lights and sat back from the wheel for a moment, savouring the silence. Suddenly the driver's door was wrenched open and Parsons spun round. 'Mr Douglas Parsons?' asked a quiet voice.

'Yes? What is it? What do you want?'

'I wonder if I might have a word?' The interior light had gone on as the door opened, and Parsons was able to see the gleam of the blade quite clearly.

Harold Engel sat alone in his study, an empty whisky glass beside the tape recorder on the desk in front of him as he forced himself to listen once more to the last tortured moments of Professor Malcolm Highcroft. Leaning forward over the tape, with the single lamp on his desk throwing dark shadows across the room, Engel pressed the tips of his fingers fiercely against his temples as the voice of his friend coughed, rasped, and then choked off into final, terrible silence. He sat back then with shaking hands, banged the 'stop' button, and almost tore the cassette out of the machine as that voice sawed across his nerves like some curse flung back from the grave. If he had known it was going to lead to this, he would never have agreed – never! If he—

'Harold?' He started, and swung round violently. Joyce was standing in the doorway, a tray of coffee things in her hands. She came forward slowly into the study, her eyes fixed upon his face and what she saw there, so that for one awful moment he thought she had heard the recording. 'What is it?' she asked, her voice almost a whisper in the shadows. 'What's the matter?' Her husband shook his head, unable to speak. The memory of what he had heard was too recent, the terror too close for talking. Joyce set the tray on the edge of his desk, replaced whisky glass with coffee cup and added one sugar with slow deliberation. Then she sat down and leaned forward. 'What *is* it, Harold?' she repeated. 'Tell me.'

He groaned and rocked back in his chair, hands linked

behind his head. 'Oh, I don't know.' He forced a travesty of a smile. 'I'm just tired, that's all. With Cardocol less than—'

'It's not Cardocol at all, is it?' she interrupted quietly.

The hands came down slowly as he tried to look surprised. 'What do you mean?'

'It's something else.'

'Something else?' he laughed bitterly. 'Good God, woman, do you have the slightest idea what sort of pressure I've—'

'Harold – stop it!' she almost shouted. 'Just . . . look at me, will you? Please.' He turned slowly and saw the fear in his wife's eyes. 'It's got nothing to do with Cardocol, has it? This thing that's tearing you apart.' He rubbed both eyes with the heels of his hands, and Joyce reached forward and grasped his arm. 'Tell me!' she commanded fiercely. 'I want to help, can't you see that?'

The seconds ticked away as the silence built into a wall between them. Then – 'I can't,' he admitted, the words a husky whisper. 'I can't, don't you see? I'd like to, I . . . I want to, but . . . I can't.' He pulled open a drawer, tossed Highcroft's tape inside and slammed the drawer shut with a force that made the brass handles rattle.

'Please: just . . . just tell me. Where are we going?' Douglas Parsons begged again, with a tremor of fear in his voice. It was quite unmistakable this time, and Ridley smiled grimly to himself in the darkness of the moving car. He enjoyed planting terror in others and had come to relish the inevitable transition from bluster and indignation to dawning horror and the slow, curdling realization that death was suddenly very close.

'Nearly there,' he soothed, the butcher's knife a dull gleam on his lap as Parsons drove them away from the lights and safety of Gleninver towards the darkness and seclusion of the open countryside. Parsons glanced across at Ridley, his eyes white and round in a pale, frightened face. As he took his eyes off the road, the car swerved suddenly towards the ditch. Ridley sprang forward, his knife at Parsons' throat in an instant.

'No! . . . I'm sorry! I didn't . . . I just . . . ' gabbled Parsons, as the point of the blade stopped less than an inch from his throbbing Adam's apple.

'Look where you're going!' Ridley ordered curtly, before relaxing back into his seat and lowering the knife. He wrinkled his nose in disgust. He could smell the man's fear, almost taste it beside him in the closeness of the car. They drove on for several minutes in silence along dark, empty country lanes, until suddenly Parsons could bear it no longer.

'Look – whoever you are. If it's . . . if it's money you want . . . ' He fumbled in his jacket and took out his wallet with trembling fingers. 'Here – take it. It's yours. That's all . . . all I have on me, I swear it!'

Ridley plucked the wallet from his hand, glanced briefly at its contents and slipped it into his own pocket. Parsons seemed to take that as some sort of agreement, some gesture that a deal had been struck between them. He sighed with relief. 'Now, please – put that knife away and let me turn this car round. You've got what you wanted. I won't tell the police, I promise you.'

Ridley laughed quietly. It was a chilling, unnerving sound, devoid of humour, warmth or feeling of any kind.

'Why . . . why are you laughing?' asked Parsons tremulously, the fear drying his mouth so that he was unable to swallow. This nightmare wasn't real; it wasn't happening to him. It couldn't be . . .

Ridley didn't bother to answer. Another minute passed in unnerving silence, then—

'Slow down,' Ridley ordered. 'There's a turning coming up on your left. A track. There! Turn down there.'

'Where are you—?'

'Do it!'

The words lashed out, and Parsons braked the car and turned off the road. They bumped slowly along an overgrown track, with the long grass swishing against the underside of the car as their headlights carved a swathe of milky brilliance through the thick summer woodland that crowded down towards them from either side of the narrow, choked little lane. Ridley had found the track in daylight and had chosen it with care: the nearest cottage was half a mile away through the woods and, once they had passed the bend in the track, they would be invisible from the road.

They passed the bend in the track.

'Right – this'll do. Stop here.' Parsons obeyed. 'Turn off the engine. Lights too.' More compliance, until the only sound was the pant of Parsons' frightened breathing in the pressing darkness. Ridley reached up and turned on the interior light. Parsons cowered away.

'What . . . what are you going to do?' he managed fearfully. 'Why have you brought me here?' More silence. And with it, a chilling glimmer of realization. 'It's not . . . not just the money, is it?'

Ridley slowly shook his head, enjoying the game, the tease. 'No. It's not just the money.'

Parsons tried to lick dry lips. 'Then I . . . I don't . . . '

'Jackman has hired me to kill you.'

The words didn't register, not at first. When they did, what little colour there was remaining in Parsons' face drained away as though someone had pulled a plug. He sagged sideways against the door, his face putty-grey, quivering with shock. 'To . . . to *kill* me?' Ridley nodded slowly. He might have been a sympathetic doctor confirming diagnosis to a terminal cancer patient. 'But that's . . . that's ridiculous! Jackman would never get away with . . . with murder! There must be some mistake! Surely to God you—' Another shake of the head. A gesture of finality.

'No mistake.' Ridley moved closer.

'Wait! Please – listen to me!' beseeched Parsons, clawing after the final moments of life even as they slipped through his fingers. 'It's . . . it's because of Highcroft, isn't it? Because I saw Highcroft die?'

'You tried to apply pressure. You—'

'But I wasn't the only one!' Parsons protested, like a small boy caught stealing apples while the rest of the gang slip through a hole in the hedge. 'What about the others?'

Ridley looked up slowly. 'What others?'

'Calvert! Calvert and Steevenson! They were on duty too – they saw it as well!' Parsons explained eagerly, in a desperate attempt to deflect attention from himself.

'Those names again?'

'Calvert. Calvert and Steevenson.'

'Thank you.' Ridley leaned suddenly closer, knife raised. Parsons shrank away from him, and Ridley smiled. 'Listen to me,' he ordered quietly, in a voice of velvet menace. 'You don't have to die. Do what I tell you, instantly and without question, and you will live, I promise you. Do you understand?' Parsons swallowed, but did not reply. He couldn't. The words, the sudden switch, the offer of reprieve, made speech impossible. Ridley pricked him under the chin with the tip of the butcher's knife. 'Tell me you understand,' he coaxed.

Parsons found his voice at last. 'I . . . I understand.'

Ridley nodded patiently. 'You are to stay exactly where you are, is that clear? Do not move. Try to get out, try to escape, and I will kill you. Do you understand that?'

'Yes,' Parsons whispered, the word almost a croak.

'Hands on the steering-wheel. Keep them there.'

Parsons hurried to do what he was told as Ridley reached slowly across his lap and removed the keys from the ignition, his eyes never leaving Parsons' face for an instant. Getting out, he moved round to the rear door, reached inside his plastic carrier bag lying on the back seat and took out a pair of motorcycle gauntlets and a roll of thick carpet tape.

Parsons glanced round once, fearfully, hands never leaving the steering-wheel as he sat hypnotized by the man's menace. Ridley closed the door softly and stood for a moment in the darkness of the forgotten lane, listening intently. Nothing. Just the sigh of the wind in the trees. He moved round to the driver's door, pulled it open and held the gauntlets out towards his prisoner. 'Put them on!' he ordered.

Parsons looked from the gauntlets to Ridley's lean, hard face in total bewilderment.

'What are—?'

Ridley raised the knife the merest fraction, and Parsons pulled on the gauntlets without another word.

'Hands together.'

Parsons did as he was told. Ridley laid the knife within easy reach on the roof of the car, gripped both of Parsons' plump wrists with the fingers of one lean hand and began binding the carpet tape around his wrists. Too late, Parsons saw the look on his face and began to struggle.

'You don't—'

'Quiet!' Ridley hissed, twisting the tape rapidly around wrists and fingers until both hands were trussed tightly together.

'Why . . . Why are you doing this?' blurted Parsons, as Ridley passed the roll of tape through the centre of the steering-wheel and round the steering-column, forcing Parsons forward until his chin was almost touching the wheel. Ridley worked on swiftly, paying no more attention to Parsons now than he would to a piece of meat.

He stood back and examined his handiwork, his face set and hard. He was panting a little now, perhaps from exertion. He moved back to the rear of the car, reached inside that plastic bag of his and returned with a towel he had taken from his motel bedroom. Folding this into a thin bandage, he squatted down beside the sill of the driver's door, swept Parsons' legs towards him and wrapped the towel swiftly around his ankles. Then he bound more tape over the towel until ankles too were bound securely, both to one another and to the steering-column above. 'All done,' Ridley announced briefly, tugging on Parsons' bindings.

'Please . . . ' Parsons begged with a terrible earnestness, as he sensed through a rising tide of panic that somehow he had been tricked, fatally duped. 'Please: I . . . I beg you. You promised you'd let me live if—' He got no further. Ridley pinched his cheeks tightly together, prised his jaws apart and jammed a napkin into his mouth, forcing it back down his throat until his eyes bulged from their sockets. Then he stepped back and studied his victim with cold, flat eyes, noting the face covered in a sheen of sweat, and the hair plastered in wet disarray across his scalp as he strained at the tape. Ridley watched his futile efforts with a little smile of amusement.

'I know I did,' Ridley said softly, kissing the tips of his own fingers and then laying them gently against Parsons' cheek like some obscene form of papal benediction. 'I lied.'

Parsons began to scream then – a weird, sub-human sound of terror and naked supplication from somewhere deep down in his throat. Ridley watched him a moment longer and then hurried round to the rear of the car.

He took a length of garden hosepipe and another large towel from his plastic bag, crouched down in the long grass and jammed one end of the hosepipe into the exhaust and trailed the rest round to the front of the car. Opening the nearside front passenger window, he draped the hosepipe inside, closed the door carefully and got into the back of the car. Reaching forward, he wound up the front window until the hosepipe was trapped against the top of the door, and then pushed the towel into the gap that was left, forming an airtight seal around the pipe.

Ridley checked each of the other windows in turn and then returned to the driver's door. He took the ignition key out of his pocket and held it up. Parsons saw the key, saw the hosepipe, realized what was coming, and began straining and twisting at the tape like a man demented, his eyes starting from his head as his back arched out of his seat. Ridley slipped the key unhurriedly into the ignition and straightened up. 'It's just a job, that's all,' he said quietly. 'Nothing personal.'

He turned the key in the ignition. The engine caught obediently, and the first fumes of carbon monoxide began to fill the car.

Ridley smoothed Parsons' hair over his forehead, patted his cheek in farewell, closed the door firmly and moved away. The interior light was still on, but that was deliberate. Ridley always liked to watch.

It didn't take very long. Parsons was panicking and thus hyperventilating, dragging the poisonous fumes down into his lungs, just as fast as he inhaled them through his nose.

Nine, ten minutes went by with Ridley sitting quietly on a flat stone five yards away, listening to the hoot of an owl in the distance and the soft, ominous bubbling of the exhaust closer to hand. Gradually, the level of colourless, odourless carbon monoxide rose inside the car as Parsons twisted and heaved, fighting to delay the inevitable. At last his struggles slowed, and then ceased altogether, and he collapsed against the steering-wheel.

'More coffee, madam? Sir?' Tony gestured at their empty cups, and the waiter poured. Tony and Jenny were sitting in the French restaurant, *Chez Simone*, down by the quay in Gleninver. Tony had chosen the table with care when he first came in alone, just in case Jenny had decided to join him, rejecting the offer of an intimate table *à deux* in one of the wooden-walled alcoves for a place by the wide bay window with a good view of the boats bobbing to their lights on the tide. They were moving towards friendship, not lovers bent on an exchange of confidences. Now Jenny leaned forward, fingers playing nervously with the sugar spoon on the edge of her saucer. 'I . . . I just thought it was what he needed, you know?' She spoke so quietly that Tony had to lean forward until his face was warmed by the flame from the candle to hear what she was saying. 'A chance to spread his wings a bit, get away from home and build some memories of his own. Gain a little confidence.' She looked up, her eyes a mirror of some deep inner pain. 'I remember . . . I remember even *now* thinking: should I go with them? Just to be on the safe side. And I . . . I deliberately decided not to. That's what's so . . . so awful. I deliberately let him go off with Robbie on his own. It's not even as if—'

'From what you say, I think you did the right thing,' Tony offered quietly.

'You do?'

'I like to think I'd have done the same thing, put in your position. The easy thing would have been to go with him. The *hard* thing was to let him go off alone. You can't wrap a child in cotton wool forever. What happened later . . . ' He shrugged. 'You were just unlucky, that's all. It could have happened to anyone.'

'Unlucky?' Jenny pushed granules of brown sugar into a little pattern on the starched white tablecloth. 'I don't think I was just unlucky.' She looked up. 'I think there was something else.'

Ridley was waiting. A dark, motionless shadow lost amidst an army of shadows. At last the engine of Parsons' car faltered and then cut out completely, and in its place was left a waiting, brooding silence.

Ridley rose to his feet and walked slowly forward, the butcher's knife held down at his side, the long grass swishing against his shoes. He peered in at the driver's window and saw Parsons slumped sideways across the wheel, eyes closed. He tugged open the driver's door and stepped back as the gas swirled out into the cool, clean air of late evening. He let another full minute slide by as he watched for the slightest sign of movement, of revival. Nothing. Holding his breath and ducking down into the car, he reached across the body and prised back an eyelid in the bright cherry-red face. It stared back, fully dilated.

When he was quite satisfied Parsons was dead, Ridley tugged the napkin carefully out of the slack, gaping mouth and sliced through the bands of carpet tape binding wrists and ankles together. Taking the motorcycle gauntlets off the limp, unresisting hands, Ridley inspected the wrists carefully and saw that, as he had intended, the thick leather padding on the deep cuffs had prevented the tape sawing into raw flesh as Parsons had struggled desperately to free himself. Ridley looked at the ankles and then rose to his feet, well satisfied: there was not the slightest mark anywhere that might cause a coroner familiar with suicide by carbon monoxide poisoning to raise so much as an eyebrow.

Thrusting tape, gauntlets, napkin and towel into his plastic bag, Ridley arranged Parsons' body carefully behind the wheel, started the engine again and closed the door. As the car began to fill once more with carbon monoxide, he painstakingly erased every trace of his presence in the lane and then set off westwards through the woods. There was a little moon to help him on his way and, with luck, he would be back in his motel bedroom well before dawn.

CHAPTER THIRTEEN

'Miss Macrae?' called a voice, and Jenny glanced up from the dog-eared, two-year-old copy of *Country Life* she had been reading. It was the next morning and she was sitting in one of the straight-backed wooden chairs that lined Dr Erskine's old-fashioned surgery behind Gleninver's Market Hall Square. Morning surgery was almost over, and the queue of waiting patients had dwindled steadily until Jenny was almost alone in the waiting-room. 'Dr Erskine will see you now, Miss Macrae,' said the receptionist, pointing. 'Down the corridor, second door on your left.' Jenny nodded. She'd been coming here as long as she could remember.

She walked down the corridor, conscious of that familiar sense of trepidation that was present whenever she went to doctor or dentist. But this time, she reminded herself, it wasn't her health she was concerned with but somebody else's, and that knowledge gave her confidence as she knocked on the doctor's door.

'Come along in!' Dr Erskine was sitting behind his roll-top desk, writing something on one of the forms in front of him. Now he looked up and laid his pen aside as a genial smile creased his craggy face. 'Ah – if it isn't Jenny, my very favourite patient. Sit you down, lassie – sit you down.'

Jenny smiled. 'Bet you say that to all the girls, you old rogue.'

Dr Erskine held up an admonishing finger. 'Not at all, not at all.' His eyes twinkled merrily. 'Only those under eighty-five. So – Jenny lass: how're you keeping? I was sorry to see the back of that doctor friend of yours, Danny . . . What was the man's name, now?'

'Kindersley – Danny Kindersley. Yes, I was too,' Jenny

admitted simply. Dr Erskine nodded, watching her shrewdly over the top of his glasses.

'I read about what happened in the papers,' he said quietly. 'Oh – I'm not going to go on about it,' he held up a hand, 'but equally, I'm not one to sit with my head in the sand pretending I don't know what's going on in my own town. I'm very, very sorry for you, Jenny – and I'd just maybe add this: not all of us here are as ready as some to attribute blame. You've still got a lot of friends here, lass – a lot of friends.' He cleared his throat. 'Now then – that receptionist of mine tells me you wanted to see me about a personal matter. Am I right in thinking it's got something to do with what happened out in the bay? If it's just a few tranquillizers you're after, just to tide you through—'

Jenny shook her head. 'It's . . . er . . . it's about that, yes. But it's not about tranquillizers. It's . . . it's about a couple of your patients.'

'My patients, d'you say? Well now . . . what passes between a doctor and those who come to see him is strictly confidential, as I'm sure you're aware.'

Jenny nodded. 'I realize that, yes.'

'Well, you must have a reason for asking. Who are they, anyway? You have their names, I take it?'

'One's Mrs Proctor – you know, my landlady. She went into hospital yesterday.'

Dr Erskine nodded. 'Aye. And the other?'

'A man called Roberts. Robbie Roberts. He lives out in Ardtornish. Or rather—'

Dr Erskine sighed. 'The man in the boat with the wee boy, you mean?'

Jenny nodded, took out Mrs Proctor's Cardocol pills and leaned forward. 'Both Robbie and Mrs Proctor were taking these,' she said, her eyes on his face. 'I went down to Archie Hooper's here in the town, but he's never filled a prescription for Cardocol. In fact, he's never even *seen* pills like these before.' She paused. 'Then, when I saw Mrs Proctor in hospital yesterday she told me she got the pills not from a chemist, but from you. Is that right?'

There was silence while Dr Erskine picked up the green

packet and studied it carefully, as though he too was seeing it for the first time. 'She . . . she must have been mistaken,' he muttered, his eyes sliding away.

Hamish Owen was in the front office at Gleninver police station doing routine morning calls. A handbag had been stolen from an unlocked car behind the sea front, a teenage motorcyclist from Birmingham was in hospital with severe head and leg injuries, and there had been a brief scuffle outside one of the pubs down by the quay at closing time – all just routine. Nothing so far worth more than a paragraph or two on the front page. 'Anything else?' asked Hamish, disappointed, leaning across the counter and twisting his head to one side to get a better look at the incident book.

Sergeant McInnes shook his head. 'That's your lot for today, Hamish.'

He glanced down at his notebook and turned back several pages. 'What about that man who went missing? The one who worked at Highland Pharmaceuticals? Anything more on that?'

The Sergeant shook his head. 'Professor Highcroft, you mean?' He scratched at a bare arm and shook his head, remembering Mrs Highcroft standing in front of him across the counter. 'He hasn't turned up, I know that for a fact. But you're wasting your time there: it's a domestic – between him—' he jerked a thumb to one side – 'and her.'

'You mean he walked out on his wife?' Hamish asked ingenuously. 'Just walked out on her?'

'Aye, that's right. Just like that.' He leaned forward. 'And when that happens, we stay right out of it, thank God. You'd be well advised to do the same.'

'Thanks for the advice.' Hamish shut his notebook. 'Right then. See you tomorrow.'

'I'll be looking forward to it,' replied Sergeant McInnes dryly.

Hamish was about to push through the swing doors into the street when a side door behind the station desk opened and a young PC in shirtsleeves came through into the main office, reached for the incident book, laid a report on the counter beside it and began the laborious business of transcription. Something about his concentration, his air of urgent preoccupation, made Hamish pause and then turn back towards the counter. He didn't know it then, but he was beginning to be a reporter, a journalist. 'Morning,' he tried conversationally. 'Anything interesting?'

The policeman glanced up briefly and then looked down again. 'Who're you?' he demanded shortly.

'Press. *Gleninver Times*.' Like it was *Newsweek* or the *Sunday Times*. Surprisingly, the policeman nodded.

'Might have something for you, as it happens. Bloke's gone and gassed himself in a car a few miles outside town. Couple of campers found him an hour or so back. My oppo's just gone to break the news to the next of kin.'

Hamish had his notebook out in a flash. This was more like it! 'Can you . . . can you tell me the man's name?' he asked eagerly, pencil poised.

'Don't see why not,' shrugged the policeman. 'Wife's going to find out soon enough, anyway.' He traced a finger across the form. 'The deceased's name was Parsons. Douglas Walter Parsons.'

In the main reception area at Highland Pharmaceuticals, Helen Highcroft was sitting on one of the plush brown couches beside the potted plants that arched gracefully over the smoked-glass entrance doors. Overalled decorators were working nearby on stepladders, sprucing the place up for launch day, but Helen sat alone, glancing at her watch with increasing impatience.

She had lain awake most of the night, twisting restlessly as she saw again and again the Christmas snapshot of Malcolm and his colleagues she had found at the back of the family photograph album, heard over and over again her conversation with Jackman twenty-four hours earlier, here in this very building. Now, what with the photograph and the business of the Volvo booked in for a service less than twelve hours before Malcolm was supposed to have run off with that girl in the photograph, Helen's frustration had crystallized into a decision that had brought her hurrying back to her husband's company first thing in the morning. Any moment now, Helen intended to confront Jackman with her fears, her suspicions, stupid and groundless though they might prove to be.

Stupid and groundless? Helen paused at that, turning the words over slowly in her mind like coins in a pocket. No, she didn't believe them to be either stupid or groundless – not any more. For she had made another discovery last night as she lay in bed, staring dry-eyed up at the darkened ceiling, conscious of the unfamiliar absence in the wide bed beside her. She had discovered that she did not, could not, believe in the evidence of Malcolm's desertion and infidelity, in the 'proof' that had fallen from her husband's diary. Such a conviction might very well be illogical, but the discovery of that girl's picture had forced Helen to examine the warp and weft of their marriage with brutal honesty. She had done so and she had found nothing, *not one thing* that would allow her to believe Malcolm would willingly have turned his back on all that he had worked for, all that they had shared together.

Strengthened by that knowledge, Helen's anxiety centred now not upon her husband's fidelity or supposed preference for some younger woman, but upon something quite different: his safety.

Something was wrong, deeply wrong, she was sure of it. Something was going on – here, at the company. Something that linked her husband's disappearance to that office not fifty yards from where she was waiting. An office that had curtains, not blinds.

She had been waiting for Jackman for almost forty minutes. She had called through from the phone at reception when she arrived unannounced, to be told by some unseen secretary that he would be down directly – and here she was, still waiting. Now, for the first time, it dawned upon her that her arrival might be embarrassing to the firm that had supported their family with monthly pay cheques these last few years. Well, if that was the case it was just too bad. Having formulated her questions, Helen was now in the mood for some answers.

Another glance at her watch: forty-three minutes. On impulse, Helen rose to her feet suddenly and crossed to the reception desk. 'Look – I'm sorry to be a nuisance, but do you think you could call Mr Jackman's office for me again?'

'Certainly, Mrs Highcroft. Just one moment.' Long, slender fingernails toyed elegantly at the face of the telephone, and Helen waited, conscious, by contrast, of her own dishevelled appearance. The receptionist listened, replaced the receiver, and switched on another smile. This one expressed mild, professional regret. 'No, I'm terribly sorry, Mrs Highcroft. His line appears to be engaged. I do happen to know Mr Jackman has a very busy schedule this morning. Perhaps if you wouldn't mind waiting just a little bit longer . . . ' Helen returned to her seat and sat down. Five minutes, she told herself angrily. I'll give him just five more minutes – and not a moment longer.

Jenny turned off the main road, drove a few yards down the private lane leading to Highland Pharmaceuticals and stopped at the white gatehouse that stood sentinel at the entrance to the company's property. As she waited for the elderly security guard to come forward and ask her business, she studied the site stretched out before her. Like everyone else in Gleninver, she had known about HPL for years, seen its picture in the newspaper a dozen times, but this was the first occasion she had actually seen the place for herself. She had no idea the site was so . . . so big, so established. From where she sat at the wheel of her Citroën, rolling lawns stretched away in well-groomed waves and curves towards a modern, three-storey building whose tinted windows glittered and shone in the morning sunlight. Beyond and over to her right she could see thick plantations of rowan, fir and ash, and beyond the trees, the blue gleam of Loch Linnhe and the heather-clad hills that tumbled down steeply to its far shore.

'Good morning, miss. Can I help you?' The elderly security guard bent down to her window.

'I'd like to see someone about one of your products,'

Jenny replied. The man nodded, produced a large plastic-covered VISITOR sign and handed it through the window.

'Would you mind leaving this in your windscreen when you park?' He pointed ahead. 'Follow the signs to the car park, go through the double glass doors directly facing you, and someone at reception will be able to help you from there.'

Jenny smiled. 'Thanks very much.'

The man touched a hand to his cap, made a note of Jenny's registration number and the time of her arrival, and waved her on. She drove forward impressed, as she was meant to be, by the scale and friendly efficiency of Gleninver's largest employer.

Helen twisted round as the smoked-glass doors behind her sighed back, and a young woman in her slim mid-to-late twenties entered the building and walked up to the reception desk, distracting the receptionist completely.

Helen glanced around casually. Apart from the two painters working halfway up their stepladders over in a corner, the reception area was empty. Another quick glance at the receptionist and Helen rose to her feet and moved swiftly towards the swing doors leading to the corridor Jackman had showed her earlier. The corridor and the office that was supposed to be Malcolm's . . .

'And your name?' asked the receptionist politely, cradling the phone against an immaculate shoulder as she dialled a number.

'Jenny Macrae.'

The girl nodded.

'Oh, Richard? Carole here, in reception. I wonder if you could help me. There's a Miss Jenny Macrae down here who'd very much like to talk to someone about one of our products. No, no, I don't think so. Hang on a moment and I'll just ask.' She covered the mouthpiece with her hand. 'You're not with any particular firm or organization, are you?' Jenny shook her head, and the girl spoke into the phone once more. 'No, she's not. She says she'd just like some advice, that's all. Yes . . . yes, that's what I thought. No . . . about Cardocol.' She listened a moment longer and then replaced the receiver. 'Someone will be down to see you in a moment. Oh—' She looked round at the deserted reception area and frowned. Where had that other woman disappeared to, that Mrs Highcroft?

Helen hurried down the empty corridor, her feet making no sound on the rubber matting as she counted off the doors to her right, tensed for the call behind her and the polite, frosty summons back to reception that must shatter the silence at any moment. She had very little time, perhaps only seconds, before the receptionist came looking for her. This was the door. Helen glanced down the empty corridor and then hesitated, suddenly unsure, for the name-holder beside the door which had displayed Malcolm's name was now empty. She tried the handle, the door opened and she slipped inside. Closing the door swiftly behind her, she looked round. Yes, this was it, quite definitely – and she had been right. The office *did* have curtains.

Helen went further into the office and saw that, apart from the telephone, the desk was now bare and there was no sign anywhere of either her husband's diary or the framed photograph that had been there the day before. Now she opened each drawer of the desk in turn. Empty. Not a letter, not a file or a paperclip in sight. Nothing. She looked around the walls. They too were bare. No calendar, no wall chart, no company poster – and no marks, either. The place looked as if it had never been used.

Helen went over to the metal filing cabinet and tried the top drawer experimentally. It was locked, but the whole cabinet rocked gently towards her. The reason was obvious: it was empty. And this was supposed to be where Malcolm had spent the last three years of his working life?

She sat down on the edge of the bare desk and tried to think, to work out what it all meant. Surely they wouldn't have cleared out Malcolm's desk already? Not if they really believed he had just run off with some young woman, decided to have a mid-life fling, add a little spice to sedentary, respectable middle age. He was too valuable, too senior to be just . . . written off. Wasn't he? Helen twisted the phone idly towards her, and then she froze. The extension number was different. If she wanted to call Malcolm at work she asked for extension 650. This was extension 476.

Helen felt the walls of the little office begin to close in around her and suddenly she began to feel very alone, very frightened. Something quite terrible had happened to Malcolm, she knew it.

Pushing the phone slowly away, as though from a great distance, she watched her hand begin to shake as she stood up, her worst suspicions ruthlessly confirmed. This had never been Malcolm's office. It didn't look like his office, it didn't feel like his office – it looked exactly what it was, a shell, a facade placed in her path to deceive.

And the only question was: why?

Helen went to the door and eased it open a few inches. She heard the sudden sigh of the swing doors at the end of the corridor and shrank back, steeling herself for discovery. A young man hurried past the door, clutching a file of papers. Helen stepped out into the corridor and closed the door softly behind her. 'Excuse me,' she called.

The young man turned. 'Yes?'

'Can you tell me: who works along here, please?' She gestured up and down the empty corridor.

The young man shrugged. 'No one. They're not used yet.'

'What, none of them?'

'Not as far as I know. Who're you looking for?'

'Oh . . . er . . . no one. No one special. Thank you. Thank you very much.'

The young man nodded and turned on his heel. As Helen walked back towards the main entrance, the receptionist pushed through the swing doors and came hurrying towards her. Without a trace of a smile. 'Mrs Highcroft – please!' she called. 'I've been looking everywhere for you! This area is restricted to visitors. Didn't you see the signs?'

'What signs?' Helen asked vaguely, taking sudden

enjoyment from the other's annoyance, from the slipping of that brittle, impersonal mask.

'The signs, back here! Please – come along with me. Mr Jackman would be most annoyed to learn you had ignored directions.' They went back through the swing doors, the receptionist hurrying towards her desk as though it was her own private refuge, an island in a hostile sea. Perhaps it was. 'Oh – by the way.' She threw back over her shoulder. 'Mr Jackman called down. He sends his apologies but he's been called away to a meeting.'

Helen sighed. 'All right, then – I'll wait.'

The receptionist shook her head. 'He . . . er . . . he told me to tell you he'll be tied up most of the day. He won't be able to see you at all. I'm sorry.'

There was a stunned silence.

'What, not at all? Not even for five minutes?' Helen demanded incredulously, her raised voice drawing the attention of both the painters on their ladders and the young woman sitting waiting patiently nearby.

'I'm afraid not, no. But if you'd care to make another appointment I'm sure . . . '

Helen stalked up to the reception desk. 'Where is Mr Jackman's office?'

The girl looked up, startled. 'On the . . . on the first floor. But you can't . . . ' Helen could. She crossed the foyer to the lift and pressed the call button. The indicator showed the lift was at the third floor. As Helen waited impatiently, the receptionist pressed a button beside her knee and hurried out from behind her desk. 'Mrs Highcroft – wait! Visitors are not permitted on to the working levels! Now I'm sure if you—'

Helen swung round. 'A visitor? Is that all I am now? Well, let me tell you something. For the last three and a half *years*, my husband has been working all the hours God sent to get Cardocol on to the market on schedule, and now, just days before the launch, he's just . . . disappeared – vanished! Mr Jackman thinks he's gone off with some young woman, but he hasn't, I . . . I know he hasn't! Something . . . something terrible's happened to him, only I

. . . I can't find out what it is, don't you understand? I can't do anything to help him!' The words broke off into a choking sob and Helen reached angrily for her scrap of handkerchief, hating herself for her lack of control, for this sign of weakness.

'Now then – what's all this?' The receptionist turned with relief towards the comforting bulk of the security guard, summoned by the press of her buzzer alarm under her desk.

'Oh, George – perhaps you'd like to help Mrs Highcroft. She's . . . very distressed. She's had to wait almost an hour for a meeting with Mr Jackman. Unfortunately he's now been called away, and although he's sent his apologies she's really become . . . well, as you can see . . . quite irrational.' Told like that it sounded very reasonable. One more menopausal housewife trundling gently off her trolley. Nothing that a nice cup of tea wouldn't put right, of course. Or a handful of Valium. The security guard put a well-meaning hand around her shoulder.

'There now, Mrs Highcroft – don't you fret. You just come along with me.'

Helen threw off his arm. 'Leave me! Just leave me alone! I want to see Mr Jackman! He knows what's happened to my husband, I know he does!'

'Come along, Mrs Highcroft. No point getting yourself up into a state now, is there?'

With a great effort of will, Helen stopped the tears and looked up, both her voice and her emotions under tight control.

'Look. Just listen to me for a moment – please. Just *listen*!' Reluctantly, they turned and listened. 'My husband has disappeared, do you understand? He hasn't been home now for almost three days! There's been no phone call, no letter – nothing! Something's happened to him!'

The security guard nodded simply. 'Aye. I read something about that in the paper, I recall. I shouldn't worry if I was you, Mrs Highcroft. He's bound to turn up sooner or later.' As though he was just a little late home from the pub. Helen groaned with exasperation and decided to give it one last try.

'The office Mr Jackman showed me,' she explained patiently, 'the one he said my husband had been using: it's been empty for months!'

'Mrs Highcroft, I can see you've maybe been under a great deal of strain just recently – but please, be reasonable: there's nothing you can do here, now is there? If Mr Jackman says he's busy and he'll see you some other time, well . . . that seems fair enough to me. You take my advice and give Mr Jackman another call in a day or so, eh? When all this launch business has died down a wee bit. Now, why don't you just go home and . . . '

Helen saw that it was hopeless. Nothing she could say or do would achieve anything. It was enough that she was making a spectacle of herself in the foyer of Highland Pharmaceuticals. It was his job to nip that sort of thing in the bud. Unprotesting, Helen allowed herself to be guided outside into the sunshine. He left her there with a final little pat on the arm, and she walked alone to her car, her shoulders slumped in defeat. She felt beaten, exhausted, the clarity and resolve of those nocturnal thoughts clouded now by the blinkered misunderstanding of others and by her own confused emotions. She took the car keys out of her handbag and bent down to unlock the door.

'Mrs Highcroft?' She turned suddenly, for she had not heard the footsteps running lightly up behind her. It was the woman who had been sitting alone in HPL's reception area a few minutes earlier.

'Yes?' she acknowledged warily.

'I'm sorry to trouble you at a time like this, but I couldn't help hearing what you were saying just now about your husband and about his work with Cardocol. I . . . I wonder if I could talk to you somewhere for a few minutes?' She held out a slim hand and smiled. 'My name's Jenny. Jenny Macrae.'

In his office on the first floor of the administrative building, Jackman was standing by the window in silence, waiting for Ridley to finish reporting back to Baxter in London. Used to dominating others by force of will,

Jackman did not enjoy Ridley's presence here in his office, for there was something intangible and dangerous, something . . . unleashed, about the man's attitude towards his task that Jackman found unsettling.

Ridley had been on the phone for almost ten minutes. As soon as he had begun to talk to London, Jackman had risen to his feet, turned his back on his dangerous visitor sitting in front of the only telephone for several hundred miles that could be neither tapped nor intercepted, and gazed for long, silent minutes out of the window towards the outskirts of Gleninver glimpsed through the trees in the distance, his thoughts locked away, hidden behind an impenetrable mask.

He had thus been able to watch from above as Helen Highcroft was escorted from the building by the security guard, and had smiled with satisfaction as he watched her walk slowly across the tarmac towards the visitors' car park, her shoulders slumped in defeat.

Then that same smile had turned into a frown as another woman suddenly pushed through the smoked-glass doors and hurried after her. Now Jackman watched as they spoke for a few minutes and then separated. The younger of the two walked across to a yellow Citroën Dyane and reversed quickly out of her parking space. Then the two cars followed one another slowly down the approach road in a manner that suggested they were now in convoy, linked by whatever had passed between their owners in the car park a few short moments ago.

Ridley was still on the phone to London. Jackman crossed to another phone, swept up the receiver and dialled a number. 'Who was it who just left the building after Mrs Highcroft, Carole? Young woman, twenty-five, thirty, dark hair?'

'Miss Jennifer Macrae, Mr Jackman,' the receptionist answered promptly. He scribbled the name down.

'What was she doing here?'

'I don't really know. I mean she . . . she came in about ten minutes ago asking to speak to somebody about Cardocol. Richard Connor was coming down to see her and then she . . . well . . . she just left.'

'What d'you mean, woman, she just left?' he snapped.

'I don't know, Mr Jackman, honestly. She just got up and left. She said something I couldn't quite catch about it not mattering any more and hurried outside.'

'Did she talk to Mrs Highcroft? While she was waiting for Mr Connor to come down?'

'No. Not that I know of, anyway.'

Jackman thought for a moment, then – 'What's the number of the main gate?'

'217.'

Jackman rang off, dialled again, and asked the security guard for the registration number of the yellow Citroën that was about to leave. The number had been logged on entry as a matter of company policy, and he was able to read it back to Jackman almost immediately. Jackman replaced the receiver then and sat forward over his notepad, joining the name 'Jenny Macrae' to her car number inside a little pencilled box. He drummed his pencil absently against his notepad. Perhaps it was nothing. But just possibly it might be something; perhaps even trouble. Until now, Jackman had been satisfied Helen Highcroft was containing her loss within the immediate family, looking no further than the planted photograph and her own relationship with her husband for an explanation that would justify his disappearance. Now, for the first time, he was not so sure. The realization worried him. He was still worrying when Ridley replaced the receiver carefully and turned round.

'Thank you,' he said quietly. Always so polite.

'I take it London is satisfied?'

'With Parsons? Oh yes, I think so.' Ridley reached forward, picked up a single sheet of paper, glanced at the notes he had made and let the paper slide gently back on to the desk. 'I understand it was you who vouched for Calvert and Steevenson. To Baxter,' he enquired idly. Something about the tone of voice made Jackman look up sharply.

'That's right, yes. So I did. They're both good men.'

'Careless men,' corrected Ridley softly.

'I'm sorry?'

'You told Baxter they could be trusted. You told Baxter they would be discreet – both of them. You also told London they knew how to keep their mouths shut.' It was almost an accusation.

'What the hell are you driving at?' Jackman demanded shortly.

Ridley smiled. 'I did a little . . . investigating of my own this morning. Before coming here.'

'Oh?'

'A bit of . . . checking. For Baxter. London always insists on a thorough job. That's why they use me.'

'Let's stop playing silly buggers, Mr Ridley,' snapped Jackman. 'Get to the point, will you? What did you find?'

Ridley glanced down at his notes. 'Your Mr Calvert,' he said softly, 'has just booked a holiday for himself and his girl in Hawaii. First class all the way. And paid for, in advance, in cash. Steevenson's just put a fifteen hundred pound deposit on a BMW. That deposit, again, was paid in cash.' He looked up reproachfully with those cold, dead eyes. 'Now, Mr Jackman, I ask you: you'd hardly call that discreet, would you? I mean, not here. Not in a pisspot little town the size of Gleninver.'

'I'll have a word with them. Tell them—'

Ridley shook his head slowly. 'Tell them nothing, Mr Jackman.'

'Nothing? But you said—'

'Nothing. There is no need.'

'And just what the hell is *that* supposed to mean?'

'It means you are not to worry, Mr Jackman. It is out of your hands. Baxter wants me to take care of it.'

Jackman went very still. 'You're not serious?' he managed, appalled. 'London's ordered you to take care of Steevenson and Calvert? As well?'

Ridley paused before replying, then: 'There's too much at stake,' he said obliquely.

'But you can't go round just . . . *murdering* people! What the hell does Baxter think he's up to? Four deaths, all from the same department within the same *week*?'

'How many people here know they all worked together –

Highcroft, Parsons, Calvert and Steevenson?'

'No one. But that—'

'Precisely. And who said anything about murder?' Ridley asked mildly. 'No one's been murdered. Have they?'

'No? What about Parsons?'

'Parsons wasn't *murdered*,' corrected Ridley. 'Parsons committed suicide. He succumbed to the pressure of work.'

'And Calvert? And Steevenson – what about them? Does Baxter seriously expect them to "succumb to the pressure of work" too, like a couple of industrial lemmings?' he demanded scathingly.

Ridley did not understand sarcasm. He considered this possibility with a sincerity that made even Jackman's blood run cold.

'No, not suicide,' he decided finally. 'I think perhaps they should have an accident. Together.'

CHAPTER FOURTEEN

'More tea?'

'Mmm, thanks.'

'Help yourself to biscuits. There's plenty more in the tin.'

Jenny reached over gratefully. She was in Helen Highcroft's kitchen, and Helen was pouring a second cup of tea for them both. It was a large, cheerful room with a pine table set in against a bay window-seat that looked out across the lawn; a room that was at odds with the haunted, care-worn face of the woman who pushed Jenny's cup carefully across the table towards her.

They had been sitting talking quietly together for perhaps forty minutes. Slowly, an initial wariness had given way to mutual liking and trust as they began to exchange confidences. Jenny had no need to tell Helen about the fire or about the deaths of both Jamie and Robbie out in the bay – a copy of the *Gleninver Times* had been left casually on the kitchen table, and its presence, coupled to Helen's efforts to push it out of sight, had caused the only moment of real embarrassment between them.

On the drive home from Highland Pharmaceuticals with Jenny's car stuck like an insect in the centre of her driving mirror, Helen had told herself that she would say as little as possible, give away nothing to the woman who had approached her so unexpectedly in the car park. For all she knew she might have been planted, sent after her by Jackman to sound out her suspicions, find out what she knew. The way Helen was feeling just now, anything seemed possible . . .

And yet, once they had come inside the house together, once they had broken the ice of initial awkwardness and begun to talk, such caution had become unnecessary. For Jenny Macrae wasn't a plant, she couldn't be. There was too much honesty, too much pain and fresh suffering in her face as she told Helen about the fire and what had followed – suffering that, in Helen, had struck a deep chord of sympathy. Soon Helen found herself voicing fears and confiding thoughts she had not shared even with her brother or the rest of the family as she told Jenny about the photograph of Malcolm at the office party, about the Volvo, about the anonymous, late-night telephone call telling her that Malcolm was dead, and about the empty office with the wrong extension number – private thoughts and fears dragged out into the open. It was good, suddenly, to talk. To share a burden.

'What did your husband actually *do* at Highland Pharmaceuticals?' Jenny asked, halfway through her second cup as she tried to decide whether to tell Helen about the pills Robbie and Mrs Proctor had shared, and about her own suspicions centred around the product Malcolm Highcroft had apparently spent years of his life trying to perfect.

Helen twisted her fingers together nervously, her eyes on her teacup. 'He was a scientist,' she said quietly.

'I heard you say to that girl in reception that he's spent the last three years working on Cardocol, is that right?' prompted Jenny, knowing the answer but needing to keep up the flow of confidences.

Helen nodded. 'That's right, yes. We . . . we moved here when Sarah was ten. That's three and a half years ago. Malcolm was involved in the project right from the start.'

Jenny opened her handbag, took out Mrs Proctor's pills and placed them slowly on the table. 'With these, you mean?'

Helen picked up the emerald-green packet, saw the name and nodded abstractedly. 'I suppose so, yes.'

'You suppose so? You mean you're not sure?'

Helen shrugged and looked up. 'I . . . I tended not to get involved with Malcolm's work.' She made it sound like some dark admission of guilt. In a way it was. If she had been more involved, if Malcolm had felt she had more interest and a better understanding of his work, his pressures, then perhaps . . .

'You mean you've never actually *seen* them before?' Jenny asked. It was becoming a familiar question.

Helen shook her head. 'Not like that, no. Not as a finished product.'

Jenny leaned forward. 'What exactly *is* Cardocol? I mean – what's it for?'

'It's some new kind of heart drug. For people with high blood pressure. At least, that's what I think—' She broke off then and turned towards the door as someone came running down the corridor towards the kitchen.

'Mummy! Mummy! Did you—?' The door was flung open, and Sarah burst into the kitchen in denim skirt and skimpy T-shirt, only to pull up short as she saw unexpected company. 'Oh. I thought . . . '

'Sarah, this is Miss Macrae.' Helen turned towards Jenny. 'This is Sarah, my eldest.' She turned back. 'What is it, darling?'

'It's . . . oh, nothing. Doesn't matter.' Although it obviously did.

'Tell me,' urged her mother.

Sarah shifted awkwardly. 'Well, it's just that . . . when I saw the cars outside, I . . . I thought Daddy might have come home. Did you find out anything?'

Helen shook her head. 'No,' she admitted softly. 'No, I didn't. Where are Mark and Simon?'

Sarah gestured outside. 'Next door. Mrs Fielding says we can all stay to lunch. Can we?'

'I don't see why not. Don't forget to thank her, will you?'

Sarah gave her a long-suffering look. 'No, Mummy. Of course not. 'Bye.' A quick smile, a swirl of long hair and she was gone.

There was a moment's silence as Helen drifted back from some private reverie triggered by the closing of the door behind her daughter. 'It's the not knowing,' she said finally, in a voice pitched so low she might almost have been talking to herself. 'That's what she finds the hardest, I think: the just not knowing.' She sighed. 'Mark and Simon are too young, of course – they think Daddy's just . . . just gone off for a few days. But Sarah . . . Sarah's almost a woman. She feels what I feel. When she speaks sometimes it's . . . well,' Helen shrugged, 'it's like hearing myself, twenty-five years ago.' She paused. 'When I went up to her room late last night she was still awake. Just looking up at the darkness, crying.'

'I'm sorry,' Jenny offered inadequately.

Helen glanced up and forced a sudden smile. 'I am too. I didn't mean to go on like that. Now then: where had we got to?'

'You were telling me about Cardocol,' reminded Jenny gently.

Helen nodded. 'So I was. Now, let's see . . . ' She paused again, gathering her thoughts. 'Well, as I said, it's a new kind of heart drug. For people with high blood pressure.'

'New? How new?'

'Very new. It's not even out yet.' Helen smiled to rob her next words of any offence. 'Where have you been living these last few weeks? That's what all the fuss was about up at HPL. Those painters and gardeners all over the place.' She traced the shape of a sign in the air: 'The Grand Launching.'

'You mean it isn't even on the market yet? Officially?'

'Not as far as I know.'

Jenny nodded slowly. 'So that's why Hooper, the chemist, didn't recognize them,' she mused, more to herself than to Helen. 'They hadn't reached him yet.'

Helen picked up Mrs Proctor's pills, studied them for a long moment and then looked up. 'So where did you get them?' she asked quietly: 'If you don't mind me asking.'

Jenny paused, not because she minded the question but because she was not at all sure Helen would like the implications of her answer. 'It's . . . a little complicated,' she said finally.

'But it has to do with Malcolm? With my husband?'

Jenny shrugged. 'I'm not sure. But I think it might have, yes.'

'Tell me – please,' Helen urged.

Still Jenny hesitated. Then she sighed. It was bound to come out sooner or later. And besides, perhaps Helen would be able to shed a little light of her own.

'Well . . . to begin at the beginning, as they say. I . . . I live on the ground floor of a house in Elgin Terrace. My landlady, Mrs Proctor, lives upstairs . . . ' Jenny launched into her story, telling Helen first about the pills Mrs Roberts had shown her after Robbie's death, and then about Mrs Proctor's collapse and Jenny's discovery of those same pills on her bedside table. She told Helen about her visit to the hospital, and about Dr Erskine's denial that he had ever given Cardocol to the old lady. Jenny paused then, conscious of how complicated, how tentative and convoluted it all sounded. 'But he *must* have given her the pills, don't you see? Mrs Proctor would never have invented something like that, not in her condition.'

'You're saying there's some connection? Between this drug and my husband's disappearance?'

'Don't you think it's possible?'

Helen shrugged helplessly. 'I'm sorry, you've lost me,' she said.

Jenny leaned forward, suddenly conscious of the need to make Helen an ally, a believer. '*Could* something have gone wrong – with the drug, I mean? What if . . . what if your husband found out something? What if he . . . I don't know . . . What if he threatened to make that knowledge public? Could that be a reason?'

'A reason for what?'

'For . . . perhaps—'

'A reason for killing Malcolm? Is that what you mean?' Helen demanded, appalled. 'You think they'd . . . they'd *kill* him – just because he found out something that might harm the company? That's insane!'

'Yes. Yes, you're right. I'm . . . I'm sorry. I shouldn't have said that,' apologized Jenny, genuinely contrite as she saw the look on Helen's face. There were horrors enough in her mind already, she realized, without adding any more. Besides, dragged out into the open like that it sounded preposterous. As though she was insane, too. 'How important is Cardocol? To the company?' she asked.

'It's vital,' Helen replied immediately. 'It's their

flagship.' She shook her head impatiently, still thinking about what Jenny had suggested earlier. 'But that doesn't mean they'd take steps like that to cover up a mistake! If something was wrong, better to find out about it now, invent some excuse for postponing the launch and put things right rather than risk a scandal of that magnitude. Think of the publicity – they'd go out of business overnight!'

Jenny nodded. She had known something like that all along. 'You're right. Of course they wouldn't do that.' She paused, and then added slowly: 'But if you *are* right, then what other possible explanation is there? Why else would this man Jackman go to such lengths to mislead you if there wasn't something to hide?'

'I don't know,' Helen answered, suddenly close to tears as she realized how hopeless it all was. 'I don't know anything any more.'

There was an awkward silence. Then Jenny glanced round and saw the telephone on the side of the dresser. 'D'you think I could use your telephone for a minute, please?'

Helen nodded dully and gestured over her shoulder. 'Help yourself.' She looked up as Jenny pushed to her feet. 'Who're you going to call?'

'I thought I'd try Dr Erskine again,' replied Jenny. 'I've just had an idea.' She dialled the surgery number and waited. 'Dr Erskine, please. It's Jenny Macrae. I came to see him earlier this morning.' She listened for several seconds, then: 'Oh. Oh, I see. Well, not to worry. D'you have any idea when he'll be back? He will? Grand. I'll call again then. No . . . no message.' She replaced the receiver as Helen twisted round.

'No luck?'

Jenny returned to the table and sat down. 'He's at the hospital.'

It was very quiet in the medical ward, but even so, Dr Erskine had to lean down until his head was almost touching the sheets to catch what she was saying.

'I'm not . . . not going to die, am I, Doctor?' Mrs Proctor whispered weakly, a pale wraith of her usual self as she lay in the hospital bed.

Dr Erskine smiled that gruff, craggy smile of his and patted the thin, bony hand reassuringly.

'No, no, Mrs Proctor – you're not going to die,' he soothed, leaning closer as old fingers gripped his hand tightly, like the claws of a bird.

'You're not just saying that, are you, Doctor?' she whispered. 'Tell me honestly now . . . '

Erskine shook his head, smiled, and patted the hand again. 'You're good for a few more years yet, Mrs Proctor, don't you worry.' But she *was* worrying, he could see it in her eyes. 'You don't believe me? You should, for it is a well-known medical fact that Dr Erskine never tells an untruth to his patients, did you know that? A well-known medical fact.' Mrs Proctor didn't reply, but her eyes still watched him anxiously, filled with those doubts and fears that stalk the faltering steps of old age, of illness and loneliness. 'Did you?' he insisted.

Her head moved slightly on the pillows. 'I didn't know that . . . '

'Well, it's true. True as I'm standing here. And do you know why I never tell an untruth to my patients?' He tapped the side of his nose conspiratorially. 'I'll let you in on a little secret: it's bad for business. If you tell someone they're going to live and then they pop off, they tend to feel a bit aggrieved. They begin to lose faith in the medical profession.' The weak joke provoked the weak smile he had been looking for, the smile that said it would be all right now to leave her alone. 'That's a wonderful smile you've got there,' he said quietly. 'I bet you've bowled over a few in your time, eh? Eh?'

'One or two,' she managed, her eyes taking on an unexpected sparkle as she dimpled with pleasure. Dr Erskine nodded, picked up her limp wrist and felt her pulse. He always made a point of doing that before leaving a patient's bedside, for the gesture caused no alarm and yet gave an excuse for contact, for the simple act of touching: a laying on of hands that comforted patients of every age. Dr Erskine might have difficulty keeping abreast of the latest pharmaceutical developments, in remembering the latest brand names and the multitude of commercial variations upon a tired theme that were hailed by their progenitors as yet another major breakthrough, but he had learned about pain and fear and compassion a very long time ago. Now he looked up at the pale, anxious face sunk back in its valley of crisp white pillows and smiled reassuringly.

'You'll be out of here in no time, Mrs Proctor – no time at all, so don't you worry. A fall, a faint, a wee bang on the head – it's all been a bit of a shock to the system. But don't you worry: you'll soon be as right as rain, you have my word.' He rose from her bedside and patted her hand in farewell. 'Now then – you're to get plenty of sleep, plenty of rest, d'you hear? I'll look in on you again just as soon as you get home. Goodbye for now, Mrs Proctor.' He turned towards the door.

'Doctor?' she called faintly. He turned back.

'Aye?'

'Thank you. For everything,' she managed in a whisper that didn't carry more than five paces. Dr Erskine nodded and slipped out into the corridor. He closed the door softly behind him, his smile of professional reassurance replaced now by a frown of concern.

That frown was still there when Dr Erskine stopped a young nurse wheeling a trolley down the corridor and asked where he might find the duty houseman, for by then he was a very worried man.

John Ennis wasn't worried – he was angry, fuming with impatience, and his anger had built into a towering rage as he waited outside the Fiscal's office inside the sombre, brownstone Sheriff-clerk's office in Gleninver's Market Hall Square. He shared the office with a young secretary typing at a desk opposite, and so bitter, so palpable was that anger that he had caused a rash of nervous typing errors in a young woman specifically chosen for the task because of her speed and accuracy.

Now the telephone rang on the girl's desk and she picked up the receiver, listened for a moment, and then replaced the phone with a sense of relief. She got up and moved round from behind her typewriter. 'Mr Smithson will see you now, Mr Ennis,' she announced, knocking briefly and then holding the door wide. Ennis strode through with a curt nod, and she closed the door gratefully behind him.

The Procurator-fiscal was seated behind a large desk, formal and businesslike in dark suit and tie, a pile of files bound with pink ribbon heaped to one side. He rose courteously from behind his desk and stretched out a hand gravely.

'Mr Ennis, I'm sorry I had to keep you waiting. Please – sit down.'

John Ennis sat down and hunched forward, a big man with powerful shoulders and an anger building up inside him like a head of steam. 'You know why I've come, I take it, Mr Smithson?' he began shortly.

Smithson nodded. 'Aye, Mr Ennis, I believe I do. I was very sorry indeed to hear of the unfortunate death of your son. Please accept my condolences.'

Ennis shifted impatiently. 'Unfortunate? Is that what you think it was? It was more than that – it was criminal! Why else d'you think I'm here?'

Smithson looked up, puzzled now and sensing trouble. 'I don't think I quite follow you.'

Ennis sighed with exasperation. 'I'm a plain man, Mr Smithson, given to plain speaking. What I want to know is this: what do you intend doing about that woman?'

'Which woman would that be, Mr Ennis?' asked Smithson civilly.

'Which woman?' Ennis exploded angrily. 'Which woman? Christ, man, you know damn well which woman! The woman responsible for the death of my son! Miss Jennifer bloody Macrae!'

'I did see Miss Macrae earlier this morning,' Smithson admitted carefully, after a pause.

Ennis nodded. 'And?' he demanded abruptly.

The Procurator-fiscal contrived to look blank. He

seldom warmed to members of the public who ruffled the measured calm of his professional deliberations. Or to local councillors and powerful businessmen who tried throwing their weight about, looking for special treatment.

' "And" what, Mr Ennis?'

'What did she say?'

'Miss Macrae was most co-operative. She made a full and detailed statement.' He looked up.

'Go on.'

Smithson shrugged. 'I am sorry, Mr Ennis, but I am not at liberty to go into details.'

Ennis leaned slowly forward as an awful possibility suddenly presented itself. 'There will *be* a prosecution?'

'That is not for me to say,' Smithson replied carefully. 'Not at this stage, anyway.'

Ennis erupted to his feet. 'You mean to tell me there's a chance she *won't* be prosecuted – is that what you're saying? That she'll get off?'

Smithson sighed tiredly. 'Mr Ennis, if Miss Macrae is guilty of any crime, then—'

'*If*? What d'you mean – "if"?' Ennis stormed. 'Of course she's guilty! Everyone knows Jamie's death was her fault! There were hundreds of witnesses!' He pushed to his feet and loomed menacingly over Smithson's desk. 'I swear – if you let her—'

'Mr Ennis, please!' Smithson ordered sharply. 'Just . . . be seated. I accept that you have gone through a terrible personal ordeal and for that I am prepared to make allowances, but I must insist that you remain seated. Please.' Slowly, reluctantly, Ennis sat. 'Thank you,' nodded Smithson calmly, at length. 'Now then, if I can just explain. Before this office will institute criminal proceedings there must be evidence of something called "criminal intent", do I make myself clear?'

'Criminal intent?' snapped Ennis. 'Look, Mr Smithson. All I know is my son is dead. That . . . that woman let him go out to sea with some geriatric he'd never even set eyes on before. He was in her charge, her care!'

Smithson nodded gravely. 'Nevertheless, Mr Ennis, I am

afraid that does not constitute criminal intent.'

'So you're not going to prosecute, is that it?'

Smithson steepled his fingers. 'Let me put it this way,' he said quietly. 'What would it achieve? Who would it bring back?'

'What would it achieve? It would make her pay for what she did!'

'Don't you think she's paying now, Mr Ennis? Don't you think she's going to go on paying just as long as she lives?'

Ennis' head snapped up and his eyes blazed with anger. 'That woman killed my son, and *you* ask *me* if she's suffered enough?' John Ennis shook his head. 'No, Mr Smithson,' he said emphatically. 'I don't think she's suffered enough. Not nearly enough.'

Calvert and Steevenson were sitting in Jackman's office, their chairs pulled up to the far side of his desk. An Ordnance Survey landranger map of the area was unfolded across the desk, and Jackman was leaning forward, tapping the tip of a pencil against the little village of Dalrean eleven miles further along the coast. 'He'll be waiting for you both there,' said Jackman.

Steevenson and Calvert exchanged glances. 'Seems a helluva long way to go just for a chat,' Steevenson observed doubtfully. 'Why couldn't we meet him here?'

Jackman had an answer for that. 'With Professor Highcroft's disappearance still fresh in everyone's minds, Mr Baxter thought it would be . . . politic if he steered clear of the plant for a few weeks. Just in case someone did put two and two together.'

'Did he say what it was about?' queried Calvert.

Jackman looked up at the two doomed men sitting opposite, and smiled a confident smile.

'You acquitted yourselves well the other night,' he confided. 'I said as much in my report to London. When Baxter read it he felt you might both be suitable for involvement in another similar project further south. I gathered that, if you were both interested, there could well be a fairly substantial salary increase – plus, of course, all the usual . . . ah, fringe benefits.' Calvert and Steevenson both smiled. 'But gentlemen—' Jackman held up a hand as though to forestall premature optimism – 'I think we're all jumping the gun a bit here, don't you? Any offer London may wish to make will come from Baxter, not me.' He tapped the map again with the tip of his pencil. 'The sooner you meet him, the sooner you'll hear what he has in mind, from the horse's mouth, so to speak.'

Calvert glanced at his watch. 'Half past eleven, you say?'

Jackman nodded. 'That's right, yes. So I'd suggest you get a move on. He'll be in a white Rover in the car park behind a pub called the Clansman. Oh—' He appeared to suddenly remember something as he reached down, opened a drawer, and took out a set of car keys. 'You can take one of the reps' cars parked outside.' He tossed the keys across to Steevenson and nodded pleasantly, signalling that the meeting was over. Steevenson and Calvert rose to their feet and made for the door. 'Just one more thing.' They turned. 'You haven't spoken to Douglas Parsons recently, have you?'

'Parsons? No,' shrugged Steevenson, a hand on the doorknob. 'Not since the night of the accident.'

'Mr Calvert?'

Calvert shook his head. 'No, sorry.'

Jackman nodded, evidently satisfied. 'Right, then, gentlemen. That will be all. Thank you very much.' He leant forward over the papers that littered his desk.

'Oh – Mr Jackman?' He glanced up. It was Calvert.

'Yes?'

'Thank you . . . you know . . . ' Calvert gestured awkwardly. 'For putting in the word.'

Jackman smiled. 'Not at all.'

Both men left his office then and went down the empty corridor towards the lifts, joking and laughing quietly together at this sudden break in their routine, at this unexpected upturn in their fortunes. Down to reception and outside where they found the car Jackman had placed at their disposal. Steevenson slipped behind the wheel, while Calvert got into the passenger seat beside him.

From his window above, Jackman watched them go. As they drove out of sight down the approach road, he turned back to his desk, unlocked a drawer and took out a slip of paper. He smoothed it out on the blotter and reached for the phone. He asked for an outside line and dialled the number written down in front of him. The call was answered immediately. 'They've just left,' Jackman reported quietly, with one eye on the office door and the secretary working beyond. 'Both travelling together in a dark-blue Vauxhall Cavalier, registration number DRX 652Y. They should be on the coast road in about twenty mintues.'

'Twenty minutes – got it. You're sure that's the road they'll use?'

'Positive. They haven't any choice.'

'Thank you. I shall be in touch directly.'

'Look – I've been thinking. Isn't there some other way we—?'

'Thank you for your co-operation.'

The line went dead, and Jackman replaced the receiver slowly. Then he sat back in his chair, swivelled round towards the window, took a clean, folded handkerchief from his breast pocket and began polishing the lenses with quick, agitated little movements. It should never have got as far as this, he thought, with the first faint stirrings of panic. Never.

Fifteen minutes later, the dark-blue Vauxhall Cavalier began winding up the steep coast road that twisted along the sheer cliffs towards Dalrean. Since the opening of the new road through the pass to the east, this stretch of the old north-south pack route was little used, and Steevenson and Calvert made good time as they negotiated the sharp bends and climbed slowly higher, the waters of Loch Linnhe's eastern shoreline a glittering, ribbed mosaic of blues, greens and greys lapping against the tumbled rocks in the sunshine sixty feet below their nearside wheels. Steevenson changed down for another bend, swung tightly into the corner, and had just begun to straighten up when Calvert suddenly tapped him on the arm and pointed. 'What the hell's he up to?' he demanded.

A man in his mid-thirties was running down the middle of the road towards them, his jacket flapping behind him in the wind.

'Christ knows,' Steevenson muttered. 'Maybe there's been an accident.' The man had seen them now and was waving them to a stop. Steevenson brought the car to a halt, hauled on the handbrake and wound down the window. 'What's up?' he called pleasantly, elbow resting against the windowsill as they waited for Ridley to draw level.

Jenny banged the door of her flat shut behind her and walked slowly through to her sitting-room, deep in thought. She dumped her bag on the sofa and sat down, her thoughts not upon her surroundings, or even upon Jamie Ennis, but upon Helen Highcroft and the mysterious disappearance of her husband. Linked in there too – somewhere – was a whole series of questions about Cardocol; about Dr Erskine, Robbie Roberts, Mrs Proctor, and the company that had come to dominate the town of her birth in a few short years.

She had approached Helen Highcroft on impulse, reacting almost instinctively to her anguished mention of the drug's name in the reception foyer at Highland Pharmaceuticals. The rest, too, had been more or less instinctive as she had followed Helen home and there questioned her about her husband's involvement with a drug, a product, that seemed to be becoming more and more of a mystery. She had gone to Helen expecting if not actual answers, then at least some measure of illumination. Instead, she had driven home more baffled, more confused than ever. Jenny sighed, alone in her flat. If only Danny were here; he'd know what to do. At the very least he'd be able to put the strange denials of a fellow doctor into some sort of context . . .

The thought had no sooner entered her mind than Jenny found herself crossing to the phone. She hesitated then, her hand hovering over the receiver as her courage, her confidence, suddenly deserted her. Then she remembered what he'd said the night he phoned; the night she had seen herself on the nine o'clock news and had shrunk away into a corner and wept bitter, wretched tears. If you want help, if you need anything, anything at all, all you have to do is call. Just like in the song.

She lifted the receiver and dialled his number. From memory. The call rang in some surgery all those miles away to the south, and twice Jenny almost banged the receiver back into place. But when the call was answered, she was still there.

'Doctor's surgery,' answered the efficient voice of the receptionist. Jenny took a deep breath.

'Dr Kindersley, please. It's a . . . a personal call.'

'Oh. One moment, please.' The moment passed, with Jenny picturing him working at some desk, listening to—

'Dr Kindersley.'

'Danny? It's . . . it's me.'

'Jen! How are you, kid?' So clear, so close, he might have been standing beside her, a hand on her shoulder.

'I'm . . . I'm fine,' she managed. 'Bearing up under the strain, as they say. Am I calling at a bad time?'

'No. No, of course not.'

'If you like I can call back later . . . '

'Really. Now's fine.'

Jenny hesitated nervously, suddenly unsure how to go on, how to explain why she was calling without sounding as though she had gone quietly bonkers. Or that she was just phoning with an invented excuse that would somehow throw them together again. That she was chasing after him. There was a sudden awkward silence between them, and Jenny closed her eyes. This was awful. If only they weren't so far apart . . . 'Are they keeping you busy?' she tried, regretting the words even as they were spoken, wishing she could bite back their stilted banality. What's happening to us, she thought with sick dismay? We shouldn't have to manufacture conversation, not after all we've shared . . .

'Pretty busy,' Danny replied breezily, playing the same game. 'I've just done morning surgery. There's—'

'I'm . . . I'm suspended, Danny,' she interrupted suddenly, as the words, and the pain, came tumbling out. 'Corbett told me personally. There's to be a full departmental investigation after the inquiry. And . . . and guess what? The Fiscal came by too. I may be prosecuted for . . . for Jamie's death. That'll be fun, won't it?' She tried to make it sound almost incidental, all part of Jenny's Jolly Japes. She failed miserably. What began as an attempt at a carefree offhand little laugh turned into a raw sob of anguish.

'Jenny . . . ?'

'I'm . . . I'm sorry,' she sniffed. 'I didn't . . . I didn't mean to just . . . break down on you. I promised myself I'd be so . . . so . . . ' Danny murmured quiet, soothing words down the phone as slowly, gradually, Jenny fought the tears and the pain back below the surface. 'I'm . . . I'm sorry,' she managed at last. 'God, how stupid of me, you know? That's the last thing I wanted to do – bawl on your shoulder like one of your patients.' She sniffed again. 'I . . . I called because I wanted to ask you something,' she continued more firmly. 'As a doctor, I mean . . . '

'Private or National Health?' Danny replied, trying a joke.

'I . . . it's about a drug, OK? I . . . I know it'll probably sound crazy but I'd . . . I'd just like you to listen – would you do that?'

'OK, I'm listening,' promised Danny, suddenly serious. 'Fire away.'

'Have you heard of a new heart drug called Cardocol? It's manufactured up here by Highland Pharmaceuticals.' Danny laughed suddenly. 'What's so funny?' demanded Jenny suspiciously. So low was her stock of self-esteem just then that she feared he might be laughing at her.

'Yes, I've heard of Cardocol. So has every other GP by now, I shouldn't wonder, if he isn't deaf or blind.'

'Why's that?'

'The post's been full of the stuff for days.'

'What? You mean pills? Cardocol pills?'

'I mean pamphlets, hand-outs, information; clever promotional gimmicks – that sort of thing. They're spending a small fortune. There's even a four or five page supplement in this week's BMJ, now I come to think of it.'

'Is there? Are you sure?'

'Is it important?'

'Yes. Yes, it is. Would you mind checking, Danny, please?'

'Hang on just a minute.' He put down the phone and was back in a moment. 'Yes, here we go—' Jenny heard pages being flicked over in the background – ' "Cardocol – A Heartbeat Closer: HPL pushes back the frontiers of preventative medication—" D'you want me to read on?'

Jenny had cradled the phone against her shoulder and was writing furiously. 'What was that? After "Heartbeat Closer"?'

' "HPL pushes back the frontiers of preventative medication." It's just a long-winded way of saying they think they've found something new.'

'And haven't they?'

Danny thought for a moment, then – 'No,' he said shortly. 'At least, it's unlikely.'

'Why's that?'

Danny shrugged. 'They're just not big enough. As a useful rule of thumb, the more a medium-sized company like HPL spends on promotion, the less they've got to back it up. Real drug breakthroughs are usually left to the big boys like ICI, Glaxo or Geigy. Without reading the promotional material in any detail, I'd say this looks like just another "Me-tooer".'

'What on earth's that?'

'A Me-tooer? A variation on a pharmacological theme that's just different enough to skirt around the original patent.' Danny paused. 'Jen – d'you want to tell me what this is all about? Why the sudden interest in Cardocol?'

Why indeed? Perhaps she was just clutching at straws, searching for someone else to take the blame for Jamie's death. Jenny hesitated. 'I'm not sure,' she admitted finally. 'It's just that there's something funny going on up at HPL that involves a missing scientist whose wife—'

'Funny? In what way?'

'Strange. Wrong,' Jenny said thoughtfully. 'As though something's going on just below the surface and no one knows what it is. No one on the outside, anyway.' She paused. 'Cardocol's not available yet, is it?'

'To GPs, you mean? No, not officially.'

'What would you say if I told you I know of two people who were both given Cardocol by the same doctor more than a week ago – and that one of them is now dead and the other is in hospital?'

There was silence for a moment. 'Which doctor?'

'Dr Erskine.'

'Down by Market Hall Square?'

'The very same.'

Another pause.

'I'd have to say you'd probably got your facts wrong,' Danny replied carefully, subconsciously closing ranks behind another professional colleague. 'Erskine wouldn't prescribe a drug before date of licence. No doctor would.'

'That's just my point, Danny – he didn't even bother with a prescription! He just gave them the pills over the counter! In his surgery!'

'You sure?'

'Pretty sure, yes. Remember Mrs Proctor? The old woman upstairs?'

'Mrs Proctor? Of course,' Danny replied dryly. He had taken to creeping into Jenny's flat on tiptoe once Mrs Proctor discovered Jenny's boyfriend was a newly qualified doctor.

'Well, she's one of them. I've got her pills here. She collapsed yesterday morning and had to be rushed into hospital. When I went to take her some flowers, she insisted she'd been given the pills by Erskine himself. Personally.'

'Perhaps she just confused Cardocol with something else. Was she taking any other medication?'

'Any number. Her bedside table was groaning with bottles.'

'Well, there's your answer, then—'

'But Cardocol was *there*, right at the front!' Jenny insisted emphatically. 'Danny – listen to me. When I took the pills down to Hooper's to ask what they were for, he said he'd never even seen them before! She *must* have got them from Dr Erskine!'

'All right. What does Dr Erskine say?'

'He practically threw me out on my ear and denied giving the pills to anyone – but he was lying, I know he was.'

'Why should he do that?'

'Well, wouldn't you? If you'd been caught giving pills to patients before you were supposed to?'

'I might be a bit embarrassed, but I certainly don't think I'd deliberately lie about it,' Danny replied. 'Who's the other one? This person who's supposed to have died?'

'Robbie. Robbie Roberts. He'd been given Cardocol too. That's what started me off, you see. His wife showed me these pills he'd been taking right up to the time of the accident. She told me he'd got the pills from Dr Erskine too.'

'Roberts? The old man in the boat?'

'Yes, that's the one.'

'Ah! I see . . . '

'What's that supposed to mean?' Jenny challenged defensively, alive to every nuance of blame, of possible criticism.

'Nothing. I just . . . '

'You just what?'

'I just wondered what you were trying to prove, that's all . . . '

'I'm not trying to *prove* a damn thing!' Jenny exploded.

'Just because this man Roberts *may* have been given Cardocol doesn't necessarily mean that—'

'But it might, don't you see, Danny? It might! Why else would he suddenly collapse like that? If I could only prove those pills contributed in some way to Robbie's accident, then I . . . then I wouldn't be to blame for Jamie's death, would I? Not entirely.'

'No, you wouldn't,' Danny agreed cautiously. 'Not if you could prove it.'

'Well, it's possible, isn't it? For there to be something wrong with the drug?'

Danny sighed. 'You want my honest opinion?'

'Of course!'

'I'd have thought the chances were remote, quite frankly.'

'Why?'

'Because it's too late in the day, Jenny! All the tests have been done – not last week or last month but last year – and the year before that! The surveys, the clinical trials, the—'

'But it's still *possible*, isn't it?' insisted Jenny doggedly. 'I mean – look at what happened to Opren, and that other one . . . Debendox. Everyone thought they were OK too, didn't they? Until things started to go wrong.'

'Yes, that's true,' Danny admitted reluctantly. 'But . . .'

'But what? Go on.'

'I just don't think you should pin your hopes on a miracle, that's all. It's an outside chance, Jen, that's all; an outside chance. The odds must be . . . oh . . . a thousand, ten thousand to one?'

CHAPTER FIFTEEN

Tony Lockhart, Dave Bourne and Pete Sleaman were airborne in RESCUE 44 on a training flight across the bay. Officially, it was supposed to be their day off. Unofficially, a broken collarbone and a court of inquiry in Edinburgh had left RAF Glenhaddon a crew light. The result had been an early-morning phone call and the briefest of apologies from Flight Lieutenant Bill Churchill: he was sorry, but there was no one else. They were to come to Available just as soon as they could make it.

Twenty minutes earlier they'd taken off and flown low along the coast, the shadow of their aircraft chasing along the glittering wave crests as Tony and Pete crouched in the open door and waved at the boats and windsurfers, before startling a couple of girls sunbathing topless in the sand dunes as they banked steeply to starboard and raced out to sea. Dave brought them down to thirty feet. 'OK, Winchie. Anywhere around here.'

Tony reached behind him for a battered metal drum, glanced down at the empty sea and tossed the drum out of the door. 'Drum gone, Dave. It's all yours,' he reported briefly.

'Drums' was part of any SAR aircrew's monthly training programme. Toss a metal canister into the sea and try to recover same in the shortest possible time, using a special grappling hook on the end of the cable. The exercise was designed to sharpen pilot/winch operator co-operation as they ran down on to an object in the sea. Sometimes it went like clockwork. And at other times—

'Ten . . . eight . . . six . . . five . . . four and – right three! Right! Dead ahead one! Steady . . . Steady . . . bugger! Back ten and start again, Boss. Must be that lager,' Pete advised laconically.

Tony leaned out of the door and watched the drum slide past the hook thirty feet below. 'Give that man a coconut,' he grinned.

'Come right . . . right . . . steady. Height is good. Ten . . . eight . . . six—'

'RESCUE 44, RESCUE 44, this is Oban. Immediate.' Pete and Dave tensed as, above them, Dave acknowledged, then: 'RESCUE 44, this is Oban. We have a report of a vehicle over the cliffs two miles south of Dalrean. Can you respond, over?'

Down in the cabin, Pete was already unfastening his monkey-harness prior to wriggling back to the navigator's seat as Tony began bringing in the winch cable, the drum forgotten. Drums could wait – cars over cliffs could not. There might be people inside.

'Oban, this is RESCUE 44. Responding, over.'

'RESCUE 44, this is Oban. Many thanks. That location: two miles south of Dalrean. Picnickers reported seeing something down on the rocks twenty minutes ago. Coastguard Mobile at the scene has just confirmed the sighting; it's definitely a car . . . '

'Er . . . all copied, Oban. Suggest you have the Coastguard vehicle point its headlights out to sea. We shall be closing from the south-west, over.'

'All noted, RESCUE 44. Listening out.'

Pete was now busy with his maps up beside the pilot. 'Come right to zero three zero, Boss. We can correct once we have them visual. ETA now nine minutes.'

As Dave reported course and estimated time of arrival to Oban Control, Tony hauled the door closed and struggled into bo's'un's harness even as he thought ahead and tried to anticipate what he might need down there on the rocks, conscious of the minutes slipping away as they flew towards the cliffs and the coast road. He unclipped the first-aid backpack from the cabin wall and began adjusting the straps.

'RESCUE 44, this is Oban. Cliff Rescue estimate their arrival that location forty minutes, repeat: four zero minutes.'

Dave acknowledged, then—

'There we are, Boss! See the lights? Your two o'clock.' That was Pete.

'Yeah, I have them now. Coming left to zero two five. Fuel is down to twenty-one hundred pounds.'

Tony thrust the Pye pocket-phone down the front of his lifevest and hauled back the door. Pete wriggled down into the cabin. The aircraft banked steeply to port and began flying up the coast at two hundred feet as Tony studied the cliffs with the total concentration of a man about to become intimately acquainted with their dangers – overhangs, earth-slides, and slate, scree-choked gullies; a wicked, crumbling, devil's playground of a place plagued by up-draughts and sudden, treacherous gusts of wind. A bad place for helicopters.

Forty yards from the cliff-face . . . thirty . . . twenty . . . ten . . . Dave edged the aircraft closer, as Pete crowded into the door beside Tony, his head twisting up and round, his lips moving ceaselessly as he kept up his patter into Dave's headphones as the gap between whirling rotor-blades and cliff-face steadily diminished. Tony clipped himself on to the winch cable and sat forward into the door. Now they could see the Coastguard Land Rover. Four people stood near the edge of the cliff, pointing downwards and waving as the elderly Coastguard raised a hand briefly in greeting, his hat tucked under his arm as the down-draught of their rotors blasted the hair away from his face.

'There!' Pete pointed suddenly. 'See it? Jesus . . . ' Tony followed his pointing finger down one hundred and thirty feet of sloping, crumbling rock-face and nodded, his mouth suddenly dry. Oh, beautiful. Just terrific . . .

A dark-blue Vauxhall Cavalier lay crumpled at the base of a narrow ledge of sloping scree, its front wheels and bonnet hanging over empty space. Right side up, precariously balanced, the car looked as if it was waiting for no more than a sudden gust of wind before starting that final death-plunge to the rocks that waited eighty feet below like a row of rotten, hungry teeth.

Hands and feet feather-light upon the controls, Dave

manoeuvred RESCUE 44 away from the cliffs, lost height and brought them into the hover exactly opposite the damaged car and about sixty feet away from the cliffs. Tony took out a pair of binoculars and focused them on the vehicle. No one said a word.

The car looked like something out of a wrecker's yard. The windscreen was broken, the roof and panelling buckled and dented. There was no sign of movement, no sign of life. Tony closed his mind deliberately to what might be waiting for him inside the car out of sight, and swung the glasses away from the wreckage. He focused instead upon the rocks above, trying to plan the best approach.

'How d'you want to play it, Tony?' Dave asked over the intercom. The three crewmen discussed the options, then Dave brought RESCUE 44 round in an easy, climbing curve until they were thirty feet above the cliff-top and the Coastguard Land Rover that was surrounded now by a cluster of upturned faces.

'Ready to winch out,' Pete intoned, as Tony disconnected his headset and nodded. Pete grinned reassuringly and reached up. 'Winching out.' A slight tug and Tony was swinging gently down from the aircraft, head and shoulders buffeted by the down-draught. Looking up, conscious of the weight of the first-aid pack between his shoulders, Tony watched Pete's face recede as the cable came off the drum.

Tony kicked round to the left as he spun slowly clockwise and the cliff-top came up to meet him. Down . . . down . . . A few more feet and Tony had touched. Leaning into his harness he began walking down the cliff, back towards the sea, his boots bouncing off the slabs of sun-warmed slate as the helicopter dwindled away to a small yellow square in the sky, and the world became quieter around him. Tony dropped into a shallow gully and then started violently as a black-coated guillemot exploded suddenly from a ledge beside his hand and clattered away with that high, characteristic wheezy squeak of alarm. Tony wedged himself into a cleft of rock and paused, suddenly aware of the sweat running down the inside of his sealed rubber suit and of the sharpness of the slate beneath his hands. He reached for the pocket-phone. 'Dave – this is Tony. Do you read, over?'

'Loud and clear, Tony. How's it looking?'

'OK so far. Another thirty feet or so and I'll have to go off the wire, OK? I don't want it chafing against that overhang, over.'

Leaning back on to the cable, Tony gestured downwards. He was out on more than one hundred and fifty feet of wire, and at that distance from the cabin his hand signals were little more than specks of orange movement against the greys and whites of the rocks below. Feeling for a toehold in his soft rubber boots, Tony edged slowly backwards, working his way across and down towards the overhang. Presently he pressed the transmit button on the radio. 'OK, Boss. I'm near the overhang. About to go off the wire.'

'OK, Tony. We'll bog off for a bit and try and help with the route-finding.'

'Coming off . . . now.' Tony twisted the quick-release box, came off the wire and waved upwards. The cable snaked away, and Tony was left alone and unsupported on the cliff-face. The easy part was over.

RESCUE 44 swung out to sea and stood off like some benevolent guardian angel, the steady, reassuring thwop-thwop-thwop of its rotors drowning out the crash of the waves and the scream of the seagulls wheeling nearby.

'Tony, this is Pete. You're now about thirty feet above and slightly left of the car, over.'

Tony climbed carefully into another shallow gully and moved slowly downwards. Body pressed tightly against the cliff-face, bare fingers locked into every offered crevice, he inched his way round the overhang. One step, then another, and the rear of the car slid into view. It was then that Tony almost trod on the body.

The gully he was climbing down acted as a natural gutter for the rain and debris of soil and rock clitter that trickled down continually from above. A man in a light-blue suit lay crumpled face downwards in the bottom of this channel, his body hidden from above by the overhang. Tony shrugged out of the shoulder straps of the first-aid pack, straddled the gutter with a foot on either side and slithered down beside the body. One look was enough. The crown of the man's head was matted with dark blood and pulpy to the touch. When Tony tried to ease back the head just a fraction so he could feel for a pulse, the neck lolled brokenly, giving him a quick glance of a slack, gaping mouth in a face masked with blood and smeared with dust. From the way the body lay it was obvious there were other injuries as well. Tony sat back on his haunches and twisted round to look back up the slope. Thrown from a car anywhere up there, the poor sod hadn't had a prayer. He pulled out the radio.

'Found one, Dave,' he reported flatly, his nostrils full of the smell of blood on sun-dried rock, of the tang of the sea and the sharp, pungent smell of bird droppings. 'Bloke's lying in a gully about twenty feet above and to the right of the start of the slope. There's nothing I can do for him. All copied so far, over?'

'Roger, Tony.'

'OK. I'm now going to move down to the car. See if anyone's still inside. If it's empty I'll start searching the rest of this gully area, over.' Tony signed off and stowed the radio back inside his lifevest.

It was easier going now as he moved out from the cliff-face and began walking warily down the sloping shelf of scree towards the wrecked car. Easier, but no less dangerous. Without a single handhold there was nothing between him and an eighty-foot drop to the rocks but the loose scree underfoot that carpeted the ledge until it dropped away into nothing, thirty feet from where Tony was standing. Slowly, gently, one foot at a time, Tony moved towards the boot of the car and the edge of the slope. He could see the helicopter hovering about fifty yards directly ahead with Pete sitting in the door, a pair of binoculars clamped to his eyes as he followed Tony's progress. Twenty feet now, with each step a cold-blooded gamble that he was not about to start a rock slide that would sweep the car over the cliff and take him with it. Ten feet to the boot of the car. Five . . . there! He'd made it. Tony reached out automatically for the support of something solid, and then pulled back as if the metal was red hot as the car began to sway and groan alarmingly on the metal belly that was the pivot of its own centre of balance, the crushed rocks trapped underneath screeching against the metal.

Edging slowly round to the back window, Tony looked inside. No one in the back. Thank God. Another careful foot forward and Tony peered over the front of the driver's seat – and froze as everything seemed to go suddenly cold inside him and the sweat broke out on the palms of his hands. Another man lay crumpled under the dashboard, slumped sideways across the passenger seat with both legs twisted at an impossible angle under the mangled remains of the steering-column. Oh, Jesus . . . Tony moved back a few paces, sat down, and leant back carefully against the rear wheel. Then he reached for the radio. 'Dave?'

'We're still here.'

'Found another one. Driver's side and fallen left across the front passenger seat.'

'Alive?'

'Don't know. Shouldn't have thought so. He . . . wait one.' Tony broke off suddenly and cocked his head to one side. With the noise of the rotors swamping everything else he might have imagined it, only . . . Tony tore off his helmet and pushed to his feet. There it was again – and this time there was no mistaking either the sound or where it was coming from: a low, almost inaudible moan of pain from the front of the car. Tony leant as far forward as he dared, and was rewarded by the slightest movement of a bloody hand as the car began to rock and sway once again.

'It's all right, mate – don't worry,' he called. 'Soon have you out of there, OK? Only don't try to move. Stay where you are.' Tony stepped back and crouched down. 'Dave – the guy's alive! I just saw him move.'

'Can you reach him?'

'Negative. He's right in the front of the car. If I start

clambering around in there after him, the extra weight'll just topple us over the cliff.'

There was a pause. 'Want to wait for the Cliff Rescue team?'

It was tempting. Why not? Why not just pass the buck? Let someone else stick his neck out for a change.

'The way this thing's balanced? It may not be here by the time they arrive. No thanks, Boss. There isn't the time. I've . . . er . . . I've had an idea.' He shared it with them and there was a brief, stunned silence. Then—

'You're raving mad,' advised Pete, from the safety of his cabin high in the sky.

'Anyone got any better idea?' Dave asked briskly. Another silence. 'All happy? Right then, we'll give it a whirl. Pete? Let him have all the cable you can.'

With that, RESCUE 44 began to climb as the cable unwound steadily. Tony stood up and watched as the helicopter came in high and then began crabbing gingerly along the cliff-face towards him, the winch hook trailing below at the full extent of the cable. Tony craned up at the tiny pale dot that was Pete's face as he leant out of the cabin door and guided Dave forward, the rotor-disc less than six feet from the edge of the rocks as Dave jockeyed the cable within reach. It was pilot/winchman co-operation of a very high order indeed. The hook swung closer, earthed as it touched down and Tony grabbed it. He pressed the transmit button. 'OK, Boss. Hold it there. Moving forward now.'

'Roger,' came the reply as, high above his head, pilot Dave Bourne reached out a gloved hand and slid back the red cover shielding one of the switches on the control panel in front of him. It was labelled: CABLE SEVER. The instant Dave pressed it, the cable would be cut. An admission of professional failure or misjudgement, cutting that cable was considered a desperate, last-ditch measure they had talked about often but never had to do for real. Now, in the next few minutes, that drill might become reality.

Tony gripped the cable hook firmly, inched his way along

the body of the Vauxhall Cavalier, and then paused. He had hoped to be able to loop the cable through the broken windscreen and round the steering-column, but he discovered now that he couldn't reach. Instead, he had to settle for the offside door pillar. He looped the cable round, snapped the hook back upon itself and edged away. A quick look through into the bloody shambles of the front two seats. No movement, no sound. 'Soon have you out of there,' he encouraged loudly. 'Only don't move, OK? Stay exactly where you are.' The man was almost certainly unconscious, but the words couldn't do any harm and might even penetrate even though the man was incapable of responding. Tony pressed the transmit button. 'It's fixed, Dave. You're anchored to the offside front pillar support.'

'Understood,' Dave acknowledged tersely, all his concentration focused now upon holding six tons of yellow helicopter motionless in the sky.

'Up one foot,' ordered Tony.

'Up one foot. Roger,' Dave repeated.

Eyes locked on the winch cable, Tony watched as the aircraft's downward thrust moved the car's point of balance back a precious couple of feet.

'Steady . . . Steady . . . Hold it there,' Tony ordered, as the helicopter took the strain, the winch cable became bar-taut, and the bonnet of the car lifted level. Moving round to the rear door, Tony took hold of one of the handles and pulled savagely. Nothing happened. Once, twice, three times he tugged, grunting with the effort until he felt the muscles in his shoulders begin to crackle. Finally, just as he thought it was hopeless, the door burst open and the way was clear into the back of the car. Tony stood back, panting with effort, and began struggling out of bo's'un's harness and lifevest. Then, ducking down, he reached forward for the seat-tilt lever and racked the driver's seat back towards him until it was almost horizontal. He did the same with the passenger seat, and then began worming gently forward into the car, the radio held in one hand. As he reached for the shoulder of the unconscious driver, the car suddenly began to rock and sway. He froze. 'Up six inches, Dave! Quick as you can! Up six inches!'

'Will do,' Dave's voice came back calmly. The bonnet rose fractionally, the swaying ceased, and Tony allowed himself to breathe again. He shook the casualty urgently.

'Oi! Can you hear me?' No response, no movement. Tony didn't waste any more time. The priority now was to get them both out of the wreck before the rear wheels slipped, the car toppled forward, and they ended up on the rocks eighty feet below. Gripping the man unceremoniously under the armpits, Tony pulled him backwards. The heavy body slid towards him and, for a moment, Tony thought he had got him clear – then the legs snagged in the tangle of wreckage where the pedals ought to have been and the body refused to move any further. 'Come on, you bastard . . . ' Tony muttered under his breath as he grunted and strained. It was no use. He couldn't get anywhere near the pedals from where he crouched, he would have to go in further. So far, in fact, that if the car did begin to slide or overbalance . . . Cursing steadily, Tony wriggled into the car and squeezed down between the trapped man's hips and the driver's door. Again the car began to sway – and again Tony held his breath as he waited for that final, terrifying plunge as he stared without daring to move at the floor of the Cavalier, the sweat running into his eyes. Slowly, slowly, it stopped. There. Good. Stay there. Please. Just a few more minutes.

Hooking his hands under the sole of one shoe, Tony eased the twisted foot sideways, ignored the gleam of white shin bone protruding from blood-soaked trousers, and pulled the foot sharply towards him. And again. There! It was free. Panting loudly, Tony wriggled slowly back across the driver's seat and pushed back into the open air. Hauling the man after him out of the car, Tony dragged him away from the edge of the slope and lowered him down to the ground. He bent forward. Unconscious but still breathing, the man was still alive. Out came the radio. 'This one's still alive, Boss,' he panted.

'Stretcher's on its way down,' Dave acknowledged.

'Nice one, Winchie,' Pete called down from above, the

words failing to conceal his relief now that his friend was out of immediate danger.

Tony nodded and waved his radio vaguely up at the helicopter, too spent to come up with some quick, flip reply as he crouched beside the man he had saved. A brief examination told him the casualty was critically injured, probably dying; a special pass in his bloodstained wallet told him Thomas Steevenson was cleared by Internal Security to work at Highland Pharmaceuticals in a restricted area described simply as RD7. The wallet also contained a special pass to the staff's celebratory lunch to mark the launch of Cardocol, HPL's breakthrough new heart drug.

As Tony Lockhart waited for the stretcher to come down on the wire towards him, Jenny sat back from the polished wooden table in the reference section of Gleninver's public library, and closed the magazine she had been reading with a feeling of total inadequacy. She had gone to the library to read for herself the BMJ article on Cardocol that Danny had read to her over the phone earlier that same morning.

The Cardocol supplement ran over five glossy, full-colour pages. Headlined: CARDOCOL – A HEARTBEAT CLOSER, the supplement carried impressive-looking graphs and toxicity curves, and column after column of technical text peppered with phrases like 'random sample', 'statistically significant', 'probability indices', and 'minimal contra-indications'. The trouble was, Jenny didn't understand a word of it. Or rather, she understood the broad thrust of its message but was quite incapable of assessing either the independence and validity of the report itself, or the efficiency of the drug it was advocating. One thing, however, was clear: taking the promotional supplement at face value, Cardocol appeared to be the most significant pharmacological development since the introduction of penicillin and the sulphonamides in the nineteen thirties; a drug of such proven therapeutic value that the prescribing habits of a generation of family practitioners were about to undergo a sea change – or so the writer of Highland Pharmaceuticals' advertising copy would have the reader believe. Cardocol was *stable* – that was the point that was hammered home, time and time again. Absorption, metabolic and excretion rates had all been tested and carefully monitored, first in the laboratory, then on rats and mice and finally on human volunteers in a whole series of integrated, expensive clinical trials. The release of Cardocol on to the drug market of the United Kingdom would revolutionize the treatment of hypertension – high blood pressure – because HPL had at last developed a drug without any of the unpleasant side-effects that had defeated their rivals and sent them scuttling off into less thankless, more profitable areas of pharmaceutical research. Agonists and acetylcholine, alpha-blockers and guanethidine; neurones, double-blind techniques and the problems of postural hypotension and unsightly oedema – it was all there for the cognoscente, neatly stapled into the BMJ between pages thirty-nine and forty. But Jenny was a speech therapist, not a cardiologist. Or even a doctor.

Jonathan Tomalin was a neat, dapper little man in his mid-fifties in a light grey suit with a rose in his buttonhole and a bright-red tie, who made a very good living advising companies with better things to do how best to cater for the needs of Press and public whenever they wished to launch a new product, create a favourable impression or, more usually, do both. His had been the hand behind the successful reception for marathon runner Sandy Tulloch, and it was he who was now co-ordinating the final details for the Press reception at the Cardocol launch in just two days' time. Nodding at David Eckett, HPL's Marketing and Promotions Manager who had just resumed his seat, Tomalin ran a hand over a carefully groomed head of fashionably cut, silver-grey hair, stepped up to the display board propped against a lightweight aluminium stand at the far end of HPL's boardroom, and glanced towards Harold Engel, the sunlight flashing on his square, horn-rimmed spectacles. Sitting in his shirtsleeves at the head of the table, with Maurice Jackman seated to his right, Engel nodded for him to continue, vaguely irritated by the man's obsequious efficiency.

'If I may press on,' Tomalin resumed, tapping the tip of his pointer briskly against a large white letter H in the middle of the company's spacious grounds on the diagram in front of him. 'The first helicopter from Glasgow Airport is scheduled to arrive at eleven-thirty precisely. Thereafter, flights will be arriving at approximately twenty-five-minute intervals. Each party of doctors and medical journalists – with, of course, their dear lady-friends – will then be escorted by one of my young men along this path . . . here . . . towards the main marquee, where they will be presented with one of the company folders—' David Eckett held up the emerald-green Cardocol folder briefly – 'and served with champagne and canapés before moving indoors for the formal briefing and presentation that is scheduled to commence at one-thirty. Yes?' A hand had been raised further down the table.

'What . . . er . . . what champagne?'

There was a brief smile from one or two of the other directors. Frank Beamish was responsible for company finance. Hence the question.

'Bollinger '75. Vintage.'

Beamish didn't know much about champagne but he winced anyway. It sounded expensive. 'And do we know exactly how many flights this . . . this shuttle service of ours will be required to make?' Beamish again, counting the pennies.

Jonathan Tomalin flicked over some notes and found the answer immediately. They wouldn't catch him like that. He smiled confidently.

'The company sent out a total of one hundred and forty-six double invitations. So far, one hundred and nine have replied saying they wish to attend. Discounting our local guests – Press, GPs and so forth – seventy-seven have indicated that they wish to travel here from Glasgow Airport by helicopter. Most of those, of course, will have travelled up from the south some time the previous day. That being the case, we can expect—'

'How many, Mr Tomalin?' Harold Engel interrupted wearily, suddenly tired of the whole expensive, drawn-out business of product planning and promotion. 'How many flights?'

'Er . . . six, Mr Engel. Possibly seven. It will depend upon—' He broke off there and turned as the boardroom door opened and one of the senior company secretaries stood framed in the doorway, looking pale and shaken. As if she was the bearer of bad news.

'I'm . . . I'm sorry to interrupt, Mr Engel,' she faltered, wringing her hands together, 'but I . . . I wonder if I might speak to you a moment, please? Outside if . . . if you don't mind.'

Engel rose to his feet, every professional instinct sensing trouble. 'Yes. Yes, of course,' he said quietly. 'Gentlemen? If you will excuse me for one moment?' He moved towards the door, followed by a turning line of silent, curious faces. He stepped outside and closed the door softly behind him. They were alone in the corridor.

'I . . . I'm sorry to burst in on you like that, Mr Engel,' the girl began haltingly. 'I know how busy you all are just now, what with the launch and everything, but I thought . . . that is, we all thought . . . you ought to be told straight away.'

'What ought I to be told, Lucy?'

The girl swallowed. 'There's . . . there's been a terrible accident,' she managed, her eyes swimming with tears.

Engel leant forward. 'An accident? What sort of accident?' he demanded, thinking immediately of some mechanical, production-line disaster.

'Martin Calvert and Tom Steevenson, Mr Engel. Their . . . their car went over the cliffs! Martin's dead, and Tom's been taken away to hospital! They say he may die too . . . '

'Calvert and Steevenson – is that what you said? When was this?' demanded Engel roughly, shocked not by the news of the accident but by the names of those involved. Both men had worked in RD7 with Douglas Parsons, the man who had committed suicide just the previous night. Or so he had been led to believe. Until . . . A sudden chill dread of suspicion, almost of certainty. *Three* deaths in twenty-four hours – all from the same department? It wasn't possible . . .

'Mr Engel? Sir? Are you all right?'

Harold Engel forced himself to concentrate, to pay attention. As far as people like Lucy and the rest of HPL's clerical and administrative staff were concerned, RD7 was engaged solely in secret commercial research into the next generation of heart drugs . . .

'What? Yes, yes – perfectly all right, thank you, Lucy.'

'I . . . I was just saying: the accident happened about ten miles away – two miles this side of Dalrean.'

Engel nodded, picturing the road, twisting and winding its way up the side of those steep, sheer cliffs with the rocks waiting far below. He closed his eyes briefly. 'Was anyone else involved?'

'Anyone else, Mr Engel?'

'Any other vehicle? Was any other vehicle involved?'

She shook her head. 'No, no – the police didn't think so. They just . . . went over the edge.' She shuddered, and Engel nodded. No, there wouldn't be, he thought grimly: not if that bastard Jackman was up to his usual standard of chilling, cold-blooded efficiency. A sudden sense of proprietorial anger, of outrage, welled up inside him. How dare he? How bloody well dare he? All this was Jackman's fault, and London's, all this subterfuge, all these sudden accidents and deaths . . . 'Can I get you something, Mr Engel?' asked Lucy. 'You look all . . . well . . . sort of funny.'

Engel forced himself to smile, to present that calm, bland exterior which people like Lucy with their hundred-words-a-minute shorthand and fifty typing had a right to expect from a man in his position.

'Yes. You can bring me their files, if you would, Lucy. And then ask Mr Jackman to come to my office, would you? In about five minutes' time.'

'Certainly, Mr Engel.'

'Thank you. Oh – and Lucy . . . '

'Yes, Mr Engel?'

'Don't worry. Everything's going to be all right.'

She gave HPL's Chairman and Chief Executive a puzzled glance and then nodded uncertainly. 'Yes, Mr Engel.'

But they might have been speaking different languages. Lucy was distraught because one man she knew was dead, and another she had chatted to in the canteen was critically injured. But Harold Engel's final, strange words of reassurance had been directed not at her, but at himself. Despite Jackman, despite London and Baxter and all that RD7 had come to represent over the years since he had first allowed himself to be lured into such a partnership through a mixture of flattery, greed, and polite, sophisticated blackmail, Highland Pharmaceuticals Limited was still *his* company, *his* creation. Cardocol was *his* triumph, these people *his* employees. So – it would be all right. For he would make it so.

Eight minutes later there was a soft tap on his door and Jackman entered his office. Engel waved him to a chair without looking up, for he was still on the phone to the police station, the telephone wedged against his shoulder as he made rapid notes on the pad in front of him. 'Yes . . . yes, I see. No. No, I don't suppose there is. Thanks very much.' He replaced the receiver slowly, his eyes on Calvert and Steevenson's personal files lying together on his desk. At least both men were bachelors, unattached. He had been spared that much, at least.

'I understand you wanted to see me,' Jackman began.

Engel looked up. 'You told me this morning that Douglas Parsons, one of the men in RD7, had committed suicide. "Pressure of work" I believe was the phrase you used.'

Jackman nodded warily. 'Yes, that's right. He'd been under a lot of pressure.' A casual shrug. 'Always did push himself too hard in my view. Took Highcroft's accident particularly badly, so I was told – felt he was partly to blame, although that'll never come out into the open, of course.'

'Of course not,' Engel murmured, with a deceptive quietness to his voice Jackman had never heard before. Engel studied Jackman calmly from across his desk.

Remarkable how once he thought he might have been able to like the man. 'And Calvert? And Steevenson – what about them?' he asked softly.

Jackman affected uncertainty. 'I'm sorry? I'm afraid I don't know what you mean.'

'Don't you?' challenged Engel. 'Calvert is dead. Steevenson is in hospital critically injured. Their car – one of our cars – went over the cliff on the road to Dalrean some time after ten this morning.'

'Oh.' There was silence. Engel stared at him.

'One man dies, another man lies critically injured in hospital even as we speak, and all you can say is "Oh"? Is that all?'

'What would you like me to say?' Jackman countered coolly.

Engel hunched forward. 'I want, Mr Jackman, to hear you tell me this "accident" has nothing whatever to do with you, nothing to do with London.'

There was a long, stretching silence, then – 'Tricky bit of road, that,' Jackman observed quietly, the truth lying there in those cold, pale eyes.

CHAPTER SIXTEEN

Ridley stepped through from the bathroom adjoining his bedroom on the second floor of the Seaview Motel on the hilly outskirts of Gleninver, his bare feet leaving damp patches on the carpet. Apart from a white towel wrapped around his waist he was naked, the clothes he had worn for the cliff job lying in a heap at the foot of the bed in a plastic bag, never to be worn again. Ridley stepped in front of the mirror, comb in hand – and then paused to stare through his own unsmiling, gaunt reflection at the memory of that moment as he steered the Vauxhall Cavalier towards the edge of the cliff road, the two passengers lolling unconscious and unprotesting in their seats as the car jolted over the grassy verge, gathered speed, tipped up and plunged headlong over the edge. Ridley began combing his hair slowly. Another scene, this time more than an hour later as the yellow helicopter raised one body strapped in a white canvas shroud, and the second man came up in that stretcher with the winchman in his orange suit hanging on to the side of the cradle. Watching and waiting from higher up the road with a pair of binoculars, Ridley had moved down closer to the Coastguard Land Rover then and mingled with the cluster of spellbound holiday-makers as they watched the drama unfolding before their very eyes. Standing there beside the open door of the Land Rover, with the Coastguard radio relaying the helicopter's messages through the speaker system, he had arrived just in time to have his worst suspicions confirmed: one man was dead, certainly – but one, the driver, was still alive. Still alive. Ridley brushed his hair carefully, opened his suitcase and took out clean socks, shirt, underwear and newly pressed trousers, the need for fresh clothes almost a physical hunger after the soiling contact with the fear and the smell of the men he had been targeted to kill. Now, after his bath, he felt clean, sated, relieved. He dressed slowly, savouring the crispness as he shrugged into a new shirt. When he had finished dressing he sat down on the bed and lifted the telephone towards him. 'Would you put me through to the local hospital, please?'

The call went through and Ridley asked for the casualty department. 'Good afternoon,' he began politely. 'I understand a Mr Steevenson was admitted to your department shortly before lunchtime?'

'One moment, please.' Ridley waited. 'Who is this calling?'

'A friend. I just wanted to know how he is.'

'Well, Mr . . . er . . . '

'Henderson.'

'—Mr Henderson. We don't usually disclose information of that nature over the telephone. When he arrived here, you see, he was very severely injured. If—'

'But he is still alive?'

'Och, yes, Mr Henderson, he's still alive. He—'

'I see. Thank you. Thank you very much indeed.' He replaced the receiver slowly.

In the crewroom at RAF Glenhaddon, the duty Corporal stuck his head round the door, saw Tony filling in his report at one of the desks beneath the cluttered Flight noticeboard and flight hazard posters, and pointed: 'There's your man.' Tony glanced round as a tall, broad-shouldered police constable in shirtsleeves came into the crewroom, stooping warily as though from long habit in knocking his head against door lintels. He came forward uncertainly, his service cap wedged under his arm.

'Flight Sergeant Lockhart?'

Tony tossed down his biro and swung round. He'd peeled down the immersion suit as far as his waist and was sitting at the desk in his T-shirt like some half-deflated Michelin Man.

'That's me.'

'Police Constable Ayres, Flight Sergeant. I wonder if I

might have a few words? It's about that wee job up on the cliffs there.'

Tony nodded. 'Sure. Fire away.' He gestured at the forms in front of him. 'I'm just making out the paperwork.' The policeman nodded sympathetically, recognizing a kindred spirit. 'Tea? Coffee?' The policeman nodded and laid his hat carefully on the bench beside him as he sat down.

'Aye, thank you. That would be grand.' Hot and flushed in blue service trousers and with dark sweat marks at each armpit, he looked as though he could damage a pint into the bargain. Tony leaned far back in his chair and swung round. 'Corporal Deakin!' he shouted. The face popped back round the door.

'Already on its way, Flight.'

Tony grinned and then turned back to PC Ayres, suddenly serious. 'That bloke Steevenson going to make it?' he asked. He'd just risked his own life for the man. It would be nice if there was a return, a dividend.

PC Ayres hauled a bulky black notebook out of his breast pocket, folded it open and blew out his cheeks. 'Now then – fractured skull; fractured clavicle; four broken ribs; ruptured spleen – I wouldn't bet money on it, myself . . . Oh, and they lost the car, did they tell you? Went over the edge about two minutes after your lot had left.'

Tony nodded, not in the least surprised. 'Will they recover it?'

The policeman shook his head. 'Not worth the candle. It's under water now, wedged in among the rocks even at low tide. My guess is they'll leave well alone – there's been enough risks taken over that car to my way of thinking.' He glanced up speculatively. 'Unless, that is, you know of some reason why they shouldn't?'

Tony frowned. 'Come again?'

'Well, apart from the two men inside, you're the only one who got a good look at the car.'

'I was after the people inside,' Tony protested. 'Not doing a bloody MOT.' The tea arrived and PC Ayres spooned in sugar patiently.

'Aye, I appreciate that, Flight Sergeant. But still, you might have seen something. That's why I'm here. Just to tidy away any loose-ends.'

'It all looked pretty straightforward to me. He'd just driven off the road and over the edge. Don't ask me why.'

'Steering? Brakes?'

Tony shrugged. 'Could be, I don't know. There wasn't much of it left. There wasn't much of anything left.'

'Were they strapped in?'

Tony shook his head. 'No.'

'You're sure?'

'Yeah, I'm sure. The seatbelts were still there, reeled in against the pillar supports.'

'What about identification?'

'Steevenson had a wallet in his pocket,' Tony remembered slowly. 'That's how I found out his name. There was a permit inside issued by Highland Pharmaceuticals for some department or other called RD7. The bloke who died had one too.'

'Is that a fact?' said PC Ayres, leaning forward and taking out that bulky black notebook once more. 'You didn't hang on to those passes, I suppose?'

Tony shook his head. 'They went up with the body. In the stretcher. They'd be at the hospital now, I suppose, if you want to look at them.'

Jenny sat in the window seat of Helen Highcroft's kitchen, and watched as a cluster of children played around the climbing frame in the garden, her thoughts not on them but upon Danny and the BMJ Cardocol supplement she had read in the library. Behind her, Helen Highcroft sighed, and Jenny turned back into the room. They were sitting opposite one another at the pine kitchen table, their cups of tea in front of them. They had been drinking a lot of tea recently. Helen tapped the five photocopied pages of the Cardocol supplement into a neat pile and slid it back across the table. 'Well . . . ' she began, searching for something useful to say. 'It all sounds very . . . thorough, doesn't it? Very responsible.'

'You mean you could actually *understand* it?' A fleeting smile.

'About one word in four, if you want the honest truth. The technical stuff just went over my head.'

Jenny nodded. 'Me too.' She hunched forward. 'But Malcolm never mentioned any of this to you? There's nothing here that rings a bell?' Helen shook her head as Jenny leafed through the pages and then pointed at a column of text. 'What about these things – clinical trials? Could he have been involved in those, d'you think?'

Helen tilted her head to glance at the upside-down headline and shrugged helplessly. 'I . . . I don't know. He might have been, I suppose . . . '

'But you're not sure?'

'I'm not sure of anything,' replied Helen miserably, pushing a hand through her hair. 'God, I just wish I'd *listened* more, you know? If only I'd asked more questions, taken more interest in what he was doing. I never—' The phone rang on the dresser. Helen spun round and pushed to her feet, the speed of her reaction revealing more clearly than words just how desperately she hungered for news of her husband. Seeing that hunger, Jenny cursed her own thoughtlessness as she guessed who the caller might be almost before Helen had lifted the receiver.

'Hello? Yes?' said Helen, her whole body tensed, expectant. Then, as Jenny watched, the shoulders slumped dejectedly. 'Oh. Yes. Yes, she is. Will you wait one moment, please? I'll just get her.' She turned. 'For you,' she said simply. 'A Dr Kindersley.'

Jenny squeezed round the end of the table to take the call. 'I'm sorry, that was thoughtless of me,' she apologized. 'I knew I was coming here so I gave him your number. He's . . . a friend of mine. I thought he might be able to interpret for us.' Jenny took the outstretched receiver. 'Danny?'

'How many other Dr Kindersleys do you know?' replied the friendly voice in faraway Newcastle. Jenny smiled.

'Oh, half a dozen, at least.'

'Sorry I couldn't talk earlier, Jen. It just wasn't possible.'

'Are you clear now?'

'For the next forty minutes, anyway.'

'It shouldn't take that long – please God,' Jenny replied, trying to keep their conversation on a cheerfully detached, professional plane. Defeated by the Cardocol supplement's technical outer-shell, she had called Danny almost in desperation the moment she returned home from the library, and had pleaded for what she described as an 'idiot's guide'. She was after information now, that was all – understanding. The fact that they had once been lovers was immaterial – or so she tried to tell herself. 'Have you read the supplement?'

'I have, yes, ma'am. From cover to cover, as per your instructions,' Danny replied, playing the same game. 'Oh – by the way: some more stuff arrived in the post this morning from HPL's promotions people. They're really pushing the boat out. It must be costing them an absolute fortune.' It had been on the tip of his tongue to make some joke about the Caribbean holiday for two on the island of the winner's choice, but he had stopped himself just in time. That would have been a little too near the knuckle for both of them.

'What did you make of it?'

'From a professional standpoint? I found it rather impressive, actually.'

'What? You mean you'd use it? On the strength of just one article and a couple of free hand-outs?' demanded Jenny.

'No, I'm not saying that,' Danny hedged cautiously. 'I just found it . . . interesting. I'd like to know more about it, that's all.'

'You said it was just another "Me-tooer",' Jenny accused, the curious phrase still fresh in her mind.

'I know I did. But now that I've read the promotional material I can see what they're getting at. I . . . I may have been wrong, that's all. It's certainly an intriguing possibility.'

'Why? What makes it so intriguing?'

'Well, they're billing it as an anti-hypertensive adrenergic neurone-blocker. That means it—'

'Whoa, Danny—' Jenny interrupted in alarm. 'This is me you're talking to, remember? Little old me? Just put all that into English, will you?'

'Sorry, Jen. Right, let's see. It's a heart drug, OK? A drug aimed at reducing high blood pressure, particularly among the elderly. No one really knows for sure what causes high blood pressure – what *is* known, however, is that blood pressure goes up when you get old because the arteries narrow, and it therefore takes more effort – more pressure – to force blood along the arteries from the heart – OK so far?'

'OK so far,' echoed Jenny faithfully, like a co-pilot verifying cockpit checks.

'Good. Now then, the heart, as you know, is self-running – we don't have to do anything to make it go, it just works. When it doesn't—'

'Er . . . Danny – I know I asked for an idiot's guide, but I didn't mean the complete and unabridged Northern Ireland edition. I do have some medical knowledge, you know?'

'Patience, Jen – patience,' counselled the expert. 'It's all about to become just a mite more complicated.' He paused. 'Although the heart works without conscious control, its activity is adjusted by nervous impulses from the brain sent along something called the autonomic nervous system. This in turn has two parts, or outflows. The—'

'—Sympathetic and parasympathetic outflows,' Jenny supplied smugly. 'There – you see?'

'Excellento, smartie-pants,' retorted Danny. 'In that case, I fail to see why you require the services of a humble general practitioner. You quite obviously—'

'No, no – really, Danny, that's it: that really is the sum total of my medical knowledge. I won't interrupt again.'

'Promise?'

'Cross my heart.'

'OK. Both those outflows are constantly at work; both have opposite effects upon the heart. The parasympathetic outflow *restrains* the heart's action and slows it down. But the sympathetic outflow has just the opposite effect – it increases the rate and force of contraction. One of its major effects upon the human body is vasoconstriction – the tubes the blood runs along get smaller in diameter, and thus the pressure needed to force the blood along those narrowing tubes increases. Result? High blood pressure. It's this outflow – or, at least, the chemical transmitters at the end of the nerves – that Cardocol's chiefly concerned with.'

'It is?'

'It is. Now – the narrowing of those arteries is controlled by the release of certain chemicals which in turn are controlled by nervous impulses from the brain. We haven't yet learned how to control those nervous impulses – but we *have* learned to block that signal on its way down from the brain and so stop the release of those chemicals – adrenaline and noradrenaline – at the end of the nerve fibres. Further up the chain of command, as it were, are things called ganglia – ganglion, singular – a sort of impulse transmitter fuelled by another chemical called acctylcholinc. Wc'vc lcarned to block that, too. I'll come back to that in a moment.'

'Acety—?'

'Acetylcholine. Still with me?'

'By the skin of my teeth,' Jenny muttered, concentrating for all she was worth as Danny breezed on.

'Basically, Cardocol's what is known as a blocker – blockers are drugs that block either the impulse transmitter – that's the ganglion; the nerve ending – the neurone; or the receptor site at the end of the adrenergic nerve – the alpha or beta receptor. Stimulate those alpha receptors and you trigger constriction of the blood vessels. *Block* that stimulation—'

'—By stopping the release of those chemicals—'

'—Correct—'

'—And blood pressure does not rise, yes?'

'You've got it, kid.'

Jenny sighed with relief. 'Thank God for that.' She paused, suddenly puzzled. 'And all that's *new*? I mean, that's what HPL have discovered, all on their own in little old Gleninver?'

Danny laughed at the ingenuous question; he couldn't help it. 'No, no – there's nothing new about neurone-blockers – or alpha- or beta-blockers either, for that matter. Guanethidine's been in use for . . . oh . . . must be all of fifteen, twenty years by now.'

'Then you've lost me,' Jenny announced. 'I don't see why—'

'Because there's always a problem, Jen – a price to be paid. With any drug you're interfering not just with the body mechanism you're aiming at, but with everything else as well. It's . . . it's like firing a shotgun at one particular flower in a crowded flowerbed – everything else gets hit as well. So, with drugs, you have to try and balance the benefit you hope to achieve against the side-effects you'd much rather do without.'

'What sort of side-effects?'

'There's a whole list of them.'

'Such as?'

'With guanethidine monosulphate? It all depends upon the particular patient, but let me see: diarrhoea, dizziness, breathlessness, nausea, nasal obstruction, postural hypotension, failure of ejaculation—'

'And people put up with that?' Jenny interrupted incredulously. 'They just go on taking pills that do that to them, day after day?'

'If the choice is between a bit of nausea and sickness or an early death due to a stroke, which would you choose?' demanded Danny simply. 'Anyway, guanethidine's a thing of the past now, by and large.'

'Why's that?'

'Oh, because of its basic crudeness, its lack of discrimination. It was cumulative, too. It took a long time to build up adequate control levels, by which time the patients were taking fairly hefty doses of the stuff each day. If a doctor wanted *immediate* control then he had to resort to a different drug altogether – which in turn triggered off a whole series of additional side-effects as that drug reacted not only to the human body but to the presence of the primary drug as well . . . Is this helping at all, Jen, or am I getting off course?'

'No, no, it's fascinating,' Jenny replied, thinking ahead. 'I never realized it was all so . . . so complex. Where do HPL and Cardocol fit into all this?'

'Ah! Now, they've been very crafty. When everyone else wrote off guanethidine as a dead-end and went haring off after vasodilators and beta-blockers, HPL looked round, saw the field wellnigh empty of competition, and put their maximum research effort into overcoming guanethidine's side-effects and bringing high blood pressure under immediate control. Still with me?'

'I'll tell you when you've lost me. Keep going.'

'It's called creating a gap in the market.'

'How did they manage it? A company the size of HPL, I mean? I know it's big as far as Gleninver's concerned, but compared to the big boys it hardly rates, does it?'

'God knows how they managed it. An industrial secret like that must be worth an absolute fortune. All they're giving away in the brochure is that it's tied in somchow with a special delay-release formulation in the pill's outer coating – its matrix – that dissolves evenly over a twenty-four-hour cycle, giving – and I quote . . . hang on a second – "consistently low systolic and diastolic pressure readings over a statistically significant range of hypertensive conditions" unquote. And there's virtually no risk of postural hypotension. Or so they say.'

'Postural hypotension? What on earth's that?'

'One of the unwanted side-effects I was telling you about – the major side-effect, in fact. It was an absolute killer in terms of marketability and commercial appeal. Guanethidine was so effective at preventing constriction that if a patient stood up suddenly and actually *needed* the blood vessels to constrict, to pump blood up to the brain, it took a fair old while for the message to get through. By which time you'd blacked out.'

Jenny suddenly found herself listening very hard. 'Blacked out, did you say?'

'That's right. All the blood's still down in the trunk and feet, you see. The brain's starved of oxygen, it needs more blood, but the blood can't get up there fast enough. Result? You fall to the ground like a felled oak. Quite spectacular to watch, actually.'

'Or to the bottom of a boat,' Jenny said quietly, almost to herself.

'Sorry?'

'I was thinking of Robbie Roberts,' admitted Jenny. 'He had high blood pressure, I know he had. His wife told me.'

'So now you think he collapsed because of postural hypotension, is that it?' demanded Danny, more scathingly than he had intended. 'Maybe with guanethidine he might have done, Jen, but not with this new drug, Cardocol. That's the very problem HPL claim they've overcome!'

'I know it is,' Jenny said quietly. 'But what if they're wrong, Danny? Just suppose – what if they're *wrong*?'

In the Editor's office of the *Gleninver Times*, Bob Harris was sitting at his desk in his shirtsleeves, working on the layout for the first early pages of the next week's edition, his heavy face hot and flushed in the stuffy little office whose windows, as usual, were firmly closed. In exchange for the promise of extensive news coverage of the Cardocol launch in two days' time, Harris had been able to generate four more pages of local advertising, two of them whole-page advertisements taken out by Highland Pharmaceuticals itself, as the company thanked the local work-force for their efficiency and predicted even greater prosperity in the future. Now Harris laid his ruler aside, poked around in the litter of papers on his desk for cigarettes, and lit up, the flare of his match and the first deep drag of smoke adding their contribution to the closeness of the stale little room. There was a sudden tap on the frosted glass door. 'Come,' Harris called out, without either looking up or removing the cigarette from the corner of his mouth. A plug of ash fell on to his pages, and he brushed it away impatiently with the back of a heavy hand as the door opened and Hamish Owen stood in the doorway, notebook in hand.

'I've been thinking . . . ' he began.

Harris sighed. 'Christ, laddie, not again. I don't think I can bear it. Have you got that picture for me yet?'

Hamish Owen shook his head. Harris had sent him round to the home of the suicide to borrow a photograph to go with the story of Douglas Parsons' sudden death. Hamish had got no further than the front step. When he had told Mrs Parsons who he was, the door had shut firmly in his face and he had been forced to return to the office empty-handed. Harris had pounced upon his failure with relish and hailed it as yet another example of the futility of academic training.

'—About that suicide,' Hamish persisted doggedly. 'Douglas Parsons – and those two men in the car that went over the cliff this morning, Steevenson and Calvert.'

'What about them?' asked Harris shortly, his chair creaking and groaning suddenly as he leant back and linked his hands behind his head.

'They all came from the same company, HPL.'

Harris nodded. 'Aye, laddie, so they did. What about it?'

Hamish made a helpless gesture with his notebook. 'Well, don't you think that's a bit of a coincidence? Two men dead and a third critically injured, all from the same company, all in the same week? And that other man who disappeared: the Professor. Put him in with the others and that's four – four, all from the same company!'

Harris rocked forward suddenly and slammed a hand down angrily on his desk. 'You've been a reporter – how long?'

Hamish sighed, knowing what was coming. 'Twelve weeks.'

Harris nodded. 'Aye. Twelve weeks. And in that time, have you learned to hand in a decent Women's Institute report? No. Can you write up the results of a flower show without spelling half the names wrong? No. Can you do a simple bloody thing like borrow a photograph from the next of kin without having the door slammed in your face? You cannot. But give yourself half a bloody chance and you'll find murder under every stone. You'll—'

'But three, four people have had accidents, or killed themselves . . . or disappeared in the last week! From the same company! The statistical chances of that happening—'

'I don't give a bugger about your "statistical chances"!' Harris stormed, pushing angrily to his feet. 'Professor whatshisname didn't disappear – he went off with a younger bit of stuff, OK? It happens all the time, although you wouldn't know that, would you, you with your head stuffed full of all that university rubbish!' He turned and flung a hand towards the town stretched out beyond the grimy windows. 'Look out there!' he ordered. 'Go on, laddie – look out there and tell me what you see.'

Hamish moved to the window. 'Well . . . I can see the town. The streets . . . harbour. The—'

Harris nodded impatiently. 'Aye, laddie – so you do. So you do. What else do you see?'

Hamish shrugged. 'There's the square with—'

'You see people, laddie – people and jobs! At least half the jobs in this town revolve around HPL, either directly up at the plant or by providing some of the service industries that support it. Half! You and your pet theories about murder and suicide,' he scoffed. 'No doubt if you were working in Birmingham and heard about three fatal accidents you'd be rushing in to your Editor screaming "Hold the front page – I've found a link between these three deaths: they all work at British Leyland!" ' He spun round. 'Birmingham *is* the British motor industry, Mister high and mighty junior reporter, and Gleninver *is* Highland Pharmaceuticals. It's about time a man as brainy as you're supposed to be sorted that out, d'you hear what I'm saying?'

CHAPTER SEVENTEEN

It was dusk as Jenny locked the Citroën and walked towards her flat, her bag swinging from her shoulder as she remembered how she and Helen had sat on, talking at the kitchen table as the shadows lengthened outside and the children came in from the garden for their tea, their heads full of the day's adventures. It was only as they changed drowsily into pyjamas and got ready for bed that the questions at the back of everyone's minds came bubbling to the surface: When's Daddy coming home? Can't Daddy read me a story, Mummy . . . ? Jenny had decided it was time to leave. Now she stopped at the garden gate and felt in her bag for the door key. As she rummaged around, a figure loomed suddenly out of the darkness beside her and she spun round, startled.

'Jenny?' A man in uniform. She caught the gleam of his cap visor, recognized the face beneath and let out a sigh of relief.

'Phew – Tony. You made me jump.'

'Sorry. How're you?'

'Fine.'

'Can I have a word? Inside?'

'Well, I . . . '

'Yeah, I know: it's late. It's about that drug you were telling me about, OK?'

Jenny looked up sharply. 'Cardocol?' She sensed Tony nod in the darkness.

'That's the one.'

A fractional pause, then – 'You'd better come in. Mind the step.' She led the way up the path, closed the door behind them and went through into the sitting-room where she turned on the lights and drew the curtains. 'Like a drink? Sherry? It's all I've got, I'm afraid. A speech therapist's salary doesn't run to a fully stocked drinks' cabinet.' Tony shook his head. Jenny gestured to a seat and sat down on the sofa.

'We had a job today,' Tony began quietly, turning his hat round and round in his hands as he spoke. 'Car went over the cliffs at a place called Dalrean, about ten miles or so down the coast.'

Jenny nodded. 'I heard something about that on the car radio. One man was killed, wasn't he?'

'One killed, one critically injured.' Tony took out the Cardocol lunch invitation he had found in Steevenson's wallet, smoothed it out and offered it to Jenny. 'One of the casualties in the car had this in his pocket. After what you were saying about the drug . . . ' He shrugged. 'I thought you might be interested.'

Jenny took the card, glanced at it briefly and then handed it back, puzzled and at a loss to fathom why he should come all this way just to show her that . . .

'Do the names Steevenson and Calvert mean anything to you? Tom Steevenson and Martin Calvert?'

Jenny looked blank. 'No. Should they?'

'They're the names of the two men in the car. They both worked for HPL. Calvert's the bloke who died.'

'I see,' Jenny said slowly, not seeing anything at all. What did any of this have to do with her? There was a brief silence. Then Tony got up and walked restlessly towards the window. He turned.

'I probably shouldn't be telling you this, but both those men – the two in the car – they both carried special passes that had been issued by Internal Security. I found them in their wallets when I had to look for identification.'

That went straight over Jenny's head. 'HPL's internal security? I don't see what—'

'No. Not HPL's internal security. Listen to what I'm telling you, will you?' he ordered roughly. 'That's not what I said.'

Jenny looked baffled. 'You said—'

'I said: Internal Security. I didn't mention HPL.' He paused. 'They were issued by MoD, all right? In London.'

'The Ministry of *Defence*? But that's . . . that's crazy! I thought—'

'Internal Security's part of MI5. It deals with the screening and security clearance of civilians who work in sensitive government areas – GCHQ, the Ministry of Defence – places like that. Windscale's another one.'

Jenny hunched forward. 'HPL's not a . . . a military installation, for goodness' sake! But . . . those two men with the passes. They were working there – you said so yourself, just now!'

Tony nodded. 'That's right, so I did. In somewhere called RD7. *Now* are you getting it?'

'—I'm sorry, Mr Henderson, but your friend Mr Thomas Steevenson died forty minutes ago.' In his room in the Seaview Motel, Ridley's face blossomed into a slow smile. 'Hello, Mr Henderson – are you still there? Hello? I—' Ridley replaced the receiver slowly and sat back against his pillows with both hands linked behind his head as he relived that moment of pleasure as the dark-blue Vauxhall tipped forward and plunged slowly over the edge of the cliffs.

Presently, Ridley lifted the receiver once more. 'I'd like to place a call to London, please,' he said, giving Baxter's private and unlisted number. It was time to report in. And receive further instructions.

'Anyway – time I was going.' Tony pushed to his feet, and Jenny watched from the sofa as he turned towards the door, service cap in hand.

'Tony?'

He turned. 'Yeah?'

'Tell me something – why are you bothering? With all this, I mean? With me?'

'I thought you'd like to know, that's all.'

Jenny shook her head. 'I don't mean just now,' she said softly. 'I mean yesterday, last night in the restaurant. Coming here this evening.'

Tony shrugged, suddenly awkward. 'Does it matter?'

'To me it does, yes.'

Tony paused. 'After the accident out there in the bay? I think you got a rough deal, as it happens – from the papers, the Press, and that – even your own people here in the town could have been a bit more understanding, couldn't they?'

'A bit,' agreed Jenny, smiling slightly. The understatement of the year.

'I suppose too . . . because the boy reminded me of Paul.'

'Paul?'

'My son,' Tony explained briefly. 'They were the same sort of age.'

'I didn't know you had a son.'

'Didn't I tell you?' Tony asked, knowing full well that he hadn't, and surprised, now, that he had.

'You didn't tell me very much at all,' smiled Jenny. 'You just listened, mostly. I want you to know I appreciate it. You've been . . . very kind.'

He gave another awkward little shrug. 'There's not much to tell. Maureen – that's my wife – she packed her bags at the start of the summer. I came home off shift one day to find a note on top of the fridge,' he admitted, the bitterness in his voice unmistakable. 'She took Paul with her, back down to her parents in the south.' He paused. 'She's got custody, of course. I tried to fight it at first, but with my job? No chance. They said I must be joking.' He forced a smile and tried to match it with a lightness he did not feel. 'Still, it could be worse. I'll be able to see him every four months – once the papers have gone through.'

'I'm sorry,' she said inadequately.

'So am I,' agreed Tony. 'So am I. It's what we call an occupational hazard. It comes with the territory.' He looked up. 'So what I suppose I'm saying is: when you ask me why I'm bothering, let's just say I know a little bit about loneliness too, OK?'

' . . . And that ties up all the loose-ends, I think you'll find. As per our agreement,' Ridley concluded quietly into the mouthpiece as he sat back against the pillows in the shadows thrown by the single bedside light. There was silence for a moment as, in faraway London, a dinner-suited Ewan Baxter drew a jotting pad towards the phone. On it were two names. Earlier that same evening he had been talking to somebody else in Gleninver: Maurice Jackman.

'Not . . . not quite all,' he mused. 'I'd like you to stay on a few more days if you wouldn't mind.'

'What?' snapped Ridley. 'You didn't say anything about—'

'Keep your hair on, old man. This would be an additional, of course. That goes without saying.'

'What do you want done?'

'Just a watching brief at this stage, I think,' soothed the man in London. 'Who they're seeing, what they're up to – the usual sort of thing. Our mutual friend seems to think they have the capacity to cause a certain amount of embarrassment, given time.'

'You'd better give me their names then, hadn't you?'

In London, Baxter glanced down at the notepad in front of him. 'The names are: Helen Highcroft and Jennifer Macrae – have you got that?'

'Got it,' Ridley confirmed quietly.

Jenny watched from the window as Tony slid behind the wheel of his Escort and pulled away from the kerb. As the car disappeared down the road, she let the curtains fall back into place and hurried over to the table she used as a desk. Sweeping up pencil and paper, she began jotting down what Tony had told her, hurrying to get the words down before she forgot them. What was it he had said? 'Internal Security is part of MI5 and deals with the screening and security clearance of civilians who work in particularly sensitive government areas'? Yes, that was it! Jenny thought, her mind racing. So what about Helen's husband – had he carried one of those passes too? Had he also been working in a 'particularly sensitive government area'? And what about RD7? What about that?

Jenny hurried to the phone, looked up Helen's number and began dialling. Then, on impulse, she suddenly broke the connection and looked up a different number in the phone book. Finding it took only moments, for the size of the typeface dominated its column.

'Good evening. Highland Pharmaceuticals – may I help you?'

'RD7, please.' There was a moment's silence. Jenny wasn't to know that those who knew of RD7's existence were required to refer to it only by an innocuous-sounding series of extension numbers.

'I'm sorry?'

'Put me through to RD7, please,' tried Jenny, her confidence eggshell-thin as she tried to bluster her way past the telephonist.

'I'm sorry, caller, but we have no department listed by that designation. Who is it you are trying to contact, please? Perhaps I can be of assistance.'

'No. It . . . it doesn't matter.'

'Who is this calling?'

Jenny hung up hurriedly, angry at her own stupidity and worrying now in case the girl recognized her voice from her visit to the firm earlier that same morning. Jenny made herself pause and calm down, gather her thoughts before dialling once more. This time it was Helen's home number.

'Hello?' A girl's voice. Her daughter, perhaps. Jenny racked her brains for a name.

'Hello, Sarah – it's Jenny Macrae, you remember? I was round at your house talking to your mother earlier on.'

'Oh, yes. D'you want her?'

'Is she there?'

'She's just gone out. I'm baby-sitting.'

'Oh, I see. D'you know when she'll be back?'

'Don't know. She didn't say. She's gone round to see Mrs Engel.'

The name rang a bell. 'Would that be Harold Engel's wife, d'you know? The man who owns Highland Pharmaceuticals?'

'That's right,' Sarah agreed readily. 'Dad's boss.'

Helen Highcroft stood under the bright porch light of

Harold Engel's expensive home, and waited nervously for the front door to open. Although there were still lights on downstairs it was now a quarter to eleven, and she wondered belatedly if she should not have waited until morning. But it was Harold, not Joyce she wanted to see and that would have meant getting past the receptionist again at the plant. Now she heard heels tapping over the hall towards her. A chain was thrown off the lock and the door opened.

'Helen! Come in!' greeted Joyce, standing back and holding the door wide. Helen hesitated.

'It's not too late? You're not just off to bed or anything?' she asked, noticing the lines of strain around the eyes for the first time. Or perhaps it was just tiredness. Joyce shook her head and there was another quick, ready smile.

'Of course not. Please – do come in.' Helen stepped across the threshold as Joyce asked: 'Any news? Has he rung?'

Helen shook her head. 'No. Not a word. I—'

'Joyce? Who is it?' called a man's voice. The study door opened and Harold Engel came into the hallway, a glass in his hand.

'It's Helen. Helen Highcroft,' Joyce called over her shoulder.

'So I . . . so I see,' replied Harold Engel, standing there by the study. He raised his glass and took a quick, nervous little swallow. 'What can . . . what can we do for you, hmm?' he asked, with the slightest slur to his voice. He might have been addressing a casual acquaintance rather than the wife of a senior colleague and friend, who had dined at his home on at least two occasions. Helen felt she was looking suddenly at a stranger.

Joyce was deeply embarrassed. 'I'm afraid Harold's been drinking,' she warned.

Helen nodded. Good, she thought; so much the better. 'I tried to see you today. At the office,' she began.

'About Malcolm. Yes, yes, I know,' Harold Engel nodded, waving his free hand about as though to dispel some minor irritation.

'Harold—' interrupted his wife, who had been listening with mounting alarm. 'This is Malcolm we're talking about, for goodness' sake! Malcolm and Helen – our friends!' She turned towards Helen. 'I really am terribly sorry. He—'

'I was . . . tied up,' Engel apologized, with a generous wave of his glass. 'All this . . . all this damn launch business, I'm afraid.'

'I understand,' Helen replied in a low, controlled voice, as Joyce took her arm and steered her firmly towards the drawing-room.

'Come and sit down, Helen. Can I get you something? Tea or coffee? A drink, perhaps?'

Helen shook her head, unwilling to be distracted from the purpose of her visit as she sensed that Malcolm's disappearance, and Harold Engel's sudden, uncharacteristic transformation from cool-headed executive to domestic drunk, might somehow be connected.

'No, really. Would you mind if I asked a few questions now, Harold? About Malcolm?'

'Not . . . not at all,' he managed, following them into an elegant drawing-room with deep armchairs and drawn, heavy velvet curtains. Helen knew the room well. She and Malcolm had been guests at a small dinner party that had withdrawn to this very room less than six weeks earlier. As the two women sat down together on the sofa, Harold Engel helped himself to a fresh drink from the cabinet. There was the chink of glass against bottles carelessly handled, and Joyce forced another tight, apologetic little smile.

'When did you last see Malcolm?' Helen asked. There was the squirt of a soda siphon.

'Well now, let me see. Must have been . . . yes . . . Monday morning.'

Helen had to twist round awkwardly on the sofa to watch his face. His reactions. 'And did he seem . . . normal, then?'

Harold Engel thought for a moment. 'Yes,' he said finally. 'Yes, he did. Far as I could tell, anyway.'

'He didn't seem upset? Moody or distracted about something?'

Engel shrugged. 'No. He seemed perfectly normal.'

'Can you remember what time this was?'

'About ten-thirty, I think. Maybe a little later.'

Helen thought for a moment, studying her hands. Then she looked up. 'Harold – tell me honestly, as a friend. Did Malcolm ever say anything to you about a woman called Monica? I need to know.' The name was etched into Helen's mind like acid into soft metal.

'No. No, he didn't.' Engel paused, remembering he was supposed to have first heard about the photograph from Jackman when he returned upstairs to the boardroom. 'I'm sorry, Helen. About the photograph and everything. Mr Jackman told me, of course. After you left.'

'That's very kind of you,' Helen replied. 'Anyway, I don't believe it.'

Engel leant forward, not sure if he had heard right. 'I'm sorry?'

'I don't believe it,' Helen repeated simply. 'I don't believe Malcolm did have a mistress tucked away somewhere.'

'You . . . don't believe it?' echoed Harold Engel, sobering up fast.

'No.'

'But the . . . the photograph you found in Malcolm's diary. Surely that—'

'Yes, I know about the photograph,' Helen replied calmly. 'But I also know my husband. If he had had a mistress, an . . . an affair – if he was about to go off and live with someone else, then I would have known about it.' She looked defiantly from one face to another, challenging them to contradict her. 'I'd *know*.' She shrugged helplessly. 'We just had that kind of relationship, that's all.'

'What do you think's happened to him, then?' asked Joyce. 'Something must have made him . . . well . . disappear like that.'

If they'd been alone, Helen would have told Joyce

about Jenny Macrae. With Harold there in the room she just shrugged again.

'I don't know. That's what I'm trying to find out. But I certainly don't believe he's just run off with some woman or other half his age.' Turning once more to Harold Engel: 'What did Malcolm actually *do* at HPL? Specifically, I mean?'

The question seemed to take him by surprise. 'That's a bit difficult to define without going into technicalities,' he replied evasively. 'Malcolm was one of half a dozen senior research scientists who—'

'He was working on Cardocol, wasn't he?' Helen asked, conscious of Joyce sitting tensely at her side.

Engel seemed to hesitate. 'Well, yes. Indirectly. He . . . he was involved in research. Much of his work was very secret, naturally.'

'Where did he work?' Helen asked innocently.

'I'm sorry?'

'Where did he work? Where was Malcolm's office?'

Harold Engel relaxed. 'Oh, I see. I'm sorry. In the administration building.'

'Was that where you last saw him?'

'That's right. He was just coming out of his office, and we travelled down in the lift together.'

'You travelled down together in the lift?' asked Helen quietly, as casually as she dared.

'Yes, that's right.' He paused. 'Why? What's the matter?'

'I'm not sure,' Helen replied slowly. 'It's just that when Mr Jackman showed me Malcolm's office . . . it was on the ground floor.'

Lights were still burning in a downstairs office at the *Gleninver Times*. Hamish Owen was in the morgue, leafing through large, leather-bound, dust-covered volumes of back copies. Nearby, Katie, his petite, dark-haired girlfriend of a few precarious weeks, sat on a hard wooden stool and waited impatiently for him to finish. Nineteen, a trainee hairdresser more into discos, fashion and fantasy than newspapers and facts, she looked at her watch, sighed pointedly, and wrapped a thin shawl tighter around bare, angular shoulders. This wasn't her idea of a night out. The place gave you the creeps, anyway, what with all those musty old newspapers. She shivered.

'You said we were going to the cinema,' she accused. Mum thought this one was better, different from all the others. Just because he'd gone to university. But Katie was already having second thoughts. If this was different, you could keep it.

'I know. I'm sorry,' Hamish said automatically, without looking up as he turned another page. Week by week he was working his way through the year *before* Highland Pharmaceuticals arrived in Gleninver. Beside him was the bound volume of the following year, open at the week when the company first brought new hope to the valley with the creation of three thousand new jobs. The news of the company's arrival filled the front page, and had inspired one of Harris' better headlines: HIGHLAND TONIC FOR GLENINVER! But Hamish wasn't after fancy headlines. He was looking for background; digging into the past.

'Well, how much longer, then?' The pubs would be shut too if they left it much longer.

'Nearly there. Just a few more minutes.'

'You said that half an hour ago.'

'I . . . I know. Just a couple more minutes.'

A quarter of an hour later, Hamish found what he was looking for: a brief background piece on the man heading the company that was coming to Gleninver. Hamish made notes and then hurried upstairs, with Katie following plaintively in his wake. A flick through Willing's *Press Guide* and he was dialling a number in faraway Surrey as he called up the local weekly newspaper in Leatherhead.

For Leatherhead, he had discovered, took in a place called Bookham. And Bookham, according to the files, had once been home to a company called Engel Laboratories.

By the time he had finished talking to Surrey, it wasn't just the cinema that had closed. The pubs had too.

CHAPTER EIGHTEEN

The insistent shrill ringing of the telephone downstairs hauled Tony from the depths of deep sleep. As some concession to filling in yesterday's duty schedule, Tony had been promised he would be left alone. Now he swung his legs to the floor, padded downstairs to the hall and reached drowsily for the phone, confident that this time, at least, it wouldn't be work. He should have known better.

'Tony? John Murdoch. Sorry to haul you out of your pit.' John Murdoch, another winchie on SAR Flight. Tony squinted at his watch. Eight o'clock. Eight-oh-sodding clock. He groaned.

'You're a bloody liar, John-boy,' he retorted. 'Where were you yesterday when they needed you?' He could have done without the cliff job.

'I was off, mate, wasn't I?' Murdoch said cheerfully. 'Manchester.'

'So was I,' accused Tony. 'Until Winston hauled me in.'

'Shouldn't answer the phone then, should you? Take my advice – the moment they sign you off, take the bloody thing off the hook and leave it there.'

Tony nodded, still half asleep, but he knew he never would. He just wasn't made that way.

'So – what's up?'

'Boss wants you in here right away.'

'What? I'm off duty, for Chrissake! Get him to look at the flying roster, will you, John? Tell him to take a look at my hours!'

'I'm not talking about flying, chum. There's a couple of blokes from S.5 who'd like a word with you.'

'S.5? What the hell do they want from me?' S.5 was a division of Military Security.

'Don't ask me, mate, I haven't a clue. I'm just passing the message, OK? Only I wouldn't keep 'em waiting too long, if I were you. They look a mean couple of bastards to me.'

John Murdoch was right. They were a mean couple of bastards. Warrant Officer Metcalf and Sergeant Eason were waiting for Tony in the Flight Commander's office opposite the crewroom – two lean, hard-looking men in their late thirties in civilian suits with sharp creases, highly polished shoes, and calm, watchful eyes that missed nothing. Tony's Commanding Officer, Flight Lieutenant Churchill, was waiting for him too, standing with his back to the room, looking out across the airfield with his arms folded as Warrant Officer Metcalf sat at his desk with Eason at his right. Tony could sense the tension, the mutual dislike, between those who flew and those who investigated service betrayal and breaches of national security, the moment he stepped into the office. S.5 was universally detested throughout the Royal Air Force, a fact that bothered Metcalf, Eason and their colleagues not at all. Cynical and case-hardened to a man, they would have been instantly suspicious if they had encountered friendship or an easy-going smile. Now Tony closed the door firmly behind him and turned, his hat under his arm. 'I'm Lockhart,' he admitted warily.

Which would have been fine – except that Metcalf didn't want to play it like that at all. He watched silently as Tony looked towards Flight Lieutenant Churchill, his own flight commander, waiting for a lead. Churchill shrugged and gestured him forward to the desk. Warrant Officer Metcalf let him stand there for a moment like some errant schoolboy while he consulted some papers in a file in front of him. Then he looked up.

'You are Anthony Peter Lockhart, service number 2542844?'

'That's right, yes.'

'And you are currently serving as a Winchman Flight Sergeant with "A" Flight, 29 Squadron, engaged on Search and Rescue duties stationed at RAF Glenhaddon?'

Tony looked around him carefully. 'Unless they've moved everything around overnight without telling me, yeah.'

Warrant Officer Metcalf looked up slowly. 'Oh. I see. A funnyman. And it's "Yes, *sir*",' he corrected, deadpan. Inwardly, Tony groaned. So that was the kind of bastard he was dealing with.

'Yes, sir.' Tony took a short step closer. 'I'd like to know who you are too, if it's all the same to you.'

Eason and Metcalf exchanged brief, world-weary glances and slid their formal warrants on to the desk for a moment before slipping them back into their pockets. They were well-used to smart-arses like Flight Sergeant Lockhart, too.

'Right, let's stop this pissing about, shall we, Flight Sergeant? You were on a job yesterday afternoon, yes? Flight Lieutenant Bourne, Flight Lieutenant Sleaman, and yourself – correct?'

'Correct,' Tony acknowledged.

Warrant Officer Metcalf closed the file in front of him and leaned forward. 'Tell me about it,' he encouraged. 'From the moment you were diverted from routine training.'

Tony glanced across at Churchill, who nodded.

He complied. In brief, sparse sentences, Tony told the two men from S.5 about the walk down the cliff-face on the wire, about the position of the car, and about the two casualties. He made it sound almost routine and certainly devoid of any fear, or courage, or heroism. Eason began to make notes, for by then Tony was referring to the two casualties by name.

'Steevenson and Calvert,' mused Metcalf. 'Not friends of yours, by any chance?'

Tony shook his head. 'Never seen them before in my life.'

'But you knew their names. How did you know their names, Flight Sergeant?'

Tony sighed. 'You've seen my report – or if you haven't, you should have. It's all in there. When I got to the second man – Steevenson – he was trapped in the car. When I'd got him outside and sorted him out, I went through his pockets for identification – that's standard procedure, by the way, just in case you got the idea I was looking for five-pound notes. I found a pass in his wallet with his name on it. Calvert had one too, OK? Satisfied?'

Metcalf didn't even blink. He was used to being spoken to like this. In his line of work there was often a pay-off. Aggression and rudeness were very often hiding guilt.

'What sort of pass?' he asked quietly.

'A security pass, issued by the Ministry of Defence.'

'Go on.'

'Authorizing the holder to enter somewhere called RD7 at Highland Pharmaceuticals. That's a big local drug firm in Gleninver, six miles or so down the coast.'

'So we understand,' Metcalf nodded dryly. 'Go on.'

Tony shrugged. 'That's it. Then the stretcher came down and up we all went – Calvert in a body-bag, Steevenson in the cradle. Look, what is all this? You've got all that information already. If you—'

'—What happened to those passes, Flight Sergeant? The ones issued by the Ministry in London?'

'They went back in the wallets. I assume the police and hospital staff took care of them when they were looking for personal effects.'

Metcalf studied Tony in silence for several seconds, then reached down to a briefcase propped against the leg of the desk, took out a cellophane envelope and laid it on the desk. 'Are these the passes you saw?'

Tony studied them briefly. 'That's them.'

The passes disappeared back into the briefcase and the locks snapped shut. Warrant Officer Metcalf looked up. 'You told a PC Ayres about the passes.' It wasn't even a question.

Tony nodded. 'Yes. He was the Incident Officer on the cliff-top.'

'Who else have you told?' Instinctively, without pausing to ask himself why, Tony decided to lie, to shield

Jenny from this cold, clinical man from Military Intelligence. She had enough problems.

'No one.'

'You're sure?'

Tony stared him straight in the eyes. 'Yes. Sir.'

'What about your wife?' He glanced down at the file. 'Maureen?'

Bastard. 'No, sir. We're separated.'

'Ah, yes. Yes, of course.' Metcalf closed the file. 'I will remind you, Flight Sergeant, that as a serving non-commissioned officer in Her Majesty's Royal Air Force, you have signed the Official Secrets Act, and that any unauthorized disclosure which may be considered a breach of national security will—'

'Look – what the hell's going on?' Tony exploded. 'All I did was follow SOPs, all right? What's all this "national security" crap?'

Metcalf looked up with calm, cold eyes. 'Forget what you saw down there on those cliffs, Flight Sergeant, is that clear? Forget about Steevenson, forget about Calvert, and forget about those passes, understand? They do not exist. They have never existed.'

Jenny glanced round impatiently at the closed door marked 'Pathology', and then smiled what she hoped was a brisk, confident, I-have-every-right-to-be-here sort of smile at the white-coated medical technician who came hurrying towards her, his heels clipping importantly on the marble-flagged corridor, a sheaf of papers thrust under one arm. He swept past with an answering smile, and Jenny breathed a sigh of relief. Come on, come on . . . What's keeping you, Annie? she muttered under her breath, as another laboratory assistant came down the corridor towards her, and Jenny swung away to study the noticeboard. It was now shortly after ten o'clock, and Jenny was waiting for an old classmate who worked here at the Alanby Annexe of Gleninver hospital, where District Pathologist Dr Cousins carried out his post mortems. If Procurator-fiscal Smithson's sense of professional propriety prevented him from discussing the accident before the Fatal Accident Inquiry, no such scruples stopped Jenny from begging a favour from a distant friend. At last the door at the end of the corridor swung open, and Annie Barnard came hurrying towards her, a pale folder held down at her side. As though to dissociate herself from what she was about to do, Jenny saw that Dr Cousins' assistant had shed her white lab coat.

'Did you get it?' Jenny whispered eagerly, her voice echoing along the empty corridor.

Annie made a furious gesture of silence and pressed a finger to her lips. 'Sssh!' she hissed. 'You'll get me shot, you will.' She took Jenny's arm and hurried her towards the exit. 'Where are you parked? We can talk in the car.'

Jenny pointed. 'Over there.' They walked quickly out into the sunshine, down the ramp and across the tarmac car park away from the hospital. They got into the Citroën. As the front passenger door slammed shut, Jenny turned impatiently towards her friend. 'Can I see it?' she asked.

Annie hesitated, the file gripped tightly in her hand. 'I can only stay a moment.' She looked up. 'Not a word to anyone, promise me, Jenny. If Cousins ever got to hear I'd been discussing one of his precious post mortems with an outsider . . . ' She closed her eyes and shuddered. 'Well, let's just say I'd be out on my ear, OK?'

'Not a word, I promise,' Jenny pledged.

Annie nodded, glanced round guiltily, and then flicked open the folder. 'What d'you want to know?'

'Have they set a date for the FAI?'

Annie nodded. 'Next Wednesday morning.'

'And the . . . the autopsies? The post mortems?'

'Cousins did them yesterday afternoon.'

'Both of them?' Annie nodded and laid a hand briefly upon the file on her lap. 'Could I see them? Please?'

Annie looked up, saw the pain already there in Jenny's eyes, and shook her head. 'Better if you didn't. Really. It's . . . well, it's a bit clinical, you know? It's all right if you don't know the people. Otherwise it's . . . well . . . it's just better if you don't read it, OK? If you've got any questions, fire away – but please, be as quick as you can, all right? If

Cousins starts wondering where I've got to . . . '

Jenny nodded. After Tony's visit to her flat the previous evening, there was only one question that really mattered. She asked it.

'How did Robbie Roberts die?'

'The old man? He drowned,' Annie replied simply.

Jenny waited for something more. Nothing came. 'That's . . . that's all?' she asked. 'He just drowned?'

Annie shrugged. 'He inhaled saltwater. Death was consistent with drowning, yes.'

'But . . . what about the burns? The burns around the face and neck? I was talking to the helicopter winchman who said—'

'Yes, there were burns too. There was also some contused bruising near the left temple, but that wasn't what killed him. He drowned.'

'You're sure about that?' pressed Jenny earnestly.

Annie looked up, puzzled. 'Yes, we're sure about that. Why?'

'Would you . . . I mean . . . could you tell me why you're so sure?'

Annie looked at her doubtfully. 'D'you really want to know?'

Jenny swallowed. 'I don't *want* to know, I *need* to know. Please. It might be important.'

Annie sighed and glanced down at the file. 'We removed and examined his internal organs, all right?' she explained gently. 'Having done that, we found that the lungs weighed twice as much as normal. They were waterlogged. There was a fine froth in the trachea and the bronchi – that's the windpipe and the air passages inside the lungs – caused by the seawater washing away the lung lining. If you want the technical name for it, death was caused by asphyxia. Not enough oxygen was getting into the body.'

'But the burns. The burns and the bruising. Surely they—'

'They looked pretty bad, certainly, but, like I said, they didn't kill him.'

'You're sure?'

'Definitely. One hundred per cent certain.'

'How do'you think he got the burns?'

Annie shrugged. 'That's not for me to say, is it?' She flicked over several closely typed pages.

'But you can guess, surely?'

'Off the record? I'd say that when the boat caught fire, the old man slipped trying to put out the flames. He banged his head as he fell over, became unconscious, and lay in the bottom of the boat while it burned around him. Then, as the boat sank under him, he drowned.'

'And . . . and Jamie? What about the little boy?' Jenny had been steeling herself to ask that, yet dreading the answer more than anything else in the world. But she had to know.

'He drowned too.'

'That's all?'

'That's all,' Annie softly reassured. 'No burns, no disfigurement – nothing. He just drowned, I promise.'

Jenny nodded. 'Thank you,' she managed. 'Thank you very much. I'm . . . I'm sorry I had to ask you to do all this.'

Annie closed the file and reached out for the door catch. 'That's all right. Only please, just remember. I haven't told you a thing. When it comes out at the FAI, you're hearing it for the first time – agreed?'

Jenny nodded. 'Oh – Annie?'

She turned. 'Yes?'

'If . . . just suppose Robbie's collapse had been caused by a . . . well . . . by something else. Would you have found it?'

Annie frowned. 'What d'you mean?'

'Well, say it had been caused by a . . . a drug of some kind. Would that have shown up? On the post mortem?'

'The hospital labs here carry out simple blood tests for aspirin, barbiturate and carbon-monoxide poisoning, yes.'

'But what about other drugs – heart drugs, for example?' Jenny persisted, as Annie's puzzlement deepened.

'I'm not sure I know what you're getting at. If Dr Cousins feels there's a need for that sort of detailed analysis, then we can send organs and blood samples off to the Home

Office labs in Chepstow for toxicology tests, yes.'

'But that's not usual?'

Annie shook her head. 'No, it's not. There just isn't the time – or the money. It's an expensive process. We've only done that . . . oh . . . once? Twice? Twice in the last five years that I'm aware of.'

'And it wasn't done for Robbie Roberts?'

'Mr Roberts? No, why should it be? We already know how he died. There's no mystery. I told you: death was consistent with drowning.'

By mid-morning, the rolling, well-kept grounds in front of Highland Pharmaceuticals' administrative buildings were a hive of activity. Brawny, shirtsleeved contractors wrestled to erect huge marquees, gardeners watched sourly as workmen hammered tent-pegs into clipped green lawns, and all was noise and apparent confusion as they raced to have everything ready for the influx of guests, doctors and reporters the next day. If time was against them, then the weather, at least, was on their side: bright blue skies with a few fluffy clouds and a gentle south-westerly wind.

Buttonhole ablaze with colour, every silver-flecked hair carefully in place, Jonathan Tomalin hurried importantly across the concrete landing circle, past the company helicopter that was Engel's pride and joy, and down the wine-red carpet towards the main marquee, clipboard in hand. To the sweating workmen hauling on their ropes, and to the HPL management team charged with the responsibility of bringing every last detail of the Cardocol launch to a triumphant climax at exactly the right moment, this sudden proliferation of strange faces, turning vans, and endless deliveries of everything from extra chairs and microphones to carnations and ice cream, was something to be worked through, to be endured and co-ordinated with gritted teeth. Jonathan Tomalin, however, was a man in his element. Now he consulted his clipboard, stepped carefully over another taut guy-rope, and tapped Jackman gently on the sleeve. Jackman had been watching the men struggle with a tangle of canvas and ropes. His thoughts, however, had been elsewhere. Less than an hour earlier, he had been told someone had called the company switchboard late the previous evening and asked to be put through to RD7. No name, but the caller had been a woman. Jackman swung round.

'Ah, there you are, Mr Jackman! It's all coming along just splendidly, don't you think? Splendidly!' enthused Jonathan Tomalin with a happy smile, as he swept a ringed hand around the chaotic scene.

'Splendidly,' Jackman agreed, with rather less enthusiasm. 'Were you looking for me?'

'Ah, well, yes, I was really. It's about the champagne, I'm afraid – the Bollinger. Tiresome really, but those catering johnnies swear . . . oh, one moment . . . ' As he turned, Tomalin caught sight of Harold Engel moving across the lawns towards them. Self-centred to a fault, Tomalin assumed it was him Engel was now coming to see. His busy mind filled with a thousand interlocking administrative details, he didn't notice that Engel was looking not at him but at Maurice Jackman. Nor, at first, did he register the look on Engel's face.

'Good morning, Mr Chairman,' Tomalin greeted effusively, planting himself in Engel's path and turning on that smile. 'I wonder if I might have a few moments? It's about the Bollinger.'

Engel frowned. 'The Bollinger? Later, Mr Tomalin, if you don't mind.' He made to move on.

'Those catering people swear the company has only ordered a dozen crates, Mr Chairman,' Tomalin rattled on, with scarcely a pause for breath. 'A dozen, I ask you – that's less than a hundred and fifty bottles between four hundred people! Quite, quite ridiculous, in my opinion! If each guest has three glasses – and if this weather continues they're *bound* to – we're going to need fifteen crates. Fifteen at the very least!' He sighed theatrically. 'If there's one thing that makes or mars an important occasion like this, Mr Chairman, it's the supply of champagne. Especially where the media are concerned. I remember when I had to organize the—'

'Fifteen crates, Mr Tomalin,' Engel interrupted quietly, when he could bear it no longer. 'Whatever you consider appropriate. It really doesn't matter.'

Tomalin looked nonplussed. 'Oh. But it does matter, Mr Chairman. It matters very much indeed. I would be doing less than my duty if—'

'Mr Tomalin, the catering arrangements for tomorrow's reception are *your* responsibility – that's what we're paying you for. If you can't sort out a simple matter like how many bottles of champagne we're going to need without calling a board meeting, I'll find someone else who can. Do I make myself clear?'

Jonathan Tomalin paled. Nearby, workmen looked up, grinned, and then bent over their work.

'Er . . . yes. Yes, of course. I only meant . . . thank . . . thank you. Fifteen crates it is.' Tomalin hurried away into the refuge of the marquee, as Engel turned and caught Jackman's eye.

'A word,' he said briefly, turning on his heel and walking away towards the trees where they could talk freely without being overheard. As Jackman came up beside him – 'I had a visitor last night. At my home.' They walked slowly along the edge of the flowerbeds, heads bowed.

'Anyone I need to know about?' Jackman asked casually.

Engel stopped and faced him, eyes glittering with anger. 'Yes, I think so.' He paused. 'Helen Highcroft. Ring a bell?' If he was expecting a gasp of surprise, Engel was disappointed.

'Oh? What did she want?' asked Jackman, his face a mask.

'What the hell d'you think she wanted?' Engel snapped. 'She wanted news about her husband.'

'What did you tell her?'

'That's the whole point: I didn't have to *tell* her a damn thing! She told me!'

'What d'you mean?' Jackman demanded shortly.

'Did you really think you'd be able to pull the wool over her eyes indefinitely with that switched offices idea of yours? You must have been out of your mind – the woman's not a complete fool, you know. Didn't it occur to you that—'

'Tell me what she said.'

'She asked me where I last saw Malcolm. Not when. *Where*.'

'And?'

'I told her the last time I saw her husband he was coming out of his office.'

'Go on.'

'She asked where his office was. I lied. I told her it was in the administration building.' He jerked a thumb over his shoulder, and Jackman nodded.

'Then I don't see any problem.'

'Don't you?' Engel laughed bitterly. 'I also told her we went down in the lift together. From his office.'

Jackman's head snapped up. 'God! You—'

'Don't blame me, Jackman! How the hell was I supposed to know you'd shown her an empty office on the ground floor? I can't read your bloody mind, can I?'

Jackman removed his spectacles and began polishing them carefully with a folded handkerchief as he paused before replying. 'No,' he said quietly. 'No, you can't.' For he had been thinking not about Helen Highcroft, but about someone else.

Ridley.

'But it wasn't his office, don't you understand?' Helen Highcroft repeated dully. 'It wasn't. It had been made to *look* as though it was, with his diary and everything, but it wasn't.'

'I see. You'd been there before, had you, madam?' asked Police Sergeant McInnes patiently, looking up from his notes. She'd had a good night's rest, he reckoned, and some of the pain and exhaustion had left her face, but she still looked tense and coiled, ready to crack into a thousand pieces at the slightest provocation. They were sitting opposite one another across a bare brown table in the bare, brown little interview room with frosted glass windows across the hall from the charge room in Gleninver police station.

Helen shook her head reluctantly. 'No. I hadn't been there before.'

Sergeant McInnes made a careful note on his sheet of ruled foolscap paper and leaned forward. 'Then if you'll forgive the impertinence, Mrs Highcroft,' he said, not unkindly, 'how do you know it wasn't his office? Maybe he'd been moved. Transferred.'

'I just know, that's . . . that's all,' Helen replied helplessly. 'It didn't . . . it just didn't *feel* like his office.' Helen watched that go down on the record with a sick, helpless feeling of despair in the pit of her stomach. God, how lame, how slender it all sounded! Then she remembered the photograph. 'Look – look at this.' She fumbled in her handbag, took out the Christmas party snapshot she had found pushed into the back of the family photograph album, and slid it across the table towards the policeman. Sergeant McInnes examined the photograph dutifully, tapped a finger against the central figure seated behind the desk, and looked up.

'That's the Professor, I take it?'

'That's him, yes – the one in the middle.' She leaned over, arm outstretched. 'And there – see the blinds?'

'The blinds?'

Helen nodded eagerly. 'The blinds, yes. The office Mr Jackman took me to had curtains. I checked.'

There was silence for a moment, then Sergeant McInnes sighed. 'Mrs Highcroft – just because a company the size of HPL decides to change the interior decorations of one of its offices, doesn't automatically mean—'

'But it's there, can't you see?' insisted Helen, with a note of desperation creeping into her voice. 'That *proves* it's not the same office!'

Sergeant McInnes shook his head. 'I have to tell you, Mrs Highcroft, that it proves no such thing. Look – I sympathize with what you're going through, truly I do. God knows, in your position I'd be clutching at straws myself.'

'I am not clutching at straws – something's happened to

my husband! What have I got to do to make you see that?'

'Mrs Highcroft: your husband's vehicle was found parked at the station. The keys—'

'Somebody . . . somebody else must have parked it there! To . . . to make it *look* as though he'd left, as though he'd taken the train! Look – Sergeant. The morning he disappeared, the very same morning, my husband booked that car in for a major service *the next day*. I know that for a fact. I've got witnesses if you want them. Now: would he really have gone to all that trouble if he'd known he was going to dump the car at the station less than twelve hours later? Would he?'

'Mrs Highcroft, like I said. I appreciate what you're going through, but—'

'You don't believe me, do you?' she interrupted. 'You don't believe any of it. You think I'm making it all up – I can see it in your face. You think I'm just some menopausal, middle-aged housewife who's been deserted by her husband, don't you? Go on – admit it.'

'I'm thinking no such thing, Mrs Highcroft,' Sergeant McInnes replied wearily. 'And I will remind you that whatever my failings may happen to be, I'm still sitting here listening to what you tell me and trying to help you with your difficulty.' Which was true.

'I'm sorry, Sergeant,' Helen apologized, and meaning it. 'You're quite right. That was uncalled for. You've been very patient, thank you.' She clasped her hands together tightly and leant forward across the table, forcing herself to appear rational. Normal. 'All right, then. What about Harold Engel? Will you at least send someone to see him? Please.'

'About the office, you mean?' Sergeant McInnes shook his head. 'I don't see how I can do anything about that – they'd think I was cracked if I went up there demanding a formal police investigation just because someone decided to change the office curtains for blinds. And as for this . . . this other business, this conversation you claim you had with Mr Engel last night in his home—'

'You think he just made an innocent mistake, is that it?'

Sergeant McInnes looked up. 'It's not unheard of, you know, Mrs Highcroft. Such things do happen. Tell me – what did he say? When you challenged him? About this business of the lift and your husband's office being on the first floor?'

'He backtracked immediately, like I said. As soon as I told him that Mr Jackman had taken me to a ground-floor office, he pretended to remember that it hadn't been Malcolm's office after all that he'd been coming out of, but somebody else's. He tried to put the confusion down to the fact that he'd had a few drinks and that he was tired because of all this Cardocol business – but he was lying, Sergeant, I know he was. You could see it in his eyes.'

Sergeant McInnes nodded soberly. The nod of a man who has heard it all before. 'What you mean is,' he corrected quietly, 'you *think* he was lying. There's a world of difference, you know. Especially in a court of law.'

'All right. I *think* he was lying.'

Sergeant McInnes leant back in his chair and studied Mrs Highcroft in silence for a long moment. 'Just suppose – just suppose, mind – that I did go and see him. What's he going to say to me, eh?'

Helen shrugged. 'I've no idea. But at least you'd be able to form an opinion, judge for yourself.'

The policeman blew out his cheeks. 'You're a one for the timing, Mrs Highcroft, I'll say that much for you. With all that launch business going on tomorrow? I'd just be wasting my time. Perhaps, in a few days, after all the fuss has died down . . . '

Helen took the hint. 'Thank you for seeing me, Sergeant. I think I've wasted enough of your time for one morning, don't you?' She rose to her feet, gathered up her handbag and made for the door. Sergeant McInnes stood up too.

'I'm sorry I couldn't be of more help, Mrs Highcroft.'

Helen looked back from the doorway. 'So am I, Sergeant. So am I.'

The door closed softly behind her. Sergeant McInnes listened as her footsteps receded and the swing doors creaked shut behind her, then shook his head slowly and let out his breath in a long-suffering sigh. Crumpling the notes into a ball, he tossed them into the wastepaper basket and rose wearily to his feet.

It was a morning for screwing up bits of paper and throwing them into wastepaper baskets.

Gleninver Times Editor, Bob Harris, was on the phone to Photographic, finalizing details of the next day's coverage of the official launch at HPL. 'I don't give a monkey's about the sea-angling competition,' he was saying. 'I want Mike on the job, covering the helipad arrivals by eleven at the latest. Angus should be in the main building by then too, got it? Yes . . . yes, I know. Well, he'll just have to bloody well *unfix* it, won't he?' Harris slammed down the phone with a crash, pushed suddenly to his feet and went through to Editorial.

Hamish Owen was sitting at his desk, making notes from a newspaper spread open in front of him. 'Before I forget, laddie, when you get to Highland Pharmaceuticals in the morning—' Harris broke off, frowning. 'What the hell are you doing with that?'

Hamish looked up. 'It's the *Leatherhead Advertiser*.' He held up the paper so Harris could read the masthead for himself. Harris had spent a working lifetime reading copy upside-down and required very little help. And none at all from Hamish Owen, trainee reporter and university graduate . . .

'I can see that, laddie – I can see that. What's it doing here?'

'Oh. I ordered it.'

'You *ordered* it?'

'That's right, yes,' Hamish admitted, still confident, imagining Harris might yet applaud such initiative. 'They stuck it on the train last night. I was checking back in the files – about HPL. We only reported the fact that HPL was coming to the valley – there was nothing about Engel's previous company down in Surrey. Then I remembered that the paper down there would have covered the closure of Engel Laboratories just as closely as we're going to cover this launch tomorrow, so I gave them a call. They remembered it well – it was a big story at the time, see?' He turned the paper round so Harris could see the headline: ENGEL LABS – SHOCK CLOSURE AS GOVT STEPS IN.

Harris brushed the paper aside and it slid to the floor. 'Who the hell told you to start ordering copy, eh?'

Hamish looked blank. 'Well, I—'

'The only person authorized to order copy on behalf of this newspaper is the Editor, got it, laddie? That's me, understand?' He tapped a finger against his own chest.

'I'm sorry. I just assumed—'

'You just "assumed", did you? And who do you think's going to pay for this ordered copy of yours, eh?'

'I thought petty cash would—'

'Petty cash? Petty cash? Over my dead body, it will!' stormed Harris. 'Suffering Christ – I'll tell you who's going to pay for it, laddie – you are!'

Sitting there silently, taking it, watching the overweight journalist ranting and raving on about something his intellect told him another less bigoted editor would have put right with a few calm words, Hamish felt his patience suddenly run through his fingers. He might be inexperienced, but even *he* could see that the *Gleninver Times* should have carried more about Engel's background, about the mystery man who had suddenly arrived in their midst promising jobs and prosperity – and that the blame for such an omission lay with Harris himself. He pushed back his chair and rose recklessly to his feet, Harris' words, his belligerence, goading him beyond endurance.

'All right – *I'll* pay for the bloody thing! But doesn't it strike you as just a little bit *strange* that the same man who's forced to shut down Engel Laboratories because of certain—' he snatched up his notebook and flicked back a couple of pages – '"unspecified but serious irregularities" should turn up here, in Gleninver, less than three years later, with apparently limitless funding and a product licence issued by the same government bloody department that put out the Press release I just quoted? Doesn't it?'

Hamish demanded scathingly.

It was the first time he had hit back like that, and the outburst took them both by surprise. In the silence that ensued, Harris stepped up menacingly to Hamish's desk and stabbed out a short, blunt finger. 'You ever pull another little stunt like that, laddie,' he said finally, 'and you'll find yourself on the next train back to that university of yours, I bloody well promise you, d'you hear?' Hamish held his gaze defiantly. Then Harris reached down to the floor with a grunt of effort, mashed the scattered pages of the *Leatherhead Advertiser* into a large, untidy ball, and tossed it angrily towards the wastepaper basket. Then he turned on his heel and stormed back to his office, slamming the half-glass door with such force that Hamish expected to be showered with broken glass.

Hamish stared at the closed door for long moments. Then he rose from behind his desk, retrieved the crumpled pages of the *Leatherhead Advertiser* and carefully cut out the feature on the sudden, unexpected collapse of Engel Laboratories.

Jenny was unloading shopping on to the kitchen table, and the sealed orange envelope containing the photographs was at the bottom of her basket. When everything else was stored away, Jenny picked up the packet of prints and went through with them into the sitting-room, holding them carefully in her hands as though they were fragile, precious. To Jenny, at that moment, they were more than that: they were unique, irreplaceable. They were her one link with the past. With Danny – and with the child whose trust she believed she had betrayed.

She sat down slowly by the window, the little wallet of photographs on the bare table in front of her. She opened the wallet, tipped out the photographs, and spread them out quickly, face-up, in front of her, as though she was dealing out cards. Jenny sat back and paused to push the hair away from her temples, then leant forward and studied each photograph in turn, bracing herself for the pain of guilt and recollection.

The first three photographs had been taken in her father's vegetable garden – amateur, slightly fuzzy close-ups of rhubarb, cauliflowers and sweetpeas, each with a proud, grey-haired old man crouching down beside the vegetables in braces and frayed carpet-slippers.

The next one was of Pam, sitting smiling, bare-legged, on the steps outside the clinic. It had been taken one lunchtime, Jenny remembered, when they had eaten their sandwiches outside together in the first of the summer sunshine.

Then the pain began.

The next one was of Danny, clowning around in the stern of a dinghy they had hired, grinning inanely into the camera with Jenny's straw hat pushed forward over his eyes. Jenny closed hers for a moment, and remembered the day so clearly she could almost smell the salt-stained paintwork of the little dinghy, almost feel the sun burning her shoulders, it was all so close, so poignant.

There were three more photographs of Danny, a couple of general views taken in the hills, and then one or two of her, all taken that same sunny weekend. With not a cloud on the horizon.

The last photograph was of Jamie Ennis.

He was sitting on the breakwater at Ardtornish harbour on the last day of his life, bare feet dangling over the edge as he twisted round with that lopsided grin of his and looked up into the camera. Jenny studied that photograph for long, precariously balanced moments, and then the tears began to slide down her cheeks. She tried to stop them at first, tried to stem the pain that flowed out of her at the sight of a child so full of life, so . . . so *happy*, but it was no use. Her sobs became louder until finally Jenny buried her face in her hands, and the sound of her wrenching tears filled the empty, silent flat as she remembered now the little things: the way she and Jamie had held hands as they skipped happily across the road to buy ice creams; the vee of the bow-wave as Robbie's boat chugged innocently out across the bay with Jamie standing proudly in the bows, Robbie's outsized binoculars slung around his neck; the light in

Jamie's eyes, the magical difference, the sheer joy in his face at being away from that mother of his and off on an adventure of his very own. Of being young and curious and free of responsibility. Of simply being alive to feel the sun on his back on a warm, sunny day.

Jenny wept for him. She wept for Robbie and Mrs Roberts and for Mr and Mrs Ennis. She wept for Danny and for what might have been. She wept for them all.

But even pain ends. Or at least loses the sharp, cutting edge of intensity. At length, Jenny pushed the photographs into a pile and slid them back into their orange wallet – all except the picture of Jamie, which she took through into her kitchen and pinned carefully on to her noticeboard beside the reminders and the shopping lists, the Snoopy cartoons and the colourful postcards from friends on holiday.

When she stood back from her noticeboard, Jenny was no longer crying. The picture of Jamie was there as a reminder, as a private pledge to a victim, to a small boy no longer able to fight for himself. Presently, standing there alone in the silence of her narrow kitchen, Jenny tried to marshal her thoughts.

She had called Danny about Cardocol because she wanted to understand about drugs, to rule out any possible connection between the fire, Robbie's death, and the packets of Cardocol pills she had found in both Mrs Proctor's bedroom and on Robbie Roberts' kitchen table. She had persuaded Annie Barnard, the pathologist's assistant up at Gleninver hospital, to disclose privileged information about Robbie's post mortem because she needed to be told that such a connection between the fire, the deaths at sea, and the drug had been examined and ruled out by detailed, unequivocal forensic examination. Yet she had been told no such thing, and the absence of such reassurance had served only to add fuel to her suspicion.

Jenny walked slowly back into the sitting-room, remembering the look on Dr Erskine's face when she asked him about Cardocol, and heard again Tony Lockhart's warning about something called RD7 at Highland Pharmaceuticals, heard again the fears and suspicions of her new friend and ally Helen Highcroft as she searched for something that might explain her husband's sudden disappearance. No, the questions weren't over yet – and nor were her obligations. It was now time to put weight upon the next link in the chain of enquiry, of suspicion.

Jenny picked up her notebook, pulled the phone towards her and dialled Directory Enquiries.

'Town please.'

'London, please. Central London,' Jenny answered in a firm voice.

'And the name?'

'The Committee on the Safety of Medicines.'

Helen Highcroft was upstairs making the children's beds, with the sounds of Radio Two washing through from the bedside radio next door. The children were out again with friends, and it occurred to her dimly that she had hardly seen them these last few days as one well-meaning friend after another stepped in unobtrusively to help lighten her load. But if the children had gone, then so too had the noise and laughter she had taken for granted, leaving in their place an oppressive silence that seemed to crowd closer with every passing hour. She found now, as she performed the mechanical, almost mindless act of smoothing down the sheets and tucking in the blankets, that she needed the radio to blot out that silence, to push away the ugly thoughts and fill the brooding emptiness that told her Malcolm was never coming home.

The last bed was finished. Throwing a counterpane over the eiderdown, Helen straightened up, went through into her own bedroom and turned off the radio. There it was again, that silence, whispering to her in the empty house as she recalled what Sergeant McInnes had told her, and remembered again that look of stoic disbelief as she poured out her story. She was alone, that was the hardest thing. To be alone with no one to turn to.

But not quite alone, she remembered, thinking suddenly of Jenny – Jenny Macrae. If Sergeant McInnes couldn't help, Jenny at least could understand. Could listen. Yes, that was it: she'd go and see her. Right now. At least the drive would get her out of the house . . .

Helen hurried downstairs, swept up her car keys and handbag, scrawled a note for the children and slammed the front door behind her.

Ridley watched her leave.

He watched her slam the front door, cross the gravel drive, enter the garage and emerge a moment later behind the wheel of the Volvo. He made a note of the registration number together with the time of departure for, among much else, Ridley was a methodical, painstaking professional. Slipping his notebook into an inside pocket, he waited until the Volvo had swung into the main road at the bottom of the hill and then pulled away from the kerb and set off quietly in pursuit. Nobody noticed the hired Ford Capri tuck itself neatly into the traffic and follow the Volvo all the way across town until it braked to a halt outside Jenny's ground-floor flat in Elgin Terrace.

But then, nobody was supposed to.

CHAPTER NINETEEN

Jenny was still on the phone to the Committee on the Safety of Medicines in London. 'Yes, I can see that,' she was saying, the phone wedged against her shoulder as she tried to listen, make notes, and think of intelligent questions all at the same time. 'But you mean to tell me no one actually *checks* the submissions made to the Committee? No one bothers to go through them line by line?'

The man on the other end of the phone sighed impatiently. Ever since Opren they'd been getting a lot of calls like this.

'Of course we *bother*, Miss Macrae. Each submission is examined most carefully. But we're hardly in a position to test each and every application individually, there simply aren't the facilities. It's a question of time. Of money.'

'But you're the people who issue the licences! We're . . . we're talking here about drugs that affect people's lives!' protested Jenny.

'Do you have any idea just how many submissions the Committee receives each year, Miss Macrae?'

'How many?'

'Between six and seven hundred.'

'Each year?' Jenny echoed incredulously.

'Each year. Not only do we have to process an increasing number of product licence applications,' the clerk continued remorselessly, 'but we also have a statutory obligation to monitor the safety of some sixteen *thousand* products already on the market.' He paused. 'I tell you this, Miss Macrae, not to sound like some bleeding heart but to give you some idea of *scale*.'

Just then the doorbell rang. Jenny glanced over her shoulder. 'Could you hold on one second?'

'Certainly.'

Jenny put down the phone and hurried down the hall, conscious of peak time and the cost of a daytime telephone call to London. She pulled the door open cautiously, and then smiled with relief when she saw who it was. 'Oh, Helen. Hello – come along in.'

'I hope you don't mind my popping round. Only I—'

'Not at all. I'm on the phone, OK? Won't be a moment. Come through.' Jenny hurried back up the hall as Helen closed the door behind her. 'I'm on to the Committee on the Safety of Medicines,' Jenny threw back over her shoulder. 'About Cardocol.' She picked up the phone again. 'Hello? Are you still there?'

'Yes, I'm still here.' Jenny beckoned Helen to a chair next to her.

'You . . . you were saying it was impossible to inspect every application individually, is that right?'

'To *test* each and every individual application would be impossible, yes. But detailed testing is seldom necessary, Miss Macrae. Many applications are merely minor chemical variations upon a successful drug that has already passed the test of time.'

'Nevertheless, what you're saying is that you have to rely heavily upon the integrity of the drug firms themselves? Upon what they choose to tell you?' She sensed him bristle at that.

'There has to be a certain measure of trust, of course. But the very fact that a drug is being presented for licence is often its own best safeguard.'

Jenny tried to work that out. 'I'm sorry, I don't follow.'

Another sigh. 'An application for licensing only reaches us after a great deal of time and money has been spent on research – in the case of one of the larger companies about to launch a major new product, we could be talking here about forty million pounds, and perhaps ten years' research and development. After all, a flawed product is in no one's interest. Word would soon get back if a new drug started piling up yellow cards.'

'Yellow cards?'

'Miss Macrae, really. I—'

'Please. I'm sorry to be so dense.'

'The final test of any drug intended for human use is Man himself, agreed? It's obvious: you can run your clinical trials on relatively small numbers of human volunteers, you can experiment on animals until you're blue in the face – but the only way you will ever really know if a drug is one hundred per cent safe with, say, forty thousand patients—'

'—Is to give it to forty thousand patients and see what happens?' Jenny finished for him. There was a brief silence.

'I wouldn't have put it quite as crudely as that, Miss Macrae, but yes, that's what it boils down to. There is no substitute for practical application in the field, no.'

'Where does this yellow card business come in?'

'We send pre-paid yellow cards to every GP and hospital doctor in the country. If they use a drug that throws up some unexpected adverse reaction in the patient, then we ask them to send the card back to us with all the relevant details. If enough yellow cards come in, registering the same adverse reaction to the same drug . . . well, then the alarm bells start to ring, don't they?'

'And then what happens? Is the drug withdrawn?'

'In extreme cases it can be, yes.'

Jenny frowned. Was she just being slow, or was there some basic flaw in the organized logic of such a system?

'You *ask* them to send the card back – that's all? There's no legal obligation on them to do so? No law?'

'Doctors aren't children,' the clerk replied testily. 'You can't force a doctor to yellow card something if he doesn't consider it necessary. Doctors have a perfect right to prescribe whatever they choose – within reason – *despite* the risk of adverse effects. They may feel that, under a particular set of circumstances – terminal cancer, for example – the benefits outweigh the discomfort.'

'But this . . . yellow card business: it's only done *after* a drug has been put on the market?'

'Yes. Of course. We are attempting to monitor a significant number of adverse reactions – and we are only likely to get that sort of quantitative feedback after the drug has been exposed to a large number of patients.'

'But – and I'm sorry to labour the point – isn't that all a bit late in the day?' Jenny persisted. 'The damage could have been done by then, surely?'

'Miss Macrae, forgive me, but I really cannot afford to go on discussing a purely hypothetical situation that—'

'One last question, please, then I'll go away and leave you in peace. If I . . . if I wanted to look at the results of those clinical trials you mentioned earlier – the ones on Cardocol – where would I have to go?'

'Nowhere, I'm afraid. Clinical trials are part of the company's product licence application.'

Now it was Jenny's turn to sigh. 'All right, then. Where can I see HPL's product licence application?'

'I'm trying to tell you, Miss Macrae. You can't. It's just not possible.'

'Why isn't it possible?'

'For the simple reason that all PLAs are dealt with in the strictest confidence. Whatever transpires between ourselves and the various drug companies is never disclosed to a third party.'

'Oh. There isn't a . . . library somewhere, or a register perhaps, where members of the public can—'

'Good gracious me, no! Apart from our own records here, the only place you'll find a copy of that application would be at Highland Pharmaceuticals itself.'

'Highland Pharmaceuticals itself, did you say?' Jenny mused, echoing his last words.

'Highland Pharmaceuticals, yes,' the man in London replied testily. 'That's what I just said.'

'Thank you . . . Thank you very much indeed. You've been very helpful.' Jenny replaced the phone and looked up slowly. He had just given her an idea.

Ridley sat patiently outside Jenny's flat for more than half an hour. He attracted little attention, for the street was crowded with parked cars and there was a book on his lap to suggest his presence there was wholly innocent: a salesman perhaps, killing time in a quiet side-road before his next appointment.

But Ridley's eyes were not on the printed page. They were fixed on the front bay window of the ground-floor flat opposite. There was a pair of french windows at the garden end of Jenny's sitting-room, and he was able to see both women clearly against the light as Jenny replaced the telephone and turned towards Helen. He could not hear what was said, of course, but he was able to form an impression of their relationship as Jenny leant suddenly across the table towards her visitor. He watched as Helen listened and then shook her head emphatically, pushed to her feet, and took to pacing the length of the room. They appeared to be arguing. Presently, Ridley had seen enough. Enough, that is, to realize that the two women were more than chance acquaintances who had just happened to share the same departure time from Highland Pharmaceuticals the previous afternoon. They were partners in something, he decided. Conspirators, perhaps.

It was time Jackman was told.

Ridley tossed his paperback into the glove compartment, started the Capri, and drove slowly round on to the main road towards the nearest telephone kiosk. As he did so, he turned on the car radio, for it was news time. There, at the bottom of the local bulletin, was the announcement that the man injured in the car-over-the-cliff drama the previous day, had died in hospital. Ridley smiled. Two hours ago the same story had been higher up the running order. Another hour, another bad accident or traffic jam somewhere else on Argyllshire's busy roads, and the story would have slipped out of the news altogether. It would be forgotten.

But there Ridley was wrong. In the offices of the *Gleninver Times*, Hamish Owen was on the phone to HPL, asking for the usual biographical details to go with the story of the fatal car crash. And this time, just for once, he was acting on the Editor's instructions.

'And can you tell me something about their work with the company, Mr Jackman? What were they working on at the time of the accident?'

'Both men were engaged by the company as laboratory technicians as part of our Forward Planning Development team. You . . . ah . . . appreciate, Mr Owen, that I'd rather not be drawn on specific details. For obvious reasons.'

Hamish presumed after a moment's thought that Jackman was referring to commercial rivalry.

'Yes, of course. I understand.'

'What I feel I can say is that both Martin and Tom will be sadly missed. Not just as business colleagues who will be difficult to replace, you understand, but as friends – friends of us all. HPL prides itself on being a happy, closely knit company, as I'm sure you sensed the other night at our reception for Sandy Tulloch. These two deaths will be felt as a personal loss by us all.' He might have been reading the eulogy.

'Yes. Yes, of course,' Hamish Owen agreed, dutifully recording every false word in his notebook. 'You've . . . er . . . you've had a tragic time recently, haven't you?'

'I'm sorry?'

'What with Douglas Parsons committing suicide . . . '

'Oh, I see what you mean. Yes, indeed we have.'

'—And Professor Highcroft. Just disappearing like that . . . '

'Professor Highcroft? Oh—' Jackman tried a little off-hand laugh. 'I'd hardly lump that in with the others, Mr Owen.' He paused. 'If . . . if I may speak off the record for a moment?'

'Please.'

'Well, strictly not for quoting, you understand, but it appears the Professor had been having an affair for quite some time. Those "in the know" hardly expected things to come to a head in so . . . ah . . . dramatic a fashion, but it does at least take some of the mystery out of his disappearance – that, as I say, is all *strictly* off the record.'

'Yes. Yes, of course,' Hamish agreed, his mind already elsewhere. 'Going back to the accident, Mr Jackman, I . . . I was just wondering – they were killed on their way north, weren't they?'

'Er . . . yes. I do believe they were.'

'Going away from the town? Away from HPL?'

'That would be so, yes,' Jackman conceded cautiously. He had marked Hamish Owen down as a lightweight, a man of no consequence and little perception. Now, for the first time, he wondered if, thanks to that fool Harris, he might have dangerously underestimated the young reporter. 'What are you suggesting, Mr Owen?'

Hamish wasn't even sure himself. Not yet. 'Well . . . it's probably nothing, but—'

'Please. Perhaps I can help clear up any . . . misunderstanding.'

'It's just that . . . the accident happened in the middle of a working morning. I . . . I just wondered what two lab technicians were doing going *away* from the company at that time, that's all. Shouldn't they have been at work?'

The question took Jackman by surprise. 'I've really no idea, Mr Owen. They might have had the day off for all I know.'

'Could you find out for me, please?'

'I'll . . . I'll make a few enquiries if you like, yes.'

'That would be very kind of you. Oh – there was one other thing: their ages. D'you happen to know how old they were?'

'Yes, I can tell you that straight away. Martin Calvert was thirty-seven. Thomas Steevenson was thirty-five.'

'And both were single?'

'Both were single, yes. Their parents lived down in the south somewhere, I believe.' Jackman had their addresses in the folder in front of him, but he wasn't going to pass them on to the reporter. He might start asking more questions, digging deeper. The object of this exercise in Press liaison was to nip conjecture in the bud; to be helpful but not *too* helpful; to present a brief, encapsulated, watertight picture of personal and professional loss and then leave it at that. With no loose-ends. 'Was there anything else, Mr Owen?' Jackman asked. With just the politest hint of impatience.

'I can't think of anything. You've been very helpful, Mr

Jackman, thanks very much.'

'Not at all. Goodbye, Mr—'

'Oh. Yes – sorry: there was just one more thing. How long had they been with the company?'

Jackman relaxed. They were back on safe ground. 'Since we started here. They were in at the very beginning.'

'And before that?'

'I've really no idea.' He had, of course. But he had no intention of passing on the information to a young reporter who had already exceeded his quota of permissible questions.

'Oh. Perhaps someone in your personnel department could—'

'I'm afraid not, Mr Owen. They really are far too busy just at the moment. In any event, it's hardly important, is it?'

'No. No, of course not. Thanks for your help, Mr Jackman. I'm much obliged.'

'Not at all.' He rang off.

Hamish Owen sat back in his chair, a pencil tapping thoughtfully against his teeth as he checked over his notes. Sure as God made little apples, Harris was going to want to know why he hadn't tracked down the dead men's next of kin, why he hadn't found out where they worked before joining HPL . . . He flicked open his contact book, ran a finger down the 'A's, and a moment later was dialling the London number of ASTMS, the white-collar, scientific trades union. When his call was answered, he asked to be put through to the Membership Secretary. Presently – 'Steevenson and . . . what was the other one?' asked a young clerk in Records.

'Calvert. Martin Calvert.'

'D'you know their date of birth?'

'Steevenson would have been . . . 1950. Calvert, 1948.'

'Half a mo.' Hamish waited, chewing absently on the end of his pencil. At last: 'I've got a T. W. Steevenson, that any good?'

'That sounds like him, yes. D'you have an address?'

'Well . . . I'm not sure it'll be much use,' the girl replied doubtfully. 'It's eight years old, isn't it? After that it's NLN.'

'Doesn't matter,' Hamish replied, clutching at an answer that would keep Harris off his back, at least. 'It's a start, anyway.' He paused, pencil poised over his notepad. 'What's NLN?'

'NLN? It means he's taken himself off the register, hasn't he? No Longer Notified.'

'No longer notified of what?'

'Jobs, pension rights, arbitration decisions, local area meetings – all that sort of thing.'

'Why would he do that – go off the register, I mean?'

The girl shrugged. 'I dunno, really. Quite a lot of 'em do that when they move into more sensitive areas – electronics, fibre optics, defence contracts, stuff like that. They like to cover their tracks a bit, don't they? Stops rival companies picking up on the competition. Head-hunting, they call it.'

'Can you give me that address, anyway?'

'Don't see why not. It's number eleven, Springfield Lane, Pitton, Wiltshire.'

Hamish wrote it down. If he drew a blank with someone called Steevenson through the local phone book at that address, he could trace the occupant through the county electoral rolls.

'Thanks a lot. What about the other one – Calvert?'

Another delay ensued, then – 'That's funny . . . '

'What is?'

'Well . . . he's down as NLN too.'

'What, Calvert?'

'That's what it says here. His address is five years out of date an' all.'

'Where was he living – can you tell me?'

'It's down as Fairwinds, School Avenue, Lower Woodford, Wiltshire.'

'Wiltshire? Again?'

'What d'you think I'm doin', makin' it up?'

'No. No, of course not.' Hamish scribbled down the address. And found himself looking at a third name on his notepad. On impulse, he decided to throw that in too. 'Could you try one more?'

The girl hesitated. 'You don't want much, do you?'

'Please. Just one.'

She sighed. 'Go on, then.'

'Thanks. The bloke's name is Parsons, OK? Douglas Parsons. I don't know his date of birth.'

'Hang about.' He waited once again, then – ''Ere – you having me on?' demanded the girl suddenly, suspiciously.

Hamish sat forward. 'What d'you mean?'

'I mean, he's the same as the other two, ain't he? An' guess where he lived . . . ?'

'Wiltshire?'

'Yeah, Wiltshire. Place called Allington.' She hesitated, curiosity aroused. 'What have all these blokes bin up to, then?'

'I'm not sure,' Hamish replied slowly, truthfully. As far as he was concerned, until a few moments ago all they had shared was a place of work and a time of death. Now, suddenly, it seemed that they might have shared a great deal more.

Hamish rang off and did some more thinking, playing with the names on his jotter. Then he rose to his feet, took down the office atlas and looked up the first of the three Wiltshire villages in the index.

Pitton, he discovered, lay a few miles east of Salisbury. Allington was just south of Bulford. Lower Woodford was on the banks of the River Avon.

Another name seemed to leap out of the page towards him, and Hamish felt a sudden shiver of excitement. For there, roughly in the centre of a triangle formed by Pitton, Allington and Lower Woodford, and within easy commuting distance of all three, lay the village of Porton.

Porton as in Porton Down, the government's chemical warfare establishment.

CHAPTER TWENTY

Dr Stanley Erskine was sitting in a doctors' surgery, waiting. It was a novel experience.

He had spent most of the morning driving northwards along the eastern bank of Loch Linnhe, towards North Ballachulish and Fort William. It had been a long, tedious and irritating journey in the last of the crawling summer traffic, but his irritation had stemmed not from the clogged roads, nor even from the less-than-dependable behaviour of his ancient Rover, but rather from the pricking of his own professional conscience. Now he glanced round the crowded waiting-room and felt an unfamiliar and wholly refreshing sympathy with the cluster of patients who waited, like him, to see Dr Hastings, the duty GP at this, one of several doctors' surgeries in Fort William.

Glancing down at the worn leather briefcase at his feet and picturing its contents, Erskine wondered just how many of Dr Hastings' patients would have understood why he felt compelled to drive all this way along the coast instead of simply using the telephone – or why his own sense of professional pride had prevented him from making these same enquiries in his own home town forty miles away to the south. He was not at all sure that he knew himself. What he *did* know was that his presence here in Fort William had to do with a young woman called Jenny Macrae, and a new heart drug called Cardocol that was about to burst upon the marketplace with the promotional incandescence of Halley's Comet; that it had to do with two of his patients, one of whom was already dead – and that it had to do, finally, with a sense of personal shame at the realization that he had, however briefly, traded the traditional cynicism of his calling for the suspension of disbelief and a handsome set of leather-bound medical reference books. And of therefore having broken faith with those he was pledged to serve.

'Dr Erskine?' He looked up at the receptionist. 'Dr Hastings will see you now.' He picked up his briefcase and followed her pointing finger, conscious that the prefix 'Doctor' had drawn attention to his presence and set him instantly apart from the rest. He walked down a short length of corridor and entered Dr Hastings' consulting-room.

Twenty years his junior, Dr Hastings rose from behind his desk and stretched out a hand. Florid, fair-haired, and with a firm, crisp handshake, he exuded an air of over-worked, likeable efficiency. 'Sorry I had to ask you to wait out there with the others,' he began. 'We're a bit short of space just now as you probably noticed.' Compared to Erskine's own little surgery behind Gleninver's Market Hall Square, it had seemed positively palatial.

'That's perfectly all right,' Erskine replied, clutching his briefcase under his arm. 'I'd forgotten what it was like, you know. Being on the receiving end, so to speak. It was a salutary experience, Doctor – most salutary.' He smiled as Hastings gestured him to a chair.

'Well now – what brings you to our neck of the woods?' asked Dr Hastings directly, as he studied the territorial interloper over the ridge of his knuckles. 'You sounded a little vague. Over the phone.'

'Aye, so I did. I apologize,' Erskine agreed. 'It seemed better to discuss things face to face.'

Hastings opened his hands in a gesture of invitation. 'I am at your disposal.'

Dr Erskine bent down, opened his briefcase, took out a sheaf of notes and laid them carefully on his lap. He looked up.

'It's about Highland Pharmaceuticals, the drug firm away down in my neck of the woods, as you might say. I understand one of their representative chappies calls here fairly regularly?' He leant forward and endorsed his words by tapping a finger lightly against the desk-tidy that adorned Hastings' desk. Made of dark brown plastic, with the letters HPL and company logo embossed across the front of the pencil tray, it was identical to the one on his own desk back in Gleninver. There were probably thousands of them scattered up and down the country, Dr Erskine thought bleakly.

Hastings nodded. 'You mean Mr Langley? Yes, that's right. Comes in once every six weeks or so. Seems a pleasant enough sort of chap.'

'I take it he's been . . . ah . . . extolling the virtues of this new drug of theirs just recently?'

'The neurone-blocker? Cardocol? Naturally.' Dr Hastings spun his chair gently to one side, reached across to a shelf and took down a pile of glossy HPL promotional brochures. He dropped them on to the centre of his desk, and Dr Erskine leaned forward.

'You'll be going along to this launch of theirs, I take it? This symposium or whatever it is they call these things nowadays?' he observed, picking up the emerald-and-green personalized invitation.

'Of course.' Dr Hastings frowned. 'Look, Doctor. Forgive me, but could you perhaps tell me what all this is about?'

Erskine held up a hand. 'I'm sorry, Doctor, I'm sorry. I was forgetting what a busy lot we all are.' He smiled disarmingly, rummaged around in the pockets of his baggy sports coat and pulled out a packet of Cardocol pills. 'I take it you've received a few of these already, have you not?'

The younger man nodded. 'A few, yes. As promotional samples.'

'Aye, that would be it: promotional samples.' Dr Erskine weighed his man shrewdly across the width of his own desk. 'Would I be right in saying you've maybe given one or two of these "promotional samples" to a couple of your patients already, Doctor?'

Hastings stirred restlessly, visibly irritated now by the elderly GP with his scruffy old suit and his string of obscure, unsettling questions. 'Yes. As a matter of fact, I have,' he admitted stiffly.

'Ah! And would you consider it a breach of medical

ethics to tell me just how many?'

'Look, Dr Erskine. With the best will in the world, I fail to see—'

'Please. If you don't mind.'

Hastings sighed. 'Well, let me think. Three. Possibly more. I couldn't be certain, not off the top of my head. Not without checking my case notes.'

Dr Erskine nodded. 'But three, anyway. Three that you know of, yes?' He paused. 'Tell me this, if you will, then: were there any adverse reactions?'

'Adverse reactions? Some, of course. But nothing serious. No—'

'No postural hypotension, for example?'

'No, of course not!' Hastings objected impatiently.

Erskine regarded him quizzically. 'You sound very sure, Doctor.'

'That's because I make a point of studying the relevant medical literature,' retorted the younger man a little pompously. 'The whole point of Cardocol, as I understand it, is that they've eliminated the risk of an inconsistent blood-pressure reading *and* postural hypotension! That's what the whole thing's about!'

'You mean that's what they're *claiming* they've done,' Erskine corrected gently. 'The two don't necessarily add up to the same thing in my experience – not the same thing at all.' He paused. 'You're quite sure all your patients have taken to this new drug quite satisfactorily?'

'As far as I am aware – yes. I had one of 'em in here just this morning. Claimed Cardocol was the best thing that had ever happened to her!'

'And your colleagues here in the surgery: they've been trying out these promotional samples too, no doubt?'

'Presumably, yes.'

'And they've not mentioned any problems?'

'To me? No. Dr Erskine – I don't mean to be rude, but I have a waiting-room of patients out there who—'

'I know – you're a very busy man,' Dr Erskine nodded, refusing to be ruffled as he picked up the notes he had compiled after talking to the houseman at County

Royal Hospital and examining Mrs Proctor's blood samples. 'But I would still like you to spare a couple more minutes just to read these.' He handed over the notes. 'Your patient this morning may very well be right when she says Cardocol's the best thing that's happened to her since her wedding night – I don't know, I'm not qualified to judge. What I do know is that one of my patients was admitted to Intensive Care yesterday morning with all the *initial* symptoms of postural hypotension, and later developed a blood pressure of 230/130! She's lucky to be alive.'

Dr Hastings looked blank. 'I'm sorry, I don't see the connection.'

'She's been on two hundred milligrammes of Cardocol for the last six days,' Erskine explained quietly. 'What happened to her was supposed to be statistically impossible.'

In the crewroom at RAF Glenhaddon, Tony Lockhart clumped up to the availability board in orange immersion suit and rubber boots, rubbed out his own name opposite the words DUTY W/MAN, and tossed a piece of chalk across the room at his replacement sorting through the flying gear in his locker as he came on duty. 'There you go, chum – you can keep it.' With that, Tony pushed through the swing doors, and the swish of his baggy suit and the thump of his boots receded down the corridor towards the changing-rooms. Officially, Tony was still rostered off. Unofficially, anyone inside the building without a cough or a cold or an arm in plaster was considered fair game if a crew was light, and Tony had been nobbled. Normally, he wouldn't have minded. Normally, but not today. Not after spending time with the men from S.5.

In an easy chair over by the video, Flight Lieutenant Churchill chucked a well-thumbed paperback into an empty chair, rose suddenly to his feet, and followed Tony down the corridor towards the changing-rooms. As he entered, he heard a metal locker door crash back angrily as Tony reached inside for a towel and headed off to the showers.

'Tony?' He turned. 'Like a word.'

'I'm having a shower, all right?'

'I'd still like a word. Now.'

Tony hesitated, then walked warily back to his locker and sat down on one of the wooden benches. Churchill sat down opposite. 'All right, let's have it. What's eating you?'

'Nothing's eating me.'

'Bollocks,' Churchill replied briefly. 'You've been snapping people's heads off ever since you came in. I want to know why.'

Tony hunched forward, lips pursed. 'All right, I'll tell you. I'm pissed off. I'm pissed off with you, I'm pissed off with this,' he swung a hand around the changing-room, 'and I'm pissed off with the whole sodding Air Force, just as it happens, OK?' He rose to his feet and stood over Churchill menacingly, a finger stabbing down into his Flight Commander's face. 'I've been in this man's Air Force fifteen years, OK? Fifteen sodding years – and what I don't need is a lecture in loyalty from a couple of shits from S.5. And what I really, *really* don't need is to find my own Flight Lieutenant has gone running off to service Security about a couple of passes I find in some stiff's pocket, without telling his winchman first. That's about loyalty too, OK?'

'You finished?' Churchill asked quietly.

'Yeah. Just about.'

'Fine.' Churchill rose to his feet. 'What makes you think I was the one who called in S.5?'

Tony turned. 'You saying you didn't give them the word?'

'If I had, you would have been told. You ought to know that.'

'Then who the hell did?'

Churchill shrugged. 'The word went down "through channels", according to Warrant Officer Metcalf.'

'Through channels? And just what the hell is that supposed to mean?'

Another shrug from Churchill. 'He didn't say and I didn't ask. But for my money . . . ? Someone at Group read that report of yours.'

'The Incident SITREP? Jesus.' Tony sat down again slowly as the implications of that sank in. 'What's going on, then – up at HPL? What's so bloody important that a winchie's routine Incident report on the contents of some guy's pockets has a couple of heavies from S.5 legging it all the way up from London?'

Churchill rose to his feet. 'Don't ask me, Tony. I'm just like one of the three little monkeys. From what they were saying, you'd be well advised to be like one too – you know: eyes, ears and mouth, all firmly closed.'

In Fort William, Dr Hastings finished reading Dr Erskine's detailed notes, laid them carefully in the centre of his desk and rocked back slowly in his chair, frowning with a mixture of worry and concentration. In the last forty minutes his opinion of the elderly doctor sitting opposite had undergone a radical transformation.

Dr Erskine watched him in silence, aware that he had just won some sort of battle and that at the very least he had managed to breach the younger doctor's wall of professional scepticism. In one sense, Dr Erskine already had his reward. It had been paid in Hastings' silence as he read the results of Mrs Proctor's various tests; in his sparse, incisive questions, and in his lengthy phone call to the consultant at County Royal Hospital.

Now Dr Hastings leaned forward, rose to his feet and crossed to a metal filing cabinet in the corner. He unlocked the top drawer and began leafing through his patients' case notes. He then extracted four files, closed the drawer and returned to his desk. Then he pulled the phone towards him, looked up and tapped Dr Erskine's notes thoughtfully.

'Who are you going to call?' Dr Erskine asked.

'My partners,' Hastings decided. 'I think they ought to see these right away.' He lifted the receiver and began dialling.

Ridley made another careful, timed entry in his notebook and glanced up from behind the wheel of the Capri. The

Volvo hadn't moved. The two women were still sitting inside facing one another, talking.

Ten minutes earlier, almost exactly, Helen Highcroft and Jenny Macrae had left the flat in Elgin Terrace, got into Helen's Volvo and driven here to this lay-by halfway along the country road that led past Highland Pharmaceuticals. They had pulled in suddenly, as though on impulse, causing another car to swerve and brake suddenly. Ridley had turned in more sedately a few minutes later and tucked himself away behind a caravanette to watch and make notes.

Ridley was puzzled, intrigued. They were up to something, definitely. The two women, Helen Highcroft and Jennifer Macrae, had spent most of the afternoon sitting together in the living-room of Macrae's flat, drinking tea or coffee, talking and looking frequently at their watches. As though they were waiting for something to happen or someone to arrive; killing time, perhaps. Seated behind the wheel of his hired car, Ridley had no need to look at his watch other than to record events for the sake of his operational report to Baxter in London, for while the two women waited for something to happen, for some particular moment to arrive, Ridley waited, simply, for them. Where they went, he would follow. Time had ceased to have any meaning, its only relevance related to light and darkness, brightness and shadow. Once Ridley had spent six days lying in an open field under a tiny piece of scrim netting, watching a farmhouse across the border in Northern Ireland. Six days, withdrawing only at night to gulp a mug of hot tea, collect his rations and make his report. In January. He had the endless, feral patience of the hunter, the stalker, had Ridley. After Northern Ireland in January, sitting in a nice warm car on a summer's evening in the Scottish Highlands watching a couple of civilians through an open window was a doddle; a piece of piss . . .

'I still think you're mad!' Helen was saying, twisting round to face Jenny in the Volvo beside her. 'You'll never get away with it!'

Jenny sighed impatiently. They'd been over all this in her flat. 'Why not?' she challenged reasonably. 'You did.'

'That was different!' Helen insisted. 'I was only in there a moment, anyway. And even then the receptionist was breathing down my neck.'

'When you came out the receptionist was breathing down your neck,' corrected Jenny. 'Isn't that what you said? When you came *out*. Not when you were in there. Besides, the offices aren't even used yet – none of them are: they're empty.'

'That's only what the man told me,' Helen pointed out with increasing desperation. 'What if . . . if he's wrong? Then what will you do?'

'I only need one. I'll use the office you did, the one that was supposed to be Malcolm's. There was a lock on the door, wasn't there?'

'Yes, but . . . '

'Well, there you are then – nothing could be simpler. I'll just lock the door from the inside and wait. Then, when everyone else has gone home, I'll slip out.'

Helen leant across earnestly and grasped her arm. 'Look – Jenny. I . . . I appreciate what you're trying to do, really I do. But it's . . . it's madness! You can't go creeping around someone else's property. It's . . . well . . . it's illegal, for one thing.'

'So? So it's illegal – so what?' Jenny countered recklessly. 'So's giving out pills before you're supposed to; so's swopping people's offices round and then lying to their wives, you know? Or it should be.' Jenny paused and then added, going for the clincher: 'Or don't you really want to find out what happened to Malcolm?'

'Of course I do, you know that. That's not the point.'

'Yes, it is! That's exactly the point! There's no other way – you told me yourself your questions get nowhere. Look – Helen. Something *has* to be going on up there, agreed? Why else would Jackman lie? Why else would Harold Engel make such a crass mistake about the lift?'

'What if you're caught?'

Jenny shrugged. 'I'd have to tell the truth then, wouldn't

I? At worst I'd get a fine. HPL wouldn't dare prosecute, anyway. They'd never risk it all coming out in the open. The police round here don't—'

'I didn't mean the police,' Helen interrupted. Something in her voice brought Jenny up short.

'What d'you mean?'

Helen glanced involuntarily over her shoulder and gave a little shudder. 'Oh, I don't know. Jackman, for example. You haven't met him yet, but there's something . . . horrible about him. Sinister. I felt it in that office. What if *he* found you?'

'In the middle of the night? Don't be silly – Jackman won't be within a hundred miles of the place! Nor will anyone else, apart from a few geriatric night-watchmen with flat feet. I'll hear them coming a mile off.'

'Then at least let me come with you,' Helen offered impulsively. 'That way at least there'd be two of us and you wouldn't be alone. We could—'

'Wonderful. And whose car's going to be out there all alone in the car park, sticking out like a sore thumb when everyone else has gone home?'

'Oh. I hadn't thought of that.'

'I had. Besides, you've got the children to look after. Just help me to get inside, OK? I'll manage the rest. Now—' she glanced at the clock on the Volvo's dashboard – 'are you with me or against me, as they say? If we sit around here chatting much longer we'll miss the five-thirty rush.'

Helen thought for a moment, then nodded. 'I'm with you.'

Jenny reached over and kissed her impulsively on the cheek. As Ridley watched.

'D'you think we should just run over things once more – you know, just to be sure we haven't forgotten anything?'

Jenny shook her head emphatically, her stomach already churning with nerves. 'No. If we're going to do it, then for goodness' sake let's get on with it, OK?' She turned away, a hand on the door catch.

'You're *sure* you've got everything?' Helen persisted.

Jenny patted her large, cavernous handbag. 'Yep.

Torch. Sandwiches. Thermos. Notebook and pencil. Gloves. A book to read – oh, and a clean handkerchief.'

Helen smiled nervously. 'Sorry. Didn't mean to nag. What are you reading?'

'*One Flew Over the Cuckoo's Nest*,' Jenny answered with a grin. They both laughed then, a welcome release of tension. 'What about the morning? Coming out?'

'Like we agreed,' Helen repeated. 'At nine-thirty, from reception, I'll ask for extension 476. I'll let it ring four times, then hang up. That's your signal. When it stops ringing, I'll go straight up to the desk and start talking to that girl again.' Helen smiled grimly. 'When she sees me coming at her for the third time, she'll be distracted all right, I guarantee it. You shouldn't have any trouble slipping back into reception. Just go straight out to the car and wait for me there. If there's space, I'll be in the same car park where we met.'

'And if there's not?'

Helen shrugged. 'Well . . . you'll just have to try and blend into the scenery, I suppose. Anyway, tomorrow's launch day – nobody's going to be paying you much attention.'

'Thanks very much,' Jenny said dryly, the butterflies now practising circuits and bumps as she thought of the long hours of silence and darkness stretching ahead.

Jenny got out, opened the back door and slid across the rear seat. She glanced quickly through the rear window, saw the caravanette with its portly owners sitting in their camp chairs, faces tilted towards the sun, and totally failed to notice Ridley's Capri a little further back in the lay-by. She would pay for that dearly, later. 'All clear,' she called. Shaking out the travel rug on the back seat, Jenny dropped to hands and knees on the floor and crouched down. 'There. How's that?'

Helen twisted round and draped the rug carefully over her back, head and shoulders until Jenny was completely covered. The tartan lump looked terribly obvious, thought Helen, panicking suddenly, but it was too late for changes now and time was pressing on.

'Fine. It looks fine. Can't see a thing. Comfortable?'

'Are you kidding?'

Helen took a final glance over her shoulder and reached down for the ignition. 'Right then – here we go.' She brought the car to life and drove out of the lay-by. 'We're on the road,' she reported. Behind her, Jenny crouched down in the warm darkness among the sticky sweet papers and the used car-park tickets, and listened to the drumming of the tyres on the road a few inches below her face.

Behind them both came Ridley, eyes narrowing with suspicion as the heavy Volvo gathered speed towards Highland Pharmaceuticals.

A few minutes later – 'Gate coming up,' Helen said, without turning round, her hands suddenly damp on the steering-wheel as she slowed down. Fifty yards . . . twenty yards . . . ten, with Helen relieved to see a steady flow of outgoing traffic being waved through without a pause, as she brought the car to a halt for the man on the gate and wound down the window. She forced a smile and wondered if he could hear the thud of her heart. 'Hello there. Good afternoon.' Wider went the smile.

'Afternoon, ma'am,' replied the grizzled, elderly security guard as he stepped closer and bent down towards her window.

'Mrs Highcroft to see . . . er . . . Mr Engel. Harold Engel,' she hurried, rattling off the first name that came into her head. Don't check, she prayed silently as soon as the words had left her mouth: please don't check. 'It's all right,' she smiled with a confidence she didn't feel. 'I know the way.' The security man nodded slowly as he made a careful note of the car's registration number on his clipboard. It seemed to take an age. Then, at last, he handed a visitor's pass in through the window. Helen pushed the pass on to the dashboard, slipped the car into gear and took off the handbrake. As she did so—

'Oh. Mrs Highcroft.' She spun round, smile still stitched into place. What had he seen?

'Yes?'

'I'm . . . that is to say . . . we're all very sorry – about the

Professor, an' that.' He shrugged apologetically and gestured back at the gatehouse. 'One of the . . . the lads had a paper.'

Helen nodded, the relief washing over her. 'That's . . . that's very nice of you. Thank you.' She drove forward, and let out a long sigh of relief as they cleared the first bend and the gatehouse was lost from sight. 'All clear,' Helen announced, her voice not quite steady. 'We're through, Jenny! He never even glanced in the back!'

'Thank God for that.' Jenny tossed the rug aside, sat up and pushed her hair straight in the driving mirror. Then she scrambled over into the passenger seat just before another car came towards them and Helen slowed down for the car-park turning. A minute later they were getting out together, the tension mounting again now as they walked casually towards the main entrance and the stream of people emerging homeward-bound from HPL's administration building. Jenny looked at her watch: 5.27. They had only just made it. As they paused beneath the tinted windows, brushed now with burnished gold by the late-afternoon sunshine, Jenny felt a hand rest lightly on her shoulder.

'Good luck, Jenny,' Helen whispered. 'See you in the morning.' Jenny nodded imperceptibly.

Once through the revolving doors, the two women separated immediately – Helen to make straight for the reception desk, Jenny to walk casually towards the sofa nearest the door leading to the ground-floor corridor and what was supposed to have been Professor Highcroft's office. She sat down. And waited for her cue.

Although the painters with their dust-sheets and stepladders had gone, Helen was relieved to see the reception area was much busier now than it had been the last time she had made a scene. She and Jenny had banked heavily on that. Apart from HPL employees emptying out of the lifts and hurrying outside to the car parks, there were half a dozen workmen putting the finishing touches to a Cardocol promotional display in the foyer. Two girls in fashion-pink coveralls were arranging tubs of ferns and plants in the space between the two lifts and there was quite a crowd of people clustered around the receptionist, noticing Helen as she walked closer. Good.

Jenny glanced towards the door leading to the corridor. Before they had left the flat, she had made Helen draw her a diagram, a ground plan showing exactly where she had to go. Now Jenny waited, poised for the next part of their plan, her bag over her shoulder.

'Excuse me . . . ' called a familiar voice over by the reception desk as Helen pushed forward into the cluster of waiting people. 'I said: excuse me . . . ' Jenny didn't wait any longer. Looking neither to right nor left, she rose to her feet, went straight through the door and hurried down the deserted corridor. Past one door . . . and another. There! There was the third. A quick look round: no one in sight. She turned the handle, the door opened and Jenny stepped inside. One bare desk, one chair and a filing cabinet. Apart from that the office was empty. Jenny whipped the door shut, turned the lock and froze, ear pressed against the door as she listened fearfully for the sudden voice saying, Oi! Where d'you think you're going . . . ? Nothing. Not a sound. Jenny relaxed and moved away from the door. Leaning back against the wall, she slid down slowly to the carpet, eyes closed. There. She'd done it. Presently she opened her bag, took out sandwiches, torch, notebook and thermos and arranged them all neatly around her. Another look at her watch: 5.29. It wouldn't be dark much before nine. Jenny took out her novel and settled down to wait.

Ridley glanced at the dashboard clock as the Volvo paused at the mouth of the lane leading to Highland Pharmaceuticals before turning left back along the road towards Gleninver. Out came pencil and notebook as Ridley wrote in neat, small capitals: 17.38: VOLVO LEAVES HPL. DIRECTION GLENINVER. ONE OCCUPANT. Stowing away his notebook, Ridley started the Capri, swung it round in a cloud of dust from the dry verge and set off after the Volvo. So that was their little game. It was enough to make you weep.

Ridley remembered there had been a telephone box a mile or so further along the road. He had been trained to remember and store away little details like that. He pulled in off the road, dug coins from his pocket and pushed into the hot, stuffy little call-box. He'd better check in, let Jackman know what the Macrae woman was up to. He dialled the number, asked for Jackman's extension and waited. There was no reply. 'Would you like me to have him paged, caller?'

Ridley was about to say yes when he had a better idea. If Macrae was still inside HPL then her flat would be empty, wouldn't it? And Ridley enjoyed searching women's flats, he really did.

'No,' he decided quietly. 'No, don't do that. I'll call back. Thank you.'

Jackman paused inside the lift on the third floor of RD7 and studied the control console and the gleaming laboratories beyond for one last time, making sure nothing had been missed. The place was empty, temporarily closed down – and would remain so until the Cardocol launch was behind him and they could get quietly back to business, breaking in the new replacements for OMAHA who had been arriving by car and train from Porton. He'd met all four off site and told them peremptorily to disappear, to vanish; take a few days off and settle in, find their way around. Satisfied now that nothing had been forgotten or overlooked, Jackman pressed the button for the ground floor and the doors sighed shut. Down at ground level he took a large printed sign and wooden stand from the store cupboard and then reached on to a shelf for a bundle of bright-orange marker tape.

He tied the tape at waist height across the complete width of RD7's entrance foyer and positioned the cardboard placard on its stand directly behind the tape, facing the glass doors he would lock on his way out. He had long realized you did not need barbed wire or searchlights to protect a secret and deter the curious, for they served only to advertise the presence of something worth investigation. Instead, he reasoned, all you needed was marker tape and a little psychology, a little understanding of your fellow man. Such a tenet, indeed, was fundamental to OMAHA's very existence here in the centre of a legitimate pharmaceutical enterprise. All you needed was tape, psychology and a placard reading:

QUARANTINED AREA. IMMUNOLOGICAL EXPERIMENT IN PROGRESS.
DO NOT CROSS TAPE.

It worked every time.

CHAPTER TWENTY-ONE

Helen Highcroft turned into her own driveway and braked sharply to a halt. An ancient, maroon-coloured Morris Minor was blocking the entrance to her garage, and there was a tall, thin young man she had never seen before standing outside her front door. At the sound of her car he turned, raised a hand and came down the steps towards her. Helen leaned across the passenger seat and wound down the window. 'Yes? Can I help you?'

'Mrs Highcroft?'

'That's right. What d'you want?'

'Hamish Owen, Mrs Highcroft – *Gleninver Times*,' he said, catching the look on her face, seeing the way she closed up when he identified himself. 'I'd like to ask you one or two questions.'

Helen shook her head emphatically. She'd heard first-hand what Jenny had gone through with the Press.

'Sorry – no. There's nothing more I want to say.'

'It's not just about your husband, Mrs Highcroft. Not just about his disappearance, anyway.'

Helen paused, a hand on the windowsill. 'What d'you mean: not *just* about my husband?'

'I'm not interested in private details about your marriage. About why he left you,' hurried Hamish. 'That's not why I've come to see you, honestly.'

Helen got out of the car and slammed the driver's door angrily. 'My husband didn't "leave" me, as you put it, Mister whatever-your-name-is,' she snapped. 'My husband has disappeared! Vanished! There's a difference. Now, if you don't mind, you can move that heap of rust that's blocking my driveway and let me—'

'Please, Mrs Highcroft – could you just tell me: have you and your husband ever lived in Wiltshire?'

Helen looked at the young reporter for a moment as though he was quite mad. Then – 'How on earth did you know that?' she asked quietly.

Ridley went up the garden path to the front door of Jenny's flat in Elgin Terrace, saw the individual name-plates beside the bell push and let himself into the communal hallway with the main staircase and the two doors off, one on either side. He waited there a moment, listening to the sounds of the silent house around him, acclimatizing himself to alien surroundings. That had once been part of his training too. Listen to your body, to your senses: give them the chance to work for you – they can save your life.

Now Ridley rang Jenny's doorbell and waited with a plausible story, an excuse, ready on his lips. He knew she wasn't in there, of course, knew she couldn't possibly have got back before him – but recognized too that he had not been watching the flat long enough to be absolutely, one hundred per cent *sure* that there wasn't a boyfriend, a bed-bound granny or a yapping bloody poodle waiting for him once he got over the threshold. So he rang the doorbell and waited. Silence. No boyfriend; no yapping poodle.

A careful glance round as he unzipped the neat, soft leather wallet he carried in his hip pocket, an expert squint at the lock and he was in with the door pushed closed behind him in the time it took ordinary people to find the front-door key.

Ridley was not like ordinary people.

He moved slowly down the hall. Looking, listening, taking his time. A quick look round to make sure gran wasn't straining away on the lav – he'd almost been caught like that once – and he was moving swiftly through to the kitchen to unlock the back door and open up an escape route, just in case. Then he was ready to start.

He began as he always did with women, in the bedroom, gloved fingers moving along her racks of clothes, his eyes panning slowly along softness and femininity to linger on blouse and discarded bra over the back of a chair, on the lipstick and make-up that cluttered her small dressing-table.

He found her packet of contraceptive pills in her dressing-table drawer and he found her unopened packet of Tampax. He saw everything and he found nothing. Nothing of any importance, anyway. Not there.

He picked up the leather-framed photograph on her bedside table and studied it carefully, for it offered another small window into the private world of Jennifer Macrae: Mum, Dad and a little girl with a pony-tail, sitting together on some windswept, long-forgotten beach eating ice cream, the girl in shorts and checked shirt, the mother in headscarf and round black sunglasses, the father in baggy brown shorts and the kind of open-toed sandals worn with dark socks in the fifties.

Ridley found another photograph in the wastepaper basket, only this one was in colour and had been torn in two. Piecing the two halves together he saw a man grinning into the camera from the stern of some dinghy, a girl's straw hat pushed forward over his eyes. Ridley tapped the pieces thoughtfully against the palm of a gloved hand, let them flutter down into the wastebasket and went through into Jenny's living-room: you sometimes say more about yourself by what you discard than by what you keep.

He found Helen's diagram without the slightest difficulty.

Crumpled into a ball, it had been thrown away, discarded. Ridley smoothed it out on the table. It was not a particularly good sketch, but then it didn't have to be. HPL had been doodled across the top of the paper, plain as day. So too was the word 'Reception'. And a child of five could have followed the pencilled arrow through the door and down the corridor to the office marked 'X' on the plan. Just like Cluedo, thought Ridley scornfully, putting it all together with what he had seen in the kitchen.

Ridley looked round for the phone – and froze. A man was coming up the path.

Tony pushed open the front door, crossed the hall and rang the bell to Jenny's flat. He waited. Nothing happened. He rang again. As he did so, he noticed that the door was slightly ajar and pushed gently. The door swung open and he took a cautious half-step forward. 'Hello?' he called. 'Jenny? It's me, Tony.' Still no reply.

He walked slowly down the hall, listening for sounds from the kitchen, for the flush of a toilet, perhaps. Nothing. 'Jenny?' More silence. Tony looked right to the living-room and then started suddenly. A man of about his own age was sitting on Jenny's sofa, a newspaper open in his lap. 'Who the hell are you?' demanded Tony suspiciously. 'Didn't you hear me calling?'

Ridley turned a page and then looked up and studied him impassively. 'Could ask you the same question,' he countered calmly. To get to the kitchen door he would have had to cross the hall. Instead he had decided to stay, brazen it out. Perhaps even learn something into the bargain . . .

'Flight Sergeant Lockhart. A friend of Jenny's.' He gestured over his shoulder. 'The door was ajar. And you?'

'Just a friend.' Ridley affected to return to his newspaper.

'Where's Jenny?'

Ridley looked up. 'She's gone out. Shopping.' Ridley returned to his paper as Tony studied him in silence. Because there was something . . .

'Jenny gave you a key, did she?' he asked casually.

'That's right. Jenny gave me a key.' And over went another page. You're too cool, thought Tony suddenly, suspicion crystallizing into certainty as he remembered the two visitors to RAF Glenhaddon early that same morning. Men with the same polite, icy hardness, the same lurking cruelty beneath the sharp creases and the short, regulation haircuts—

'You're not a friend of hers at all, are you?' Tony accused suddenly. 'You're another of those bastards from S.5.'

Ridley looked up, laid the paper slowly aside and rose casually to his feet. 'That's right,' he admitted agreeably. 'I'm just another of those bastards from S.5.' Whatever that was.

Tony nodded grimly and glanced round. S.5 were taking an interest in Flight Sergeant Lockhart; Flight Sergeant Lockhart was taking an interest in Jennifer Macrae; ergo,

S.5 would take an interest in her too. Or so he thought.

'You've been searching here, haven't you? I can bloody well smell it! You've been turning over her things!'

'Something like that,' admitted Ridley softly. Stepping closer.

Tony stopped him with a raised hand and an impatient click of the fingers. 'Right, sunshine: let's see some ID.'

'Sure.' Ridley reached obligingly inside his jacket, took out his soft leather wallet and held it out. 'Help yourself,' he smiled easily. Tony took the wallet. And looked down.

Jumbled, fractured impressions then of several slender black tools in a case; of a swirling, rushing movement towards him and of a brief, sharp, agonizing pain between neck and collarbone. And then darkness. Oblivion.

Ridley watched his mark fall sideways without a flicker of pleasure or satisfaction. Flight Sergeant Lockhart, lying there in a crumpled, ungainly heap with his head against the leg of the sofa, represented an additional complication, that was all. The matter of his life or death, his survival or disposal, a thing of professional indifference to the man sent from London to tidy up loose-ends. Now Ridley stepped over the body, retrieved his wallet of skeleton keys, zipped it shut and crossed to the telephone. As he dialled Highland Pharmaceuticals and asked once more for Jackman's private extension, he wasn't even breathing heavily.

'Maurice Jackman.'

'You know who this is, Mr Jackman,' Ridley said quietly.

'Where are you?'

'Gleninver. Inside Macrae's flat.'

'You're *where*? Good God, man – is she with you?'

Ridley permitted himself a brief, mirthless little laugh. 'No, Squire.' He paused, enjoying it. 'She's with you.'

'What? With me? Don't be fatuous! She's—'

'Don't you start calling me names, Mr Jackman,' rebuked Ridley with quiet, calm menace as he twisted his head to one side and inspected the blank, expressionless face of the body sprawled at his feet. 'I don't like having to repeat myself. Listen to what I'm saying. She's with you. In the main building.'

'What is this?' Jackman hissed. 'Some sort of game? If she was here, in this building, I can assure you—'

'That you would know about it? Ah, that's where you're wrong, Mr Jackman,' corrected Ridley patiently. 'Not if she wanted a crafty little look round, you wouldn't. Not if she planned a little snoop round after lights out.' He paused and then added softly: 'And she *does* plan a little snoop round, believe me.'

'How do you know?'

'Because I made it my business to find out. That's what they're paying me for.'

'Where is she now? If she's—'

'Where she's not doing any harm. It's all right, Mr Jackman – just relax. She won't do anything until it gets dark.'

'You sound very certain.'

'I am very certain.'

'What has she found out? What is she after?'

'I don't know, do I? That's why I'd better come and collect her. When everything is nice and quiet. When everyone's gone home.'

'You're *sure* you know where she is?'

'Oh yes, Mr Jackman,' Ridley soothed, turning Helen's sketch slowly towards him. 'I know where she is all right. To the inch.'

Jenny screwed the cap on to her thermos, crawled across the office floor until she was beneath the window, and then rose to her feet, body flattened against the wall as she peered outside. From where she was hidden she could see a triangular wedge of HPL car park and a slice of the road winding down through the trees to the security gate and the main road. The car park was almost empty now and the number of cars, lorries and sub-contractors' vans using the road had dropped to a trickle. If she crossed to the other side of the window she could see the white-taped 'H' of the helicopter landing circle beside the main marquee area in front of HPL's administration building, the smooth convexity of the lawns outside cluttered now with the business of tent-pegs, trestle tables, hospitality tents and guy-ropes. In the last hour the noise had dwindled away considerably as the florists and the catering firms had departed and the workmen had at last stopped their interminable hammering.

Everyone was going home. Except her.

Jenny dropped to her knees, slid across the carpet and picked up her novel again. Earlier when, ironically, there had been noise and bustle outside, she had managed to read a few pages, even lose herself completely for minutes at a time as she drifted away on the printed word. But now noise had been replaced by an unnerving, lonely silence and she found it impossible to concentrate. The shadows were lengthening outside and, like the sunshine, her confidence was fading.

She glanced at her watch for the hundredth time. She must have been out of her tiny mind to come up with a crazy idea like this. What did she hope to find? To prove? Jenny sat back hugging her knees, a lone, frail, frightened figure waiting for darkness in an empty office.

Dr Erskine sat back in his borrowed chair, folded his arms and regarded the group of fellow doctors over the top of his spectacles. There were eight of them now, including himself, all crowded into the one surgery in Fort William with a pile of confidential medical case notes on Dr Hastings' desk in front of him. Each surgery in Fort William used a different colour coding for their files to prevent confusion in the town's hospitals, and the top of the desk now looked like a multi-coloured quilt.

Two hours ago these same doctors had crowded into the surgery, each resenting beneath the facade of conventional politeness this sudden request to pool their knowledge and experience of the town's cardiovascular patients and listen to an elderly GP from Gleninver none of them had ever met before. Now, however, after each doctor had studied Mrs Proctor's case notes and asked whatever supplementary questions they considered necessary, that individual resentment had been replaced in most cases by an air of attentive concern.

In most cases, but not all. Dr Harrard was sitting back against the edge of the desk, arms folded and holding forth. '... if we take the simple business of numbers, gentlemen,' he was saying, 'then we *know* that forty-seven patients in and around the Fort William area have already switched to Cardocol from one or other of the usual beta-blockers or vasodilators. Of these—' he glanced down at a notepad – 'something in the region of ninety-four per cent have reported an immediate and significant reduction in blood pressure sustained over the full twenty-four-hour cycle without resort to additional drugs or medication.' He paused. 'To my own personal knowledge, gentlemen, one of these patients even had a persistent hypertensive characteristic of 106mmHg diastolic – and yet has made the change-over to this new drug with almost negligible side-effects and certainly not the slightest hint of end-organ damage. Not one of the patients canvassed thus far has expressed the slightest reservation about continuing with—'

'If I can stop you a moment there, Doctor,' Erskine interrupted. 'Would you mind telling us what side-effects you *have* seen? What adverse reactions? Just for the record, so to speak?'

Dr Harrard glanced down at his notes, scarcely bothering to conceal his irritation or the fact that he considered it all a gross waste of his very valuable time. He had suspected as much from the start: this didn't concern him at all. Dr Erskine's patient showed worrying symptoms, certainly, but that was a problem for Gleninver, not Fort William. And certainly not for Cardocol. He had read the promotional literature that had come through his letterbox: the drug was a breakthrough, a major step forward. It had been tested exhaustively, its success now, on the very eve of its launch, almost a foregone conclusion. What was more, he had no intention of letting this scruffy stranger with his half-formed theories and suspicions spoil his enjoyment of a free trip to Glasgow and a brief appearance at a medical symposium afterwards, all at the expense of Highland Pharmaceuticals Limited. He found the entry he was looking for and glanced up.

'A slight dry cough, that's all,' he said shortly. 'Which disappeared completely with the use of ordinary cough-mixture. A small price to pay, I should have thought, for the relief of symptoms which—'

'I'm sorry to interrupt you in full flow again,' said Dr Erskine. 'But I wonder how many of us here in this room are familiar with that?'

'With what, exactly?' demanded Dr Harrard acidly.

'With the fact that Cardocol causes a wee bit of bronchial inflammation?' There was a brief exchange of glances and then the hands began to go up. One . . . two . . . three . . .

Over the next few minutes they established that out of forty-seven patients, no fewer than seventeen had developed a dry, irritating cough soon after starting the new heart drug. Seventeen that they knew of definitely, here in this room. Predictably, it was Harrard who chose to ignore the significance of the discovery.

'What exactly is the point you wish to make, Doctor? Even if one hundred per cent of Cardocol patients developed a slight dry cough, I am sure that they, like me – like most of us here – would consider it cheap at the price.'

Dr Erskine nodded thoughtfully. 'I don't know,' he admitted candidly. 'I don't know that I am making a point at all,' he mused slowly. 'Except to say that if we are representative of the British Isles, then if twenty thousand people start taking this Cardocol as a matter of course, then . . . ' he spread his hands, 'at the very least that's an awful lot of coughs, would you not agree? Doctor?'

Hamish Owen leant forward slowly towards the coffee table in Helen Highcroft's sitting-room, the silence eggshell-thin between them as he waited for her to go on. Out in the hall a grandfather clock chimed the quarter as Helen shrugged helplessly, her fingers laced tightly over one knee as she gazed sightlessly into her empty coffee cup. Into the past. 'I . . . I thought all that was over, you see – finished,' she whispered. 'At least, I suppose I pretended I did. After we came back from America we . . . we never talked about his work any more. I suppose deep down I may have realized he was still involved, but I wanted to believe he'd kept his word. That he'd got out. I *needed* to believe that, do you see?'

'When did you live in America?' Hamish probed, his excitement crushed ruthlessly below the surface. This was dynamite.

'When the children were quite small. Between 1972 and 1975. That's what started the arguments, I suppose: seeing them growing up and knowing all the time what he was doing. It seemed . . . well, monstrous, somehow. Obscene.'

'Where were you living? In America?' Hamish asked quietly, waiting until she had looked away before picking up his pencil, aware that a sudden movement might stop the flow of words as quickly as they had started; that an insensitive, badly timed question could smash the fragile bond of trust he had managed to build between them ever since he had told her about Calvert, Steevenson and Parsons and about their link with Porton Down. It was as though he had thrown a switch. Turned a key.

'Where were we living? Oh . . . near a place called Pine Bluff, Arkansas. It sounds rather nice, doesn't it?'

'Well, I—'

'It wasn't,' she said bitterly, shaking her head and giving a sudden, nervous little shudder. 'It wasn't nice at all. Malcolm worked at Fort Detrick, you see.'

'Fort Detrick? I don't think I've ever heard of that.'

'You're not supposed to have,' Helen replied, with a tight, grim little smile that had nothing whatever to do with laughter. 'That's where we . . . that's where the Pentagon put the Army Medical Research Institute of Infectious Diseases when America renounced germ warfare and handed the whole place over to the National Cancer Institute. Malcolm worked on there in secret for months as an exchange microbiologist.'

'But we're not supposed to have any germ warfare capability, are we? No NATO countries are, including the United States.'

'Oh, we do,' sighed Helen cynically. 'We do, just like anyone else. Only our work is always "purely defensive",' she said, the sarcasm heavy in her voice. 'We do research just to keep up with what the other side may use against us. They, of course, are doing exactly the same thing for exactly the same reason. It's madness.'

'And your husband? Malcolm?'

'He was part of something called the "Watchtower Capability" – peering into the scientific future and helping to devise new, better, more economical ways of killing other human beings. That's what he was doing at Fort Detrick,' she sighed tiredly. 'And at Porton, too, I suppose.'

'And here, Mrs Highcroft? What about up here – at Highland Pharmaceuticals?' Hamish asked.

There was a long moment of silence before Helen looked up slowly and shrugged. 'I don't know, Mr Owen,' she said quietly. 'I . . . I think so, but I honestly don't know. I never had the courage to ask.'

CHAPTER TWENTY-TWO

It was dark.

Fifteen minutes ago, Jackman had pulled his Rover on to the soft shoulder of the perimeter track and doused the lights. He was a mile from the main entrance, and about thirty yards from one of the locked chain-link gates set into the perimeter fencing that enclosed Highland Pharmaceuticals on three sides and which provided alternative entry points for fire appliances in the event of a major emergency. The provision of those gates, ironically, was one of the very few conditions the Council had insisted upon when the site first opened. So far there had never been such an emergency and the perimeter track was little used, the verge lush with rank grass and wild flowers. It could have been some place of desolation, an abandoned wartime airfield perhaps, except for the hunched square block of darker shadow that was the HPL complex of buildings silhouetted against the dull gleam of Loch Linnhe beyond. A gentle breeze sighed through the woods nearby. The only light came from the car park and the main reception area three hundred metres from where Jackman waited now impatiently in the darkness. Taking a small pair of binoculars from the glove compartment, Jackman focused on the distant reception hall and watched as an elderly security guard reading a newspaper yawned, stretched, and then rose heavily to his feet with the air of a man who sees a long night stretching ahead of him.

'You won't find her there, Mr Jackman,' said a voice quietly. Jackman jumped. He hadn't heard Ridley come up beside him even though that was precisely the sound he was waiting for. He hadn't heard the door snick open, hadn't heard a thing. There had just been the faintest breeze on the side of his face and then that quiet, mocking voice of his out of the darkness as Ridley slid into the passenger seat beside him. Jackman sensed Ridley grin at his discomfort, at his unease in Ridley's private world of stealth.

'Any change?'

Jackman shook his head. 'She must still be in there. I checked with Security a while ago. Helen Highcroft went in and out on her own either side of half past five. No one called Jennifer Macrae's been anywhere near the place.'

'Not officially, anyway,' corrected Ridley quietly.

Jackman twisted round towards him. 'Look, are you *sure* all this is strictly necessary? Perhaps she changed her mind. If you—'

'Mr Jackman,' Ridley interrupted wearily. 'If you don't like it, if you're not happy, give Baxter a call in London. I'm telling you: she's in there. She's in there with a thermos of coffee and a packet of cheese-and-pickle sandwiches just waiting for—'

'Cheese and pickle? Come on! You can't possibly—'

'Can't possibly know? Oh, but I can, Mr Jackman – I can. She hadn't bothered to wash up, you see. All the stuff was still out on the draining-board, waiting to be read by nosy little people like me, OK?' He peeled back a cuff and activated his watch. 'Right – time I was away. Give the gate the word, will you?'

Jackman reached for the car-phone on the console beside him.

'Security.'

'Security, this is Maurice Jackman. I'm doing a perimeter check out on the east side. Will you please isolate gate four and leave in that condition until further notice.'

'I'll need the code of the day before I can do that, Mr Jackman.'

'Indeed. The code is: November Quebec Uniform, Zero Nine Alpha.'

'November Quebec Uniform, Zero Nine Alpha. Right you are then, Mr Jackman. If you can wait a moment, I'll have that done in a jiffy.' Jackman waited. 'Gate four is now isolated, Mr Jackman. Alarms are registered at inert.'

Jackman replaced the receiver and glanced across. 'Satisfied?'

'Thank you,' nodded Ridley. He held out a gloved hand. 'Keys?'

Jackman handed them across. 'What about the security men? Inside the building?' he asked.

'What about them?' Ridley countered, a hand on the door catch.

'If they see you—'

'They'd better be careful, hadn't they?' There was a soft chuckle followed by the faintest click and Jackman turned to find himself alone.

Ridley was off, running: a dark, fleeting shadow heading soundlessly towards HPL, towards Jenny. A man unleashed.

The lump of shadow on the floor of the darkened flat in Elgin Terrace stirred, groaned and tried to sit up. There was another cry, more of pain than of awakening, as Tony tried to focus on a corner of the rug and the skirt of the sofa that seemed to be hanging like some black cliff above his head. He felt the room tilt and sway beneath him, felt the dizziness turn to nausea and closed his eyes again as he tried to hang on to consciousness, fight the gnawing pain in his left shoulder and work out what the hell had happened to him. Why was everything so dark?

It came back slowly, piece by piece, and he groaned again as he remembered the man reading the newspaper, that sudden swirling movement towards him as he looked down, and then the blazing pain knifing down through his shoulder. The bastard, he thought, the medic inside him recognizing the anger for what it was and welcoming it as an aid to recovery. The bastard he'd thought was from S.5 but who couldn't be: S.5 didn't need to go round breaking people's collarbones and knocking them unconscious; S.5 had access to a different sort of sandbag. They could hit people behind the ears with the Official Secrets Act, threaten them with the Tower and Christ knows what. They had proper passes too, not skeleton keys in soft leather wallets.

Tony forced himself to open his eyes, gritted his teeth and hauled himself up the side of the sofa-mountain, left shoulder hunched high as the room began its slipping-away act and he sagged, half-sitting, half-lying, on to the sofa just in time. Presently the room settled on to a more or less even keel, and Tony edged his way gingerly towards the bathroom, left hand grasping right shoulder.

He tugged on the light, looked at himself in Jenny's bathroom mirror, wished he hadn't made the effort, ran water into the hand-basin and gingerly dunked his head in cold, clear water. That helped, it helped a great deal. It cleared his head but didn't do much for the throbbing agony in his shoulder as he wiped his head over with a towel, jerked open the linen cupboard and searched for anything that would do as a makeshift sling, the water still running off his head and down the inside of his shirt. He improvised with a tea towel, gulped down a couple of paracetamol from a bottle he found in Jenny's medicine cupboard, and eased himself slowly, carefully, through to the kitchen, grimacing with effort as he tried to push aside and discard the pain and remember something important, something to do with the man who had been waiting for him in Jenny's sitting-room, reading that sodding paper . . .

That was it, wasn't it? That was the whole bloody point! He hadn't been waiting for him, had he? He'd been waiting for *her* – for Jenny. And if he wasn't from S.5, then that meant . . . God. He had to warn her. So – think: where would she be? He looked at his watch and saw with a slow, curdling feeling of fear and realization that he had been out for hours. Jenny could be anywhere; he could already be too late, hours too late. Where? The office? No – stupid; she's been suspended. Her father, the old man in the bungalow? Possibly. What about that other woman, that Helen Highcroft, the one whose husband had walked out on her, vanished; the woman who'd listened to all those wild, crackpot theories of hers that suddenly didn't seem to be so wild and far-fetched after all?

Back into the sitting-room as quickly as he dared and

over to the telephone, panting for breath and hanging on to the edge of the table as the room threatened to take off again. Tony took the phone off the hook, dropped it on to the table with a clatter and dialled Enquiries, his left arm nursed diagonally across his chest. 'Yes. I'd . . . I'd like the number of a . . . a Professor Highcroft – you got that? Professor Malcolm Highcroft. In Gleninver. It's very urgent.'

Helen Highcroft waited until the tail-light of Hamish Owen's Morris had turned into the main road and then hurried back into the hall and shut the front door behind her.

Malcolm was dead. Somehow, somewhere, he had died. She knew that now and the knowledge brought with it a sense of release, not from grief and bitter sorrow and anger, but from the uncertainty, the self-doubt and endless self-examination that had haunted these last few days. Calvert, Steevenson and Parsons – all three had worked at Porton; all three were dead. Malcolm had worked at Porton also. Now he too was dead, she could feel it. Hamish Owen's questions and the information he had brought with him had triggered something deep inside her, dragging into the open at last those lurking fears that had been bottled up inside ever since America. Yet his probing questions had done more than that. Not only had they forced her to recognize the true nature of her husband's work, but they had opened her eyes to the danger not just to herself but to Jenny as well. Jenny, who was inside HPL right now, searching for information about Cardocol, unaware that all the while, all the while . . . Helen snatched up the phone and began dialling feverishly. If she could only reach her in time, warn her to get *out* . . .

Tony dropped the phone back on to the cradle, broke the connection and dialled the Highcroft number again. Still engaged. He slammed down the phone impatiently. The operator had given him Highcroft's address. It was only a few minutes across town if he could drive. He could wait for the line to be free, of course, but that could take hours. And he didn't have hours. He'd try the phone once more. After that . . . He dialled again, heard the engaged tone and banged down the phone. Nursing his bruised shoulder, head tilted to one side away from the pain, Tony hurried down the hall, slammed the door behind him and clambered awkwardly behind the wheel of his car. More pain as he reached down and started the engine, stretched across with his right hand for the handbrake and banged the car into gear.

Jenny rose cautiously to her feet. At last the waiting was over and it was time to move. Crouching down, scrabbling around on the carpet in the darkness, not daring yet to use her torch in case she was seen from outside, Jenny stuffed her things into her bag, pressed an ear against the door and listened intently for any sound from the corridor beyond. A moment passed in complete silence. She reached for the door handle, was actually just beginning to turn it slowly anticlockwise, when the phone rang on the desk.

Jenny whirled round – as shocked, as frightened, as though someone had suddenly shouted her name. She stared at the telephone, fluttering with panic. An automatic reflex made her reach out to take the call and then she hesitated. She might as well fling open the door and turn on all the lights, she thought. Then a little voice prompted that it might be Helen. That it *had* to be Helen, for who else knew she was there? Who else knew there was anyone inside that particular office long after everyone else had gone home? What if it was a wrong number – or someone from HPL? What if . . . what if even now someone was coming down the corridor to answer it – someone from Security, for example? That decided her. She couldn't risk it; daren't. Back to the door, a quick listen with the phone strident and demanding behind her, and Jenny stepped out into the corridor closing the door quietly behind her.

No one in sight. Not a sound apart from that muffled ringing of the telephone. Just the door with its square of yellow light showing the well-lit reception area beyond at one end of the corridor, and darkness at the other with a staircase leading up to offices on the floor above – and the office, in particular, which Harold Engel claimed Highcroft had left before they entered the lift together. A quick glance over her shoulder and Jenny was running lightly down the corridor towards the staircase. Away from the lights. And safety.

Leaving her thermos on the office floor behind her.

Helen slammed down the telephone and groaned aloud. She was too late. She had missed her.

Ridley flattened himself back against the north-eastern corner of HPL's main building and paused, his every sense alive to the sight, feel and sound of the night around him: the scud of cloud across the face of a pale moon; the feel of the bricks coarse beneath his hands; the murmur of the wind sighing through the trees and the distant murmur of traffic; the muted hum of the air-conditioning in the building beside him, and the thin weep-weep-weep of some night bird hunting nearby. Another predator.

He moved silently along the wall towards the fire-escape door at the far side of the building. Another listen, a moment's delay while he worked on the deadlock, and then he was inside among the darkness and the velvet shadows he loved with only the milky gleam of steady, unblinking eyes to betray his presence as the door closed behind him.

Up the winding steps one at a time, the sound of her own nervous breathing loud in her ears as she groped her way up the unfamiliar staircase to the first floor. At length she reached the top, although it seemed to take an age. Here, she decided with a sigh of relief, here she could risk using the torch, just to get her bearings. Shielding its face between her fingers, Jenny turned it on and was rewarded by a sudden glimpse of empty corridor with the lifts to her left and identical office doors marching away into the shadows on her right. Off went the torch.

She walked cautiously forward, hands outstretched in front of her like a child playing some nursery game. Ah.

The wall. Left a bit . . . her hands encountered first the door surround, then the door itself. It opened to her touch, and she entered what she hoped would prove to be Malcolm Highcroft's office. Another quick flash of the torch: desk, chairs, filing cabinet. Potted plants on the windowsill, medical posters and calendars, progress charts and in-jokes pinned to a noticeboard. All the signs of normal occupancy; all the signs that had been so conspicuously absent downstairs. Jenny slipped behind the desk, pulled open the top drawer and switched on her torch: pencils and paperclips, a box of elastic bands, luncheon vouchers and a stapler. An office diary. She flicked it open and looked in the flyleaf: Stuart Young.

Jenny frowned. So they had both been wrong: downstairs might not have been Malcolm's office, but this one wasn't either. It didn't look like it anyway, not on second glance. This was the office of an administrator, a paper-pusher, not a scientist. She closed the diary after a quick flick through the pages and was just about to put it back in the drawer when she saw that it had been lying on top of something that might prove even more revealing: an internal HPL telephone directory. Jenny sat down in the chair behind the desk, hunched forward and began turning over the pages under the shaded beam of her torch, looking for Malcolm's extension number. It wasn't hard to find for employees' names, predictably, were listed alphabetically: Highcroft, Prof. M. . . . 650. Helen had been right.

Jenny bent forward and looked at the face of the phone in front of her. There, beneath the instruction DIAL 0 FOR OUTSIDE LINE, she read the extension number: 482.

Dial 0 for an outside line . . . Impulsively Jenny lifted the receiver, dialled 0, winced at the noise and waited, half expecting to hear the operator demand to know what she thought she was up to. Instead, she heard the solid burr of the dialling tone. Covering the earpiece with her hand, she lowered the phone, cocked her head to one side and listened. Nothing. Not a sound. She took out her diary, looked up Helen's home number and dialled as quietly as she could. But there isn't a quiet way to dial a telephone number from a dark, empty office in the middle of the night, she discovered, as the face of the phone unwound deafeningly. The number was dialled at last, there was silence – and then the call began to ring in. Brr-brr . . . brr-brr . . . brr—

'Hello?'

'Helen? It's me – Jenny,' she whispered.

'Jenny! Thank God. I was trying to—'

'Sssh! Keep your voice down,' Jenny hissed fiercely, hunching forward with a hand cupped round the phone's mouthpiece, her eyes on the door and the faint lightness of the corridor outside. 'I'm in Malcolm's office on the first floor – at least, what we thought was Malcolm's office, next to the lifts. Only it's not – Malcolm's office, I mean. It belongs to someone called Young. He—'

'Jenny, listen to me. You—'

'—You were right about one thing, though: the extension. I've—'

'Jenny – shut up! Listen!' Helen urged desperately. She got through.

'What's the matter?'

'I . . . I want you out of there. Now. Please.'

'What? Don't be silly! I've only just—'

'I . . . I mean it. There isn't time to explain now, but there's . . . there's more going on than you think. More than just Cardocol.'

Jenny frowned into the phone. '*More* than just Cardocol?' she whispered. 'What d'you mean?'

'You remember that reporter you told me about? Hamish Owen – the one from the local rag?'

'What about him?'

'He came here to see me. I tried to call you after he'd gone, to warn you, but there was no reply.'

'To *warn* me? What about?'

'He'd . . . he'd been doing some digging – about Engel and the company. And about those . . . those other men who died, you remember?'

'Go on,' Jenny whispered, hunching closer to the phone.

'He thinks something . . . something happened to them. That their car didn't just go over the cliff by accident. He found out they'd all been working at Porton, too. He found that out as well.'

Jenny frowned. 'Too? Who else worked there? I'm sorry, I don't follow.'

'Porton Down's some sort of secret chemical warfare establishment. Malcolm . . . Malcolm used to work there too. A long time ago. Before we came up to Scotland.'

There was silence while that sank in, then – 'You never told me. You never said anything about Porton,' accused Jenny.

'I know I didn't. I just . . . didn't think it was relevant, I suppose . . . '

'Not relevant?' Jenny demanded incredulously, her voice rising. 'Malcolm used to work at Porton Down and you didn't think it was *relevant*?'

'Sssh! I . . . I'm sorry. I don't know what else I can say.'

Jenny gripped the phone tightly and forced herself to remain calm. 'All right, all right – let's just think. This . . . this Hamish Owen reckons they all worked together, is that it?'

'He doesn't know for certain yet. He—'

'Wait a second,' Jenny interrupted suddenly. 'Just . . . wait a second, all right?' She pulled pencil, paper and internal directory towards her and began turning over the pages impatiently. 'What were those names, can you remember?'

'Jenny – please. Get out of there. You—'

'In a minute, in a minute. Just give me the names . . . '

'All right: Martin Calvert. Tony . . . no . . . Thomas Steevenson and Douglas Parsons.'

'Hang about.' Jenny cradled the phone against her shoulder and ran a finger rapidly down the first page. There! Calvert, M: . . . 648. Jenny gabbled through the alphabet under her breath, her eyes flicking constantly to that open, empty doorway. M . . . N . . . O . . . – P. P for Parsons. Got it! Parsons, D: . . . 645. Then Steevenson, T, right at the back: 646. They *had* all been working together!

So what were the odds on three men who worked together all dying within the same . . . She grabbed the phone. 'Helen?' she whispered excitedly. 'Guess what?'

'What?'

'He's right! Parsons worked on extension 645, Steevenson on 646, and Calvert on 648 – they're all together! They probably worked in the same office!'

'All right, fine. Now please, will you just get out of there? Go down to the—'

But Jenny hadn't finished yet. 'A moment, OK? Just a moment,' she whispered. Beginning at the front of the HPL internal directory, Jenny began sweeping a finger not down the left-hand column of names, but down the right-hand column of numbers, searching for any other extension with a six-four prefix.

Heyer, Dr P 383
Highcroft, Prof. M 650
Inger, J 866
Jackman, M 640/483

'Malcolm and Jackman, Helen,' she said matter-of-factly. 'They worked with them too, although Jackman appears—' She leant forward suddenly, looking not at Jackman's six-four prefix but at the three-number digit that followed it. And then at the face of the phone she was using herself: 482 . . . 'Jackman has two offices, Helen,' she said urgently, her voice pitched low with excitement. 'It looks like one's next door! I'll see if it's open, OK? Then I'll—'

'Jenny, please. Don't be a fool! If you—'

'Call you back.' She rang off, pulled an anguished face at the ting! of the phone as it went down on its cradle, put diary and internal directory back where she had found them and rose to her feet. One thing, she had the building completely to herself. And there was plenty of time . . .

Helen groaned aloud with frustration, dragged a hand back through her hair and was just turning towards the kitchen when she heard the crunch of gravel outside as a car braked to a halt, a door slammed and there was a sudden long ring on the doorbell. Helen went hesitantly out into the hallway. It was too late for callers, friends to just happen by. She dropped the chain on to its catch, turned on the porch light and pulled the door cautiously towards her. 'Yes?' There was a man outside with his arm in some sort of sling. He looked pasty-faced, grey with pain as he stood there on the doorstep, a hand on the wall holding him up.

'Mrs . . . Mrs Highcroft?'

'Yes? What do you want?'

'Is Jenny with you? Jenny Macrae?'

'I don't—'

'Please, Mrs Highcroft, just tell me. It's very important.'

'Who wants to know?'

'My name's Tony Lockhart. I'm a . . . a friend.'

Ridley moved unhesitatingly down the corridor, turned left at the bottom and peered cautiously through the small square window into reception. He had spent twenty solid minutes in his motel bedroom studying the floor plan of the building and was now able to move around the labyrinth of unlit corridors and empty offices and laboratories with a confidence and a sense of direction that suggested he had been doing so all his working life.

Nothing to worry about from reception, he thought contemptuously. The security guard was leaning back in his chair, tunic buttons undone, one fat hand groping unwatched at an open tin of thick-cut sandwiches, his eyes glued to the boxing on a small portable television tucked away out of sight beneath the top of the reception desk.

Ridley turned quietly on his heel, retraced his steps and paused outside the third door along, the one marked 'X' on the diagram he had found in Jenny Macrae's flat. Then he slipped into the office, whipped the door shut behind him, turned the key and pressed back against the wall to listen intently in the darkness.

Jackman's door was unlocked. Jenny moved carefully past the dark bulk of his secretary's desk and tried the handle to the inner office. That opened, too. Another quick, surreptitious flash of the torch – same sort of office as before, same aspect, only bigger, more spacious: wide desk, chair and a row of filing cabinets; modern sofa along one wall with, nearby, a computer terminal on a polished pine table. Nothing special in the top drawer of the desk this time apart from a plastic identity tag for a Mr Maurice Jackman, Project Development Manager.

But in the bottom drawer that was deeper than the rest she found a jumble of miscellaneous personal possessions, among which was a framed photograph of three smiling children playing on a garden climbing frame, together with a bundle of internal laboratory analysis reports sent from somewhere called E11 to someone called Professor M. Highcroft, RD7.

In the shallow grey pencil tray that slid out of the top right-hand side of Jackman's desk, Jenny discovered a single round silver metal key. She took it over with her to the filing cabinets and found them shut fast. Against every hope and expectation the key fitted the centre lock, and the first heavily laden drawer rolled obediently towards her on smooth, silent runners.

Whatever else Jackman might be, he was a tidy, methodical professional who kept his files in apple-pie order. There were several at the front neatly tagged and marked simply: CARDOCOL. Jenny lifted them out, took them over to the desk, spread them out in front of her and switched on her torch.

One of the first things she found was a thick, green, ring-bound folder marked:

CONFIDENTIAL. CARDOCOL CLINICAL TRIALS
SERIES 886/FGJ

Jenny sat forward and opened the folder. Then, with a sudden little shiver of excitement, of arrival, she began to read . . .

Tony hurried down Helen Highcroft's front steps, crossed the gravel and slid awkwardly behind the wheel of his car, wincing with pain suddenly as he jarred his shoulder against the lip of the door. Helen watched him anxiously from the doorway as he reached forward for the ignition. 'What about the police?' she called suddenly. 'If you went to them surely they'd—'

'The police?' Tony shook his head and started the car. 'I'd just be wasting my time,' he shouted over the noise of the engine. 'They're out of their league!' He banged the car brutally into gear and drove out on to the main road with an angry spurt of gravel.

The silence of Jackman's office was broken by the slow turning of a page as Jenny leant forward appalled, torch in hand, and read again that final, damning paragraph. Just to be certain there was no mistake:

> . . . while volunteers undergoing clinical trials at registered out-patient clinics and surgeries have shown an incidence of adverse reaction deemed to be commercially unacceptable, those in hospitals have not. It is therefore recommended that consideration be given to the selective amalgamation of both sets of statistics shown in 17/AEK (attached) before submission to CSM. It is anticipated that an adjustment of as little as between seven and eleven per cent overall would be sufficient to deflect an adverse decision by the licensing authority. Such a finding would have catastrophic repercussions, not just upon Cardocol's short-term commercial profile, but upon the long-term viability of Highland Pharmaceuticals itself.

There was a small neat tick at the bottom of the paragraph with, beside it, one word and two initials: 'Agreed. M.J.' Maurice Jackman.

Jenny sat back in her chair, stunned. There it was, in black and white. Not satisfied with the results of their own trials and tests under legitimate conditions, HPL, with the endorsement of its own Project Development Manager, had cold-bloodedly decided to stack the deck, bend the rules; to cheat. Not by much, perhaps, but by enough to ensure that the granting of their application for a product licence was a foregone conclusion. Postural hypotension, the condition whose mastery was at the very core of

Cardocol's appeal, the essence of its claim to originality in an overstocked, cut-throat marketplace, had never been at issue with between seven and eleven per cent of those patient-volunteers who had taken part in HPL's programme of clinical trials. Because they had been *flat on their backs*, supine, bed-bound in some hospital ward.

Jenny closed the ring-bound folder, slid it into her bag and replaced the other files where she had found them, conscious of a cold, raging fury at what she had discovered; at the verbose, grandiloquent manner in which some businessman had dressed up the sordid business of deception: selective amalgamation . . . commercial profile . . . long-term viability. But there had been nothing there about people. Or illness. Or caring. Nothing about Robbie Roberts or Jamie Ennis. Just commercial considerations about profit. Profit without honour.

Ridley bent down smoothly and felt on the office floor for the object he had just brushed with his foot. He found it, identified Jenny's thermos for what it was and rose silently to his feet. She'd been here, definitely. He'd sensed it before – now a hunter's instinct had been endorsed by tangible evidence. He placed the thermos on the desk and slipped out into the deserted corridor. Then he turned right towards the staircase. And the offices above.

Jenny pushed the filing cabinet closed, turned round – and then froze as she thought she heard something. She listened carefully, straining, head cocked to one side. Then she let out her breath in a slow sigh of relief. Nothing. She must have imagined it. Picking up the piece of paper on which she had written the names Calvert, Steevenson and Parsons, Jenny went slowly towards Jackman's computer, a plan forming in her mind. She switched on her torch for a moment and recognized the model immediately. They had had an identical computer in the clinic for the last nine months, given to the local Health Service by that well-known local benefactor, Highland Pharmaceuticals.

She sat down in front of it, glanced round nervously at

the silent room watching her, and then back at the dark, inert screen, wondering if she dared. She brought the machine to life, and the screen turned her face ghostly green against the darkness of the office as the room filled with a low, scarcely audible hum. Jenny thought for a moment and then keyed in: PERSONNEL SEARCH. The words were stripped in instantly in front of her eyes, white on green, and were followed by the instruction: INPUT LOAD. Jenny's fingers worked over the keys.

CALVERT M. HIGHCROFT M. JACKMAN M. PARSONS D. STEEVENSON T. She paused then while the cursor blinked at her patiently from the screen's top left-hand corner as she tried to remember the language. SEARCH COMMONALITY she typed. Blink. Blink. Blink—

SECURITY CLEARANCE came the reply.

WRONG banged in Jenny, using lies to trick the machine into divulging more than it should.

CORRECT . . . CORRECT . . . insisted the computer, angry now. CALVERT M HIGHCROFT M JACKMAN M PARSONS D STEEVENSON T ALL CLEARED FOR ACCESS RD7.

DEFINE RD7 ACCESS tried Jenny. And blew it. The ploy was too crude, too obvious. The computer didn't buy it, not for a moment.

VERIFY OPERATOR CLEARANCE PROJECT OMAHA it demanded sternly.

OMAHA? thought Jenny. What the hell was OMAHA? If it . . . there was a noise next door: the smallest, quietest click as though a door had been softly closed. Jenny froze for a moment, then reached out a stealthy hand and turned off the terminal. The screen cleared, the low hum sighed away to silence, and Jenny slid away from the chair, crossed the office and crouched down beside Jackman's desk. Scared and worried, yes, but not terrified. Not yet, for she was still thinking in terms of detection and embarrassment, of a possible court appearance and fine, not in terms of her own survival. It was probably just the old security man from downstairs doing his rounds.

It wasn't. It was Ridley, working methodically along the first floor from one empty office to another. He paused outside Jackman's outer office door, a gloved hand on the door jamb. She had been in here. He could smell it, quite literally. He could smell the faintest hint of soap and perfume mingled with that charged, electric residue of fear, of excitement, that would pass unnoticed among nine hundred and ninety-nine men out of a thousand. He moved on, one slow, careful step at a time as he listened for the rustle of cloth, the stifled intake of nervous breathing, anything at all. Past the secretary's desk and through, his senses fine-tuned to that moment of certainty when he would know he was no longer alone. Silent as the dark that enveloped him, Ridley felt the wall smooth against his gloved fingers, sank down to his haunches and waited. She was close now, very close. He could feel it . . .

Helen stood alone and irresolute in her hallway, her fears for Jenny magnified tenfold now by Tony's visit and his brief, terse description of the man he had found waiting in Jenny's flat. If only she would leave, get out of that place. Finally, Helen could bear the waiting no longer. She picked up the phone and began dialling the number Jenny had given her a few minutes earlier. The number of Jackman's office.

The phone rang suddenly on Jackman's desk, inches from Jenny's head. She started violently and banged her head against the edge of the desk. Oh, Helen – no! In some half-thought-out attempt to repair the damage already done by that single strident ring of the bell, Jenny rose from behind the desk and reached for the phone. Her hand encountered not the smooth plastic of the receiver, but the soft leather of a glove covering a human hand.

'Snap,' said a voice softly.

CHAPTER TWENTY-THREE

Jenny let out a stifled scream and pulled her hand away as though it had been scalded. Stumbling back towards the window, she fumbled with the torch and switched it on. The beam wavered, settled on a dark-blue arm and moved up to the thin, drawn face of a man weirdly streaked with camouflage cream. The phone rang on, oblivious.

'Well?' said the man softly. 'Aren't you going to answer it?'

Jenny tried to speak but the words wouldn't come. 'I . . . I . . . '

'Go on, answer it.'

Jenny wondered wildly if she had gone suddenly mad, flipped; if this apparition, this nightmare, could possibly be real. 'Who . . . who are you?' she managed finally. 'What are you doing here like . . . like that?'

'What am *I* doing here? I might . . . ah.' The phone stopped ringing suddenly and there was silence. Ridley shook his head regretfully. 'You should always answer the telephone, didn't they ever tell you that, Jennifer?'

Jennifer. 'How do you know my name?' she whispered, as realization built horror upon horror. Ridley said nothing. He just waited there patiently, like Mr Spider. When Jenny could stand it no longer – 'If you're going to call the police, I—'

Ridley seemed to find the possibility amusing. 'Call the police, Jennifer? No. I don't think I'll do that. It would hardly be . . . appropriate. Not in this instance. I – TURN THAT OFF!' While he had been talking, Jenny had stepped forward, reached out and switched on Jackman's desk lamp. The man was clearer now, his dimensions less sinister. Jenny could see that he was wearing a two-piece, dark-blue tracksuit with the hood folded down around his neck; and that he was holding a slender-bladed knife down against his right thigh. In that instant, in that frozen moment of discovery, Jenny knew that he had nothing to do with the police or with the company security men downstairs. This man was different. This man was death.

As Ridley reached for the lamp switch, Jenny darted forward, swept the lamp off the desk towards him and lunged at the door. A fleeting impression then of Ridley swerving aside as she hurled her torch back towards him, a splintering crash as the lamp fell to the floor and the room was plunged into darkness. Through the far door and spinning right to hurtle down the corridor with Ridley somewhere behind her. Darkness, terror, and endless flight – the stuff of every child's nightmare become reality as the horror of silent, unseen pursuit, of reaching hands behind her, gave Jenny wings. Crashing through another door and flinging it back behind her, Jenny ran blindly along the first-floor corridor, not caring if there were steps or walls or the deepest hole in the world waiting for her ahead. She wanted only to get away. To escape. One second, two, three – and then bang! as shc heard Ridley flat-hand his way through the same swing door and come racing silently after her.

Round another corner with just the sob of her own breath for company. More darkness to her left, the lighter outline of a door and window to her right, the slightest delay as she hesitated – and it was too late. A hand reached out and grabbed her roughly by the hair. 'Far enough, girlie.'

Jenny screamed with fear and pain as Ridley jerked her viciously back towards him and slammed her round against the wall. 'Game over.' There was a sudden glint of steel as he moved closer.

Tony slowed down for the turning, swung the wheel to the right, grinding his teeth with the pain in his left shoulder as he trod on the brakes and the gatehouse slid into view. He sounded the car horn impatiently with the heel of his hand, and watched as the door swung open and the HPL security guard came out towards him. Tony didn't wait. As the man raised a slow hand in greeting and then moved to one side to approach the driver's window, Tony banged the car back into gear, trod on the accelerator and surged past. Round the bend and on, the headlights swinging across velvet shadow and the pale gleam of tents waiting for morning as the cries of the guard receded behind him, the road flattened out, and the main building with its ground-floor lights swung into view. Left arm and shoulder aching with the effort of movement, Tony glanced to right and left searching for a car, lights, anything that might give him a lead. Both car parks were empty. There wasn't a vehicle in sight. Well, he knew where she was, Helen Highcroft had told him that much, at least. All he had to do now was go in there and find her. Simple. Except that the moment he – there! Something, movement! Tony had been turning the car left across the far end of the larger of the two car parks when something just beyond the glare of his lights caught his eye. Instinctively, Tony tightened the turn and flicked the headlights on to main beam. Jenny! Jenny and that bastard caught together out in the open, the man forcing Jenny's arm up behind her back and pushing her forward in front of him across the grass, the pair turning now, frozen in the glare of his headlights. Tony slewed the car across the car park towards them, bumped over the raised grass hummock separating lawn from tarmac and accelerated across the grass, wheels spinning and sliding as they fought for purchase. Suddenly Jenny broke free and began to run to the right, away from Ridley. Tony didn't hesitate. Ridley was the threat, the danger. He swung the car towards him, aimed for the widening gap between Jenny and his target and kept going, eyes flinty-hard as he crouched down behind the wheel as Ridley turned now and began to run. Tony swung the car after him – thirty yards . . . twenty . . . He was aware not of the running, twisting figure as a man, another human being made up of flesh and blood, but simply as a target, something to be smashed and destroyed. Ten . . . A swerve, a slight thud and Ridley had gone, lost somewhere in the darkness behind him as he swung the car away in a wide, slithering turn across neat green lawn and twisted round, looking for Jenny. There she was! Over by the edge of the car park, one hand to her mouth. He turned towards her, bumped back on to the tarmac and screeched to a halt beside her. Reaching over, he flung open the passenger door.

'Tony! I—'

'Get in. Quickly. Before that bastard gets back—' Breathlessly, Jenny scrambled in beside him. Tony accelerated forward, throwing Jenny back against the seat as the door slammed shut. A quick glance to his left. 'You OK?'

Jenny nodded, gulping air. Quivering with shock. 'I . . . I think so. God, he – watch the road!' They swerved violently towards the grass verge, swung back on to the road with a screech of rubber and sped down towards the main gate.

Ridley rose to his feet, brushed down his arms with slow deliberation and watched as their tail-lights disappeared from sight. He had leapt aside at the last moment, banged a hand against the side of Tony's car as it swept past. He hadn't been hurt at all.

It had suddenly become very personal.

Dr Erskine closed the cottage door softly behind him and began walking slowly back down the steep cobbled lane towards his Rover, his nostrils full of the tang of the sea. He paused presently by the sea wall to light his pipe and stare unseeing out across the bay towards the whaleback hump of island, the salt-laden breeze ruffling his hair as he stood there with pipe clenched between his teeth, his mind heavy with a sense of personal guilt, of failure, that linked the small bottle of cough-mixture in his pocket to a new heart drug called Cardocol – and to a patient who had died out there by that island less than a week ago, taking a small child with him.

Dr Erskine had spent the last half-hour talking to Robbie Roberts' widow. As always, despite the lateness of the hour, she had received him with unfailing kindness and courtesy. That only made him feel worse for she, like most of his older patients, trusted him blindly. She did so for the simple reason that the family doctor, like the minister, was someone you always trusted without question. Yet now Dr Erskine believed that, although her husband's death might not have been iatrogenic, he was still personally to blame, still responsible. He stared out across the bay, conscious of a pricking tiredness behind his eyes and a stoop to his shoulders after the long drive back along the coast from Fort William, remembering a younger man who had entered the medical profession full of blazing ideals and a simple passion for healing, but who, over the years, had been overtaken by the very advances he should have welcomed. And who had become too rigid, too complacent, too set in the comfort of his ways to recognize it . . .

He turned away and walked heavily down the cobbled lane. As he got into his car, he felt the little bottle of cough-mixture he had found on Mrs Roberts' kitchen table digging into his pocket. He took it out and tossed it into the cardboard box with the others. First, he would return to the surgery. A few days ago – was it only then? – the presentation of that complete set of Groesners had seemed like a harmless perk, an innocent gesture of appreciation from local manufacturer to local doctor. Now, he saw it as a reward for professional neutrality, for compliance and the suspension of cynicism. The books would be returned in the morning – that was easy enough. Meanwhile, however, there was something he still had to do before he could sleep. He started the engine. He would go and see Harold Engel, the Managing Director of Highland Pharmaceuticals. There was something he had to tell him.

Jenny swung towards Tony as the signpost flashed past in the car's headlights. He was hunched grimly over the wheel, the pain in his shoulder pasting a waxy sheen to his face as they jolted over another darkened pot-hole. 'This isn't the way to the hospital.'

'I know,' he replied tersely, concentrating on keeping

the car on the road. HPL was a couple of miles behind them now as they drove towards Gleninver.

'Your shoulder, Tony! If we don't—'

'They'll be watching the hospital. Your place too.'

'*My* place? But—'

'That's where I got this. That bastard back there was waiting inside. For you.' He flinched. 'That'll teach me to . . . to talk to strangers.'

'But you got him, didn't you? Back there! It's over – finished! All we have to do now – what's the matter?'

'You still don't understand, do you?'

'Understand what? I understand he was going to kill me, if that's what you mean! He—'

'Just . . . just shut up a minute, will you? Shut up and listen.' He glanced across at her briefly, and there was a slight nod of apology and his eyes softened for a moment before flicking back to the road. 'Let me . . . let me try and explain something,' he said quietly. 'It isn't "finished", as you put it, until those people say it is, OK? You can't just stick your hands in the air and say "Pax" just because you feel like it. We're not playing some sort of . . . of game, understand? That's the first thing.'

'Who, for God's sake, are "*they*", Tony? Will you just tell me that?'

'Remember that policeman I told you about? The one on the cliff I gave those passes to?'

Jenny nodded, and then waited as Tony gritted his teeth against a sudden wave of pain. 'Want me to drive?' she offered.

Tony shook his head. 'That report of his went down the line – to headquarters somewhere, I don't know. Anyway, it doesn't matter. Next thing we know, blokes from Military Intelligence are crawling all over the shop asking questions about somewhere called RD7, while I'm ordered – *ordered*, mind – to forget what I saw; forget all about those passes. And when I go to your flat, the place has been turned over, right? Searched by sunny Jim back there with the healing hands.'

Jenny shuddered. 'But I'd never even *seen* him before—'

Tony glanced across pityingly. 'Doesn't that tell you something?'

The tone of superiority, of private, inner knowledge, fanned Jenny's anger, her fear, into flame. 'No, it doesn't "tell me something", Mister high-and-bloody-mighty helicopter winchman – why the hell should it? I'm not exactly *trained* for this sort of thing, you know. I'm a speech therapist, remember? I know about children and hearing and . . . speech defects, not military intelligence and . . . and . . . ' She pushed a hand through her hair and then added, more quietly, 'I'm scared, all right? I'm just bloody scared. I'm sorry, but that's the truth.' A moment's silence. 'What should it tell me – please? I'd be interested to know.'

'That this is important,' said Tony quietly. 'They're not messing around, these people. They're serious, professional.' He paused. 'You got *any* idea what you've stumbled into? It's a damn sight more important than just some minor scandal over a new heart drug, I'll tell you that for nothing.'

Jenny nodded and gazed out into the darkness as she remembered what Helen had told her on the phone and saw again that one word punched up on the computer display: OMAHA.

'HPL's some sort of cover for something to do with chemical warfare – at least, I think it is,' she said quietly. 'Malcolm Highcroft used to work at Porton Down. So did the others – Parsons, Steevenson and Calvert – they all did.'

The car swerved suddenly. 'Christ Almighty – chemical warfare!' Tony muttered. 'So that's it . . . ' They drove on in silence for a moment or two, then—

'You still haven't told me where we're going.'

Tony hesitated. He had been thinking a lot about that: the local hospital, Gleninver police, even RAF Glenhaddon – all offered more danger, variations upon a lethal theme, for he knew now who "they" were. "They" were the State, Government, the Authorities – and he and Jenny had suddenly become Very Undesirable People. Yet they couldn't just keep on driving, blundering on aimlessly through the night until they ran out of petrol. Not with a pack of hungry mice gnawing away at his shoulder. He needed time. Time to think and rest, plan and recover.

'Home,' he decided finally. 'My house – all right? Just to get this shoulder of mine sorted out. Then . . . then we'll go east. A town. Somewhere nice and big.'

'Like *Glasgow*?' Jenny asked incredulously.

'Glasgow,' Tony confirmed definitely as the idea took hold. 'Glasgow hospital. Then Glasgow newspapers, Glasgow television. Lots and lots of lovely exposure.' He paused. 'Got any better ideas?'

'—And I can only repeat: you are worrying unnecessarily,' said Jackman tiredly. They were standing over a plan of HPL's site in Harold Engel's study and running over the final details of the launch and reception in the morning. 'Nothing will go wrong. Nothing *can* go wrong. Everything's taken care of, right down to the last detail. No one will be permitted anywhere near RD7. So relax. Forget about it. Have a drink. Tomorrow's supposed to be your day, isn't it? God knows, you've worked hard enough for it.' The words weren't getting through, he could see it; sense it. 'Look—' he soothed. 'I know we've had our differences over this Highcroft business—'

Engel's head snapped up. 'Differences? *Differences*? Dear God, is that all you think they are?' he challenged harshly. 'They're more than just "differences", I assure you.'

Jackman shrugged. 'Very well, I accept that – for the sake of argument. But what is over is past, finished. You can't bring him back. So – look to the future. Another month, two at the most, and Cardocol will be a household name. Yours will be too.' He paused. 'Well? That's what you want, isn't it? That's what you've strived for. Recognition. Vindication. A chance to—'

'Don't tell me what I want, Jackman. Don't you dare tell me what I want – ever,' said Harold Engel, with quiet, cold fury. 'You don't begin to understand what I want. You and I are so far apart we might as well be on different planets.'

Jackman smiled, not in the least put out. He thought he understood the motive and psyche of Highland Pharmaceuticals' Managing Director, he really did.

'Nonsense! Results – that's all that matters,' he said briskly. 'We're after the same thing, you and I.' He paused, and then added thoughtfully, as though realizing something for the first time, 'Perhaps that's what really frightens you, hmm? Not that we are so different but that we are so *alike*. We travel to the same destination by different routes, that's all. I, at least, pride myself upon being a realist. To achieve results I accept there must inevitably be compromise, sacrifice. Decisions that are sometimes . . . unpleasant must be taken to achieve the aim. But you? You?' he scoffed. 'You choose to delude yourself that you are above all that, that you can somehow keep your hands clean in that ivory tower of yours you call clinical research, and remain detached and untainted by what is going on beneath the surface to maintain precisely that facade that permits your work to continue. RD7 would not exist without HPL – true. And the converse is also true. Highland Pharmaceuticals – Cardocol – would not exist without Tabun GA and RD7. The ends, Harold – the ends always justify the means. They always will. You choose to forget that if you hadn't been so desperate for another chance after the Bookham fiasco, our paths would never have crossed. We—'

'Bookham was not a fiasco,' corrected Engel fiercely. 'If people had only—'

'Been more patient? Had more vision, perhaps? Backed you just a little bit longer? Poured just a few more thousands into your company – is that what you were about to say?' soothed Jackman with that mocking voice of his. 'Ah, but they didn't, did they? That's just the point. And so you have to take what you can get, grasp the opportunities as they come by, even . . . even suspend those delicate sensibilities of yours occasionally if you believe in something enough, if you really want to achieve your aim – whether it's the creation of a new heart drug or the manufacture of a new chemical warfare agent in the peace and quiet of the Scottish countryside.'

'If Cardocol works—'

'If? *If*? Don't tell me you are beginning to have doubts?' Jackman mocked.

'Let me make you a promise, Jackman,' Engel said with deadly seriousness. 'If Cardocol's a success – and it will be, I think we both know that – then I will never, never permit my company to be used by you and your people again, is that quite clear? I've done things for you that will be on my conscience for the rest of my days. Well, you can find someone else to blackmail into providing you with your . . . your facilities!' He almost spat the word out.

'Blackmail? Come now, Harold, it was hardly that – aren't you being a trifle over-dramatic? Besides, I think you'll find you've left things a little late for that sort of ultimatum.'

'What d'you mean?'

Jackman shook his head sadly and smiled. 'Harold, Harold – you really can be most delightfully naive at times. Do you seriously imagine the Defence Procurement Secretariat pulled your name out of a . . . a *hat*? Do you think they went to all that trouble just to—' They both turned to a knock on the door. It opened, and Joyce Engel stood framed in the doorway.

'Sorry to interrupt. There's a . . . oh . . . ' She broke off as she sensed the atmosphere in the study. Glancing anxiously at her husband – 'There's a Dr Erskine to see you, Harold.'

The name meant nothing to her husband, nor to Jackman. Engel glanced at his watch. 'What – at this time of night?' It was after midnight.

Joyce nodded. 'I suggested waiting until morning but he . . . he said it was rather urgent.'

'Did he say what it was about?'

'About tomorrow. About Cardocol.' She gestured behind her. 'He's waiting in the hall.'

'Well, you'd better show him in.'

She nodded and turned away. 'This way, Doctor.'

Engel and Jackman waited. Presently, a short, untidy old

man in a baggy sports jacket entered the study holding a square cardboard box. He looked from one face to another, surprised, blinking earnestly in the light. He had obviously been expecting to find only Engel in the room.

'Dr Erskine? I am Harold Engel.'

Erskine nodded. 'Aye, Mr Engel. I recognize your face from the papers.'

'This is Mr Jackman, our Project Development Manager at HPL.' Dr Erskine nodded. 'I understand from my wife,' Engel continued, 'that you wanted to see me urgently. Something about Cardocol, although I can't for the life of me—'

'I've some bad news for you, Mr Engel,' the doctor began simply. 'You must cancel the launch of your new drug.'

Harold Engel snorted in disbelief. 'I *beg* your pardon?'

'I said, you'll have to cancel the Cardocol launch. Postpone it at the very least.'

'Are you . . . are you insane?' managed Harold Engel. 'Cancel it? Now? After all the work that's gone into it? The tests, the clinical trials?'

'I'm perfectly serious, Mr Engel,' Dr Erskine replied calmly. 'I only wish I wasn't.' It was the way he spoke, and the manifest, weary distaste with which he set down his cardboard box and began placing small bottles of cough-mixture on a nearby table that finally chilled Engel, convinced him that the doctor was in deadly earnest. As he watched, Erskine removed the last bottle from the box and took a packet of Cardocol pills from his jacket pocket. 'I'm what you might call one of your "tame" doctors, Mr Engel,' he began. 'At least – I was. Your technical people would come knocking on my door with their charm and their free samples, their offers of business lunches and their donations to "surgery expenses", and I'd play along. Mutual support, you might say – the perks of the profession.'

'Whatever arrangements you—'

'I even put a couple of my patients on Cardocol for you,' Dr Erskine explained, holding up a packet of pills in their emerald-green packet. 'Just to keep everyone happy. A wee bit early, perhaps, but then that's no crime, is it? Not if it helps the patient.' He paused to glance first at Engel and then at Jackman, still saying nothing. Just watching. Gauging where Erskine was taking them. 'And, I must be fair – it did its stuff – to begin with, anyway. "Cardocol",' he quoted from memory, ' "A Heartbeat Closer".'

'Would you kindly explain the point you wish—'

'The point? The *point*, Mr Engel, is that six days after starting to take this . . . this wonder-drug of yours, my patient was rushed into hospital with a blood-pressure reading that had gone through the roof!' He paused and then added, almost as an afterthought: 'She also had a little cough, by the way, although that didn't register as significant, not at the time. A dry, ticklish little cough.'

'Easy . . . easy . . . Jesus!' With a groan of pain, Tony eased himself down on to the sofa in his living-room, and Jenny stood back, panting after the struggle of helping him inside from the car. 'Lock . . . lock the door and draw the curtains,' Tony ordered, waving a hand weakly at the windows. Jenny did as she was bid, checked the back and then returned to stand over Tony, watching him critically.

'How is it?' she asked, unnecessarily. He looked awful, clammy and pain-racked with skin the colour of dirty parchment. Now Tony tried to ease himself into a more comfortable position and forced a smile, trying to make light of his injury.

'A couple . . . couple of minutes' rest and I'll . . . I'll be as right as rain. Jesus . . . ' he groaned again, eyes screwed tight against the pain as Jenny leant down and peered closely at his shoulder.

'You can't drive another fifty yards with that, far less to Glasgow,' she announced definitely. 'It's broken, you know that, don't you?'

'Just . . . just give me a couple of minutes, OK? Then we'll be off.'

Jenny began to feel angry. Why the hell did men always have to start playing the stiff-upper-lipped hero? She sat down opposite and waited in silence as Tony tried to gather his strength with head thrown back and eyes closed. After several minutes – 'Help me get upstairs, will you? To the . . . the bathroom.'

With a hand over his sound shoulder, and with Tony leaning heavily against her, they made it eventually, struggling awkwardly up the narrow staircase one step at a time. In the bathroom Tony tugged on the light and then stood in front of the basin mirror as Jenny helped him ease off shirt and jacket. He almost passed out with the pain of that and had to stop twice just to hang on to the edge of the basin as the waves of nausea and dizziness threatened to engulf him. The skin around the collarbone was puffed and swollen with the purple discoloration of heavy bruising already breaking through. There was an angular projection too that told of broken bone. Tony also saw it, and their eyes met in the mirror.

'You *must* see a doctor,' Jenny said. 'You haven't any choice.'

'In Glasgow, OK? In Glasgow . . . '

'That's miles away! You'll never make it.'

'You can drive . . . '

'What . . . what about a friend? Someone from your base?'

Tony shook his head vehemently. 'Daren't risk it.'

Jenny took another glance at his broken collarbone and made up her mind. 'This is bloody stupid.' She turned and made for the stairs. And the telephone below.

Tony lurched awkwardly to the bathroom door. 'Where are you going?'

'To call a doctor.'

'A doctor? I told you, we—'

'Don't worry, this one's OK. It's the one I was telling you about – Dr Erskine.'

'Erskine? But he . . . he's the one who lied to you, for God's sake!'

Jenny twisted round at the bottom of the stairs, opened her handbag and took out the report on the clinical trials she had stolen from Jackman's office. 'This'll change his mind – don't you think?' She went to the phone in the hall and began dialling.

The surgery number rang through and was intercepted by an answering service: 'The surgery is closed at present, but Dr Erskine can be reached in an emergency at his home on Gleninver . . . ' Jenny dialled that number too. The phone rang several times, then—

'Yes?' A woman's voice. A wife, perhaps, hauled from her bed and come downstairs in dressing-gown and slippers . . .

'May I speak to Dr Erskine, please?'

'Dr Erskine is away on a call just now, I'm sorry.'

'Oh.' Jenny thought for a moment. 'Could you tell me where I could reach him, please?'

'Is it an emergency?'

'Yes. Yes, it's an emergency.'

'One moment.' There was a brief delay, then – 'You could try and reach him on Gleninver 1455.'

Jenny scribbled down the number. 'Thanks. Thanks very much.' She rang off.

' . . . There's nothing particularly unusual about a minor irritating cough, Dr Erskine,' said Harold Engel. 'The medical data sheet we issue with each packet states quite clearly that there is some risk of bronchial inflammation – particularly among elderly patients. Somewhere in the region of four or five per cent.'

'The medical data sheet? You mean this wee thing?' Dr Erskine challenged contemptuously, the note of bitterness in his voice unmistakable as he rummaged in another pocket and pulled out a crumpled piece of paper. Filled with long lines of tiny, close-set type, a patient would need 20/20 vision and a great deal of time to read through the printed warning about the risk of adverse reactions. Such data sheets are not printed that way by accident. They are printed that way to conform to the letter, if not the spirit, of the law. 'Aye, I'll give you that much, Mr Engel. You do warn people they may get a bit of a cough.' He paused. 'What you do not say, down there in the small print, is that it's near as damnit a cast-iron certainty. That would get in the way of "commercial considerations", would it not?'

'What d'you mean – a cast-iron certainty? I told you, the incidence of bronchial irritation is no more than four or five per cent! If you mean to imply that—'

'Dr Erskine, I think this has gone quite far enough,' Jackman interrupted. 'I have no idea what possible motive you may have for—' They turned to another tap on the door. It opened, and Joyce Engel came into the room once more.

'Sorry to trouble you again,' she said, turning towards Dr Erskine. 'There's an emergency call for you, Doctor. A Miss Jenny Macrae.'

CHAPTER TWENTY-FOUR

As soon as Dr Erskine had left: 'I wonder if I might make a brief phone call?' Jackman asked politely.

'What? Oh, yes. Help yourself,' Harold Engel answered distractedly, for he wasn't really listening. He was worrying about what the doctor had told him about Cardocol, about his baby. A cough, a 'cast-iron certainty'? The man must be unhinged. And yet . . . He shrugged and tried to rid himself of a sudden sense of unease, of premonition.

'Jackman?' Jackman turned, halfway to the door. And his phone call to Ridley. 'What was all that about?'

Jackman shrugged. 'No idea. Professional jealousy, I should imagine.'

Engel shook his head. 'Hardly. He didn't strike me as the jealous type. Find out in the morning who's been seeing him, will you? Before he comes back. Perhaps one of the reps can shed a little light.'

'The phone?'

'In the hall.'

Jackman nodded and the door closed softly behind him. Jennifer Macrae, making an emergency call to that Dr Erskine? What had gone wrong? If Ridley—

'Is anything the matter, Mr Jackman?' Joyce Engel asked, coming into the hall from the drawing-room. And still calling him 'Mister' after all the months he had been working with her husband, as some tacit sign of disapproval. He switched on a smile.

'No, no – nothing at all. Your husband said I might make a call.'

'Oh. The telephone's over here.'

'Thank you.' Jackman waited until the drawing-room

door had closed politely behind her and then dialled the operator, his face a mask of stone. When she had answered – 'Pagephone 3447,' he ordered. 'Subscriber is to call—' he glanced down – 'Gleninver 1455 immediately.'

'Gleninver 1455. One moment, caller.' He replaced the receiver and waited one minute, perhaps two. Then the phone rang and he swept it up. It was Ridley.

'What happened?' Jackman snapped.

'She had a friend, didn't she? A chum. In a car. Once I've—'

'She is now at number seventeen, Bruneval Close – have you got that? Seventeen, Bruneval Close.' He glanced over his shoulder at the empty hall. 'And this time, I want it finished, understand? Finished.'

Tony was back on the sofa downstairs. Jenny watched critically as Dr Erskine eased back the collar of his shirt, inspected his shoulder and broken collarbone briefly and grunted with distaste. 'You've been to the police, I take it? You've reported the . . . the homicidal maniac who did this?'

Tony and Jenny exchanged looks over the top of the doctor's head. 'No police,' Tony said after a brief silence. 'And no hospital, either. Not in Gleninver, anyway.'

Dr Erskine looked up sharply. 'Don't be daft, man – this shoulder of yours needs proper hospital treatment. And an X-ray.'

Tony nodded, knowing it was the truth. And knowing too that such a visit was impossible. Once he was inside a hospital, an institution of any kind, he was back on *their* ground and would be at *their* mercy. They were taking enough risks just now, talking to this doctor, for wasn't this the same man who had already lied to Jenny once? About her landlady?

'Later, Doc, OK? Later.'

Dr Erskine shut his bag with an angry snap. 'Would one of you mind telling me, please, just what the hell is going on?' He glared defiantly from one face to another. There was silence for a moment, and then Jenny began to tell him. She told him if not the whole truth, then at least that part of it that touched upon him and upon Robbie Roberts; upon Jamie Ennis, Mrs Proctor and upon Cardocol itself. Finally—

'Would you read this, please?' Jenny asked, opening her bag and taking out the report she had stolen from HPL, the one that dealt with Cardocol's clinical trials and which contained Jackman's endorsement of the decision to distort the figures submitted to CSM in support of the company's product licence application.

Dr Erskine took the report, glanced at its cover with the word CONFIDENTIAL, opened his mouth to make some comment, thought better of it and began to read, the frown on his face deepening as he turned back a page to compare some figures. Then he looked up with an anger in his eyes that was directed not at Jenny, or Tony, but at HPL. 'Where did you get this?' he demanded.

'From HPL,' replied Jenny. Truthfully.

'They *gave* it to you? Lent you a copy?'

She shook her head. 'Not exactly, no. I took it. It's . . . it's quite genuine.'

'So I see.' There was silence as Dr Erskine nodded slowly. He could see that much, at least, he told himself sourly – that much and not much else. But for Jenny Macrae he'd still have been handing out Cardocol without the remotest idea that . . . It occurred to him suddenly that he owed Jenny a very great deal. 'There is something . . . something I think you ought to know,' he began, the words of explanation, perhaps of apology, strange and awkward in his mouth. 'When I told you Mrs Proctor had not received her Cardocol pills from me, that was not . . . not strictly accurate. In fact, she *had* been receiving them for the last six days. Please—' he raised a hand – 'don't misunderstand me. I am not apologizing for my actions, far from it. At the time I did not feel you had the slightest right to that sort of confidential information – I still don't, as a matter of fact. But this . . . ' He let the report drop back on to his lap. 'At the very least it supports what I was telling Harold Engel just now.'

'Just now?' asked Tony, almost missing it.

'Yes,' Dr Erskine nodded. 'He . . . he didn't believe me, of course – didn't *want* to believe me, I should say. Anyway he . . . he invited me to return to his office with all the relevant facts and figures first thing in the morning.' He leant forward. 'He simply denied that the incidence of bronchial inflammation was particularly high. I . . . I got the impression he really believed that! When I tried to tell him that my colleagues in Fort William and I—'

'Just now?' Tony repeated, his eyes on Jenny as she leant forward in the chair opposite, the stolen Cardocol report forgotten. 'You saw Mr Engel just *now*?'

Dr Erskine nodded. 'I assumed you knew. That's where I was when you called.'

Tony looked across at Jenny as she shook her head with that cold, oily creature of fear uncoiling again in her stomach.

'All your wife gave me was a . . . a telephone number. When the call was answered I . . . I just asked for you, that's all.'

'Oh, I see. Well, that's where I was – with Mr Engel. Oh – and that Project Development Manager of his, M—'

'Jackman?' supplied Jenny, her voice almost a whisper.

'That's the one, yes. Maurice Jackman. Odd-looking fellow.'

'Did you tell them you were coming here?' Tony asked casually, his voice absolutely steady, neutral.

'Well . . . yes. Yes, I did, as a matter of fact,' Dr Erskine admitted. He glanced uneasily at their faces. 'Did I . . . did I say anything wrong?'

Ridley pulled the car in to the side of the road, doused the lights and reached across to open the glove compartment.

He took out a street map, turned on a torch, and, shading its beam between gloved fingers, glanced down. Yes, that was right. Bruneval Close was the next turning on the left. The torch clicked off and the map went back into the glove compartment.

Ridley looked at his watch, glanced briefly up and down the dark, deserted road, got slowly out of the car and began putting on a lightweight, dark-blue raincoat with the slow deliberation of a man performing some careful, familiar ritual. Then he got back behind the wheel and closed the door. Reaching low beneath the driver's seat he eased out a flat, heavy package. Whatever lay inside was wrapped in a square of soft chamois leather. Working carefully and with great deliberation, as he did most things, Ridley began unfolding the cloth in the darkness.

The package was a disassembled Ingram automatic pistol. The three smaller packages he now began to unwrap and place carefully on the empty passenger seat beside him consisted of the weapon itself, a filled thirty-round box magazine in .38 calibre, and an cight-inch-long black rubber suppressor. The knife – specifically, the butcher's knife – was Ridley's weapon of choice but, like a craftsman in any other profession, Ridley believed that different tools were required for different situations. The Model 11 Ingram had long been a personal favourite. For one thing, it was inconspicuous. With the silencer detached, and the rigid wire shoulder-stock snapped fully forward into the body, the weapon was less than eleven inches long and easy to conceal beneath a raincoat. It was light, too, and weighed just a shade over six pounds. Fired from the hip with a muzzle velocity of nine hundred feet a second, and a cyclic rate of eleven hundred rounds a minute, Ridley knew that a single precise, surgical sweep of that lethal, snub-nosed barrel could paper the walls with a man's intestines before the last spent case from a three-second burst had tinkled to the floor. For he had seen it done, seen the look of magical, almost comic disbelief blossom on the faces of his victims in that Armagh ballroom as he swung back the folds of that self-same dark-blue raincoat and gave those stupid Micks their first and last glimpse of Arthur Ingram. Magic it had been, pure magic. And would be again.

Jackman didn't know anything about the Ingram Model 11, nor, for that matter, the Ingram Model 10 in .45 calibre – and he most certainly did not know that Ridley even possessed such a lethal, close-quarter weapon. Nor did Baxter in London, for Ridley was a true freelance. The Ingram, anyway, was a little surprise, something he liked to keep to himself – a personal equalizer that came out of its chamois-leather wrapping when the time for threats, for finesse, was over. Ridley smiled slowly in the darkness as he slipped the silencer over the end of the short barrel and began turning. Well, that sod Jackman only had himself to blame. He'd said he wanted it finished, hadn't he? And the Ingram could do that quickly, without the slightest shadow of doubt. There. The silencer was wound on tight. Ridley eased back the cocking handle a couple of times just to check the mechanism, picked up the box magazine, tensed the first smooth, golden round beneath the ball of his thumb and then slid the magazine into the base of the weapon's handgrip. He tapped it home, wiped the assembled weapon carefully with the chamois-leather and laid the gun on the passenger seat beside him. Then he reached forward and started the engine.

The car rolled forward and turned into Bruneval Close.

Ridley drove slowly between the rows of silent, darkened houses, his eyes moving ceaselessly as he absorbed impressions: the black bulk of the buildings behind their borders of waist-high privet; the cars parked outside identical, flat-roofed garages and along both sides of the road, their windscreens gleaming silver in the street lights; a child's trike lying forgotten on its side; the eerie glow of a television seeping through ill-matched front-room curtains. Ridley eased into the verge and turned off his lights. Switching off the engine, he wound down the window and listened intently as the sounds of the night began to ebb around him and the road settled once more into silence. A dog barked in the distance. A dustbin lid fell to the ground with a faint crash as some animal hunted for scraps. Ridley waited.

A car came suddenly up the rise towards him. Ridley leant left across the passenger seat and closed his eyes as the headlights blazed past, then straightened and watched in the rearview mirror as the ancient Rover paused on the crown of the road, indicator flashing, and then turned right towards Gleninver. Dr Erskine was driving home with Jenny's stolen report on the seat beside him, although Ridley had no way of knowing that. As the sound of the Rover's engine dwindled into the distance, Ridley took a pair of miniature binoculars from the glove compartment, hunched forward and raised them to his eyes.

He had parked outside numbers ten and twelve on the right-hand side of the road. Number seventeen, the target house, was the last on the opposite side before the cul-de-sac flared out at the bottom of thc slopc. Thc binoculars panned slowly across the front of the house and picked up the garage and the Ford Escort parked outside. Lights. Lights both upstairs and – the binoculars snapped back, and Ridley made a minute adjustment to the focus. The Ford Escort.

Minutes passed. Then Ridley unclipped the pocket-pager from his waist-belt, switched it off and locked it away inside the glove compartment. He then picked up the silenced Ingram, tucked it inside the folds of his raincoat, reached up, disconnected the roof light, opened the driver's door and stepped quietly into the road. A moment more and he had vanished into the shadows. Into his element.

Jenny was standing in the living-room with a hand to her mouth, looking down the hall towards the front door as though she expected to see it burst open at any moment.

An hour ago, even less, Tony's house had offered safety and a haven; sanctuary behind lock and chain. Now, with the departure of Dr Erskine, it suddenly seemed very small and very still, as though it too was waiting breathlessly for something terrible to happen. Jenny felt trapped, hemmed in. And very frightened. She swallowed and turned towards Tony, still sitting on the sofa. 'Perhaps if we just—'

'Hang on a sec, I'm trying to think,' Tony muttered, pushing the pain to the back of his mind as he tried to work it all out, formulate some sort of plan. Yet aware even as he delayed that he was wasting precious time, perhaps squandering the very moments that could save their lives. The temptation to run, to charge out of the house, leap into the car and go roaring off to Glasgow was almost overwhelming.

'Look, Tony—' Jenny came round the edge of the sofa and crouched down beside him, glancing involuntarily over her shoulder as though they might, even here, be somehow overheard. Wide, frightened eyes in a pale, frightened face. 'This is madness, you know that, don't you?' she whispered. 'We can't just . . . just sit here, for God's sake! You heard what Dr Erskine said. He *told* them where we are! They know! We . . . we can't tell the police, we can't get you to a hospital – you said yourself the only safe place left is Glasgow, a large town. We have to go – now!' she urged. 'It's our only chance! Listen—' she leant forward – 'I can drive; in a couple of hours, three at the outside, we—'

'Turn off the light,' Tony ordered quietly, coming to a decision and hoping to Christ he wasn't making the worst mistake of his life, as he hauled himself painfully out of the sofa, his left arm pinned across his chest by the sling Dr Erskine had given him. Tony reached across for the little screw of paper containing the painkillers. One, the good doctor had said: one every four hours or when the pain was really bad. Tony thought grimly ahead to what the night might hold, and took two. He shook the pills into the palm of his hand and swallowed them down dry. When he looked up, Jenny still hadn't moved. 'The light.' He gestured behind him. 'Turn it off. Now.'

'The *light*?'

'Don't argue, for God's sake, there isn't time.' Looking at Tony as though he was mad, Jenny turned off the standard lamp behind the sofa. The room was lit now only by the light washing through from the hall. 'Wait here.' Jenny waited, totally baffled, as Tony hurried awkwardly through to the kitchen. She heard a drawer open and close, a light was switched on and off and a door was pulled shut. Then Tony was back, standing in the shadows near the hatch with something in his hand. In the gloom, Jenny couldn't make out what it was, not at first. When she could, her stomach turned over.

'What . . . what are you going to do with that?'

'We're too late,' Tony said simply by way of explanation, the words stretching across the darkness and the silence as he held the claw-hammer down at his side. It was the only thing he had been able to find without going outside to the garage. The only weapon.

'Too late? Too late for what?'

'For Glasgow. For running.'

She shook her head. 'Don't be stupid – of course we're not! Surely, when we . . . '

'LISTEN!' That stopped her. 'Just listen, OK?' Tony said, more quietly. 'That doctor friend of yours was at Engel's home – when? An hour ago?'

'About that, yes. Maybe a little longer.'

'An hour ago,' Tony agreed softly. 'And once he'd left, once they'd got the old man out of the way, what d'you think they did?' He paused. 'They got on the blower to whoever it is they use on people like us, and passed on this address, right? And they did that . . . sixty minutes ago. At least.'

'What are you saying?'

'I'm saying, they're out there already – waiting for us. One, maybe two – I don't know. What I do know is that the moment we open that door . . . well, it'll all be over.'

'We'll be killed, you mean?'

'Something along those lines I should imagine, yes.'

'But—'

'So we don't go through that door. We don't go through the windows, either. We stay here. We let them come to us.'

Jenny nodded calmly as though it all made perfect sense. 'And then you lay about with that hammer of yours, is that it?'

'Unless you've got a couple of hand grenades in that bag of yours, yes.'

Jenny shook her head angrily. 'I don't believe this – any of it! You've got a broken collarbone! You're . . . you're insane!'

'Yeah, so they tell me,' Tony agreed, more calmly than he felt. 'We've something else too up our sleeve, don't forget.'

'What's that?'

'Surprise. We know they know we're here. But they don't *know* we know – get it? So – in a moment we'll both go upstairs to bed. We're going to turn off all the lights down here and go upstairs, just like everything's normal. Then – we'll wait.'

'We'll *wait*? Oh, terrific!' said Jenny, as all her fears exploded to the surface. 'Oh, bloody, fucking marvellous! We just lie here tucked up in bed and *wait* until that . . . that animal, or someone like him, decides to pay us a visit, is that it?'

'We're wasting time,' Tony said shortly, turning away and moving towards the stairs.

Jenny hurried after him. 'Isn't there . . . isn't there something else we could do?'

'Like what?'

Jenny thought wild thoughts for a moment and then suddenly snapped her fingers. 'I know! You . . . you know all the people around here, yes? Your neighbours?' Tony nodded. 'Well . . . what if you phoned them all up? Now! Told them . . . told them their garages were being broken into – all of them, everybody! That would get them all outside, wouldn't it? It would turn the road into broad daylight! They'd never dare do anything then, would they? They couldn't! Not in front of all those witnesses! Then, when everyone's milling around . . . ' Tony began going up the stairs. 'Well? It's an idea, isn't it?' Jenny called after him. 'It's better than nothing!'

Tony turned. 'And what if he's got a gun this time, eh? What if he starts using it? Ever think of that? All those people milling around outside in the line of fire while you and I beat a hasty retreat – that would go down a bundle, that would.'

'Oh.'

'Yeah – Oh. Anyway, how're you going to contact them? By phone?' Tony pointed. 'Be my guest.' He'd tried earlier, immediately after Dr Erskine had left. Jenny just looked at him. 'Go on. Try it.'

With her eyes on Tony's face, Jenny lifted the receiver and held it to her ear. Nothing. 'It's dead,' she said in a small voice.

Tony nodded. 'That's what I mean,' he said. 'I should have told you earlier. We haven't any choice.'

Joyce Engel lay in bed beside her husband, staring up at the ceiling with her hands clenched into fists at her sides. They'd had another awful, monumental row soon after that man Jackman had left, she remembered now with numb despair. She'd had the champagne on ice for hours, waiting for just the right moment when they were alone, but it had never materialized. What should have been a private, intimate evening of celebration, of optimistic toasts to the success of the drug her husband had devoted the best years of his life to perfecting, had turned instead into a bitter, wounding, shouting-match about Jackman, the company and the disappearance of Malcolm Highcroft, until finally

Harold had stormed into his study and slammed the door angrily behind him, leaving Joyce to go up to bed alone. He had joined her, finally, forty minutes ago with a few mumbled words of apology and a sliding hand under her nightdress which she had brushed away with cold disdain, offended that he had even imagined that by making love he could make amends. Making love? She stirred restlessly. Things had been wrong in that department for months . . .

Joyce glanced cautiously over her shoulder. She couldn't tell whether he was asleep or awake. 'Harold?' she called softly. 'Harold?' He didn't answer.

She waited a moment longer, then swung back the bedclothes and rose stealthily to her feet. Another glance – and still he hadn't stirred. Groping around for her slippers in the darkness, Joyce slung her dressing-gown over her shoulders and left the bedroom. Feeling her way along the landing past the children's bedrooms, she switched on the hall light and hurried down the wide staircase, her nightdress billowing around her ankles. She entered Harold's study, turned on the desk lamp and glanced guiltily over her shoulder, aware that she was breaking one of their rules; that she was prying, trespassing. For a moment that sense of loyalty stopped her going further. Then she remembered what had happened to their life together in the last few months, what had become of the carefree, happy man she had once married, and she reached out for the top drawer of the desk and tugged it open.

The tape was lying there beneath a pile of cheque-book stubs. She examined it carefully but it was untitled. Another glance over her shoulder and she was fitting the cassette into the machine and winding it back to the beginning. Then she pressed the play button.

Presently she heard Professor Malcolm Highcroft die. She listened, horrified, as the voice she remembered lost its measured, articulate coherence and degenerated into the panting, gibbering agony of an animal in its death-throes.

And when it was over, she turned to find Harold Engel

standing behind her.

'Right – that'll have to do,' Tony whispered, hideously conscious of the noise the banging had made, conscious of the silence of the house and of the minutes slipping away – conscious, above all, of the need for *haste*. They'd moved the hall mirror, swopped it with the water-colour at the head of the stairs beside the airing cupboard. Now Tony stepped back and inspected the mirror critically. Yes, that would do. It would bloody well have to. Back down the stairs a quiet, slow step at a time to stealthily, stealthily, draw back the narrow curtains at the bottom of the staircase, then back upstairs, quickly, ears cocked for the slightest sound. Tony reached out for Jenny's hand. 'Come on – in here,' he whispered, surprised to find he was panting, short of breath. He led Jenny through into what had been Paul's bedroom and swept down her hand with his own as she reached automatically for the light switch. He glanced round, and then got Jenny to help him push Paul's narrow little bed closer towards the wall. Then he gestured at the floor in the narrow space between bed and wall. 'Down there,' he whispered. 'Flat on your stomach and, whatever happens – stay there, understand?'

Jenny swallowed. 'But you—'

'*Stay there*. I'll be OK. Promise?' She nodded, and Tony looked round quickly in the darkness, wondering what more he could do; what more than the pitifully little that had already been done.

'Right. See you in the morning – I hope.' He forced a quick smile and then turned to the door, hammer in hand. Jenny reached out impulsively and put a hand on his arm. The good one.

'Tony?' He turned. 'I just want to say . . . I'm sorry. For getting you into this mess. If I hadn't been such a fool in the first place . . . ' She shrugged. 'I just want you to know I'm sorry, OK? And very grateful. For everything.'

She reached up suddenly and kissed him. 'Be careful,' she whispered.

Tony's tired, worn face creased into a sudden, surprised smile. 'I won't say you're welcome, but . . . you're welcome. Now – down there. And don't *move*.' He slipped out on to the landing, the door closed softly behind him, and Jenny lay down carefully on the carpet between the bed and the wall, her hands tucked under her body and her head flat on the carpet, twisted to one side as she listened to just two things – the wild thudding of her heart, and the breathless, stretching silence.

The waiting began.

'But why?' Joyce Engel begged, kneeling down in front of her husband in her nightdress with both his hands gripped tightly in hers. 'That's what I don't understand, Harold. *Why*?'

'It was a way out, I suppose. It all seemed so . . . so easy, somehow, so straightforward – to begin with, anyway. It was the obvious solution,' he replied quietly, his face thrown into relief by the single lamp on the desk as his voice filled the silent, shadowed study. 'All they said they wanted were a few laboratory facilities, that was all. Just a quiet corner of the site where they could work undisturbed. We . . . we'd be the umbrella organization, you see – the cover. By taking all the usual steps to protect our own commercial interests, we could protect theirs as well.'

'And in return?' Joyce demanded bitterly. 'What did they offer in return?'

'Funds,' Harold replied simply. 'Backing. An accelerated research programme. Favourable terms. It was . . . well, it was irresistible.'

'Irresistible?' echoed Joyce, appalled. '*Your* company, the company you fought for, lifted off the ground with your . . . your bare *hands* because you believed in a new drug, a new process – *your* company becomes some . . . some government satellite involved in chemical warfare, and you call that irresistible? After what you went through in Bookham? After what *we* went through?'

'Because of Bookham, don't you see?' urged her husband, bending forward and gripping his wife's hands tightly again with his own. '*Because* of Bookham, Joyce. I couldn't have built up again from scratch – not after that. Not without help.' He paused. 'Didn't you ever wonder where the money was coming from? Didn't you? The money for the move up to Scotland? All that plant and machinery? The laboratories and all the expensive research?'

Joyce shrugged helplessly and glanced round as though the answer might be written in the shadows. 'I presumed friends in the City, investors had—'

'Friends in the City? Investors?' Harold Engel threw back his head and laughed harshly, remembering as though it was yesterday the nightmare of collapse, the frantic ringing round and the telephone calls that were never answered, the world of the brisk empty smile and the averted gaze. The silence of defeat. Of failure. 'I hadn't *got* any friends, remember?' He gazed into the distance, into the past, remembering, and then added: 'It was only later, when it was all over and we were floating again that I realized they'd probably been behind that as well, making sure I was really, really desperate. Then, once I'd agreed . . . well, the doors started opening again, didn't they?'

'But why *you*, Harold? Why us? Why not – I don't know – why not Porton Down? Somewhere like that?'

'After all the attention places like Greenham Common and Molesworth have been getting? They stopped doing sensitive work in places like that months ago for that very reason.'

'But there must be hundreds of other companies just as suitable . . . '

Harold Engel shook his head. 'Not really, no. They found out very early on that I was interested in blockers – anti-hypertensives. That meant, inevitably, that our own research chemists would be coming into contact with two specific chemicals: cholinesterase and acetylcholine. The first controls the muscles by breaking down the second, you see; the chemical which makes the muscles contract.'

'But I don't understand. What's that got to do with this . . . this Project OMAHA thing that killed Malcolm?'

'Rather a lot,' Harold Engel admitted gently. 'The chemical nerve agents they were working with in RD7 – Tabun, Sarin and Soman – all block the release of cholinesterase. It prevents it working so that the level of acetylcholine builds up unchecked to such a level that ultimately the body poisons itself. It's . . . very effective.'

Joyce looked as if she was going to be sick. 'And you . . . you've been working on this . . . this *thing* all this time? Without telling me? All these months, these *years*? Coming home, playing with the children, talking, laughing, smiling, and all the time—'

'Not me personally, Joyce. I only—'

'But you *knew*, Harold! You *knew*! How . . . how could you?'

'Yes, I knew,' admitted her husband quietly. 'OMAHA was the price, if you like – the price of commercial survival. It was either co-operate or go under. God help me, I decided to co-operate.'

Tony had been waiting so long, his ears straining for the slightest sound, that he thought he had imagined it at first. There it was again: the faintest crunching sound, as though someone was munching an apple downstairs. Or, just possibly, using something to muffle the sound of breaking glass. Tony crouched lower and changed his grip on the shaft of the hammer as he squinted through the crack in the door and stifled a groan of pain. Ironically, it was his back that was agony now. The sling and the pills Dr Erskine had left him had dulled the pain from his broken collarbone, but they did nothing at all for a back that had been bent almost double now for . . . hours. Tony twisted the face of his watch towards his eyes: 3.15.

The hour before dawn. Dawn attack.

Jenny hadn't heard a thing – she was too busy trying to stop shivering. She had been lying on the same scrap of carpet for the last two hours hardly daring to move. After half an hour she had decided to pull the eiderdown off the bed on to the floor to give her warmth, but the nylon cover had crackled so alarmingly in the silence that she had abandoned the idea immediately and had gone back to staring at the floor in the darkness. Now she discovered she had a different problem – the dust on the carpet beside her face was making her want to sneeze. Badly.

Ridley dropped lightly into the kitchen.

He paused. Listening, looking, trusting those senses of his. The house was silent. Not a sound. Not a light. He reached up and pulled the window gently closed, twisting home the locking-catch beneath the broken pane of glass. Then he swung the silenced Ingram gently out of the folds of his raincoat and moved across the kitchen with as much noise as a cloud scudding across moonlit ground. After the recce from outside earlier, he moved now with confidence, pausing at the kitchen door to press back into the shadows and listen again. Still nothing. One hand holding the Ingram across his body, Ridley slipped off the safety catch, eased back the cocking handle and waited. He was in no hurry. He waited a full three minutes without moving a muscle, every talent he possessed channelled, focused, into eyes and ears. He isolated and identified the slow drip of a tap in the bathroom and the muted gurgle of the cold-water header tank under the eaves. Then slowly, one step at a time, he moved down the darkness of the narrow hall and paused to look out at the street through the uncurtained little window at the foot of the stairs. The fact that the curtain was not drawn meant that the glow of the street light outside was permitted to fall through on to the staircase. Ridley reached up and slowly pulled the curtain closed.

Tony watched him. Watched him through the crack in

the airing-cupboard door and cursed silently under his breath as the fear dried his mouth and tightened his stomach into a tight little ball. Fuck. He should have anticipated that. He had hoped he would miss the window, would come on up the stairs and past the airing-cupboard door with his every step back-lit against that small, innocent square of light that was reflected in the mirror he and Jenny had positioned with such haste at the top of the stairs. But now, instead of that, the stairs were in darkness. And all Tony knew for sure was that the man was there somewhere, coming steadily up the stairs towards him with an automatic pistol in his hands. Oh, Jesus.

Slowly, slowly up the stairs went Ridley, finger round the trigger, weapon sweeping gently from right to left, feet pressed wide to the exact width of each tread. Ridley knew all about floorboards that squeaked and risers that groaned and banisters that creaked under the careless pressure of a hand. Up.

Tony waited, mouth dry as tinder, heart pounding furiously against his ribs as he strained his ears and tried to guess which step the man was on now. Now. *Now.*

The slightest rustle of cloth in the darkness. Tony sensed rather than saw a movement in the reflection of the mirror and erupted from his hiding-place, smashing the door of the airing-cupboard back across the top of the landing and swinging to his right, the hammer scything out in a vicious, murderous arc that carried all of his fear and every atom of his strength behind it. The hammer glanced off metal and found yielding flesh. Ridley stumbled backwards. Tony hurled himself after him, his shoulder forgotten, the hammer swinging as he used his body, his good side, as a battering-ram, desperate to close the distance before that automatic pistol swung round and cut him to pieces. He charged into Ridley and felt the hammer strike home again, this time against the side of the man's face as he caught the gleam of teeth drawn back in an animal snarl of pain. The Ingram clattered to the landing as the dark figure lost its footing and toppled backwards. Tony didn't hesitate. Hurling the heavy hammer after the crumpling figure as it crashed down the narrow staircase, he groped feverishly for the automatic lying somewhere at his feet, found it, pointed it blindly down the stairs into the darkness and pressed the trigger. The Ingram jumped and kicked in his hands. There was a soft thudding sound, the sigh of the receiver travelling backwards and forwards, the crash of breaking glass and then silence. Tony took his finger off the trigger and crouched down by the banister rail. Panting darkness and terror amid a litter of spent cartridge cases and the acrid bite of cordite. Then the bedroom door creaked open and Tony spun round, finger back on the trigger.

'Tony?' a terrified, half-choked whisper out of the darkness.

'STAY THERE! GET DOWN!' he shouted. Christ, he'd almost shot her! Jenny dropped to her knees as Tony eased down on to his right side and changed position, trying to think tactics, wriggling round until hc could twist most of his body into the doorway of the master bedroom. He waited. No sound. No groaning, no murmur of pain. Nothing. Just darkness and silence leading down to the bottom of the stairs. He waited a few more moments, tried counting to ten, then – 'Jenny?' he whispered.

'Tony?'

'You OK?'

'I . . . I think so.'

'There's a torch in the drawer of the bedside table behind me. Get it. Only for Chrissakes don't turn it on till I tell you.' He heard her wriggle across the landing into the bedroom. Good girl. At least she wasn't standing up, turning on the fucking lights. Then she was back, crawling to his side. And still no sound from below.

'Here.' He took the torch, pushed Jenny back towards Paul's bedroom and tried to think. What if there was more than one? Someone else, waiting in the shadows at the bottom of the stairs? Hunching to his knees, Tony crawled cautiously along the landing until he guessed he was roughly above the window and the half-landing where the stairs turned down into the hall. He rose cautiously to his feet, trained the Ingram downwards, held the torch away from his body and switched it on.

Christ. He'd almost cut the man in half. Ridley lay in a tangle of arms and legs at the bottom of the stairs, eyes staring emptily into space, mouth hanging slackly open. The burst of .38 calibre shells had caught him in the stomach, blowing out most of his side before stitching a neat row of holes across the window and into the wall. Blood lay pooled and puddled on the carpet and there was the wet gleam of bulging, purple intestines in the torchlight. The curtain stirred softly in the breeze by the shattered window.

'What . . . what are you going to do now?' Jenny asked in a frightened whisper.

Tony clicked off the torch. 'I wouldn't look too closely if I was you,' he advised quietly. 'It isn't very pretty.' He had recognized the ruins of that face and he was gambling now that, as before, both at Jenny's flat and at HPL, the man was a loner who preferred to work on his own. Which might just give them their chance. Tony rose to his feet, found the safety catch, slipped it on and let the weapon drop wearily to his side. Christ, what a mess! What a fucking awful mess! He went into Paul's bedroom, twitched the bedspread off the bed and returned to the landing to find Jenny standing where he had left her, staring down into the darkness as though mesmerized.

'You killed him, didn't you? With that . . . that thing.'

Tony didn't answer. He went to the end of the landing, hung the bedspread out over the stairwell and then let it fall from his hands. It fluttered down on to the body and Tony switched on the torch. The bedspread covered most of the body but not the face, and Tony sensed Jenny start violently beside him. Then she turned, hurried into the bathroom and he heard the sound of violent retching. The toilet flushed, and presently Jenny came back into the doorway wiping the back of her hand across her mouth.

'OK?' She nodded, and Tony decided to take another chance and turned on the hall light. 'Come on,' he said, taking her hand and starting down the stairs. Towards the body.

Jenny shied back. 'I . . . I can't,' she managed.

Tony came back up the stairs, placed a hand on her shoulder and looked into her eyes, trying to give her strength, courage. 'Yes you can,' he said softly. 'We're nearly there, Jenny – nearly out of the trees. For the moment, his boss—' he gestured down the stairs, 'thinks *we're* the ones who're dead – right? And they'll go on thinking that, too – for a few more hours at least. Hours we can use, Jenny. By the time they wake up to what's happened, we can be in Glasgow. And then it will be over, OK? Finished.' He paused, watching her face. 'Or would you rather stay here? Wait for them to come back?'

Jenny closed her eyes and swallowed, gathering her strength. Then she nodded. 'OK,' she whispered.

Tony took her hand and led the way. Together they squeezed past the grotesque, sprawled bundle at the bottom of the stairs and tried to close their minds to the smell and the blood and the growing, blossoming red stains that were already seeping through the crisp white bedspread. Twenty-five minutes later they were out of Gleninver.

Out of Gleninver, but not out of the woods.

If Jenny hadn't been driving then it probably would never have happened, but she *was* driving. She was doing so because there wasn't really any choice, not with Tony with one arm in a sling. Even so, she was a dangerous liability, a driver whose mind was still numb with shock, tiredness and the horror of what she had witnessed. Just how great that liability was, they discovered on a quiet, winding stretch of country road about sixteen miles east of

Gleninver as they drove between soft, rolling moorland towards the watery promise of the rising sun. A sheep darted across the road. A sheep, that was all – but it could have been a man with a rifle or Ridley himself, for the effect upon Jenny's raw nerves and reflexes was the same. She screamed and wrenched the wheel violently to the left. The Escort slewed obediently across the road towards a stone humpbacked bridge at more than forty miles an hour. Jenny saw that coming, at least. Another wrench of the wheel. The car missed the bridge by inches, crashed through a flimsy wooden fence, bucketed down a steep earth bank and finally rammed its nose into the bed of a shallow, rocky stream, pitching Tony and Jenny forward into darkness.

CHAPTER TWENTY-FIVE

Jackman should have been asleep in bed, dreaming fond thoughts about the morning. He wasn't. He was pacing his living-room, still fully dressed, and looking constantly at his watch. The phone rang on his desk and he swept it up. 'Yes?'

'I'm sorry, caller, but I'm still getting no reply on Pagephone 3447.'

'I see.'

'Perhaps he's turned it off, you know?' the operator suggested, trying to be helpful. 'I mean, it is after four o'clock in the morning.'

'I am perfectly well aware what time it is, thank you,' Jackman replied acidly. Ridley was not permitted to turn it off. He knew that, knew it perfectly well. So why hadn't he reported in? Why?

'Perhaps if you called again in a—'

'Thank you, operator.' Jackman replaced the receiver and looked round his sparse, rented living-room. Then he opened a drawer of his desk, took out a map of the town and began looking through the street index for Bruneval Close.

Twenty minutes later he was walking cautiously up to the front door of number seventeen with both hands jammed in his coat pockets. He glanced round, conscious of the milky whiteness in the sky and the fact that dawn could not be very far off. Broken glass crunched under his feet and he looked down, took another couple of slow steps forward, and then saw the shattered window and the curtains moving gently in the breeze. He went up to the front door and pushed experimentally. The door swung open and Jackman hesitated, nervous and ill at ease in this alien world of trespass, of the

Executive. Glancing furtively to right and left, he then pushed the door wide and stepped inside.

He smelt it first. Tasted the greasy, gagging sweetness of death on the roof of his mouth long before he had pushed the door shut and turned on the torch.

A couple of minutes, perhaps less than that, and Jackman was stumbling outside with Ridley's Ingram stuffed under his coat. His face drained of colour, he pulled the door locked behind him and hurried down the path as the first rays of morning streaked the sky. It was worse than he had expected – much worse. His hands shook as he locked the Ingram into the boot of his car and slid behind the wheel, his mind racing as he tried to block out the horror of what he had found and think constructively, decide what he could do immediately to contain the damage. Not much, he decided; not alone. After finding Ridley and the Ingram discarded in the hallway, he had forced himself upstairs, expecting to find at least one more body in one of the bedrooms, but he had searched the house thoroughly and found nothing. Well, it wasn't just down to him any longer. They had contingency plans to deal with something like this, whole teams of specialists who could be called in at a moment's notice. Jackman stopped at the first phone-box he came to and dialled Cheltenham Control direct, without going through any of the usual safe-houses first. That was permitted in an emergency, just so long as you could justify it afterwards. Jackman didn't think he'd have any trouble, not with Ridley lying back there with his guts hanging out and a line of machine-gun bullets running up the wall. 'This is Jackman,' he reported, the moment he knew the tapes were running. 'Jackman for Baxter, reference OMAHA. Tell him . . . tell him we have a Code Yellow up here. Code Yellow with one of his soldiers down.'

Jenny moaned, stirred and tried to sit up. She wanted to, she really did, but something somehow . . . She gave up. It was easier then, less trouble to just drift away from the pain and the cold, aching wetness. The wetness. She stirred again, faintly irritated that this wetness kept intruding into her warm little dream-world, kept tugging her back towards sharpness and pain. She could hear the water now quite plainly, a constant muted roaring in her ears that obstinately refused to go away. She stirred again, opened her eyes, and found herself looking at something round and silver a few inches in front of her; something round and silver and buckled and covered by running water that every second or two turned suddenly red. That really was most curious. Jenny put a drowsy hand to the pain above her eyes, flinched at the touch of her own fingers, and realized with a jolt of alarm that the redness was her own blood, dripping into the water from a deep cut on her forehead. That shocked her back towards full consciousness and she became aware then of other things – of the damp moss against her cheek, of the penetrating arctic coldness of the water against her legs, and of the rocks digging sharply into her side. Of the fact that it was now light and she could see. Daylight.

It all came back to her then – the sheep, the wild skidding across the road, the humpbacked granite bridge looming suddenly out of the darkness towards them, the splintering crash as they tore through the flimsy wooden fence, the—

Tony.

Jenny twisted round and forced herself, *forced* herself, to sit up and look round. The silver thing in the water she had been staring at was one of the hub-caps; the car it belonged to was resting a dozen feet or so from where she had been lying, half in and half out of a narrow, boulder-strewn stream. The bridge was a few feet beyond that, with the road and the remains of the fence somewhere above and behind her left shoulder. But Jenny wasn't interested just then in the proximity of the road, or the bridge, or the sheep that had tottered into their path at the critical moment. All she was interested in was Tony. Gritting her teeth against a sudden wave of nausea, Jenny waited until it had passed and then hauled herself unsteadily to her feet, aware of bruises, pain, tenderness, the deep cut on her forehead and the most appalling ache in her side where she had been thrown against the rocks – but that, miraculously, was all.

She stumbled towards the battered wreck of their car in the early morning light. Her door had burst open under the impact as the Escort rammed itself to a halt against the bed of the stream, but Tony's door had stayed shut and he had been pitched forward against the windscreen. Jenny could see him now, sagging head down and deathly pale against the passenger window. He wasn't moving, his eyes were closed, and there was a thick smear of blood on the windscreen. Jenny scrambled round to the passenger door muttering his name, praying his name, aware through the pain of her own injuries that this was partly her doing. This too.

She grabbed hold of the handle and wrenched the door towards her with a sudden strength she should never have possessed. The door flew open, and she lunged forward just in time to prevent Tony falling sideways on to the rocks. She cradled his body in her arms and lowered him gently to the ground. He *must* be alive. He must! Please, please God . . . Then she heard the ragged rasp of his breathing, saw his chest rise and fall, and sat back with a groan of relief. Thank you, God. Thank you . . . She watched him anxiously for a moment, then scrambled round to the back of the car, found an old RAF mackintosh in the boot and covered him up with that, bitterly aware of the inadequacy of what she was doing, aware too that of all the people she had ever met, Tony himself, if only he was conscious, would have known exactly what to do. Jenny sat back on her heels then and tried to force down a sudden feeling of panic, of helplessness, as she realized that the accident had changed nothing. If they stayed where they were, they would be found. If she flagged someone down and called for an ambulance, she was just delaying the inevitable, playing into their hands. Tony might die if she called for help. He would probably die if she didn't. So what should she do? What would he *want* her to do? What was she missing? Was there something she'd forgotten, something she'd overlooked? Talk to me, Tony. Help me. Tell me what to do, she pleaded. The wind tugged at her hair, the stream chuckled merrily beside her and there was no reply.

The farm! They'd . . . they'd passed that farm a few miles back, hadn't they? And farms . . . farms had cars, vehicles, tractors, didn't they? So what would Tony do? Think! Jenny lurched painfully to her feet, looked down at Tony for an agonizing moment of indecision, and then began scrambling up the slope to the road. Somewhere, somehow, she would find them a car, a lorry, even a tractor, *something* that would carry them on. She must. She had lost Jamie Ennis. She was not going to lose Tony, too.

A couple of miles remembered from a speeding car is always longer when you are on foot. And longer still when you are hurt and tired or frightened. Jenny was all three. It was almost six in the morning when she climbed up on to the road and began hobbling towards the farm as fast as her injuries and the pain in her side permitted, but when she finally saw the old farmhouse with its cluster of untidy outbuildings, the sun had risen into a clear, pin-sharp blue sky and it was a few minutes after seven – a few minutes after seven on the day Highland Pharmaceuticals planned to launch a new heart drug called Cardocol upon a trusting, unsuspecting British public.

Joyce Engel watched from the doorway as her husband drove slowly out of the garage, his face set and grim. When the car had gone, she stared at the mouth of the drive for a long time, wondering how it was that a morning of triumph, a morning they had both worked towards, dreamt about for so long, could taste so bitter, leave them both with so little.

Then Joyce closed the door, went back into the hallway

and lifted the telephone. She and Harold had destroyed the Highcroft tape together, had taken it down to the incinerator at the bottom of the garden in the small hours of the morning and watched as the tape melted and then burst into flames. Now there was something else she had promised she would do, someone she had to go and see. She dialled a number and waited, feeling nothing. Numb.

'Hello?'

'Helen? It's Joyce – Joyce Engel. Sorry to call you so early. Could I come round and see you? Yes . . . yes, right away. There's something I have to tell you. It's . . . it's about Malcolm.'

In the Editor's office of the *Gleninver Times*, two journalists were at work. Bob Harris now turned over the last folio of copy and looked up, his overweight face flushed with excitement. 'Just where . . . where the hell did you get all this?' he demanded. He had been roused from his bed an hour earlier to come in and read a story which, if true, would make the lead with every national newspaper in the country. It had been presented to him, on a plate, by his one and only reporter, a young trainee with less than thirteen weeks' experience, who now expected him to run it across the front page of the *Gleninver Times*, circulation eleven thousand, six hundred and eighty-seven, excluding returns. The boy looked as though he'd been up half the night putting it all together. He probably had, thought Harris wryly, with the first stirrings of editorial pride as he remembered his own early days on a provincial newspaper many years ago.

'From Mrs Highcroft and Mrs Parsons,' Hamish replied calmly.

'And you've checked these facts?' Hamish nodded, and there was a moment's silence as Harris thought giddily about all the repercussions, the local fall-out. 'What about the company? You haven't got a quote here from the company about these allegations?'

'Which ones?'

'Which ones, laddie?' Harris flicked a ham-sized hand against the flimsy sheets of copy Hamish had laboured over most of the night. 'Which ones? I suppose you can take your bloody pick! That . . . that HPL had three men murdered . . . That the company's nothing but a . . . a front for some chemical warfare programme we're not supposed to know anything about, that—'

'No, I haven't spoken to them, not yet. I . . . I thought you might prefer to do that yourself,' Hamish replied.

Harris paused. Then he rocked forward, peered up from beneath bushy eyebrows and studied his junior for a long moment. Then he chuckled. 'Aye, Hamish,' he said at last. 'Aye, I might just do that. But first, we'll do just a wee bit more checking ourselves, eh? Just to be on the safe side. Make us nice and flameproof.'

Hamish Owen smiled. You could forget about your national Press awards, your investigative profiles and single-column photographs in the UK *Press Gazette*. Right now he would settle for something much simpler – the use of his own Christian name. Not laddie. Not ever again.

Jenny crouched down panting beside the corner of the old stone barn and tried to catch her breath as she pushed the hair out of her eyes and watched the farmyard. At last her luck – *their* luck – had changed. Even as she'd broken into a ragged, agonized little run towards the nearest of the farm outbuildings, a young labourer in a battered maroon Morris Traveller that looked as if it was held together with baling wire had driven into the farmyard, got out and sauntered into the dairy with a tweed cap pushed to the back of his head and a transistor radio swinging from one brawny hand.

The noise of the radio faded away down the length of the dairy, and Jenny heard the crash of milk-churns. Now. Crouching as low as she could with one hand pressed to her side, she hobbled forward, keeping the car between herself and the dairy as she steeled herself for the sudden shout that would tell her she had been seen. She reached the car and looked inside. He had – he'd left the key in the ignition! A quick, furtive look round and Jenny had the door open and was easing herself gingerly inside amidst a clutter of baling twine and empty oilcans, plastic fertilizer bags, wisps of straw, and the pungent reminder of sheep. She settled behind the wheel, swept her eyes over the unfamiliar dashboard – and froze, remembering the last time, seeing again that stone bridge rushing towards her . . . She had to force herself to reach down for the ignition. She twisted the key and the car shook itself into life. A quick, frightened look round, a wrestle with the strange gear-stick, an angry clashing of gears and she was lurching out of the farmyard, foot hard down on the accelerator. Jenny looked in the mirror and watched as the labourer rushed out of the dairy and stared after her, hands on hips, until she slewed round a corner and disappeared. She straightened up and laughed aloud with the sudden release of tension. At last – something had gone *right*! They were going to make it, she knew they were.

But she hadn't seen the farm-hand running inside to the telephone.

Jenny was back at the granite bridge twelve minutes later. She braked to a halt on the verge next to the broken fencing and slithered down the slope to find Tony, pale, conscious and still alive, shivering violently in the bright sunshine beneath the mackintosh exactly where she had left him. Just the look on his face, and the smile of 'welcome back' behind the pain in his eyes, sent her spirits soaring as the words of explanation, of relief that she was no longer alone, spilled out in a panting, incoherent rush.

When it was time to move, it took Jenny almost five minutes to struggle back up the slope to the Morris with Tony leaning heavily on her shoulder. They made it, eventually, and Jenny staggered round to collapse in the driver's seat with her head resting on the useless horn in the middle of the steering-wheel, as Tony leaned back beside her in the passenger seat, eyes closed and panting heavily. Both too spent for words, they were very, very vulnerable just then, but no cars came by.

That couldn't last, not in the Highlands in late summer, and Jenny knew it. She reached forward, started the engine, and then gave the fuel gauge a sharp tap. The needle swung across to FULL. Jenny looked across at Tony and grinned. Plenty of petrol, at least. She forced the car into gear, and they were off with a sudden lurch that made them both cry out in pain.

The police turned up at the farm with commendable promptness. Turning east after taking a statement from the angry farm-hand, they followed the moorland road and found the break in the fence and the abandoned Escort at the bottom of the slope twenty minutes later.

Jenny and Tony had less than forty minutes' start. In a clapped-out Morris Traveller that smelt of sheep and looked as if it was held together with baling wire.

As Tomalin kept telling anyone with the time to listen, the weather was *heavenly*; just *exactly* what he had been praying for all week – hot, clear and blue with the merest *feather* of wind, the last triumphant flaring of an Indian summer that had outlasted the predictions of even the most incautious weathermen.

By seven forty-five, the sub-contractors were rolling into Highland Pharmaceuticals in a steady stream, and Tomalin of the blazing buttonhole and immaculate grooming was quivering with anger at the deep-brown skid-marks some . . . some *lout* had left on his beautiful lawn, and starting to panic about the supply of ice and ice-buckets for the champagne in the main marquee as he dabbed delicately at his forehead with a silk handkerchief. The senior Fire Officer from Glenhaddon was discussing the siting of the fire engine near the helipad beside Harold Engel's company helicopter, workmen on tall stepladders were stringing bunting across both sides of the approach road, and a posse of locally recruited waitresses in frilly white blouses and black skirts with freshly ironed aprons were busy shaking out starched tablecloths and counting wine glasses, wondering if there would be enough cutlery and trestle tables; enough red carpet and enough champagne; enough canapés, enough soft drinks, enough everything.

Inside the main hall of the admininstrative complex, members of HPL's Press and Publicity department were wondering if they had provided enough phones, typewriters, and free hand-outs for the reporters and guests as they laid a glossy, emerald-green Cardocol promotional wallet on every one of the three hundred seats that filled the hall, and the slogan, CARDOCOL – A HEARTBEAT CLOSER became a jumble of meaningless letters before their eyes. On the raised stage at the end of the hall, men ran out the wires from a cluster of microphones and made the early morning hideous with their 'Testing testing . . . one . . . two . . . three . . . '

Harold Engel stood alone. Alone surrounded by people.

He looked about him at the men on the stage, at the young girls hurrying up and down the aisles with their arms full of promotional wallets. He had dreamt of this moment, pictured it all so clearly a thousand times, and yet now that it had arrived he felt detached from it all, apart; isolated from the excitement, the pride and professional satisfaction of the drug launch, by private knowledge and a soiled, tarnished reality. It was him that had changed, he realized bleakly – his attitude. Not towards the drug itself, but towards the way he had come to regard the personal compromise that had made it all possible. He had never really questioned that before, he realized now – not until last night with Joyce, after he discovered her listening to the tape of Malcolm's death. Until then, every problem and difficulty thrown in his path during his search to perfect the latest adrenergic neurone-blocker had hidden from him the fact that he had bartered his very soul for this one last chance of success. Until gradually, as each problem was felled, each challenge overcome and cleared like undergrowth around some ancient monument, the true price of that second chance had emerged, to stand before him like some totem of dubious merit. He bent down, picked up one of the promotional wallets they were giving away, glanced at it briefly and then dropped it back on to the seat.

'Ah, *there* you are!' He turned and sighed. That man Tomalin, advancing towards him with hand outstretched expansively at the heavens in a gesture that suggested arranging the weather was just another of his party-pieces. A little of Mr Tomalin, Engel had discovered to his cost, went a very long way indeed. 'What did I tell you? You see – you needn't have worried! A perfect day – just perfect!'

'Congratulations,' Engel managed dryly.

'Ah – but it is *I* that is to be congratulating *you*, Mr Chairman,' corrected Tomalin, the true sycophant. 'Were it not for you, then all this—'

'Yes. Well, that's very kind of you, I'm sure, Mr Tomalin. Now, if you don't mind . . . ' He turned away, and then stiffened suddenly as he saw Jackman talking earnestly to someone on the flagged terrace outside, beyond the tall windows.

Tomalin watched him go, with a vexed, petulant expression on his face. 'Well, charming,' he murmured under his breath, before twirling away to busy himself elsewhere. Some people were the absolute limit.

As Harold Engel stepped outside on to the terrace, Jackman turned to greet him. So too did Baxter, up from London on the first available flight. Baxter – Engel's initial contact. The man who'd set things up, smoothed the way. The man he blamed. Anger flared suddenly. Today belonged to *him*, to Highland Pharmaceuticals, to the people here in the valley who had given him their trust and support, who had helped nurse his concept through to the very brink of success without a single production delay or industrial dispute. Baxter, Jackman and the others from the Defence Procurement Secretariat, from RD7 – they were outsiders. Intruders. They always would be, like vultures at a gathering of swallows. Baxter smiled an urbane greeting, immaculate in dark-blue, double-breasted blazer with gold buttons and regimental tie.

'Harold! How very good to see you. My warmest congratulations.' He held out his hand. Engel ignored it.

'What are you doing here?' he demanded coldly, without preamble. 'I thought we had an agreement.'

Baxter glanced at Jackman, as if to say: I see what you mean.

'We've had . . . one or two problems. Mr Jackman called me, and I thought I'd just pop up and get the lie of the land for myself.' Which was putting it remarkably bloody mildly, thought Jackman.

'Problems?' Engel demanded sharply, swinging towards his Project Development Manager, the man with two hats but only one set of loyalties. 'What sort of problems?'

Baxter held up a hand. 'Oh, nothing for you to worry about, Harold. Just internal problems of . . . reorganization. Now then—' he rubbed his hands together briskly in the manner of the English officer classes the world over – 'd'you think we might be able to rustle up some real coffee from somewhere? The stuff they give you on the plane . . . ' He shuddered. Chit-chat, thought Engel bleakly; social chit-chat; small talk in the officers' mess. He could keep it up for hours. Observing the niceties while people choked and died in pools of their own excrement in his laboratories. The bloody niceties.

'You're not welcome here, Baxter. I'd like you to leave.'

Baxter looked mildly amused. 'To leave? Never darken your door again? That's a bit *Victorian*, isn't it, Harold?' he replied calmly, keeping his voice down and turning to lead them all gently down the path so they could continue without being overheard. 'But for me and my . . . ah . . . persuasive powers with certain government ministries, today would never have happened, you do appreciate that, I suppose?'

'You've turned my facility into a battleground with your . . . your developments,' Engel retorted thickly. 'I want our agreement terminated.' He gestured at Jackman. 'No doubt your minder here will fill you in on the details if he hasn't done so already.' He paused, watching their faces, gauging Baxter's reaction. He learnt nothing behind that bland, steady smile. 'I won't compromise your little operation, if that's what's worrying you,' he continued. 'But RD7 is to close down. Within . . . what shall we say . . . four months? Yes, four months. That seems reasonable.'

'Otherwise?' Baxter enquired mildly.

Engel shrugged. 'I don't deal in threats, Mr Baxter, you know that.'

Baxter nodded agreeably. 'I see. I had no idea you'd taken this Highcroft business so *personally*, Harold. We shall have to take more account of that in future. In the meantime, might I suggest you—' They all turned at a sudden step on the path. A uniformed police Inspector was coming towards them, the silver badges of rank glittering in the sunlight on the shoulders of his white shirt. He had the look of a man required to perform some distasteful duty.

'Ah, Inspector,' greeted Baxter. 'You know Mr Engel, I presume?' As though it was his company, his premises, his occasion.

The Inspector nodded. 'Yes, sir. We have met.' He turned to Jackman. 'Might I have a word, sir?' Jackman glanced at Baxter who nodded his consent and the two moved away.

'Inspector?'

'My men have been formally instructed to . . . co-operate with your people over this road-block business,' he began stiffly, his tone of voice making it clear he did not approve of being ordered away from routine police business to work with the cowboys from Special Effects.

Jackman nodded. 'So I understand from Mr Baxter, yes.'

'My men think they've found the car you were asking about.'

'They have? Where?'

The Inspector reached into a hip pocket, took out a notebook and flipped it open. 'Approximately fifteen miles along the road to Crianlarich. It appeared to have been involved in an accident.'

'What about the occupants?'

The Inspector shook his head. 'No, sir. Nothing.'

'Have you tried the hospitals?'

The Inspector nodded, stone-faced. Of course they'd tried the hospitals. 'Nothing there either, sir. We have checked. All of them.' He hesitated, as though reluctant to divulge a word more than protocol and orders required. 'A vehicle *was* reported stolen by a young woman from a farm a few miles to the west of where this particular car was found, shortly after seven this morning. That could be them, I suppose. One of them, anyway.'

Jackman nodded. 'It could indeed. Get me a map, will you, Inspector? Then I shall need a car and . . . No. On second thoughts, I think I'd better drive myself.'

Four minutes later he was on the road and driving fast. With the Ingram locked in the boot of his car.

The ancient Morris laboured up the steep, heather-clad hill, with Jenny hunched forward over the wheel, willing the car onwards as she listened anxiously for that sudden ominous miss to the engine and kept glancing in the mirror for another tell-tale puff of black smoke in the twisting ribbon of empty road behind them. Something was wrong – she could feel it in the way the car was straining, even along the flat; the kind of feeling that, in her own Citroën, meant she had forgotten to take the handbrake off. But with this car, this relic from another age, she thought, it could be anything. Probably the rubber band was breaking. Joke, she told herself weakly, joke.

Jenny could have done with a joke just then. Tony appeared to have gone to sleep again, and his head was lolling against his chest in a way she didn't like at all. She looked again at the dashboard – only another seventy miles to Glasgow. Only seventy. That was all. Seventy.

Jackman in his speeding Rover apart, events were already gathering momentum behind them.

The white delivery van stopped outside number seventeen, Bruneval Close, and three men got out of the driver's cab. They looked smart and efficient with their clipboards and their white coats with the words FREEZER DELIVERY SERVICE stitched in red neatly across the top breast pocket. At a nod from their leader they moved round to the rear of the van, lowered the ramp and carefully manhandled a large packing-case with FRAGILE stamped across its side on to a porter's trolley, which they then wheeled down the drive of number seventeen. The packing-case looked heavy and substantial, but that was just part of the deception. By lunchtime the broken window would have been replaced, the bullet-holes re-plastered, the wall re-painted and new carpet laid on the stairs. Bundled like so much dirty washing into the empty, plastic-lined packing-case, Ridley would leave Bruneval Close exactly as he had arrived almost twelve hours earlier: with no one seeing a thing.

Harris made a final deletion to the last folio of copy, tossed Hamish Owen's story into the copy tray, pushed back his chair, rose to his feet and belched loudly. 'Right then, Scoop,' he said, slapping his stomach, looking round at the clock on the wall and twitching his jacket off the back of the chair. 'Let's you and I go and make this bastard Engel's day for him.'

They were just about to lock the door behind them when the telephone rang. Harris went back into the office and picked it up. 'Editorial. *Gleninver Times*.' He listened for a moment and then held the phone towards

Hamish. 'For you. Helen Highcroft.'

Jackman stepped back from the wrecked Escort and climbed carefully up the slope to the waiting police car, the map he had found in the glove compartment in his hands. It had Tony's name on it. He tossed it into the back of the police car and nodded. 'That's them all right,' he confimed. 'You two know the ground. Where d'you reckon they've got to, then?'

The men shrugged, not vastly interested. Let Special Effects sort out their own problems. 'Got to be east, hasn't it, sir?' one of them offered at last.

Terrific, thought Jackman. Inter-force co-operation at its very finest. He bent closer. 'How far to the next checkpoint?'

'Want me to find out?' asked the driver.

Jackman regarded him coldly. 'Unless you feel you can make an inspired guess at it – yes, I think that might perhaps be advisable.'

The policeman sighed and unclipped the radio handset. That would teach him to open his big mouth.

'Whisky Alpha, this is Foxtrot Golf mobile. What is your present position, over?'

'Foxtrot Golf mobile, this is Whisky Alpha. We're just setting up on the outskirts of Altrunn. Nothing to report, over.' He sounded bored already.

Jackman opened out the map the Inspector had given him and traced their probable route with a finger. If they were travelling west and had left here a little over an hour ago . . . He frowned. Either they'd gone to ground, turned off somewhere along the way, or – 'You're *sure* they haven't gone through Winnoch?' he demanded.

The policeman nodded. 'Not according to Control, no, sir.'

'Right, then. Thanks for your help.' That settled it. They *had* to be somewhere in front of him, somewhere between here and the village of Altrunn. Jackman folded away the map and began walking briskly back to the Rover, calculating time and distance.

'You like us to come along with you, sir?' the driver called after him. He didn't like the look on this bastard's face. Not one bit.

Jackman shook his head. 'No need, thank you, officer – no need. We'll take it from here.' He slid behind the wheel and drove quickly away.

A mile further on he pulled in to the side of the road, glanced round to make sure no one was coming, got out, took Ridley's automatic pistol out of the boot and placed it under a coat on the passenger seat. The Rover pulled away from the verge and gathered speed.

'This way, Dr Erskine,' gestured the pretty young secretary with a bright smile. 'I think you'll find Mr Engel through in the main hall.'

'Thank you.' He glanced round uneasily at the preparations surrounding them on every side – preparations for a launch, for a ceremony, that must never take place. Not now. Not after he'd spoken to Chepstow, collated what they'd told him with what he had received from London. Clutching a copy of Jenny's stolen report under his arm, he hurried after the young girl, conscious not of a sense of victory or personal vindication but of a weary, genuine sadness that the efforts of so many were doomed to be wasted. And that he should be the one to toll the bell of failure.

The secretary pushed open the swing doors at the end of the corridor, looked round the hall at the busy publicity assistants putting the last of the promotional literature on the empty seats, and noticed a solitary figure looking out across the rolling lawns at the company helicopter on the landing circle and the slash of scarlet carpet leading to the white marquee beyond. She turned and pointed a slim, painted finger: 'There he is – over there by the window looking at the helicopter.' She laughed brightly. 'Honestly

– he's like a child with a new toy with that thing!'

Dr Erskine patted her hand distractedly and walked slowly through the forest of empty chairs towards the Chairman of Highland Pharmaceuticals.

Harold Engel turned to face him. He turned long before he could possibly have heard him coming, and Dr Erskine often wondered about that afterwards: whether somehow he had known, even then. He stopped and waited as Harold Engel came towards him.

'Dr Erskine. Good morning.'

'Mr Engel. You remember you invited me to substantiate those allegations I made in your home last night – or was it this morning?' Erskine smiled a gruff smile that robbed his words of malice. He was here to prevent a disaster, not score cheap points in some verbal duel.

Harold Engel nodded. 'This morning, I think.'

Dr Erskine raised his briefcase a few inches and glanced round. 'Would you mind if we sat down?' He sighed. 'I'm not as young as I used to be.'

Engel twisted a couple of chairs out of their neat, straight rows and gestured the doctor to be seated. Dr Erskine lifted his briefcase on to his knees, undid the old-fashioned straps, took out a thick bundle of notes and held them out. Harold Engel glanced briefly at the first few handwritten pages and looked up.

'Perhaps if you could just tell me what this has to do with Cardocol . . . ' He glanced round. 'As you've probably noticed, we're rather busy.'

'Aye. Well, I'll be as brief as I can. You remember that old man, the one who died in the fire out in the bay with that wee boy?'

'The one who was deaf? Yes, of course. A tragic accident.'

Dr Erskine nodded. 'Indeed. So it was.' He paused. Then – 'Last night, in your home, I told you I'd given Cardocol to a couple of my patients on an . . . experimental basis, you remember? Well, he was one of them: Robbie

Roberts. The PM said he drowned.' He shook his head, leant forward and tapped the notes in Engel's hands. 'Chepstow don't agree – rather, they're now prepared to go a good bit further than that. They think Robbie Roberts died because he was taking Cardocol. And because Cardocol gave him a dry, ticklish little cough. They're prepared to have that added to the statement of record.'

Harold Engel stirred restlessly. 'I don't mean to appear rude, Doctor, but would you please stop talking in riddles? I haven't the faintest idea what you're talking about.'

'Riddles, did you say? No, Mr Engel, I'm not talking in riddles – far from it. In plain language, Mr Roberts died because he mixed Cardocol with cough-mixture; cough-mixture for a cough caused by *your* drug. It was the combined side-effects of the two that caused his collapse. He drowned because he *collapsed*, not because of the fire on the boat. So you see, there *is* a connection.'

'What cough-mixture?' Engel demanded.

'He mixed Cardocol with—' Dr Erskine rummaged in a pocket and pulled out the bottle he had found on Robbie's kitchen table, the one identical to that in Mrs Proctor's bedroom – 'with this. Soothaway.' He paused, turning the bottle this way and that so Engel could get a good look at it. 'Soothaway's another new product. Just one of hundreds of new products that come flooding out of places like this every week of the year. But, unlike Cardocol, you don't need a doctor's prescription for this – you can buy it over the counter, easy as you please. A lot of people are doing just that, thanks to the advertising people.' He sighed and slipped the bottle back into his pocket. 'Patients are a gullible lot, Mr Engel, as you're doubtless aware. They're vulnerable, frightened. They'll buy what they're told to buy; what the advertisements tell them they need. Soothaway's already a rip-roaring success, so they say, and, in ninety-nine cases out of a hundred, it's perfectly harmless. Except, that is, when it's taken with—'

'Cardocol? Oh, don't be ridiculous! If—'

'—Cardocol, yes. It's an anti-spasmodic, you see,' Erskine continued with a sad smile, as though unaware of the interruption. 'It contains something called phenylpropalomine, a sympathomimetic amine taken up by the same neurones as Cardocol with its base of guanethidine. Soothaway not *only* antagonizes the action of your wonder-drug, Mr Engel, it displaces the guanethidine that's already there. Result – high blood pressure doesn't *fall*, it goes through the roof! Mix Soothaway with Cardocol's new delay-release mechanism and patients aren't taking pills any more, they're swallowing time-bombs! That's what made Robbie Roberts collapse, d'you see? Those pills of yours had nowhere to go. When the outer matrix finally eroded, they just exploded inside him.'

'Poppycock! I've . . . I've never heard such rubbish! The unfortunate death of one man, a patient under *your* supervision, Doctor, can hardly—'

'We're not talking about just one man, Mr Engel. We're talking about many thousands – not deaths perhaps, but thousands of people at risk – old, elderly people.'

'Look – Doctor. Once and for all – for this so-called interaction of yours to take place to any . . . appreciable degree, there would need to be a high incidence of bronchial inflammation, agreed? A large number of elderly patients taking Cardocol would need to get a cough, yes? That much, at least, I hope is obvious.' Erskine nodded calmly. 'Good, we're agreed on that much, at least.' Engel took a deep breath, as though to gather his thoughts. Or control his temper. 'I told you last night and I'm telling you again now: the incidence of bronchial inflammation among elderly patients taking Cardocol under medical supervision on our clinical trials programme was well within permissible levels set not by us, but by the Committee on the Safety of Medicines! Something in the region of four or five per cent, that's all! I know. I've checked! We've gone through the figures a hundred times! Your Mister whatever-his-name-is is an isolated case, that's all – an isolated case!'

‘And if he wasn’t?’ Dr Erskine asked quietly.

‘What d’you mean?’

‘What would the proven incidence of bronchial inflammation have to be before you would concede that it was too high – given that Soothaway and Cardocol were found to be incompatible?’

‘Well, I . . . that would depend.’

‘Nine per cent? Ten per cent? Higher than that? Give me a figure – purely as a hypothetical exercise.’

Engel hesitated, sensing he might be walking into a trap yet unable to think of a way to avoid what he couldn’t see.

‘All right. Eleven. Eleven per cent. Anywhere between eleven and fifteen per cent.’

Dr Erskine considered for a moment. ‘So – if eleven people out of any hundred taking Cardocol developed a cough, you would consider that number to be unacceptably high?’

‘I suppose so . . . ’

‘Yes or no?’

‘All right, then – yes. Yes, I would. Far too high, actually. I certainly wouldn’t be happy going ahead on that sort of read-back. But, as I say, our figures are much, much lower than that.’

‘Are you sure?’

Engel looked up sharply. ‘Yes, of course I’m sure! This is my company, remember? If I . . . Why? What are you getting at?’

‘I’d like you to study this for a moment, if you will,’ Dr Erskine said quietly, playing his trump card as he held out a copy of the HPL report Jenny had stolen from Jackman’s office. Harold Engel took the report, glanced at it impatiently, realized from its title and designation that it was something important, something from within his own company that he had never seen before, and began to read. Dr Erskine leant across and pointed gently: ‘I think you’ll find that’s the relevant paragraph.’

It was. Harold Engel read it quickly and the words

seemed to rear up out of the page towards him. He read the paragraph again, more slowly. And once more, just to be sure. Finally he looked up, his face ashen. There was a long silence between the two men, then: 'They've . . . they've distorted the figures,' he whispered.

'So it would appear. For the Committee.'

'Four per cent! I thought . . . I thought . . . They told me four per cent – months ago! I didn't . . . I didn't know . . . ' It is not pleasant to watch a man discover that his dreams are in ruins, and Dr Erskine looked away. 'I didn't *know*!' Harold Engel repeated, in a voice that begged belief.

Dr Erskine nodded slowly. 'I accept that. If . . . if you look at the front you will see that the distribution list was very . . . restricted.' Engel did so. Jackman. Baxter. Half a dozen names he'd never heard before. Names in London. Names in the Defence Procurement Secretariat. But Jackman's at the top. Jackman the author. The Judas.

With his own nowhere in sight.

'The true incidence of bronchial inflammation should have been higher by a factor of almost ten. If CSM had known that . . . ' Dr Erskine shrugged. There was no need to finish, but he went on anyway. 'I think you'll agree you'd never have got Cardocol anywhere near the Committee. You'd never have got your licence.' He glanced round the hall. At the chairs and the microphones, all ready, all waiting. CARDOCOL – A HEARTBEAT CLOSER. He looked at Harold Engel and saw the dazed, vacant look in his eyes. The look of defeat. 'You'll have to call it off,' he said gently. 'You do know that, don't you, Mr Engel? You'll have to call it off. Mr Engel . . . ?'

'Tony?' Jenny took her eyes off the road, reached over and shook Tony gently by the sleeve. 'Tony? Talk to me. Are you all right?' Stupid, she thought, really stupid; like waking someone up to ask if they were asleep. Tony groaned, and his head lolled across his chest. 'Can you hear me? I'm . . . I'm going to stop, OK? Just for a moment,' decided Jenny, frightened now, terrified that he was about to die on her. She glanced in the mirror, saw the road was clear, took her foot off the accelerator and eased the car to a gentle stop on the verge. Sixty-two miles to Glasgow. With Jackman coming up fast, nine miles behind.

Ten minutes later. Dr Erskine had left, and Harold Engel was alone in his office, sitting at his desk. Alone with his thoughts and shattered dreams, his realization that he had been duped, tricked by the men he had once trusted because they had offered him the chance of survival. Men who cared nothing about the integrity of his work or the safety of his product, but who wanted only that there should be a legitimate cover for their illegitimate operations, for RD7. Slowly, Engel turned the pages of the report Dr Erskine had left him, and read again in stark, clinical detail the true depths of Jackman's calculated, cynical betrayal. They had paid lip-service to his ambitions and deceived him without the slightest hesitation the moment it served their purpose. Baxter and Jackman. Baxter the manipulator, Jackman his faithful instrument.

Harold Engel rose and walked to the window, staring down from his office on to the lawns and the tables, the tents and the people he employed, the decent people who had trusted him, who were laughing and smiling down there because today was a day of celebration. A good day in their lives. One to remember.

Then he saw Baxter, standing beside the company helicopter – *his* helicopter – with a cup of coffee in his hand, talking to one of the prettier secretaries. Making her laugh. Engel turned away from the window with an idea forming in his mind. A way of getting back. God, yes.

Presently he sat down at his desk and began to write a letter. It did not take long because confessions seldom do, and it was a confession, he supposed, if not to his sins then to the sins of others he could name. And did so. He sat back when he had finished, blotted the letter carefully, sealed it in an envelope and propped it against the picture frame on the corner of his desk. He glanced up at the blue sky, conscious, suddenly, that there was little time. Soon, in a few more minutes, there would be the first glitter of sunlight on Perspex as the chartered helicopters began to arrive with the doctors and the journalists, the free-loaders and the photographers, all come at his summons to witness the arrival of Cardocol. CARDOCOL – A HEARTBEAT CLOSER. Closer, but not quite. Not now. Engel closed his eyes and shuddered, clenched fists grinding into his eyes as he tried to shut out the pain. They'd all be here in a moment or two. But not yet, please God. Not just yet. Give me a little time, for a little is all I need.

'Mr Engel? Mr Engel – are you in there? There are two reporters downstairs in reception – a Mr Owen and a Mr Harris from the *Gleninver Times*. They insist on talking to you about something called RD7. Hello, Mr Engel . . . ?'

But he'd left already. Down the back stairs with a glance at his watch and a smile as he brushed past the people he liked, the people he had worked with and trusted, as he searched for one man: Baxter. He tried to appear calm, relaxed. Like a man who didn't know his world had just ended. There. There he was. Engel walked up and laid a hand on his sleeve. Baxter turned, saw who it was and frowned with a flicker of irritation. 'Harold.' He smiled. 'I was just telling . . . ah . . . Cindy here what a tremendous achievement all this is. For you, I mean.'

Engel smiled back, he never knew how. 'Thank you. I . . . I wonder if I might have a quick word?' he began, with what he hoped Baxter would take to be just the right degree of hesitancy, the possible prelude to apology.

'By all means.' He turned to the girl and offered her his coffee cup. 'Would you mind – just for one moment? Thank you so much.' They moved away. 'Yes?'

'What . . . what I said earlier,' Engel began, looking into that sleek, well-fed face. 'I . . . I was too hasty. I hope you'll overlook what I said.'

Baxter nodded slowly. 'That's better, Harold. Just so we understand one another.'

'I was hoping perhaps you'd let me show you something – by way of amends, if you like.'

'Show me something?'

Harold Engel nodded and gestured across at the helicopter. 'It's an idea I have. Just five minutes, that's all. I think it might prove very useful.'

Baxter hesitated. He disliked flying and had already decided to return to London by train when everything was sorted out. 'Five minutes, you say?'

'Ten at the very outside. Your coffee won't even be cold.' He smiled again and gestured at the clear blue sky. 'Besides, the view should be terrific.'

Baxter put a hand up to his tie and swallowed. He hated heights, too. 'Oh, very well.'

They were airborne five minutes later, rising slowly, majestically into the sky to hover rock-steady above the site at four hundred feet. Baxter sat in the front beside Engel, clutching the metal rim of his seat and staring straight ahead. Engel turned the helicopter sedately first to the left, then to the right, and presently Baxter began to relax. Engel was quite correct – the view really was superb. And there was hardly any sensation of movement. The helicopter turned slowly through ninety degrees, rose up through another three hundred feet of clear air and set off due east away from HPL, away from Gleninver, away from that first twinkling glitter of sunlight on Perspex as the first of the chartered helicopters began to arrive from Glasgow.

'Where are we going?' asked Baxter, his voice frail and tinny in Engel's earphones. They flew on, gaining a little more height as the countryside opened up below them and houses shrank into miniature. 'Can you hear me?' Baxter asked nervously, glancing across the clear bowl of the cabin at the pilot. 'I said, where are we going?'

Harold Engel looked across and smiled.

Without warning, he suddenly flung the helicopter over

on to its side and sent it swooping down in a wide, curving spiral that sliced five hundred feet off the altimeter before Baxter could even gasp. 'Where's Jackman?' Engel asked conversationally, pulling smoothly out of the dive and rolling the helicopter through one hundred and eighty degrees until Baxter was looking down at *him*, and the gasp of the man's fear filled his headphones.

'I . . . I don't know,' Baxter answered weakly, pulling his tie away from his neck, his face white and clammy with sweat.

Harold Engel reached into one of the elasticated pockets, took out an air-sickness bag and threw it across. 'Think about it,' he advised shortly, reaching forward and flicking up the switch that cut off further conversation. They began to loop – a steep, steepening climb up the side of the sky that rammed Baxter into the back of his seat, his eyes glazed with terror. Engel glanced at his instruments, looked across at Baxter, threw back his head and laughed, for they were in his world now. On his terms. Up . . . up . . . up . . . curving over with the ground now somewhere behind and below their shoulders. Over the top, hanging in their straps with light and darkness flashing into the cabin, the world whirling round in kaleidoscopic images of terror. Corkscrew port, corkscrew starboard . . . Baxter vomited suddenly down the front of his blazer, and they levelled out. Straight and level. Ground right side up.

Engel flicked the intercom switch. 'I asked you a question,' he repeated civilly. 'I know you sent him off on one of your little errands, Baxter – so tell me, where's Jackman?' He spiked his request with a little rolling in the air, a little pitch and yaw at two thousand. It was enough.

'On . . . on the road to . . . oh God . . . to . . . Crianlarich. There's someone we . . . we have to talk to,' Baxter spluttered, retching into the bag this time. When he had finished – 'Now, please. Can . . . can we go down and land?'

Engel studied him without pity. 'Well, we certainly can't

stay up here forever now, can we?' he mused, in a quiet tone of voice that Baxter found as terrifying as the next seven minutes of aerobatics, as Engel brought them round towards the road to Crianlarich. And Jackman.

Jenny dabbed at Tony's face ineffectually with a wet handkerchief, trying to do with cold water what needed to be done in a properly equipped casualty ward. Preferably in Glasgow. But at least he was conscious again. 'There – any better?'

He managed a weak smile. 'Terrific. Makes me feel like a . . . a million dollars.' He was sitting on the ground propped against the front wheel with his legs sticking out in front of him. He looked terrible. And wonderful.

'Yes, I know – all green and wrinkled.' She smiled, relieved beyond measure that he had regained consciousness. They were going to be all right now, she knew it. She could feel it in her bones.

Thc white Rover breasted the last hill. There! By the stream. Jackman stopped the car, took out a pair of binoculars and focused impatiently on the battered, stationary Morris pulled in to the side of the road. He put away the glasses and reached across to the passenger seat. It was while he was checking the unfamiliar mechanism of the Ingram that he heard it: a faint, distant buzzing in the sky.

A white speck on the roadside: Jackman's car, stationary on an empty ribbon of twisting Highland road. Engel eased back on the stick, and they swung round closer until he was absolutely, absolutely sure, unaware of Baxter crumpled beside him as he estimated height and distance, angles of approach. Holding the aircraft steady with one hand, Engel reached into his breast pocket, took out his wallet and removed a photograph of Joyce and the children. He studied it for a moment, and Baxter felt his skin crawl as a terrible suspicion took root and blossomed in his mind. Engel switched on the intercom.

'What . . . what are you going to do?' Baxter whispered, eyes fixed, mesmerized, on that photograph of the woman and three smiling children.

Engel brought them round in a slow, sweeping turn that steadied the Rover in the exact centre of the Perspex nose and held them there, stationary in the sky, for a fragile, pendulous moment.

'I read Jackman's report,' he said quietly as they began to race forward, gathering speed with their rotor-blades skimming the ground. 'Guess.'

Baxter started to scream.

He was still screaming when they hit the Rover.